Bilge Rat - Pirate A...

Demon Pirate

(Book Three of a Series)

Kevin Charles Smith

www.piratetales.info

Journey Publications

Journey Publications, LLC

Published in the United States by Journey Publications, LLC

Library of Congress Cataloging-in-Publication Data
Smith, Kevin Charles
Bilge Rat – Pirate Adventurer / Book Three, Demon Pirate
A novel by Kevin Charles Smith
LCCN: 2017954116
ISBN-10: 0-9798171-9-6
ISBN-13: 978-0-9798171-9-9

Printed in the United States of America

Journey Publications, LLC
POBox 2442, Warminster, PA 18974

www.piratetale.info

Film/TV/Subsidiary Rights: Mark B Miller Management. (markbmiller@aol.com)

Dedicated to my partner and lifelong companion, Patricia. For the past half-century you have more than succeeded as being my loving mate, life-long companion and abiding spouse. Given my tempestuous and reclusive personality, I view this feat as miraculous and worthy of my utmost respect, admiration and outright love. Thank you from the very essence of my being!

CONTENTS

ACKNOWLEDGEMENTS

I offer my most earnest and wholehearted feelings of gratitude and appreciation to every individual collaborating and facilitating on this dream project of mine. Particular indebtedness to my wife, Patricia, for her unswerving belief and encouragement. Over time she has become my most essential and valuable critic as well as my esteemed assistant and valued and treasured word processor. To my Ayurvedic practitioner and herbal naturalist daughter, Kari, I am exceedingly indebted for her knowledgeable and invaluable counsel on natural and herbal treatments, practices and their effects. To my historically conscious and driven daughter, Shannon, I am highly appreciative for her guidance and knowledge that enabled the work to maintain historical accuracy and appropriateness. To both of my beloved sons-in-law, Clay and Ryan, my most fervent appreciation for their continued encouragement and honest critique.

To my enduring number one fan and supporter, Susan Deetjen, I revere your continuous support and patronage. To each of my brothers, sisters, relatives, friends and associates, I am humbled and blessed by your continued optimism and motivation throughout this extraordinarily lengthy process. To my departed father, Charles, and mother, Delores, I am forever grateful and indebted for their guidance, support, confidence and inspiration of which I will forever miss.

In addition, I have a considerable obligation to express by heartfelt appreciation and gratitude to the entire team of dedicated professionals who enabled my scribblings to metamorphose into a credible work. For her invaluable graphic and artistic assistance, my esteemed appreciation and thankfulness to my Creative Director, Rocio Amovadar. For the highly impactful and attention earning artwork, my sincerest tribute to my unsurpassed illustrator, Mike Saputo. To my friends, George and Karen Brigandi, I am indebted for their wise counsel and their agency's invaluable support. A heartfelt and enormous thanks to my distinguished and exceptional editor, Ali Bothwell Mancini, for her sage and constructive suggestions and recommendations that enabled my cave painting-like scribblings to transform into a credible novel.

Special thanks to all the people working in the background to provide their astute and crucial guidance, enabling my narrative to make significant headway in the intricate and perplexing modern bookselling maze. Especially among these are the leadership and member stores of American Booksellers Association (see my website for more information). Also at the top of the list, a special shout out to Mr Cevin Bryerman of Publishers' Weekly for taking time out of his schedule at London Book Fair for a mentoring breakfast.

To my proficient and highly competent digital contingent, Neil Harner, Sarah Coale and the entire Inverse Paradox team, I am beholden and indebted for the entirety of their masterful efforts. Finally, my steadfast and staunch gratitude, respect and indebtedness for my agent, publisher and most importantly my very close friend and compatriot, Mark B. Miller, whose ceaseless belief and undying faith in my work enabled it to reach fruition.

My kindest and most appreciative regards to each and every one of you!

Kevin

AUTHOR'S BIO

Kevin Charles Smith, the eldest of seven children, was born in Chicago and never outgrew his fascination with the exploits and depredations of pirates. As such, he spent his lifetime researching the celebrated and notorious antics of pirates through any available source of information. His chosen profession of marketing resulted in untold success with a number of packaged food companies including the Kellogg Company. As he matured, he remained intrigued by the rollicking exploits of famous Hollywood swashbucklers who graced the silver screen with their daring, adventurous and heroic feats of honor and triumph.

Following a thirty-five year accomplished career, culminating as Senior Vice President of Marketing Services with the Kellogg Company, Kevin set sail on his long established passion of rendering the nefarious deeds and escapades of these ocean-bound hooligans onto paper. Fully cognizant of the dearth of information on pirates in general, he set out to create his very own fictional, yet historically accurate, account of the truly fascinating pirate way of life.

As he set sail on this objective, he teamed up with an acclaimed and amazing editor, Ali Bothwell Mancini. She graciously immersed herself into this bewitching project and assisted in producing and crafting the *Bilge Rat, Pirate Adventurer Series*, which encompasses *Book One, Remarkable Rascal, Book Two, Black Tarantula* and *Book Three, Pirate Demon.*

Kevin's creative career served him well in this enterprise. His storied background afforded him a robust knowledge and affinity for the inner workings of the entertainment industry as a whole. Over his career, he partnered with a slew of the world's greatest performers and studios producing a successful series of promotional events and programs. The Bilge Rat, Pirate Adventurer Series was carefully crafted recognizing the entertainment vacuum that existed on this alluring subject matter. To satisfy this recognized need, Kevin assembled a robust team of marketing and literary professionals to assist in bringing his lifelong dream into reality. In fact, his first two novels have been recognized by numerous literary associations in both awards and accolades for their unique literary accomplishments.

With a time-tested awareness of what readers of all ages yearn for and crave, he launched his efforts to fill in the woeful gaps he found maddeningly absent in his intensive and exhaustive research of piratical life on the high seas. Concurrently, he endeavored to create an arresting and fanciful account complete with intrigue, suspense and romance that is both timeless and ageless. As a result, this novel and imaginative series has been crafted into a vastly entertaining product that even well-known reprobates such as Blackbeard and Captain Kidd would applaud, acclaim and appreciate.

After nearly half a century, Kevin remains wed to his high school sweetheart, Patricia. Together they are the extremely proud parents of Kari and Shannon, and moreover even more delighted and blessed with their grandchildren, Rowan, Lia and Van. Kevin and Pat now reside on Marco Island in Florida where Kevin can be even closer to the sea.

AUTHOR'S NOTE

Without any sort of detailed historical guide to shed full light on pirate exploits during the Golden Age of Piracy, this account is a fictional recreation of the lives and times of these merry reprobates and their fascinating lifestyles. Chocked full of imagination and whimsy, this series is a rollicking adventure tale full of romance and life-threatening escapades set in an age of long-lost but hardly forgotten history. This saga attempts to portray the true essence of the period, an arduous and brutal span where life expectancy was woefully short and stations in life were predetermined at birth and rarely altered. Spiced with captivating sailor's tales, this energetic series was scribbled as a calculated attempt to portray a authentic perception of the life and times of these notorious sea desperadoes in both an entertaining and mesmerizing fashion.

Book Three: Demon Pirate

"Poxy Doxy" (Traditional sailor's Chantey-Author Unknown)

Poxy Doxy...Poxy Doxy...Dreams Come True
Poxy Doxy...Poxy Doxy...Takin' on the Whole Crew
Poxy Doxy...Poxy Doxy...Never mind Your Name
Poxy Doxy...Poxy Doxy...Sweeter Than Sugarcane
Oh Strumpet...Oh Wench...Full Speed Ahead
Oh Strumpet...Oh Wench...Wonderful in Bed!
Poxy Doxy...Poxy Doxy...You're slay as a Fox
Poxy Doxy...Poxy Doxy...When Opportunity Knocks
Poxy Doxy...Poxy Doxy...You're Willin' to Please
Poxy Doxy...Poxy Doxy...Never One to Tease
Oh Strumpet...Oh Wench...Full Speed Ahead
Oh Strumpet...Oh Wench...Wonderful in Bed!
Poxy Doxy...Poxy Doxy...Queen of My Life
Poxy Doxy...Poxy Doxy...Never to Be My Wife
Poxy Doxy...Poxy Doxy...Quick with a Smile
Poxy Doxy...Poxy Doxy...Even Tho I'm Vile
Oh Strumpet...Oh Wench...Full Speed Ahead
Oh Strumpet...Oh Wench...Wonderful in Bed!
Poxy Doxy...Poxy Doxy...Shantytown's Fine Light
Poxy Doxy...Poxy Doxy...Mine for the Night
Poxy Doxy...Poxy Doxy...Forever on my Mind
Poxy Doxy...Poxy Doxy...Saucy and Fine
Oh Strumpet...Oh Wench...Full Speed Ahead
Oh Strumpet...Oh wench...Wonderful in Bed!
Poxy Doxy...Poxy Doxy...Sing me a Song
Poxy Doxy...Poxy Doxy...I Never Take Long
Poxy Doxy...Poxy Doxy...Without You I'd Grieve
Poxy Doxy...Poxy Doxy...Precious Coins I'll Leave
Oh Strumpet...Oh Wench...Full Speed Ahead
Oh Strumpet...Oh Wench...Wonderful in Bed!

Poxy Doxy...Poxy Doxy...The Punchhouse is Home
Poxy Doxy...Poxy Doxy...Membered by this Poem
Poxy Doxy...Poxy Doxy...Payment is Due
Poxy Doxy...Poxy Doxy...Ain't Life Cruel
  Oh Strumpet...Oh Wench...Full Speed Ahead
  Oh Strumpet...Oh Wench...Wonderful in Bed!

PROLOGUE

Shorebirds, welcome back to my perilous watery hell! Issuing a brisk scan of my immediate surroundings, I can honestly report that I am the sole survivor amongst the flotsam and wreckage encircling my ever precarious position. Carnivorous consorts continue to surround me as they await their opportunity to fill their ravenous bellies with my precious flesh. These cold-blooded fiends have already conscientiously dispatched all of the ill-fated and hapless survivors that once shared my same plight.

As I patiently and optimistically hold out for an indispensable rescuer to come to my aid, I have resolved to continue evaluating my past choices. Sadly, many of these reminisces have centered on cherished and beloved family members and friends that have tragically perished along my life's voyage. Specifically, I remain dismayed over the murder of my revered Uncle Arch and the disappearance of my beloved younger brother, Toby. Additionally, the tragic loss of my guardian and mentor, Handy dampens my spirits whenever I reminisce on his invaluable guidance, support and wise counsel. Recollecting on their stunning losses saddens me to no end. I miss each of them profoundly. This purposeful retrospection has painfully served to resurrect these beloved phantoms in order to torture and torment me anew. I am fully cognizant that I have extracted some measure of revenge to atone for their losses. However, I have come to realize that this powerful driving force does not consummately remedy or rectify grief-laden emotions and sentiments.

As such, I also recollect on the sinister and villainous forces that have crossed my wake. Included, is the memory of my intimidating and browbeating superior, Mister Bass, who I soundly defeated and permanently eliminated. I also recollect on my victorious duel over the conceited and contemptuous Sir William Brisbane III, which freed Powder Monkey from his merciless clutches. Furthermore, I harken back to outwitting and duping the determined and relentless Captain Viola. Lastly, I reminisce on decisively ending the command and eventually replacing the duplicitous and treacherous Pirate Captain Shivers. Truth be told, I have discovered the tragic reality of not dealing decisively with confirmed and formidable adversaries such as these reprobates. Painful experience has taught me well that exhibiting any measure of compassion or leniency to these types of scoundrels and villains opens the door for catastrophic misery, hardship and even potential annihilation. Consequently, I have agonizingly realized that providing even a modicum of mercy to sworn enemies can come at an exceedingly high price.

Since time remains of the essence, I will dutifully forge ahead with my detailed personal examination before my hungry confederates have a chance to make a fine meal out of me!

Chapter 1: Rescue of Captain Adams

It was now time to initiate plans and preparations to free my friend, Captain Adams from the clutches of the ruthless pirates operating out of their Tortuga stronghold. Working with the information garnered from the few sources available, I understood that success required an unconventional attack strategy. I was certain that a frontal assault would prove disastrous given the enemy's ponderous fortifications. I was also quite sure that, even if we were able to battle past the enemy's frontal defenses, Captain Adams would surely be murdered by his vicious kidnappers long before we could reach his position to free him. As I continued to ponder alternatives, I concluded that we needed the ability to infiltrate the scoundrels' lair with a nonthreatening force acting under a very convincing ruse. Once accomplished, this small faction would then need to incapacitate the bulk of his ferocious abductors before any attempt to release Captain Adams could be mounted.

Suddenly an idea struck me that might serve our needs quite nicely. My notion was to disguise a small incursion force as a volunteer medical team from Saint Domingue. As bogus medics, we would then spin a yarn that we had volunteered to sail to Tortuga to assist in combating a reportedly vicious and lethal plague. The fact that this reputed plague was totally imaginary would mean little to Hurricane Jeffers and his men once they discovered that we also had the knowledge and medicine at our disposal to cure a pirate's ultimate terror, the pox! Since this vile disease was every sailor's nightmare, I was quite sure that the miscreants who were holding Captain Adams hostage would receive my small group with open arms once they realized that we had come to cure them of this dreaded blight.

Now that I had chosen an appropriate ploy, I needed to select suitable assistants to accompany me into this den of murdering thieves. In thinking over my choices, I understood that my selections had to appear quite unthreatening, so that our foes would be given no reason to discern our true intentions. In this regard, I chose Tan, Scuttle, Powder Monkey and Long Tall Willie to serve as my fictitious medical team. Each of these crewmen were small statured individuals, who would best serve to resemble young lads dutifully assisting their attending doctor, me! We proceeded to make our numerous preparations, including altering the appropriate medical outfits that Aunt Hortence had graciously long ago provided. I also decided to tote along a small pouch filled with *Devil's Trumpet* seeds, because they were small and easily concealed as well as exceptionally potent and highly lethal. With preparations completed, I deemed it necessary to do some scouting of the pirate's stronghold, prior to attempting our actual incursion. We maneuvered *Rue's Revenge* as close as we dared to our final destination. Once stealthy anchored, we launched one of our blackened longboats, and a scout team made their way unobserved into the protected cove that formed the entrance to the Black Tarantula's pirate haven. This clandestine reconnaissance of the pirate's harbor allowed the party a first-hand peek at our enemy's schooner that rested peacefully at anchor. The patrol team reported that the ship was heavily armed, given the significant number of gunports she sported. In addition, it appeared to them that the ship was totally abandoned, in all likelihood due to the security and protection it garnered from the heavily armed fortress that loomed directly above it.

The patrol party also had a limited view of the enemy's lair, and witnessed a very daunting sight. The stronghold had indeed been built high on the bluff overlooking the tiny cove. Straining their vision, my men beheld a large battery of guns facing seaward that would provide ample protection from any invading force. They also observed several huge bonfires raging among the fortifications high above them. Given the size and intensity of these pyres, they could also make out the drunken revelry that was underway, evidenced by frenzied and mad-capped figures dancing and cavorting around these blazing conflagrations. Lastly, they noticed that this scoundrel's aerie could only be accessed by a lone set of steep steps that began at the beach and climbed up to the dizzying heights of the bluff. Having a much better visualization of the layout of the Black Tarantula's refuge, my vanguard cautiously and silently rowed out of the cove and rejoined our ship.

Once safely aboard and their observations dutifully reported, I summoned Lion and Sharkface along with my appointed medical team to discuss the scouting discoveries and to review specific plans for the following day. I explained that I and my medical team would be charged with peacefully infiltrating the fortress under the guise of providing crucial medical assistance for a rumored plague. Utilizing a special herbal ingredient from Aunt Gertrude's medicine storehouse, I planned on brewing a very debilitating potion for any suffering degenerate, which I was certain would include virtually every one of them. The medicinal leaves I would employ were called *Senna*. The elixir brewed from this substance would have quite a disastrous effect among the heathen whelps. Per Gertrude's instructions, the *Senna* tea would be both fierce and fast acting, taking full effect in two to three hours following ingestion. This tonic would act as a strong purging laxative, causing excessive gas, painful abdominal cramping and explosive dysentery, crippling conditions indeed! I informed my team that I would also employ another strong concoction from my medical cache, that when introduced into our enemies' food source, would render them utterly incapacitated and wholly defenseless. Once accomplished, my team would then search, locate and free Captain Adams. While we were performing this dangerous task, Lion and Tiger Eyes would lead a secret assault on the deserted anchored schooner with the objective of disabling its formidable guns. When my friend, Captain Adams, was liberated, we would flee the devil's citadel in our longboat and rendezvous with our ship to consummate our escape.

At this point in our conclave, I noticed a number of doubtful expressions on my compatriots faces, as they seemed quite anxious concerning our chances for success. Consequently, I also observed a very strong measure of trust and willingness on each of their parts to readily participate in this rescue mission despite all of its inherent dangers. From my point of view, I silently prayed that my ruse would prove successful, since the alternative promised a very ugly and grievous outcome!

At daybreak, my medical team loaded into our longboat and began the short trek to Tortuga. Reaching the hidden cove, we rowed brazenly passed the anchored pirate ship and landed on the small beach at the foot of the fortress. Almost immediately, we were surrounded by fierce looking rogues, who demanded to know why we had trespassed on their private holdings. Dressed in full medical regalia, I answered that I was a renowned physician from Saint Domingue, and had been sent by its concerned citizens to cure an insidious plague that had reportedly broken out on the island. Continuing, I introduced my men as my medical assistants, who had graciously agreed to accompany me on this vital mission of mercy.

Staring at me like I had completely lost my mind, the savages loudly retorted that they were not experiencing any sort of plague, and that my informational sources had sent me on a fool's errand. Regardless, they informed me that since I had made the long journey that I needed to parley with their leader prior to returning to Saint Domingue. With this announcement, they led the way up the never-ending stairway to their lofty fortress. Once topside, we were herded into a central building where the massive and daunting Hurricane Jeffers awaited us. The evil-smirking brute welcomed us graciously to his compound and listened quietly as his men recounted the reason behind our visit. After being informed of our misguided mission, the beast shook with malicious laughter and ordered us to return to our homeland immediately. Following my calculated scheme, I boldly stepped forward and addressed the chiding ogre. Informing him that I was an outstanding medical man, I offered to ply my trade amongst any of his followers who might require therapeutic attention, including anyone suffering from dreaded and allegedly incurable pox.

Well, I can tell you that my last statement produced a very dramatic effect with our mirthful hosts. The entire band of ruffians suddenly went still at the mention of the highly feared pestilence. Hurricane Jeffers peered directly into my eyes and demanded to know if I was serious or merely having fun at his expense. Understanding totally, I answered that I had extensively studied and practiced medicine in England prior to making my way to the Caribbean. As such, I had the opportunity to learn both arcane cures and newly developed remedies that no other doctor could possibly know or attempt to apply. I swore to my disbelieving audience that I could cure a man of pox if given the opportunity. This statement was greeted by a resounding roar from the entire mob surrounding us. Many of these surly dogs began begging Hurricane to allow me a short stay in order to prove the unbelievable promise I had just made. Swayed by his beseeching rabble, Hurricane finally relented and ordered one of the spare rooms of the fortress emptied so that I could establish a medical surgery. Before long, I had transformed the empty enclosure he offered into a temporary but realistic looking hospital, and I had a line of anxious pirate miscreants waiting their turn for treatment. My statement had created unbelievable excitement, and now it was up to me to prove my fictitious claim or pay for this failure with my life.

As soon as we were settled in our new facility, I had Long Tall Willie boil a full cauldron of fresh water to which I added more than a generous quantity of *Senna* leaves. After giving the mixture time to steep, I opened our surgery doors and began to admit patients. While a minority of the rogues had come for simple cures such as toothaches, infections and other assorted ailments, the vast majority were present to have me cure them of the pox. Regardless of their complaint, each individual was given a very liberal dose of the freshly brewed *Senna* elixir with explicit instructions to return in a few hours for a second dose of this special curative. Explaining to the pox victims that their affliction was caused by an internal noxious entity that required complete flushing from their innards, I warned them that my special medicine would initially cause internal stress and strife as it battled with the nasty villainous cause of their malady. I also notified each that they would experience an explosive release of their bowels, which indicated that my medicine was doing its job by driving the disease forcefully from their bodies.

Most of my anxious patients hardly heard my words, but did not hesitate to greedily gulp down the *Senna* brew, with many begging for an additional dose right then and there. Since they pleaded for more of the curative, I refilled their tankards and allowed them a generous second helping. Word spread to the waiting pirates that I was allowing a double dose of medicine, so that not long after every patient demanded and received two rations of the purging potion. My ministration continued the entire afternoon and towards early evening I had issued the last dose to my final patient.

Hurricane Jeffers suddenly made an appearance and invited me and my team to share dinner with him and his men before we returned to Saint Domingue. The fare for this evening he promised would be a superb salmagundi, a pirate specialty stew that usually included fresh meat and seafood mixed with pickled vegetables and fresh fruit that would be simmered for hours before being declared ready for consumption.

Thanking our brutal host for his marvelous hospitality, I responded that we needed to cleanse ourselves after the long day of attending to his mates, and once done would be more than honored to join him for the promised feast. As soon as he vacated our surgery, I handed Powder Monkey a fistful of *Devil's Trumpet* seeds and commissioned him to deposit them into the pirates' salmagundi in a clandestine manner. Winking his understanding, he was off to obey my command. Meanwhile, we packed up our medical stores and returned them to our longboat under the ever-watchful eyes of our pirate hosts.

As we returned for our promised feast, we were met by Powder Monkey who signaled that he had accomplished the important task given him. Before joining the pirates for dinner, I warned each of my team to avoid ingesting any of the drugged salmagundi, since it would cause them to become violently ill and induce their very worst nightmares. My advice to them if they were forced to eat any of the doctored stew was to wander off and discreetly purge the contents of their stomachs by forcing their fingers down their throats. Convinced by the dire tone of my warning, we joined our vile innkeepers for the deadly banquet.

The bubbling salmagundi cauldron was positioned in the middle of the fortress's courtyard surrounded by overturned barrels topped with doors serving as tables. The barbarian pirates had certainly not waited for our appearance to begin their feast. Spread all around the courtyard, they were busily wolfing down their portions as if they had not eaten in weeks. Barrels of ale and rum were also positioned randomly, and the liquid libations were being swilled almost as quickly as the main entrée. Glancing around, I identified that there were a number of black-hearted demons missing, a result I was sure of the explosive reactions to their earlier consumption of the *Senna* tea. I chuckled to myself as I envisioned the dim-witted degenerates doubled over with excruciating stomach cramps or squatting in seclusion scrutinizing their innards literally pouring out of them.

Glancing towards Hurricane Jeffers, I discovered that he was frantically signaling me to join him at his table-of-honor. As I approached, he shoved a plate of salmagundi into my hands commanding me to eat. I knew that I needed to avoid this drugged stew at all cost, but at the same time could not afford to offend my ferocious host. To solve this dilemma,

I announced to all present that it was my personal custom to repay any benefactor before partaking in sustenance. To that end, I proposed that I might earn my meal by relating a haunting tale that I was sure would entertain and please them all. I also was quite aware that the duration necessary to deliver this tale would allow the potent *Devil's Trumpet* seeds enough time to begin registering chaos amongst them.

As expected, my offer of storytelling was unanimously agreed to by all. As complete darkness settled around us, I launched into the familiar tale of my fictitious haunting specter, the *Black Monk*. Narrating this tale of ghostly horror proved quite effective with these superstitious and cowardly whelps. As the effects of the *Devil's Trumpet* seeds began to take hold, I witnessed some very unusual reactions to my tale of the dark clergyman, who seemed intent on haunting my every waking moment. In the midst of my story, one especially affected rogue suddenly jumped up and claimed to have witnessed the *Black Monk* roaming aimlessly atop the fortress's walls. Fearful that the demon had come to spirit him to hell, he suddenly made a mad dash to the very edge of the bluff and desperately leapt to his death.

While I feared that his drastic action would signal an end to the evening's festivities, I was sadly mistaken. The majority of my listeners were now struggling with their own inner demons as they hallucinated all manner of nightmares. One pirate far across the courtyard began rolling around on the ground locked in mortal combat with killer hellhounds. Another rogue strangled his neighbor to death, claiming the individual was a nasty old witch that needed dispatching. Even Hurricane Jeffers surprised me when he broke down in tears confessing to an imaginary lover that he was mortally sorry for the way he had treated her in life, and certainly did not intend to beat her to death with his bare hands. Before long chaos erupted everywhere, as Gertrude's devilish seeds had a much more pronounced effect than I could ever have imagined. The courtyard now resembled a lunatic asylum with inmates running amok and causing all manner of harm both to themselves as well as to their surrounding comrades. Upon witnessing these creatures demented actions, I knew it was time for my team to exit the demonic celebration and attempt to discover the location of Captain Adams!

Upon my command, my men separated and began their systematic search, constantly detouring around crazed pirate scum caught up in their dementia and posing serious danger to our rescuing efforts. I headed directly to Hurricane Jeffers room and discovered that it was nothing more than a pigsty. Discovering no evidence of Captain Adams, I closed this rat-hole's door and moved on with my search. As I maneuvered deeper into the fortress, I came across a door that had been painted entirely black and secured by a ponderous lock. Borrowing a mallet found nearby, I went to work on the device, which finally yielded to my ferocious pounding.

Upon entering the dark and dank room, I had an eerie feeling come over me but could not identify its source. The room itself was extremely cold and cheerless. While relatively neat, it was sparsely furnished with a bed, a desk and chair and nothing more. The room felt more like a prisoner's cell than an individual's living quarters. The only hint of color or sign of decoration was an old threadbare rug that covered the floor towards the center of the room. Given its out-of-place appearance, I decided to investigate this sole decoration a bit further. Tugging the aged carpet aside, I knelt down to study the floorboards directly beneath it. Using my dirk, I tapped on the planks and detected a hollow reverberation. Realizing that this discovery might reveal something of value, I pried up one of the boards to unearth an unbelievable treasure trove. Inside this highly cunning cache were a number of chests that filled the secret hiding place to capacity. Upon opening the first chest, I discovered that it was crammed with silver and gold coins of varying value. Intrigued by this discovery, I proceeded to inspect each of the hidden containers to determine their exact contents. The majority of these chests held either valuable coins or small bars of gold or silver. In a flash, I realized that I had accidentally stumbled upon the Black Tarantula's treasure horde. Continuing my examination, I noticed that there were two smaller containers among their larger cousins.

Opening the first, I found that it was crammed with English gold guineas. From past dealings, I knew that these coins were minted by machine to provide consistency and to discourage the heinous crime of counterfeiting. I reached into the chest and selected one of these gold coins for inspection. My first impression was that the coin did not feel right. My early days as a money collector working at Slugger's Sports

Emporium in London had trained me exceedingly well to instantly recognize bogus coinage. You see, I was the one responsible for making up any insufficient funds to Slugger should I happen to accept any counterfeit money. As a result, I learned very early in life what each coin of the realm should look and feel like in my hands. Since this coin felt a bit lighter than it should have, I held it up to the lantern's light and examined the images stamped on it. There was something amiss as I studied the side bearing the image of our sovereign, King George. With startling revelation, I recognized the problem in a flash. While the image of our King seemed nearly perfect, the counterfeiter had not paid close enough attention to another important detail. The image of King George faced the wrong way! A genuine guinea portrayed our leader facing right, but these bogus coins had him facing left. To be absolutely sure, I made a deep incision in the coin I had selected, and was not at all surprised to discover lead under a thick outer layer of gold. Yanking this small chest out of its hiding place, I decided to take these counterfeit coins with me. I did not have the vaguest idea of what I would do with them, but I had a very strong inclination that I would find a good use for them in the near future.

Before replacing the upraised floor planks, I reached down and liberated the other diminutive chest from its lair. When I pried this case open, I was momentarily stunned by the glistening vision of splendor that met my eyes. To my complete amazement, I found that this box was crammed with a fine and fabulous collection of both cut and raw gems of incalculable value. A quick scan revealed huge diamonds, rubies, emeralds, pearls and other precious goodies that would make their owner richer than any king on the face of the earth! Setting this chest next to its twin, I replaced the floor planks and covered the floor once again with the threadbare carpet; carefully ensuring that all appeared exactly as I had found it. Hefting both chests under each arm and covering them with my traveling cloak, I exited the Black Tarantula's quarters, replaced the lock and went in search of my men.

As I entered the courtyard filled with the delirious pirate fiends, I noticed Powder Monkey and Tan on the far side signaling to me. Hurrying over, they whispered that Captain Adams had been found and freed. They reported that he was currently being assisted to our escape craft by Long Tall Willie and Scuttle. The two frightened crewmen urged me to quickly follow, so that we could take our leave of our maniacal hosts. Nodding understanding, I ordered them to do exactly that, and promised that I would follow as soon as I accomplished one more chore. With a quick salute, my two salts turned and ran toward the descending staircase. Placing the two small chests on the ground covered by my cloak, I quickly made my way to the spot I had last seen Hurricane Jeffers. I found the rogue unconscious surrounded by a slew of slaughtered pirates. Previously informed as to its value to the rogue, I removed the silver good-luck crucifix from around his neck and dropped it into my pocket. Hurrying back, I retrieved the two small chests and scrambled down the never-ending steps to our awaiting boat.

Chapter 2: The Devil Gives Chase

As soon as I was seated, my crew hastily pushed off from the beach and rowed like madmen for our waiting vessel. As we exited the cove, Long Tall Willie questioned the contents of the two small chests that I had liberated from the pirate's stronghold. Opening only the case with the counterfeit coin, I showed them the guineas and explained why they were all bogus and completely worthless. Confused to the extreme, my men questioned my sanity for absconding with this worthless coinage. I answered that I currently had no idea on how I would put these fraudulent coins to good use, but promised them that I would surely devise a bloody good reason for doing so in the very near future. Since the second miniature chest remained closed, my men simply assumed that it also was crammed with more of the same golden impostors and nothing more was mentioned.

Taking a quick moment to inspect Captain Adams, I ascertained that his condition was beyond dreadful. While he remained unconscious, I could see that he had been bruised, battered and bloodied by his vile captors. Knowing there was little to be done for him until we arrived back at our ship, I made him as comfortable as I could. The journey back was long and torturous, but we finally arrived at our designated rendezvous spot just after daybreak. Gingerly transferring Captain Adams to our ship, I ordered him taken below to Doc's surgery and called on our esteemed medic to attend to his numerous injuries. I then hauled the two small chests aboard and secreted them amongst my belongings. When the longboat was secured, I issued crisp orders to weigh anchor and head towards Jamaica at the fastest possible speed. Lion in our second ship followed in our wake, as we employed the full complement of sail to speed our journey. Making my way to Doc's cabin, I found our medical man fussing over his newest patient. With a look of concern, he informed me that a smattering of his patient's assorted injuries appeared life-threatening. Relating that he would do all that he could prior to arrival, he promised to send for me the moment Captain Adams regained consciousness. Nodding understanding, I exited the cabin and made my way above to supervise our frantic retreat.

For the next several hours all proceeded smoothly aboard both vessels as we raced towards our intended destination. Near midday, our topman called down that he has spotted a sail far off our starboard. Reaching for my telescope, I was a mite astonished to witness the dreaded pirate schooner giving chase. While I had assumed that the brigands would eventually pursue us, I believed that the strong dose of *Devil's Trumpet* would allow us a much greater lead time given the pitiful condition of our drugged adversaries. Taking a closer look, I spotted Hurricane Jeffers on the enemy's maindeck driving his men in a furious and frantic pace to close the distance between us. Turning to Sharkface, I questioned our efforts to silence the guns on the trailing pirate ship. He winked and informed me that all had been handled and that their guns were now spiked and quite useless.

As I continued to monitor the progress of our enemy, I realized that they were running at a much faster speed and would catch us long before we reached Jamaica. Given this regrettable circumstance, I decided to turn both of our ships around and face our nemesis in battle. Issuing the order to our drummer, he beat out a simple message to Lion's ship, turn and attack! As both vessels swung around, I used my telescope to once again assess the situation on the pirate schooner. I viewed Hurricane Jeffers manically shouting orders to his crewmates to prepare for battle. Noting that the pirates had opened their gunports and were in all likelihood loading their cannons, I ordered Lion to swing wide around the villains to block their escape path. At the same time, I commanded our helmsman to adjust the course so that we could welcome our new arrivals with an unfriendly broadside. As I gazed through my scope, I was pleased to observe that Hurricane Jeffers had the same strategy in mind as he adjusted his course accordingly. With the table set, it was now time to unleash death and destruction!

As I continued to monitor our enemy, I observed Hurricane Jeffers issue the order to fire their guns. As the pirate cannon teams attempted to follow orders, they discovered that their guns had been rendered utterly useless. As I watched the confused look on Hurricane Jeffers face turn to outright terror, I ordered our gunners to commence firing. Marveling at the outright accuracy of our gunners, I issued a silent prayer of thanks for all of the long hours my men had spent practicing and preparing for this very type of engagement. Our first barrage caused devastating destruction to the pirate vessel as yards, sails and masts were completely decimated. Now in close quarters, our musket teams aligned themselves on the topdeck and began their calculated slaughter of any visible and unprotected pirate. Given the absolute brutality of the ensuing carnage, I knew within minutes that the battle was over and that we were victors. Since I judged that only a paltry number of the criminals remained alive, I ordered my men to use our grappling hooks to draw the ships together and provide us the opportunity to board our foe and finish the engagement conclusively. As we swarmed onto the pirate vessel, I witnessed Hurricane Jeffers ordering his surviving crewmen to repel boarders. His orders proved ineffectual as my men swept through his vessel leaving only death in their wake!

As I made my way onboard, I went directly to Hurricane Jeffers's position and confronted the fiend, who had somehow survived the brutal onslaught. Given my enemy's ferocity and outright size, I felt a wave of nervousness overtake me as small butterflies danced in my stomach and my throat became quite parched. Without giving these feelings time to escalate any further, I advanced on the hulking giant. As I approached, Hurricane Jeffers issued a bloodcurdling roar and attacked. I fended off his furious onslaught as our blades rang again and again in constant flashing motions. As we fought, I baited him with questions about his leader that I hoped he might mistakenly answer. Questioning Hurricane Jeffers on the Black Tarantula's location, he responded that his master was off in a search of a young French strumpet, who had captured his fancy. Paring a brutal thrust, I asked where the Black Tarantula was searching. Sneering, he responded that she has been reported hiding somewhere on Spanish soil, and that his master was currently in the process of locating her.

At this point in our skirmish, I assessed both of our conditions. While I had incurred minor cuts and scratches, my enemy had fared much worse, and was literally bleeding from all ports. Realizing that his situation was quite dire, he manically pressed his attack hoping to strike a lethal blow. His efforts proved successful as he delivered a vicious slash that laid my left arm open from my forearm to my wrist. Totally incensed by this severe wound, I decided that my questioning was over and I circled my adversary waiting for an opportunity to strike. As we continued this game, I had a sudden inspiration. Reaching into my pocket, I pulled out his purloined silver crucifix. Holding it up for him to clearly visualize, I causally tossed it over the side into the sea. I then jeered that his luck had certainly run out now that his protection was gone. As he gaped at the sinking talisman, I utilized that moment to thrust my blade into his gut, skewering him like a harpooned whale. As he sunk to his knees, he continued to curse me as a coward and a thief. Expressing fabricated gratitude for these inimical compliments, I ordered my men to secure him to a broken mast and cast him into the sea. As Doc was inspecting my wounds, Hurricane Jeffers was lashed and promptly thrown over the side. As he floated away in a rather voluminous trail of blood, the ever-present sea scavengers moved in to appease their ravenous appetites. As he was slowly carried away by the currents, he shrieked and wailed as hungry sharks tore him to pieces.

Given the precious time constraint we faced to ensure our suffering patient received proper medical attention, I chose to desert the demon's pirate schooner to the vagaries of the sea rather than add it to our small force. However, before vacating the crippled vessel, we expeditiously sacked it and seized anything of value. Since their guns had been spiked and the time necessary to transfer them would have been exorbitant, we simply left them behind even though many were superior to our current inventory. Powder, shot and a slew of ship essentials were appropriated by my crew, who scurried like rats throughout the enemy's vessel prior to her abandonment. Without another thought, we employed full sail and raced towards Jamaica, where I was certain that Captain Adams would receive expert medical attention. In the meantime, Doc treated my most vicious wound by searing it closed with a hot iron then covering it with salve and a multitude of bandages.

Upon reaching our destination, I accompanied my men carrying the unconscious officer to the Adams' mansion. I had also secreted the small chest of priceless gems under my traveling cloak to leave in the sisters' possession for safekeeping. The crew had already been paid handsomely for their efforts to rescue Captain Adams, and liberty would be allowed on a rotating basis so each would have ample opportunity to squander their earnings on their vice of choice. As soon as our medical caravan reached the Adams household, the sisters flew into a flurry of activity with Aunt Gertrude issuing commands. Captain Adams was immediately transported to his room and Gertrude chased all but me so that she could conduct a thorough examination of her injured nephew. As she went about this careful inspection, she wore a highly concerned and apprehensive scowl on her face. Upon completion, she informed me that her nephew had sustained serious internal injuries, which more than likely accounted for his unconscious state. She explained that we would first tend each of his broken bones and vicious lacerations. Once done, she instructed me to join the others for food and rest as she would personally monitor her nephew's condition over the next several days. Grateful for the opportunity to sate my raging appetite, I whispered that I would be nearby if she required further assistance.

As I exited the room, both Aunt Willamina and Hortence descended on me like seagulls after a meal of mullet. Once I had given them a detailed synopsis of their nephew's condition, they escorted me to the dining room where they had a hot meal waiting. As I wolfed down their offering, the doorman announced the arrival of the new Fort Commander, Captain Dale Houndstooth, having formally replaced the recently deceased and unlamented Toeless Hicks. Offering him a seat and a chance to sample the delectable morsels yet on the table, I questioned the reason for his visit. Swallowing a bit of savory mutton, he reported that Captain LeMerde had paid him a visit to formally accuse me of piracy. The French rascal had petitioned the good Captain to issue an arrest warrant in my name in the event that I ever returned to Jamaica. Captain Houndstooth had denied the pompous French villain's request, informing him that a formal trial was customary prior to criminal incarceration or conviction. Further, he instructed the strutting cockerel that my papers had been examined personally by him and the charge being leveled against me seemed ludicrous. Captain Houndstooth revealed that these words infuriated the Frenchman, who stormed out of his office in a state of extreme annoyance and anger. In conclusion, Captain Houndstooth advised me to remain under the sisters' care and avoid any contact with this deranged madman at all costs!

Since my sworn enemy was close-at-hand and my rescued friend was in dire need of medical assistance, I elected to remain at the Adams' mansion until Captain Houndstooth returned and informed me that it was safe to leave my shelter. I tasked Powder Monkey to act as my eyes and ears and provide any island scuttlebutt that he might uncover. The following evening my loyal friend appeared and proceeded to update me on the latest news and rumors he had uncovered. He reported that the islanders were quite happy to have their hero back alive. However, there was a great creeping fear in most of their hearts that the Black Tarantula would choose to attack their location in retaliation for our successful rescue in the near future. This general fear induced the citizens to begin mobilizing defenses in the event that the demon pirate found his way to their shores.

Continuing, Powder Monkey revealed that Captain LeMerde persisted in causing further trouble while ashore. In a one-sided duel, he had slaughtered an isle's gentry, who had the sheer audacity to secret his wife away from this brigand's interests. Powder Monkey disclosed that the unscrupulous lecher continued to spend the majority of his time ashore at *Fat Dog's Pub*. The good proprietor of this house of iniquity had been forced to suspend his highly profitable *Gator Gobble Game* due to the miscreant's dishonest antics. To remind you, this sadistic wagering game pitted a ravenous alligator against a slew of helpless young animals. Given the unholy slaughter that followed, bloodlust and gambling were the sole reasons for contest's very existence. At least, that was the case until the devious French officer had presumably ended the event in his favor by his unsanctioned slaying of the reptilian aggressor. However, given LeMerde's proficient combat skills along with the threat posed by his ever-present and subservient minions, Fat Dog was virtually powerless in any attempt to forbid the fiend's disruptive attendance at his pub night after night. Powder Monkey reported that the French miscreant spent the majority of his nights at the tavern gambling at cards. While the cocky lout was pleased and satisfied to win most hands, he could instantly revert to a spiteful and revenge-minded brute when faced with defeat. The truth of the matter was that his winning ways had much to do with his opponents' deliberate efforts to willfully lose rather than face the prospect of offending him and thereby jeopardizing their very existence!

Powder Monkey also divulged that LeMerde continued to slander my name everywhere he traveled on the island. He had publicly branded me a pirate, a highly serious and damaging allegation during these fearful times. Promising the populace that justice would eventually triumph, he was now waiting patiently for the opportunity to arrest me. While highly frustrated by being forced to bide his time, Powder Monkey confided that the madman habitually drank to excess each evening causing havoc, pain and death to anyone foolish enough to cross his wake. On any late evening, he could be observed wobbling and stumbling his way to the docks, where his longboat waited to return him to the safety of his ship.

With a concerned look on his face, Powder Monkey revealed that he had overheard a conversation between LeMerde and his two faithful subordinates discussing a plan to kidnap me and hang me at sea. To affect this result, they discussed various methods to lure me outside of the sisters' home and protection. One approach called for randomly murdering a number of my crewmen currently on liberty, which they were sure would draw me out of hiding. Listening to this ill news, I realized that I needed to devise a plan to deal with Captain LeMerde before any of his dastardly schemes were set in motion. As I began to think hard on the matter, I knew that I had to somehow separate Captain LeMerde from the protection provided by his numerous crewmen and well-armed vessel, if I ever hoped to successfully arrest him for the crime of kidnapping. Should I succeed in apprehending the fiend and rescuing Aimee, I concluded that LeMerde's loyal confederates would muster their forces and hunt me down, liberate the brigand, destroy both my ships and crews and then hang me, which was a very poor bargain indeed! Alternatively, I reasoned that I needed to uncover a method to incriminate the brute on English soil which would result in a trial, conviction and eventual incarceration enabling me to free Aimee. Just then, I remembered the counterfeit coins that I had left on *Rue's Revenge* and a very devious plan began to form in my noggin. Acting on my new scheme, I had Powder Monkey retrieve the chest of counterfeit coins. I then ordered my friend to continue his very close nightly watch on LeMerde to monitor and report all of his movements.

While I waited for Powder Monkey's next report, I assisted Gertrude in her healing efforts on her nephew. Yet unconscious, she informed me that he was still in imminent danger. All we could do now was hope and pray, as he alone battled for his life in the darkness that enveloped him. Given that we had time on our hands, Gertrude asked me to accompany her to the root cellar secreted on the far edge of their property. Entering her private domain, she led me over to an empty corner and triggered a hidden switch which opened a secret compartment containing all of the wealth I had entrusted to her, including the newest installment of the Black Tarantula's gem chest. Gertrude explained that the root cellar was actually on a separate deed from the rest of the land on which their mansion sat. She divulged that she and her sisters had decided to deed this piece of property to me, making me its legal owner. Gertrude confessed that she and her sisters had chosen this wise course of action to protect my wealth in the event that an accident or tragedy should befall them. By enacting this shrewd move, my wealth would be safe and secure and forever legally in my possession. Thanking Gertrude sincerely for her generosity and forward thinking, we closed the secret compartment and returned to the house to check once again on our patient.

Not much later, I heard a commotion at the entranceway, and was startled upon hearing the butler's hysterical cries. Moving towards his wails, I discovered the source of his extreme agitation. On the porch sat an old tattered sack that leaked blood in copious quantity. When the sack was opened, the bloody and abused body of Powder Monkey spilled out. He had been tortured, brutalized and left for dead with numerous broken bones, vicious bruises, savage slashes and an assortment of burn marks across his entire small frame. Gertrude supervised the transfer of my friend to a spare bed, while I stood by in a state of incomprehensible confusion. She turned and handed me a blood soaked note that had been pinned to my friend's clothing. Shaking with rage, I read the missive from Captain LeMerde inviting me to seek revenge for the mortal damages inflicted on the boy. Gertrude sensing my black mood urged me to calm down; sensing that any action I perpetuated in my current state of rage would only invite disastrous consequences. In the meantime, Gertrude began to minister to the lad's injuries, shouting orders to all of us to mobilize our efforts to assist her needs.

For three infinitely long days, Powder Monkey lingered on death's doorstep before finally taking a turn for the better. On the fourth day, he regained consciousness for a brief moment, and issued a grim smile before returning to darkness. The following day, he awoke dazed and totally addled but able to recognize each of us as we surrounded his bed. With supreme effort, he signed that he had been waylaid by Captain LeMerde's two loyal assistants, who had dragged him forcefully back to their ship. Once aboard, he had been interrogated by LeMerde by means of utmost brutality to force him to reveal my plans. With a proud smirk, he confided that my enemies had gained very little from this devilish exercise, other than appeasing their own savage temperaments. When they finally realized that he would choose death before revealing any pertinent information, they decided that he was nothing more than a deaf and dumb idiot, quite incapable of providing the answers they desperately sought. The only information he was able to uncover under their malicious ministrations was that Aimee was still alive aboard their vessel. While Powder Monkey did not get a chance to speak to her, he was able to catch a glimpse of her being manhandled in less than gentlemanly fashion.

Chapter 3: To Catch a Counterfeiter

Now that Powder Monkey was on the slow road to recovery, I vowed to avenge his mistreatment and bring ruin to those that had wrought his dastardly attack. Knowing that Captain LeMerde was a creature of habit, I was certain that he and his villainous cohorts could be found most nights at Fat Dog's drinking, gambling and whoring. Summoning Lion to the Adams' mansion, I laid out my detailed and diabolical plan to obliterate this unbalanced French brigand. My first requirement was the presence of a slew of my most loyal men along with the new Fort Commander and a few of his fellow soldiers at Fat Dog's for my grand appearance in two night's time. The second of my requirements was much more delicate and called for very special handling. Since Powder Monkey's assistance was out of the question, I required an individual who could stealthily and unobtrusively execute the scheme I had carefully engineered. This individual would be charged with doctoring the drinks of Captain LeMerde and his two evil accomplices with *Wormwood* elixir that very evening. This innocuous substance when mixed with hot spirits would generate moderate delusions amongst my brutish enemies before eventually rendering them unconscious. In addition, the aftereffects of the *Wormwood* draught would prevent these sea leeches from remembering little if anything of what had previously transpired, once they awoke from their drug-induced stupors. In thinking the matter through, both Lion and I agreed that Long Tall Willie was the ideal candidate for this difficult assignment. Lion promised that he would send him as soon as he returned to our ship in order to begin preparations the for the upcoming night's fun!

Later that afternoon, Long Tall Willie arrived and I briefed him on the delicate mission I needed him to accomplish. Receiving his solemn oath to succeed at any cost, I provided him the *Wormwood* elixir along with a detailed outline of my plan. The success of this mission depended on his ability to administer the drug into the drinks of Captain LeMerde and his men's without notice or suspicion. He gave me a brief salute and told me to stop fretting because the deed was as good as done. Now that the first two steps in the scheme were underway, I began my own preparations by retrieving a sizable amount of counterfeit coins. I then dressed in dark clothes and waited for time to pass. I spent the next several hours in nervous anticipation, until at last Long Tall Willie returned and informed me that our adversaries were well ensconced at their usual table at Fat Dog's and were up to their eyebrows in rum, completely oblivious to the world around them. He promised that he intended to quietly introduce the *Wormwood* elixir into their rum near the pub's closing time. I told him that we would rendezvous outside of Fat Dog's after the pub's close, so that we could shadow our foes as they attempted to navigate their way back to their ship. With a wink, I informed my accomplice that Captain LeMerde and his friends would certainly be taking a slight detour this very night!

Awhile later, I waited patiently in the deep shadows outside Fat Dog's Pub for the appointed time of closing. When it finally arrived, I observed Long Tall Willie exiting the pub, and I immediately signaled him over to my hiding spot. He whispered that we would not have a very long wait. True to his word, LeMerde and his two trusted junior officers stumbled out of the punchhouse to begin their usual saunter back to the docks. They were navigating quite erratically due to the *Wormwood* seasoning, and I breathed a sigh of relief knowing that our task would soon be successful. Stopping continuously to gauge their bearings, the trio finally collapsed on a deserted back lane, and Long Tall Willie and I hurried over to their prone bodies. Since the French commander was our primary target, we both moved to his side and carefully removed his bulging coin purse without disturbing his slumber. Extracting a prodigious horde of English guineas, I replaced them with the counterfeit coins I had toted along with me. I was quite sure that the villain would never notice the transfer nor would he be completely certain of the exact quantity of coins in his possession, so I proceeded to stuff bogus coin after coin into his purse as well as his pockets. Having completed our work, Long Tall Willie and I slipped quietly into the night, leaving our enemies sleeping off the dramatic effects of the *Wormwood* and rum. When they eventually regained consciousness, I expected them to resume their trek back to their vessel unaware that anything at all had transpired.

The next day, I employed the assistance of the Adams sisters and several of their trusted staff. Their assignment was to discreetly follow Captain LeMerde around town. Whenever he entered a business, one member of our group would also follow him into the establishment in an unobtrusive manner. If the French lunatic made a purchase, the trailing shadow had been directed to stay behind and also purchase some trifling with the counterfeit coins that I provided. The important part of this strategy was to pass these counterfeit coins at the same time as LeMerde's visit. Gertrude later reported that the prissy French officer spent the entire late morning and most of the afternoon purchasing various supplies and sundries from quite a number of the town's shops. As planned, our team members had followed him into each of these stores and passed the fake coins, once the demented rascal had paid for his goods and had vacated. By doing so, I was confident that there would be witnesses in every quarter of town once the counterfeiting scheme was made public. Now it was time for me to enter the stage.

My conspiracy called for me to innocently enter Fat Dog's that evening, and convince Captain LeMerde to allow me a seat at his nightly card game. To ensure that this madman did not attempt to take justice into his own hands, I had previously ensured that Captain Dale Houndstooth and a few of his loyal men would also be present to maintain law and order. As the time drew near, I changed into my finest evening clothes and sauntered over to the pub. Upon entering, I was warmly greeted by Lion, Long Tall Willie and several other crew members. I also made a special stop at the Fort Commander's table to pay my respects. I could judge by my quick sideway glances that LeMerde had spotted me. Having done so, he immediately stomped over to my side. Wishing him a good evening, he spat in my face and declared that I was nothing more than a cowardly pirate who purposely hid behind women's skirts

Laughing, as I brushed away his disgusting spray, I informed him that I wanted no trouble as I had merely dropped by for some friendly companionship and to enjoy a few hands of cards. Subsequently, the nefarious officer glanced around the pub and realized that he and his men were woefully outmanned. His roaming eye also detected the presence of Captain Dale Houndstooth, who would certainly thwart any attempt on his part to arrest or remove me from the premises. Having previously been warned by the Fort Commander that his authority meant absolutely nothing on Jamaica, Captain LeMerde realized that he could not so much as lay a finger on me without initiating his own serious tribulations. Frustrated to the extreme, he whispered a grave threat to end my life as soon as opportunity allowed.

Using this forced truce to my advantage, I calmly challenged him to a game of cards as a way to pass the evening in an enjoyable fashion. As I did so, I flashed my own bulging coin purse and the evil fool could not resist this tempting bait. Finding an empty table, he and his toadies sat as he began to shuffle the cards that Fat Dog had graciously provided. Noticing that there was an extra seat at the table, I invited Captain Dale Houndstooth to join in on the fun. The card game commenced and I proceeded to win the first hand and raked in a sizable pot of coins.

As I hauled the winnings toward me, I stopped abruptly and picked up one of the gold guineas giving it careful inspection. Announcing in a voice loud enough for the entire room to hear, I proclaimed that something was dreadfully wrong with the coin I held. Displaying it in front of the Fort Commander, I asked him to thoroughly inspect the offending coin. After he had done so, I could tell that he was still stymied by my announcement, so I made the task much easier by placing a legitimate guinea next to it. As soon as I did, the light of understanding came into his eyes as he immediately shouted out that our good King George was facing the wrong way. Nodding my agreement, I picked up the bogus coin and proceeded to nick it with my dirk revealing the lead hidden underneath. Shocked further by this discovery, the Fort Commander demanded to know what was happening. Responding immediately, I declared that someone at our table was deliberately passing counterfeit coins.

Propelled by my accusatory statement, Captain Houndstooth halted our game and sent one of his men to fetch the island constable, instructing each of us to leave all our coins sitting on the table. Captain LeMerde frustrated on all accounts, attempted to collect his money and leave. He was immediately detained by the sharp points of several military sabers. Upon his arrival, the policing authority along with Captain Houndstooth made a detailed inspection of all of the coins on the table. What they discovered was a slew of identical counterfeit coins amongst Captain LeMerde's holdings. The French villain was summarily arrested for the serious crime of counterfeiting and his holdings were confiscated as evidence. Screaming that a grievous injustice was taking place, LeMerde was hauled off to the city's brig accused of passing counterfeit coinage.

Well it certainly did not take long for the news of the counterfeit coins to spread throughout the entire town. A significant number of local merchants checked their own tills and realized that they too had been cheated. Incensed into action, they promptly descended on the town's prison like a pack of ravenous sharks, demanding recompense from Captain LeMerde, the villain who had passed the worthless coinage in each of their establishments. The police constable dutifully took each of their sworn statements, informing them that LeMerde was under arrest for this serious crime and would soon face this weighty charge in front of the isle's Magistrate. You see, counterfeiting was judged a very serious crime. Anyone convicted of this heinous deed was summarily treated to a hempen jig. LeMerde's trial was scheduled later that week, and I certainly looked forward to justice being served!

On the day of the trial, Captain LeMerde was hauled into court vehemently proclaiming his innocence. He furiously claimed that I had been the source of the felonious coins and as such he was totally blameless. He also charged that his French nationality along with his highly exalted and respected position did not allow him to be prosecuted on foreign soil. The irritated Magistrate informed the vexatious Frenchman that if he was convicted of this serous crime that neither his nationality nor his station-in-life held no vital importance at all in the matter. Confronted by continual outbursts during the trial's initial stages, the Magistrate in exasperation informed the officer to remain silent or face the prospect of being restrained and gagged for the duration of the proceedings. The trial continued as witness after witness was called by the Crown to testify. Each cheated merchant testified that while they could not be absolutely certain that Captain LeMerde had passed the illegal tender, he had certainly visited each of their shops and had purchased items utilizing English coinage. After more than two dozen merchants took the stand and pointed their irate fingers at Captain LeMerde for the crime, the trial's outcome certainly did not bode well for my evil nemesis.

At that point, I was called to the stand to testify any knowledge I had on the situation. I was ordered to recount the evening's events in detail, including my discovery of the fraudulent guineas. Taking my time, I related every detail that occurred that evening. I informed my rapt listeners that I probably would not have discovered the fraud had I not compared a legitimate guinea with the counterfeit version I had just won. Noting that the image of our King was facing the wrong way, I questioned the validity of this coin and requested confirmation from the Fort Commander. Upon these words, LeMerde exploded and verbally lashed out calling me a thieving lying pirate. The Magistrate ordered Captain LeMerde to be silent and probed me on my reason for being on Jamaica. In the same calm and measured voice, I explained that I and my crew had recently rescued Captain Adams from his pirate captors on Tortuga which was met by a rousing and thunderous applause. Once this clamor subsided, I explained that I had made my way to Jamaica to return him to his loved ones.

The Magistrate then questioned if I had prior dealings with Captain LeMerde. Utilizing the same serious tone, I responded that I had several disagreeable run-ins with the brute in the past. Sensing it was the right time to bury my enemy, I continued by informing the Magistrate that Captain LeMerde was a suspected kidnapper, and that I had been authorized by the Governor of Guadeloupe to arrest him and return him to French justice. As I had expected, my statement acted like a grenado exploding in the courtroom. Chaos immediately erupted with wild shouts and yells issued from all quarters, while the Magistrate banged his gavel down unmercifully in an attempt to restore a semblance of order. Once quiet was finally restored, the Magistrate demanded validation of proof for the claims that I had just made. Reaching into my coat pocket I produced the Guadeloupe Governor's formal arrest document which attested to the veracity of my claim. As the Magistrate carefully examined the document, I received a series of devilish, dark stares and mumbled threats from LeMerde. At last, the Magistrate addressed the accused and inquired whether these charges held any validity. Sputtering and fuming, Captain LeMerde answered that they were all lies, and that I was nothing more than a skilled prevaricator and a pirate!

Sensing a hint of concern on the Magistrate's part, I addressed the court and offered a simple solution to the quandary. I informed the court that if a very careful search of the French ship did not result in discovering

Aimee Turbout's presence, then I would certainly retract my testimony in its entirety. Swayed by the merits of my words, the Magistrate turned to Captain Houndstooth and commanded an immediate search party dispatched to uncover the truth of the matter. Captain LeMerde instantaneously began screaming that English authority had no right to make a search on a French vessel. The Magistrate snapped back that English law ruled the island. Continuing, he expounded that the French ship in question was currently anchored in an English harbor, and subsequently the ship was subject to search by English authority at any time for any reason. With that the Magistrate ordered a brief recess to allow for a proper search to be conducted.

The French criminal remained in irons and held prisoner at gunpoint. As I had previously formulated, Aimee was discovered on the French ship being forcibly restrained and held against her will. She was immediately liberated by the English troops and brought straight to the court to appear before the waiting Magistrate, who called the court back into session. Aimee's shabby overall condition and appearance spoke volumes concerning her mistreatment, but she was nevertheless summoned to the stand to testify. In the strongest voice she could muster, she spun her sad tale of abduction by Captain LeMerde following his failed attempt to murder me on Marie-Galant. At the end of her testimony with her tears flowing freely, the court erupted with all calling for the evil French counterfeiter and kidnapper to be hanged!

The Magistrate once again abused his gavel, as he rapped for silence. He then faced the accused with a dark scowl. Questioning if he had anything to say in his defense, Captain LeMerde erupted once again impugning my good name as well as Aimee's. He shouted that the proceedings were a complete sham and totally unlawful. Then he made the grave mistake of verbally attacking the Magistrate for his woeful lack of legal knowledge and the farce of a court over which he presided. As the Magistrate barely held his temper in check, he ordered the court officers to bind and securely gag the criminal, so that a proper sentencing could occur. Given the irrefutable evidence, Aimee's testimony and the brutish conduct of LeMerde, the judge announced to the entire court that the French officer had been judged guilty of both kidnapping and counterfeiting and was summarily sentenced to death by hanging on the following Monday, five short days away! He instructed the First Officer of the French vessel to personally supervise any needed repairs, and then to vacate the harbor and return to Guadeloupe to inform their Governor of the court proceedings. Continuing, he advised this officer that should his Governor deem to hang the rogue himself, he would be far too late since the reprobate's date with the *Grim Reaper* had already been set.

At the trial's conclusion, I made my way to Aimee's side to officially welcome her to Jamaica. As I neared, she leapt into my arms washed in tears thanking me over and over for saving her life. Returning her to the Adams' mansion, I introduced Aimee to my three aunts. Seeing her poor condition, the sisters hurried her off to attend to her pressing needs. Given some time, I wandered over to Captain Adams room to check on his progress. Upon entering, I found him still unconscious, so I quietly crept out of the room so as not to disturb him. Checking on Powder Monkey's condition, I found my friend in a state of restless sleep, so I decided to return to my ship to check on the status of matters since my absence. Upon stepping onto *Rue's Revenge*, I was updated by Lion and Sharkface that all repairs had been completed, both ships had been stocked with fresh water and food and we were ready to sail at a moment's notice. Gratified that all had been handled well in my absence, I retired to my cabin for some rest.

That same evening, I dressed in landlubbers' slops and returned to the Adams' mansion to check on Aimee's condition. As I made my entrance, I was greeted by the sight of Aimee racing down the stairway attired in a magnificent gown happily calling my name. Giving me a hug and a sensual kiss, she again thanked me for saving her a second time. While I expected a certain amount of gratitude on her part for her rescue, her fervid show of emotion caught me completely off-guard. As I contemplated her impassioned kiss, an announcement was made that dinner was served and we all sat to dine. Aunt Gertrude was the first to speak referencing that she had heard Aimee say that she had been rescued a second time. She was now quite curious to learn the details behind the first rescue. Rather than provide the answer, I turned the request over to Aimee. She informed the curious sisters of the full details of her valiant rescue from Captain Bass, and my nearly fatal battle with the escaped brigand as well as his ultimate demise.

The sisters were thrilled with the account especially upon hearing of their hated adversary's annihilation. Given this joyous scuttlebutt, they proceeded to recount the story of the plague ruse I had long ago devised that had also saved their lives. As their story unfolded, I became more and more embarrassed by the high drama of my heroism as embellished by all. At the end of both fanciful narratives, I found myself squirming and quite uncomfortable. I was saved further distress by the call for coffee, tea and dessert which was now prepared for our enjoyment on the verandah. Aimee grabbed my arm and led me out to the garden followed by the sisters. As we walked, she squeezed my arm and whispered that she was quite grateful and happy that I had been her savior once again. She promised that she would somehow find a way to repay me. Then she surprised me anew by giving me yet another ardent kiss before joining the sisters for a tour of their glorious gardens. I declined joining the tour and sipped delicious coffee while reminiscing over both of Aimee's sensuous displays! While I felt conscience-stricken over these amorous demonstrations given my commitment to my beloved Rue, I nevertheless harbored exceedingly pleasurable titillations when harkening back on them. Overall, I was quite bewildered as I continued to mentally debate whether Aimee's passionate responses were prompted by absolute gratefulness or genuine sensuality on her part. Not sure which to believe, I had to admit that her kisses were thoroughly exhilarating to say the least!

The next day, I was summoned to the Adams' mansion with the good news that Captain Adams had regained consciousness. Rushing to their home, I was ushered into the Captain's room where the sisters were bedside laughing and crying along with their nephew. Seeing me enter, he issued his well-known smile and sincerely thanked me for rescuing him from the clutches of the Black Tarantula. He wanted to say more but I realized that he was still rather weak and needed continued rest. Gertrude shooed us from the room like a mother hen as she declared that there was plenty of time later for storytelling. With a shrug and a wink, Captain Adams acquiesced, and we all shuffled out so he could get some much needed rest.

Making a quick pass by Powder Monkey's room, I found him still in a deep sleep. His numerous injuries had been skillfully treated and his broken limbs had been expertly splinted. As I stood at the foot of his bed, a white hot anger reignited in my soul that I knew would not be quenched until the convicted French hooligan was hanged. Later that evening Captain Adams announced that while still not in full health, he would like to attend dinner with us. Gertrude and his manservant attended his grooming and assisted him down to the dining room where dinner was served. Still pale and weak, he presided over the table in his usual humor and haltingly informed us of his disastrous voyage. His tale matched everything I had previously heard, including the very unlucky appearance of the French warship which had sealed his fate. Once a prisoner, his nightmarish description of the demon pirate matched all that I had also been told. Captain Adams related that his meeting with the Black Tarantula had been brief, since the fiend had to travel the very next day to locate his French songbird, having had just received invaluable information concerning her location. Given his required absence, the Black Tarantula had placed him in the capable and lethal hands of Hurricane Jeffers until his return. I could see that Captain Adams was tiring rather quickly, but waited patiently for him to finish his account. I had once burning question for my friend; "*Did the Black Tarantula say where his French songbird was hiding?*" Captain Adams thought over my query for a brief moment before sadly shaking his head in the negative. He informed me that the brutish demon made no specific reference to a location, other than fiendishly chuckling that "*her Spanish masters could not protect her forever*"! Captain Adams hoped this statement meant something to me because the statement was a complete mystery to him. In truth, it meant very little to me, but did provide vital affirmation to the information Hurricane Jeffers had spouted during our battle.

The evening ended due to fatigue on the part of both Aimee and Captain Adams. This gave me the perfect opportunity to slip off and visit Powder Monkey. When I entered his room, I found him awake and alert although in very serious discomfort due to his numerous injuries. I quickly filled him in on the Magistrate's ruling and Aimee's successful rescue. Deeply grateful for this positive scuttlebutt, he nevertheless winced in severe pain before signing that he was really pleased that everything had worked out in our favor. In a serious voice, I thanked him heartily for his demanding sacrifice to the cause. Embarrassed, he changed the subject and questioned when we would sail. In a sincere tone, I informed him that I had a pressing obligation to return Aimee to her loved ones as soon as possible. Because of Aunt Gertrude's strict orders that he remain convalescing in bed, I petitioned Powder Monkey to remain on Jamaica and guard the household until I returned. Continuing, I promised my friend that I would return as soon as possible to collect him and continue my search for Rue. Issuing a saddened expression, he signed that he understood perfectly and would protect the Adams family with his very life!

Chapter 4: Aimee's Return

Before I could direct a concerted effort to search for the nefarious Black Tarantula, I knew I had a duty to see that Aimee was returned safely to her family members. However, I also realized that I could not commence this effort until I personally witnessed the hanging of my nefarious adversary. While waiting for his rightful execution, I was approached by the new French warship's commander, Lieutenant Alexandre Devereau. This newly appointed officer insisted on forming a small convoy in order to return Aimee to Guadeloupe. In past dealings with the man, I found him to be both squeamish as well as quite cowardly, which was more than likely the reason behind his insistence that we travel together. Under Captain LeMerde's rule, Lieutenant Devereau had been cowed into submission, and as such had grudgingly accepted Aimee's presence and awful treatment onboard their vessel without question.

This craven officer seemed afraid of most everything. He was an exceedingly nervous young appointee, who remained quite thin due to his ongoing trepidation of being poisoned. The Lieutenant had also been plagued with a twitching right eye that seemed to blink and wink as if it had a life of its own. Given his unreasonable fears, he also had the bad habit of constantly glancing toward his stern. Because of these eccentric tendencies, his crew had nicknamed him Winking Blinking Alex.

Cleared of direct wrongdoing in the crimes committed against Aimee, he had been given the command of the warship on a temporary basis. Actually, Winking Blinking Alex was so cowardly that his participating in perpetrating a serious crime indeed seemed a rather ludicrous notion. For the most part, this cringing weakling was hardly first-rate officer material, but since he was next in line he had reaped the benefits of his disgraced and displaced commander. In his new role, Winking Blinking Alex had insisted that Aimee be transported back to Guadeloupe on his ship as soon as his superior was dispatched. I saw this as nothing more than a formal act of apology on his part. Given that Aimee was a French citizen, I had very little say in the matter and simply acquiesced to the coward's demands.

A day later, Winking Blinking Alex hurried onboard *Rue's Revenge* to apprise me of some very important news. In his ever nervous state, he reported that Captain LeMerde had made a successful escape from English custody. This ill-news immediately elicited my feelings of utter dead, fully cognizant that the villainous reprobate was once more at large. Alex related that his former superior had been assisted by his two loyal subordinates, who had deserted their posts as soon as the trial had ended. He further reported that the duo had smuggled pistols and swords into the prison, and the desperate trio had killed seven men and wounded a score more in their escape. This made LeMerde a murderer in addition to his convicted crimes of counterfeiting and kidnapping. It was believed that the vile threesome had fled to the safety of the island's interior. True to form, Winking Blinking Alex was convinced that the three renegades were now plotting their revenge, safe from the island's authorities. In a state of extreme anxiousness, he warned me to keep a sharp eye out for these criminals, as he believed that they would surely attempt to avenge perceived injustices done to LeMerde. Since we were scheduled to sail shortly, I was far more concerned about my Jamaican friends being targeted by these madmen than any threat the criminals posed to me personally.

Given that time was short and my concern was prodigious, I returned to the Adams mansion to collect Aimee, bid my friends farewell and ensure that steps were taken to protect them in my absence. Taking Aimee aside, I explained the need for her return to Guadeloupe on the French vessel. Consummately crestfallen on being forced to return home on her former prison, she eventually relented and reluctantly agreed to the plan. However, she urged me to make haste to initiate the journey because she was extremely anxious to return to her family. While the sisters had proved to be charming and gracious hosts, she was quite concerned over the mental stress that this ugly incident had caused her loved ones. Informing her that our departure was imminent, I urged her to ready herself and any belongings she would require for the voyage. With a nod and a despondent smile, she was off to make necessary preparations.

Utilizing this opportunity, I ventured to the root cellar to restock my traveling herbal stores. Once completed, I uncovered the small jewel chest which had had previously been deposited for safe-keeping and filled a pouch with a minuscule portion of its contents. While this pouch seemed small and insignificant, I was certain that the jewels within were of extraordinary value. In fact, I believed that my meager withdrawal constituted enough wealth to allow me to purchase several small islands should I have elected to do so. To ensure that this pouch was well protected, I neatly concealed it by sewing it to the inside of my britches.

Prior to my farewell visit and to assuage my growing trepidations, I had contacted the humongous brothers who had assisted me the night of the *Cannon Challenge* incident. Paying them a generous sum, I ordered them to act as vigilant watchdogs over the Adams household until my return. I informed them of LeMerde's escape and his thirst for revenge as the rationale behind their employment. They both were highly reluctant to accept any sort of monetary compensation to ensure the mansion and its occupants remained safe. At my strong insistence, they eventually differed and accepted my generous payment. I commanded them to locate an unobtrusive location nearby the mansion in order to keep a close watch both day and night. They gave me a mock salute and vowed to perform this function without fail. Their watchful presence somewhat mitigated my heightened unease but certainly did not serve to eliminate it entirely.

While Aimee was finalizing her preparations to leave, I hugged and kissed each of the sisters and promised them that I would return in no time at all. Questioning my reasons for a speedy return, I pointed out that I had unfinished business with the Black Tarantula as well as locating and reuniting with my beloved Rue. As if these motives were not enough, I winked and informed them that I also needed to return for Powder Monkey and end his life of leisure. Somewhat appeased, I then provided them the unfavorable scuttlebutt of LeMerde's escape. Nodding acknowledgement, they informed me that Captain Houndstooth had already sent them word of the scoundrel's dreadful deeds as well as a promise of military protection in the event of reprisal. Attempting to defuse their fears, I notified them that I believed them safe once Aimee and I departed. However, I begged them to remain vigilant nonetheless despite the promise of protection from the fort commander. Lastly, I implored them to continue to monitor any scuttlebutt on the Black

Tarantula or Rue in my absence. Promising me that my wishes would be obeyed, I kissed each sister and gave them my earnest thanks for their invaluable assistance. Before returning to my ship, I paid a visit to the recovering Captain Adams. Regretful for his numerous memory lapses, he vowed to scour the decks in my absence to dredge up any information or clues that he might have overlooked or forgot concerning the Black Tarantula or Rue.

I swore to make his household my first stop when I returned so that we could continue our discussion. Prior to making my exit, I shook his hand and wished him a speedy recovery. As I turned to depart, he suddenly sat up in his bed and repeated the words the Black Tarantula had spoken regarding Rue, "*Her Spanish masters could not protect her forever.*" Smiling excitingly, he whispered that he believed there was a hidden message behind the statement. Taking a moment, he then informed me that all West Indies' islanders considered Cuba to be the "*Master of the Caribbean*" because of its astonishing wealth and military might. Musing out loud, he stated that perhaps the Black Tarantula had referred to Cuba with his offhanded comment. While he believed this to be a wild conjecture, he informed me that somehow it just felt right. Thanking him for his continued concern, I wished him well until I returned. Before vacating the mansion, I also made a stop at Powder Monkey's room. Upon entering, I found him sleeping, but my entrance must have alerted him for his eyes fluttered open as I approached the bed. In a very weak voice, he wished me a speedy voyage and an even quicker return. In a serious tone, he once again pledged to protect and guard the household prior to promptly lapsing into unconsciousness.

The next day our convoy set sail, and we trailed the French ship transporting Aimee home to Guadelupe and then subsequently Marie-Galant. As we got underway, I ordered combat classes to resume since there was little else to do aboard except partake in drink. As we headed toward our destination, we encountered no trouble or resistance along the way. Promising at least one full week of liberty when we reached Guadeloupe, I provided Lion and Sharkface with copious coins to divide amongst their crews so that each man could enjoy their free time ashore.

We reached Guadeloupe without the slightest incident, and I was strongly petitioned by Winking Blinking Alex to join him and Aimee on reporting to the Governor. I suspected that the real reason behind his staunch insistence was his fear of being censured or possibly accused of assisting in Aimee's kidnapping. As far as I was concerned, his acceptance of the craven crime made him a willing accomplice. In any event, I decided that the meeting would provide a good opportunity to update the Governor on the numerous events that had occurred in my absence. My primary goal was to coax the Governor into providing us with yet another formal arrest order which I was sure would cost dearly. Once anchored, I put Lion and Sharkface in charge of the ships as well conducting an orderly liberty rotation for the men. I also gave Scuttle a special order to restock our grenado inventory utilizing the same local blacksmith. When these chores were completed, I joined Aimee and Winking Blinking Alex ashore for our trek to the Governor's office.

Winking Blinking Alex was the first to provide the Governor specific details of the recent events including the abduction of Aimee, the trial of Captain LeMerde and, subsequently, the rogues escape. As he related the incidents leading up to our return, I knew that he had outright lied when he claimed that LeMerde had promised to murder him if he did not acquiesce to Aimee's kidnapping. Sensing his inability to clearly communicate, I disclosed the specific details of Captain LeMerde's trial, conviction and his eventual escape. While I could tell that the Governor was quite pleased by the news of the pompous officer's demise, I also could detect extreme nervousness on his part when he was told of the villain's successful escape. After listening to my account, the Governor dismissed Winking Blinking Alex and ordered him to write up a full report on the matter which would be relayed to France. He also informed the fidgeting officer that a follow-up meeting would occur in due time to decide his fate in this matter. As he exited the Governor's office, Winking Blinking Alex's eyes were dancing up and down like a harbor buoy caught in *dirty weather*!

Turning to Aimee and me, the Governor inquired about our short term plans. I responded that I intended to return Aimee to her brother and sister as soon as possible. Upon my mention of the Turbouts, a very concerned look appeared on the Governor's face. Without delay, the Governor announced that marsh fever had been reported on Marie-Galant. The Governor then divulged to a now highly agitated Aimee that the island's best medical man had been dispatched to handle matters as soon as the dire news had been delivered. However, the Governor explained, that since a cure to this tropical malady did not exist, the doctor could really do nothing more than make sure that the infected were comforted and cared for prior to their deaths.

His drastic pronouncement sent Aimee into a frenzied state, as she pleaded with me to deliver her to her brother's home as soon as possible. Responding, I informed her that I would do so just as soon as we were able to return to my ship to procure medical supplies and a longboat to transport us. Given this new emergency, I realized that any additional business with the Governor would have to wait for another time. Meanwhile, the Governor sputtered that he was not even sure if Rene or Lille had contracted the disease, and reassuringly stammered that he was quite certain that the entire matter had been totally blown out of proportion. Not heeding these false words of hope, Aimee and I bid the Governor a good day and hurriedly made our way back to *Rue's Revenge*.

When we arrived, I sent word for Doc to meet us in my cabin. Sharkface informed me that Doc was currently on liberty and probably celebrating at some disreputable punchhouse. Calling Angry George into my cabin, I instructed our ship's storyteller to go to town and fetch Doc under my strict orders. While we waited for Doc's arrival, I took the time to collect a small medical chest which was stuffed with medicinal herbs, and secured it in the longboat intended to transport us to Marie-Galant. After what seemed like an eternity, Angry George returned to the ship with a very inebriated Doc in tow. Quite useless in his present state, I nevertheless ordered him to accompany Aimee and I to Marie-Galant, aware that he would provide valuable assistance once he had a chance to sober up a wee bit. Piling into the longboat, we made the trip in record time. Upon docking, we were greeted by the manor's *busha*, the plantation's overseer, who appraised us of the critical situation awaiting us. Contrary to the Governor's oblique report, the plantation foreman confessed that both Rene and Lille were bedridden with the fever. They had both been desperately ill for the past week, with no change other than seeming to become weaker and weaker. Doctor Baptise Broome had arrived from Guadeloupe and had been ministering to the patients but his prognosis was quite bleak.

I could tell that the man was quite concerned by the situation, and he seemed to believe that the Doc and I could do no more than what Doctor Broome had previously accomplished. He confessed that the French physician's answer to this tragedy was to continually bleed his two patients, while their plight continued to worsen with each passing hour. Questioning the foreman on how the disease had initiated, the worried overseer told me that he had absolutely no idea. It seemed that Rene and Lille had celebrated their wedding anniversary with a picnic on a secluded lagoon in the island's interior. The day had gone splendidly until late afternoon when they were suddenly swarmed by voracious flying insects. Bitten into total submission, the couple returned to the mansion in good stead but covered with bug bites. The foreman surmised that evil vapors from the lagoon must have infected them both, for not very long after the symptoms of this marauding disease emerged. From there, the couple continued to decline despite Doctor Broome's ministrations and frequent fluid drainages. Thanking him for remaining loyal and managing the plantation's business in the face of disaster, Aimee, I and Doc jumped into a waiting carriage to inspect the situation firsthand.

Chapter 5: The Cure for Marsh Fever

Arriving at the Turbout's mansion, we were admitted by the dour butler, who seemed somewhat relieved by our presence. He described the situation as extremely serious for both his charges. Asking if Doctor Broome had made any recent pronouncements on the situation, the butler actually sneered and confessed that all the good Doctor had managed to accomplish was a significant reduction of the manor's food and liquor inventory. Meanwhile, he confirmed that the pompous physician's patients continued to deteriorate at an alarming rate. Thanking him for his well-placed concern, I asked him to escort our own clearly inebriated Doc to the kitchen and attempt to sober him up with strong coffee. With his departure, Aimee and I rushed hastily to Rene's study to have a word with Doctor Broome.

Entering, we found the good Doctor seated with wine, brandy and food scattered everywhere. He had raised one of his swollen legs and seemed quite unaffected by our sudden presence. In a pompous tone, he informed us that he suffered from the gentleman's disease called gout, which I was sure was brought on by his regal appetite for rich food and drink. Aimee apprehensively questioned him on the condition of her family members, and was told that the prognosis was exceedingly bleak. The self-important healer informed her that this was the worst case of the illness that he had ever experienced, and as such, was quite concerned that the entire household was in eminent danger of also contracting the lethal disease. Promising us that he would continue his faithful ministrations despite the danger involved, he sighed and confessed that he expected the *Grim Reaper's* visit at any moment. He further expounded that traditional methods of bleeding had not producing any positive results so he had decided to double his efforts. Exasperated by the grim news, we both ran up the stairs to check on the patients firsthand.

Entering the sickroom, we discovered both Rene and Lille convalescent in separate beds in two completely divergent states. Rene was experiencing bone-numbing chills, while Lille was burning up with fever. They both sported a sickly yellow color, as they reposed on horribly soiled bed linens. Both were far too weak to acknowledge our presence, and Aimee collapsed in hysterical sobs after viewing their decimated conditions. Moving to her side, I promised to provide assistance, but urgently required her help to accomplish what had to be done. Remembering Doctor Broome's prior warning, she informed me that she was fearful of contracting the sickness but would do whatever was necessary.

After a cursory check of each patient, I decided to take control of the situation despite Doctor Broome's presence and dire warnings. The first thing I ordered was an immediate change of bed linens, which Aimee and the butler accomplished. While they were busy with this chore, I made my way back to the kitchen to prepare some proper medicine. Remembering all that Gertrude had taught me on tropical fevers, I knew with certainty that the employment of *Jesuit's Bark* was the answer. Turning to the manor's cook, I called for a fresh caldron of water to be immediately boiled. Locating my medical chest, I found the *Jesuit's Bark* and dropped several of the larger pieces into the caldron that had been placed over the fire. I then instructed the cook on the proper methods of making the tea. Once this was underway, I checked on Doc's condition. I could see that he had begun to sober up a mite due to the effects of the strong coffee, but realized it would be quite a while before he made a complete recovery.

When the tea was ready, I poured it into a small kettle and returned to my patients. When I entered, I found that both Rene and Lille had been cleansed, and that the soiled bed linens had been exchanged for duplicates that were clean and fresh. At that point, Doctor Broome entered and demanded to know what was happening. Explaining that I had been trained by a natural healer, I informed the arrogant snob that I planned on utilizing *Jesuit's Bark* tea, since it had proved highly effective in the past in curing similar tropical maladies. Acting both highly insulted as well as thoroughly incensed, he ordered me out of his hospital room so he could bleed his patients. I informed the good Doctor that I believed that his patients had lost too much blood already, and that I felt it was now time to affect a different remedy. Not really listening to me, he once again ordered me out of the room. When I refused, he called for both the butler and the *busha* and ordered them to physically remove me from the room. Confused to the extreme, the two individuals looked back and forth between themselves.

At that moment, Doc staggered into the room and sobered radically at the sight of the suffering patients. Demanding to know what was happening, I quickly filled him in on the situation and what I had planned to affect a cure. To the complete shock and amazement of Doctor Broome, Doc agreed totally with my plan. Turning to Doctor Broome, Doc informed him in broken English that I had cured several cholera patients on our ship with this treatment. Continuing, he politely suggested that all bloodletting be curtailed in favor of my proposed remedy. Doctor Broome went completely insane at that point, ordering all of us out of the room. Utilizing his native Italian, Doc shouted at him to shut his mouth and get out of my way. While the exact words were impossible to decipher for all but me, the tone and meaning were crystal clear which forced the pompous ass to wash his hands of the entire affair and return to the fine food and liquor supply. As he stomped out, Aimee turned to me and in a frightened child-like voice questioned if I was absolutely sure I knew what I was doing. Begging her to trust me, we plied each patient with the bitter tasting herbal tea, and I instructed Aimee to also partake of the curative liquid. Meanwhile, Doc, needing more time to sober completely, returned to the kitchen for more coffee. Dosing both patients every hour with the herbal tea, we attempted to make them as comfortable as we could while we waited for the curative to take effect.

The next three days were agonizing in our long wait for Rene and Lille to show some positive sign of recovery. As this time passed ever so slowly, I could sense that Aimee was quickly losing her confidence in my curative abilities. While Doc Broome was drunk or unconscious most of this time, he was able during his rare moments of lucidity to plant seeds of doubt in everyone's mind. He continually referred to me as a witch, and had successfully convinced Aimee that the foretold demise of her loved ones would be totally on her own conscience given her wrongful faith in me. Never tiring of reminding the poor tortured lass of this fact, I could see that his dire warnings and threats were taking a serious toll on her.

On the afternoon of the fourth day of treatments, Aimee confronted me demanding to know why my miraculous tea had not cured her loved ones. Informing her that my treatment came with no timetable, I urged her to remain both faithful and patient that we would soon notice some sort of improvement in our charges. Later that day, Doctor Broome accosted me in a drunken rage threatening to have me prosecuted for practicing witchcraft and demonology. Since he has been nothing but an irritating nuisance, I asked that he vacate the mansion to which he strongly refused. He then informed me that he planned on acting as the key witness at my witch trial, so it was vital that he remain nearby to be able to testify from a first-hand viewpoint. Disgusted by his threats and rants, I exited the house in search of some peace and solitude. Making my way around the plantation, I happened upon the worried *busha*, who informed me that decisions had to be made quite soon on crop management. Puzzled by this statement, I requested further clarification. The man informed me that the sugar cane required harvesting very soon, or it would start rotting in the fields. Taking responsibility, I gave him approval to initiate the harvest and he immediately was off to fulfill my orders.

Sitting down on the verandah to rest, I realized that even I was becoming skeptical on the chances of recovery for my friends. I certainly had noticed the cynical, uncertain and suspicious looks I had received from everyone around me, and these doubters had begun to erode my confidence. Whispering a short prayer to Saint Agnes, I asked for some sort of definitive sign that I had chosen the proper path in my healing efforts. In the end, I came to the conclusion that all I could really do was hold out in my uneasy and agitated state for a pronounced change in either of my patients. As I was turned to return to the house, I heard Aimee's voice calling from within shouting that her that her brother had awoken and his fever seemed to have been broken.

Racing upstairs, I made my way to our temporary hospital room to discover Rene fully conscious and smiling at his sister. Unable to speak and weak from his recent ordeal, all we could do was welcome him back to the world of the living prior to his slipping back into sleep. Not long after, Lille also came momentarily awake before also returning to her own dreams. When Doc finished his examinations, he turned to both Aimee and I and informed us that he was quite sure that our patients were now on the road to recovery. He recommended that we continue the dosage of the *Jesuit's Bark* tea, along with keeping each of our charges as comfortable as possible in the interim. Doc also announced that he believed that the real danger had passed and that our patients would recover their full health in no time at all. Shooing both Aimee and I out of the room so that we could get some much needed rest, Doc promised to watch over the infirmed and alert us if there were any further developments.

The next morning, I awoke form a very deep sleep and immediately made my way to the patients' room. Entering, I was gratified to find both Rene and Lille fully conscious and in deep conversation with Aimee. Their fevers and chills had completely broken and their appetites for food had returned. I could tell that they were both extremely weak from their ordeal, but their smiling faces finally drained the intense fear that had been building inside me since our arrival. At that moment, a very inebriated Doctor Broome burst into the room in a reeling and staggering drunken frenzy demanding to be allowed to bleed his patients to finalize their cure. Carefully managing to escort him back to the study, I asked the butler to pack his bags for his return to Guadeloupe with me in the morning. Refusing to leave the comforts of the mansion, Doctor Broome began ranting and screaming that witchcraft was a very serious crime, and that I would be burned alive for my horrid practice of these dark arts. Unable to calm him down or terminate his boisterous rants, I decided it was now time to take action.

With an upstanding medical professional proclaiming my absolute guilt, even though a blatant inebriate, the island's populace might be convinced that the good doctor was spouting the truth. Therefore, I was certain that my actions would need to be targeted on destroying my accuser's overall credibility. In order to accomplish this, I had decided to employ just a wee tad of Aunt Gertrude's newest gift, *Devil's Trumpet*! While the doctor was loaded to the gills, I took the opportunity to add a minuscule amount of the herb into his favorite brandy supply. With that, I awoke the startled drunk and announced that he and I would be returning to Guadeloupe that afternoon. I continued the planned exodus by calling for the butler to assist any preparations the good doctor required. As I exited, I glanced back and observed Doctor Broome pouring himself a strong bracer of brandy which he gulped and slurped while calling for more food.

Returning to the sleeping patients, I whispered to Aimee and Doc that since my friends were on the mend, I needed to return to Guadeloupe to petition the Governor for a special charter. At the same time, I volunteered to rid the household of Doctor Broome's odious presence. Doc nodded and promised that he and Aimee could care for the weakened pair until my return. I could sense that Aimee was not pleased by my news, but understood that my absence was necessary. As I opened the door, Aimee scurried over to me and kissed me with an intense hunger that I felt down to my very core. She then thanked me with glistening tears running down her cheeks for saving her beloved brother and sister. Her actions once again thoroughly embarrassed and astounded me as I quickly made my exit before either reaction was betrayed. As I was closing the door, I whispered a promise to conclude my business quickly and return at the earliest opportunity. With that I scampered downstairs to collect my passenger in order to return him home. Once again I was quite confounded by Aimee's actions. The question that raged in my mind was whether her ardent response was provoked once again by gratefulness or sensual passion. However, my quandary was abruptly put on hold as the pompous physician reeled into view.

Doctor Broome approached the carriage in a careening fashion with his half full bottle of brandy clutched in his pudgy fist. He immediately began the chant of witch as he neared our transport. Stopping only long enough to swallow a generous slug of liquor, the idiot seemed to know only that word, and he repeated it over and over. His temperament was quite hostile as he entered the carriage. While he greedily gulped another healthy portion of his brandy, I ordered the driver to take us to the dock at all speed. While the trip seemed to last a lifetime, I was gratified to watch the good Doctor consume the entire contents of his brandy bottle. When we reached the dock, Rene's men loaded the Doctor's possessions, and we set the small sail that would carry us back to Guadeloupe.

About midway through our passage, the doctor's eyes took on a very strange appearance and his actions became even more erratic. Sitting in the small transport, the doctor swiveled his head continuously in all directions, as if he were searching for something. At the same time, his voice became exceedingly slurred as if he was drop-dead drunk.

Continuing his manic surveillance, he began sweating and fidgeting like a madman. It was at this point in our journey that he turned and in a completely terrified voice inquired if I had also observed the devils chasing us. Taken completely by surprise, I answered that I was not quite sure what he meant. In a disgusted and superior tone, he divulged that he had viewed a number of hideous green hobgoblins that were as large as any adolescent and appeared famished and hunting for a meal. He asked that we make greater speed, since the demonic hobgoblins seemed very adept at swimming. Crouching now in the belly of our boat, the fearful medic kept peeking over the boat's transom to spot his adversaries, who he was certain were pursuing him for sustenance. Cowed and wailing manically, the trip lasted far too long and tested my sanity to its limits.

Upon docking, we made our way to the Governor's office. Upon entering, the demented medic rushed inside and immediately began screaming about the predatory hobgoblins with razor-sharp fangs and claws that were now inhabiting Guadeloupe. In a child-like screech he informed us that the demons would certainly devour anything that blundered across their paths. Running to the windows, the madman slammed all of the shutters closed casting the room into semi-darkness, as he crawled weeping and wailing across the floor. The Governor lit two candles and turned to me with a highly questioning look on his face. Frightened by the antics he had witnessed, the Governor whispered a query of exactly what was wrong with the man. As I was about to answer, Doctor Broome began screaming that the bloodthirsty beasts had discovered our hiding place and were currently storming the building. Drooling and moaning his obvious distress and mortal concern, the poor fool hardly made any sense at all given his pronounced slobbering that showered in all directions. I had to stifle my laughter as I watched him perform this impersonation of a lunatic for fear that the Governor might question my sanity at the same time.

Doctor Broome then began beating off his imaginary demonic foes to the complete horror of the Governor, who was quite shaken and confused by the invisible battle that was taking place before his eyes. Reaching the Governor's side, I divulged that I believed that the poor man was suffering from overexertion from his long hours spent battling marsh fever on Marie-Galant. I then informed the Governor that his condition developed almost immediately after his miraculous cure of Rene and Lille Turbout. Since he displayed none of the traditional symptoms of marsh fever, I whispered to the Governor that I was not quite sure what ailed him. I confessed that each time I approached the man, he would cower and scurry away sure that I was an evil witch intent on stealing his immortal soul. I advised the Governor that I believed the poor deluded and overworked medic needed complete bed rest under strict restraint, so he would not have the opportunity to seriously harm himself or anyone else.

Now terrified for his own safety, the Governor summoned his personal guards to subdue Doctor Broome and transport him to the local hospital. His specific orders called for complete immobilization and observation until the madness that haunted the medic passed. The guards latched on to the doctor, who now was shrieking and wailing in the same strange voice that witches were now assisting the green horde of hobgoblins sent to destroy him. As he was carted out of the Governor's office, the crazed doctor's screams and wails trailed him throughout the office building until silence finally returned. I was quite sure that the good doctor would continue to terrorize and frighten the citizens of Guadeloupe for some time to come. I was also entirely confident that the physician's credibility would also be utterly destroyed, so that any effort on his part to brand me as a witch would be summarily ignored. Local physicians would find his plight was quite perplexing, since he was constantly waging war with relentless and voracious imaginary green hobgoblins!

Once the raving madman had been evicted, the Governor and I returned to business. Casually questioning the condition of Rene and Lille, I informed the haughty administrator that both seemed to have made a remarkable recovery. Grunting a positive assent, we moved on to the pressing matter of my visit. When the greedy despot finally questioned me on my specific needs, I responded that I had come in search of a small favor. Realizing that this request would prompt another sizable payoff, I had liberated a sizable diamond from my stash to serve this very purpose. I informed the Governor that I was still quite committed to hunting down the Black Tarantula, but required an official arrest warrant to formally sanction this effort. As was the case with Captain LeMerde, an official document stating that I had been formally charged by French mandate to hunt down and capture this beast would never be questioned by any island's municipality or authority. It would basically allow my ships and crews free and unmolested movement throughout the Caribbean.

The Governor immediately understood my request and countered that formal warrants such as I had petitioned took time to manufacture, not to mention the administrative costs associated with this sort of document. This was my cue to unveil my sparkling present, but before I could do so the Governor continued his thought process. He confessed that he would author the official document, if I would perform a small service for him. Wary of his unethical and disreputable nature, I petitioned him to explain the nature of the favor. Unabashed, the Governor disclosed that he had been experiencing a bad run of luck in his gambling endeavors, and as such owed a local businessman a substantial sum of money. He informed me that if I were to eliminate this debt that he would immediately see to drawing up the official document I required. Questioning the Governor on the name of the local debt holder, I was more than stunned to learn that it was Andre Mimosa, the Corsican!

Chapter 6: Andre Mimosa, the Corsican

I now understood that the task before me was far from simple, since I would have to negotiate with Guadeloupe's darkest character. The Corsican was the proud owner of the island's infamous *Sanglante Noir Diable Café*, or as we English sailor's dubbed it, the *Black Demon Pub*. This notorious establishment was the lewdest, wildest and the most dangerous punchhouse on the island. If sinning was your pleasure, then the *Black Demon Pub* was certainly your choice of habitation. Since I knew little of this villain or his institution other than the loose scuttlebutt picked up from my crew, I prodded the good Governor for more information. Elated that I requested additional intelligence, the Governor launched into a detailed account of the pub and its owner. Per the Governor, the Corsican had been operating on the island for the past five years. He simply appeared one day and purchased the grogshop without arousing local suspicion or interest.

The Governor informed me that the Corsican was renowned for his nasty temperament and his unusually vengeful nature. His upbringing had instilled within him a harsh and strict vendetta code. This code strictly followed the biblical custom of an *eye-for-an-eye*, resulting in brutal and bloody feuds that could last for centuries. Protected by a small army of henchmen, these guardians followed the Corsican's orders implicitly no matter their nature. The Governor summarized the Corsican's basic nature as untrustworthy, mean, vicious, revengeful and totally bloodthirsty, a true pirate on land!

The pub itself was once a renowned smuggler's lair. It was located atop the bluff among its respectable neighbors with a spectacular harbor view. It was rumored to be equipped with an escape tunnel that had been carved directly into the island's foundation upon which it sat, and ran all the way down to a nondescript location in lower Shantytown. From there, it was an easy jaunt to a waiting ship and freedom. The pub itself had the evilest reputation on the island, probably the reason a slew of degenerate islanders and sailors alike chose to frequent it on a regular basis. It was rumored that more murders and other heinous crimes occurred within its four walls than anywhere else on the entire island!

To its marginal credit, the *Black Demon Pub* was also renowned as offering the very best entertainment on the island. The Governor informed me that a sizable locked shed that was located towards the back of the pub was the entrance to the death pit. This arena housed a ponderous fighting ring that had been painstakingly carved thirty feet into the bluff's mantle. Given its former occupants' line of work, the pit had originally been fashioned to store weapons, booty and assorted trade goods in order to keep this unlawful merchandise safe and protected. Through the escape tunnel, these goods were magically transported from the island's harbor directly into the city's center. This hand-hewed amphitheater was now utilized for savage human and animal contests. Deep enough to prevent any contestant possible escape, this huge cut of earth was as wide as it was deep. Ringing the upper sides of this pit, spectators could utilize its spacious ledge to allow them to peer down and enjoy the slaughters.

The pit's bare-knuckles fights were reputed to be the most savage and life-threatening confrontations in the entire Caribbean. The house champion was a hulking giant named Leatherface, who as yet had never been defeated. Mammoth in both height and weight, this monster had the ugly reputation for abject brutality and murder. He was famous for being outfitted in most unusual garb. His apparel consisted of a skin-tight ensemble, completed with an expertly stitched leather hood that covered the villain's entire noggin. Some rumored that the leather hood served to cloak injuries dealt by opponents, while others believed it was merely a ploy to frighten opponents into fearful paralysis. The Governor informed me that the house champion had a favorite tactic he called the *bloody bonecrush* that spelled a tragic end for any competitor. Presently, this brute was responsible for annihilating thirty foes, while seriously crippling more than threefold more. The Governor confessed that this ogre was a demonic monster who demanded avoidance at all costs!

He also reported that the death pit was home to savage and ferocious animal battles. Besides the mundane offerings of roosters and dogs, this evil cavity was the home of a profane animal terror, nicknamed Diable. This creature was a monstrous black jaguar purchased from a traveling Spanish merchant. This black demon was reputed to have been stolen from its mother while still a hapless cub. The Corsican had raised the beast, training it to be a vicious and unforgiving killing machine. The monster had grown into a gigantic and ponderous death merchant, that was easily measured chest-high to even the tallest islander. The beast had the reputation of being stronger than ten men, although any sort of measurement of this claim proved quite impossible. The creature's hind legs were shorter than its forepaws, giving the hellion a permanently hunched appearance. The brute was pure black with a ponderous head and maw. Fearless, powerful and intelligent, Diable was capable of killing utilizing either its huge wickedly sharp claws or its massively powerful jaws, God's perfect death instrument.

Diable served as the Corsican's star attraction, pitting massive fighting hounds against the beast. While these dogs were bred and trained as vicious killers, they stood little chance of survival when matched against Diable. While this sort of one-sided contest had absolutely no appeal for me, it did provide spectacular entertainment for the Corsican's bloodthirsty and inebriated patrons, a true crowd pleaser! Since the cat was unbeatable, the Corsican had devised an ingenious betting scheme of wagering on which of the canine victims would last the longest with his prodigy.

Completing his vivid and lurid description, the Governor warned me to exercise caution in my dealings with the villain since he personified evil incarnate. Contemplating on what I had been told, I was quite relieved that I would be merely repaying a gambling debt and nothing more. Despite the obvious danger, I agreed to handle the matter for the Governor. In turn, he promised to prepare the official papers I desperately required, an arrangement that I would soon regret!

Prior to repaying the Governor's debt, I commissioned Scuttle and Long Tall Willie to scout the infamous pub so I would not face unexpected surprises. Upon their return, they reported that they had uncovered some interesting intelligence. The first bit of information regarded the Corsican himself. My men had learned that the rake and Captain Shivvers were much more than good friends, they were partners! The unexpected demise of our former Captain had put a very unprofitable end to the pair's business arrangements. My men had further discovered that the Corsican had made detailed inquiries into the demise of his former associate. Scuttlebutt had it that these inquiries had led the Corsican to deduce that I was responsible for his partner's death and the sundering of their profitable dealings. Quite vocal in his blame for my complicity, the Corsican had vowed to personally handle the matter in due time.

Secondly, the pair had identified the exact location in Shantytown of the smuggling tunnel's origin. The spot was concealed by a small derelict shack that was guarded day and night by one or more of Corsican's minions. My men had even managed a look inside this shack by luring the guard on duty to temporarily desert his post. Once inside, they found the shack empty with the exception of a sturdy wheeled cage that housed Diable. They also reported that the confined and well-hidden tunnel to the death pit was compact in size at its mouth and quickly opened up to allow room for a full grown man to stand. From observations, they conjectured that Diable's cage was wheeled into place in front of the tunnel and then opened to allow the black demon access to the death pit. My scouts also learned that the Corsican held no love for his pet, as he was known to unmercifully tease and torment the beast whenever the opportunity safely presented itself. Now armed with this valuable information, I decided it was time to pay the villain a visit.

That night I ventured into his den of iniquity along with Long Tall Willie and Lion. Prior to making any formal overtures to the Corsican, I decided to do a little scouting of my own. As we entered, an announcement was made that a bare knuckle brawl was about to begin in the death pit. Curious, I joined my crewmates and we ventured out the pub's backdoor. The shed harboring the arena was stoutly built and its massive wood and iron framed doors could be secured from either side by utilizing thick iron bars that slid through sturdy housings. Inside, it was quite dark and dank with the edges of the enormous depression equipped with oil lanterns that shed illumination down its unending rock-hewed sides. Finding an open spot, we curiously peered down into the massive cavity, awaiting the start of the contest.

The match combatants were announced to the extreme disappointment of all, since Leatherface was not brawling this evening. The crowd's boos and hisses continued well into the third round, as spectators let the house know their huge dissatisfaction. Finally growing tired of complaining, they settled down to enjoy the inferior contest. For me it was more comparable to a bar brawl than a fistfight, with the two brutes continually rolling and wrestling on the stone floor. Several head-butts, elbows, and kicks were delivered with sloppy form and casual intention. Well into the match, one of the ruffians managed to get his opponent in a somewhat effective chokehold, and clung desperately on to his flopping foe until he went slack from lack of air. Deeply dissatisfied, the crowd showered both fighters with food, drink, and all manner of personal detritus. The fighters climbed out of the ring via a ladder that was lowered from above to receive even more crowd abuse before making their escape through the massive shed doors. The pit was hastily cleaned by a few scampering lads and the crowd began to settle down in anticipation of Diable's performance.

The cat's canine opponents were dragged into the shed barking and snarling. There were four dogs in all, mostly mixed breeds of undeterminable origin. They did have common traits such as massive size, sheer strength and savage ferocity. In observing their vicious snaps and snarls, I began to doubt whether any creature on earth could emerge victorious battling them. The hounds were shoved into sturdy cages and lowered by pulley to the floor of the death pit to await their opponent. Their handlers climbed down the ladder, released their charges and scurried back up to safety, terrorized by Diable's imminent arrival. The ladder and cages were extracted and the crowd went silent awaiting the black fiend's appearance. As the dogs stood snarling and growling, a black shadow raced into view. Staring transfixed, I could not believe my eyes as the jaguar was truly immense. While it was difficult to fully visualize the beast due to the poor lighting and its deep ebony color, I beheld its demonic yellow eyes as it agilely stalked the hounds.

One overly anxious mongrel decided to take the initiative and lunged snapping at the creature. With lightning speed, Diable simply lashed out with its massive forepaw and nearly tore off the poor mutt's head. Mortally wounded, the dog collapsed mid-lunge and expired. Well, I can tell you that my worries for the mammoth cat ended right there and then. The remaining whelps turned heels and began their useless efforts to scramble for safety, while the black monster stalked and tore them apart one-by-one. The jaguar saved a special treat for the last cur.

Completely engulfing the dog's head with its enormous maw, the beast proceeded to chomp down with incredible force and with a resounding crack crushed the poor cur's skull. The crowd stunned into silence by this exhibition of sheer domination, finally woke from their trance and began to clap, whistle and yell their appreciation for the slaughter they had just witnessed.

As the mob around the pit continued its boisterous adulation, I took a moment to study the beast. As if sensing my presence, the black devil raised its unique yellow eyes to meet my gaze. Staring down, I felt that there was something familiar in the beast's face. As if reading my mind, the black demon seemed to wink up at me with one of its satanic orbs, and then turned and disappeared from view. Sure that my imagination was playing a nasty trick on me, I exited the stinking slaughterhouse along with the delighted and delirious spectators.

Now that I had a first-hand view of the pub, I was ready to conduct my business and return to Marie-Galant to check on the Turbouts. The following evening, I ventured back to the alehouse with more than enough coin to free the Governor of his debt. I chose Long Tall Willie and Lion to accompany me on my mission. Entering the *Sanglante Noir Diable Café*, I could see that festivities were well underway. Finding an empty table, we sat as I scanned the premises in search of the pub's nefarious owner. He was sitting alone at a corner table, so I decided to take this opportunity to confront him. Telling my crewmates to remain vigilant, I strode over to his table.

As I approached, I decided that a friendly demeanor was called for so as to minimize any nasty complications. As I reached his side, I flashed my best smile and introduced myself. Barely looking in my direction, the thug questioned what I wanted with him. Continuing my amicable manner, I informed him that I was on a mission for the Governor, and had been authorized to repay his gambling debt. I then plunked a full purse of coin on the table informing the Corsican that as far as I was concerned the matter was settled. Giving me an extremely hateful and evil smirk, the rascal asked if I was sure that my statement was true. Confused by his reply, I questioned the black-hearted villain on his meaning. Signaling me to take a seat, he informed me that there were two further topics that the we needed to discuss. Impatient, I asked exactly what he was babbling about. With an odious sneer, he shocked me by divulging that he was well aware of my quest for my beloved barmaid, Rue. Finally finding my tongue, I questioned the sneaky brigand on what he actually knew about the girl. Laughing, he informed me that all intelligence came at a price, which I had rudely neglected to pay. Questioning the proposed fee, he again snorted in my face and informed me that I did not have enough coin to uncover the truth behind the girl's disappearance.

Totally intrigued now, I once again demanded the cost for obtaining this information. With a repugnant laugh that resembled a shrieking gull, he disclosed that his information was far too valuable to part with no matter the offer. Frustrated by his games, I announced that I believed he actually had no information on the girl's location. With eyes flashing white-hot anger, he shouted that he had several close business associates on Saint Domingue who had directly supplied this vital and timely news to him. Fully curious to uncover specifics, I pressed the rascal to name his price. Shrieking in loathsome mirth, he spat that he would need to ponder the matter a while longer. Far beyond frustrated, I got to my feet and turned to vacate his odious presence. As I took my first step, he called out that there was yet another matter to be discussed.

Turning back, I stared down at the knave and demanded to know exactly what it was. With eyes narrowing and face reddening, he disclosed that he was well aware of my plot to destroy my former captain. Now raging, he bellowed that Captain Dirk Shivvers was his business partner, and that my mutinous effort to dislodge him as leader had caused him nothing but pain and hardship, not to mention a significant loss of profit. This belligerent announcement came as no real surprise, given the information unearthed by my mates. The Corsican then snarled that his homeland was noted for loyalty among friends. With his temper blazing, the villain hissed that I had created a vendetta against him by my nefarious actions. Continuing, he menacingly sneered that he was now sworn to end my life in order to repay the debt to his former partner.

Attempting to defuse the dangerous situation, I chuckled as if his last threat-laden statement was totally ludicrous. Continuing in an unruffled voice, I questioned the lunatic on exactly how he intended go about making good on his threat. With a continued flare of his famous temper, the Corsican retorted, that if he proved unsuccessful in achieving his desired revenge on me, that his men had been tasked with wreaking vengeance on my dear friends, the Turbouts. Now it was my turn to lose my temper. In answer to his dark forewarning, I promised him a very grim ending should anything evil happened to my comrades. Waving away my furious retort, he revealed that he had a method to stop the feud, as well as paying for the information on my French lover. Fully intrigued, I probed the loathsome trickster on what he required. Cackling now, the lowlife scamp revealed that all I had to accomplish was surviving a bare knuckle contest with his champion, Leatherface. His words hit me like a rogue wave, but I was more than determined to discover Rue's current location. Undaunted by his fighter's nasty reputation, I agreed to the match, but warned the blackguard that we would resume our serious conversation once the match concluded.

The battle was scheduled for the following evening. I obviously felt a strong measure of fear at facing the monstrous brute despite my stalwart confidence in my pugilistic abilities. However, my burning desire to uncover Rue's location mitigated this grisly sensation. That afternoon, Tan made an appearance to provide some last-minute survival tips. He informed me that my opponent's superior physique and stamina would make my chore exceedingly difficult, especially if the monster were able to execute his famous *bloody bonecrush*. Tan confided that my only option was to slaughter him outright. Confused now, I questioned the method he had in mind. Grinning, he told me that there was a way of accomplishing this daunting deed. He then laid out a detailed explanation of this unique technique that brought a sinister smile to my face.

That night, I found myself on the floor of the pit listening to the spectator's roar while I awaited my barbarous opponent. Preceded by the crowd's hysterical reaction, Leatherface shambled down the ladder to engage me in battle. Glancing at my opponent, I could see that he was monstrously huge, much larger than any man I had ever fought! Because he was wearing the tight fitting hood, I could not discern his facial features. However, in studying his movements, I noticed that he progressed in a shuffling, halting and waddling manner, which resembled the motions of an upright bear. Our names were announced, the ladder extracted and the bell was rung to signal the start of promised brutality. As we closed on one another, the brute stopped his advance and in a hissing whisper wished me well on my way to hell!

As I warily circled him, I was certainly fearful of injury or death, but given my rigorous training and Tan's sound advice I felt prepared. Considering myself capable of victory gave me confidence, but I was soon to learn a valuable lesson on the difference between confidence and arrogance. Given that I was anxious to conclude the match expeditiously, I immediately went on the attack. Since my opponent was slow and ponderous, I used it to my advantage and outmaneuvered him landing several brutally lethal blows. These strikes would have felled an ordinary man, but Leatherface seemed to barely even register their devastating effects. He simply shook his head, as if groggily waking from a deep sleep, and continued to lumber after me in the tight quarters of the pit. Confounded and a bit shocked at his endurance and ability to absorb my nasty strikes, I continued to deftly avoid the reach of his tree-trunk arms that promised mortal harm. I bashed him again and again to no avail. It seemed as if I was striking a mountain of dead flesh devoid of feeling.

As I continued my ineffectual attack, I was suddenly jolted to the floor of the pit by a brick that had been hurled by one of the spectators. Dazed and fighting to regain my senses, Leatherface seized the opportunity and wrapped his ponderous arms around my torso and began to squeeze me to death with his *bloody bonecrush* gambit. Instantly, I realized that I was not only going to lose the match, but would summarily perish in my assailant's powerful grip. Staring at the leather-masked fiend as stars began dancing in my head, I calmly prepared to execute Tan's gambit. As my world filled with sparks and shooting stars, I cupped both my hands and slammed them against my opponent's ears. As Tan had predicted, this strike momentarily dazed the behemoth as his deadly grip loosened just a mite. Given this respite, I then reared back with my right palm and slammed it into his nose at a sharp upward angle. You see, Tan had instructed me that this lethal blow would drive an opponent's soft nasal bones directly into his brain, killing him instantly. Upon delivering this strike, the brute reeled back in agony, went deathly still as he toppled to the stone floor with thunderous crash. The mob above went ghostly silent, as they awaited the giant to revive and finish the battle. Well, they never got their wish, as the hulking giant never so much as twitched. He was quite dead and I was declared the victor!

At that point, the Corsican ordered the ladder placed in the pit and quickly descended to face me. With his facial features now bright crimson with utmost rage, he screamed that I had cheated and as such could not claim victory. The crowd, dissatisfied with the outcome, came alive and launched bottles, tankards, food scraps and all manner of objects upon us. One half-empty bottle of rum struck the Corsican square in his face and he joined his former champion on the pit's floor. Realizing that my foe was beyond any further questioning regarding Rue, I utilized this distraction to climb out of the profane hole and flee the den of iniquity.

Back aboard my ship, I called a war council of my trusted leaders and laid out a plan to deal with the Corsican and his minions that very night. Fully aware that special care was required to keep us blameless in the matter, I instructed my team to return to the enemy's pub long after closing time. Their orders were to assault the building from all entry ports when the hooligans inside were sloshed with *hot spirits*, insuring that they would be caught totally off-guard. Once they had overrun and secured these miscreants, Angry George and No Nose were tasked with wrapping the Corsican in old sailcloth and carting him unobserved to Dible's home for a private and confidential discussion. The fiend's remaining minions would then be escorted to the floor of the death pit. I commanded my arresting contingent to utilize their weapons with extreme malice to ensure the evil gang's complete silence and total cooperation. Consequently, I empowered Lion and Sharkface to proceed to the Shantytown shack and dispatch its guards prior to the villain's arrival.

After giving my team time to complete these instructions, I made my way to the secreted hut to confront my enemy. Secured by stout ropes in a chair, the Corsican seemed to gain a semblance of courage as I entered. In fact, he shouted a promise that I would surely die before the night was over for my devious actions. Laughing in his face, I informed him that I hoped to soon return the favor. Glancing around the shack, I observed Diable's mammoth cage covered by large black cloth. Moving over to it, I pulled the cover partially to the side revealing the black monster that stared curiously at me. Once again, I had the strangest sensation that something was quite familiar about this gigantic hellion. Almost inquisitive in its fixed stare, I could not decide if the fiend was a potential friend or foe. Just then, Diable spied its owner trussed behind me and issued a bloodcurdling growl. Relieved to discover that my intelligence was accurate, I had a sudden inspiration on the best method to encourage the wily pub owner to divulge his secrets. Fully uncovering the cage, I judged by his frightened expression that my adversary would soon sing like a canary.

Sauntering to my foe's side, I demanded he tell me what he knew of Rue's present location. Sputtering and spitting curses, the Corsican responded defiantly that he would never divulge the information. Grinning, I turned to Lion and instructed him on how our game would advance. Following my orders, Lion dragged the chair containing the bound Corsican closer to Diable's cage. Although consumed with abject fear, the revenge-minded scum repeated his promise of silence. I informed the Corsican scoundrel that should he continue on his present course that I would allow his pet ample opportunity to slowly tear him asunder piece-by-piece. The Corsican's false courage persisted until Lion positioned his chair adjacent to Diable's cage. With a coughing roar, the black beast shot across his prison cell and managed to rake the Corsican's shoulder with its massive claw. As soon as this occurred, the Frenchman began wailing like a toddler, as the blood from his shoulder began running down his chest.

Dragging the moaning blackguard away from the cat's enclosure, I once again demanded an answer to my question. Receiving no response, I thundered that he left me no other option. At the same time, the black demon unleashed a bloodcurdling roar that caused the Corsican even greater alarm. Signaling Lion, we positioned ourselves on either side of the bound criminal and began slowly dragging him back towards the object of his utmost dread. Pleading for us to stop, he finally began to confess all.

In between his pitiful mewling and begging, he informed me that Rue had indeed vacated Saint Domingue. She had found sanctuary with close friends on Cuba, somewhere near the town of Havana. The terrified fool also informed me that he understood that the Black Tarantula was also aware of her present location. While she was yet safe, the Corsican sneered that it would not be long before the despicable villain would finally succeed in seizing his prize. I quizzed him on any further knowledge he could provide on Rue, but was quite disappointed to discover that the miscreant had recounted all that he knew on the subject.

I then questioned him on his intended plan for me. With a cruel smirk, he informed me that he had given specific orders to his men to murder me that very evening. Additionally, his brutes were charged with covertly boarding and burning both of my vessels, while slaughtering everyone found aboard. Convinced that we had drained the very last dregs of useful information from the swine, I proceeded to the next phase of my plan. While my scheme was fraught with complications, I felt reasonably assured that I would succeed with the planned extermination of the villain along with his minions without implicating myself or my crew.

The first step of my strategy was accomplished by my team's subjugation of his assistants and dragging them to the death pit. To that end, Tan arrived and informed me that the raid had been successful and the scum had been assembled as ordered. I then commanded my loyal crewman to return to the pub's arena and announce his arrival with a single pistol shot. Once accomplished, I charged him to release their charges in the pit, exit the hellhole, remove the access ladder, gather our men and return to our ship as their duties were at an end.

After waiting for what seemed like an eternity, I was finally rewarded by a distant pistol shot that resounded down the tunnel signaling Tan's compliance. I then turned to my prisoner and secured his hands tightly behind him, while stuffing a filthy rag in his mouth to negate the chance of ruining my surprise party. Once done, I released him from his bindings. Shoving him over to the tunnel's mouth, I informed him that his men were waiting for him at the other end. Nodding furiously, he began his stumbling and awkward climb upward.

As soon as I lost sight of him, we wheeled Diable's cage over to the tunnel's entrance and slid the door open so that the demonic feline could pursue its detested owner. Before the cat moved, it glanced at me with that same look of familiarity and once again winked one of its luminous yellow orbs. Taken completely by surprise, I informed the creature that I would move the cage away from the exit and leave the door open should the black demon desire to make his escape. Winking once again, as if able to comprehend my words, Diable turned and raced after its owner. Not waiting for the initiation of the upcoming brutality, Lion and I pushed the cage away from the tunnel entrance and scurried out the door, leaving it wide open in our wake.

The next morning, I went ashore to pay a visit to the Governor. Upon entering his office, the self-important politician rushed over to warmly shake my hand. Since he was in such a celebratory mood, I waited patiently to hear his news. The Governor confided that his problems with the Corsican had officially ended, since the villain had died sometime during the night. Acting innocently astounded, I questioned the Governor on what had transpired. The beaming fool began explaining everything that had been reported to him. It seemed that sometime during the night, the Corsican and his men had entered the death pit for reasons unknown, and had been viciously torn apart by Diable. The destruction wrought by this vicious beast was exceedingly devastating, as only scraps of clothing, gnawed bones and chunks of flesh remained for the authorities to discover. Curious as to the fate of the cat, I questioned the Governor on what was planned for the offending feline. With a very nervous glance, he confessed that the marauding beast had escaped with only its bloody footprints left in its wake as evidence of its presence. He then reported that an extensive search conducted by the fort's soldiers had yielded no further sightings of the jaguar. In a conspiratorial manner, he whispered that it was assumed that the beast had probably fled to the safety of the island's interior. Making the sign-of-the-cross on his chest, the Governor acknowledged that he hoped that the demon cat would never be heard from again!

Since the Governor was in an accommodating mood, I asked about the Black Tarantula's arrest warrant. Smiling, he reached into a pile of official documents and pulled out the writ, which he presented with undo pomp. Accepting the valuable piece of paper, I shook the Governor's hand and thanked him for his kind assistance. Arriving back on Marie-Galant, I hurriedly made my way to the manor house intent on checking the condition of my patients. Ushered by a jubilant Aimee, I entered the Turbout bedroom to find both patients sitting in their beds conversing amongst themselves. Upon spotting me, both Rene and Lille jumped up from their beds and rushed to my side. Lille gave me a most grateful kiss and thanked me for saving their lives. Rene then shook my hand in a most vigorous manner, and informed me that he owed me yet another great debt. Curious about my future plans, the three Turbouts plied me with question after question. Waving my hand in abject surrender, I informed them that I had been officially sanctioned by the Governor to hunt down the most notorious sea bandit alive, the Black Tarantula! Shocked and visibly upset by my announcement, Aimee questioned my timing for this grand endeavor. Informing them all that recent news dictated an immediate departure, I promised to return to their lovely island in very short order.

With abject concern dominating their features, an exhausted Rene and Lille wished me the best of luck and retreated back to their beds. Waving to them both, I exited the room with Aimee trailing in my wake. On the way downstairs, I bumped into Doc who had been liberally sampling Rene's marvelous inventory of fine wine. Tipsy and incoherent, Doc pronounced that both patients had recovered and no longer faced any danger so he had been freed to drink to his heart's content. I informed him, that once we rejoined our mates, that we planned to set sail immediately. Cradling his precious bottle of wine along with medical bag, he unsteadily navigated his way down the stairs to await my arrival in the transport carriage. Turning to Aimee, I instructed her to continue the *Jesuit's Bark* tea once a day for the remainder of the week. Promising her that this dosage was merely precautionary, I demurely kissed her cheek and turned to make my exit. Aimee had other intentions, as she urgently reached out and grabbed my shoulder turning me back towards her. With eyes glistening with fervent tears, she leapt into my arms and delivered a very long and passionate kiss, informing me that she was deeply in love with me and would pray for my safe return. Before I could respond, she spun around and headed back to her patients as I stood transfixed by her bold announcement! Her sincere declaration of love cleared up an earlier mystery for me. I was now fully aware of the lass's true intentions behind her amorous and exceedingly profound shows of emotion, both here and earlier on Jamaica. While I found myself sorely tempted to return her ardent and highly desirable affections, I was emotionally precluded from doing so due to my professed and highly deep-seated love for Rue. Given this serious dilemma, conflicting emotions raged throughout my entire being as I stumbled down the stairway in a fog of abject perplexity!

Chapter 7: Disaster on Jamaica

Yet highly conflicted by Aimee's love declaration but anxious to return to Jamaica to rescue Powder Monkey from his life of leisure, I was quite pleased to discover that both Lion and Sharkface had nearly finalized the necessary preparations to allow for a speedy departure. In less than a week, we were comfortably slicing through the turquoise waters on our way home.

As I roamed the vessel monitoring operations, I found myself in the galley as a new recruit had just begun a strange tale that occurred on Guadeloupe immediately prior to our departure. The new recruit's name was Rambling Roberto, an innocuous sailor of Spanish decent. From his serious tone, I concluded that Roberto's account was something beyond the usual seafaring yarn heard aboard any sailing vessel. In fact, every tar in the galley appeared totally mesmerized by Roberto's account. Intrigued, I found a comfortable perch in a dark corner and made myself at home. Roberto was in the midst of explaining the background of the characters central to his recital. The gist of Roberto's account concerned the irrational behavior between two island doxies, Ostrich Katie and Molly Hatpin. At this point, I came to the realization why the story held such great importance to my mates. You see, these two madams and their respective establishments were the most infamous houses of pleasure on the island. As any sailor on leave would attest, sumptuous chow, amorous women and hot spirits were very high on their list of onshore demands. Since each of these renown cathouses offered to gratify all three in regal fashion, they were held in utmost regard. As such, the two madams in question were essentially viewed by sojourning sailors as island royalty. In continuing his tale, Roberto explained that these two trollops were in constant competition with each other for the affections of island men searching for carnal gratification. While the two ladies operated out of different establishments, Guadeloupe was a relatively small island with a limited population, so detailed scuttlebutt of each other's exploits was routinely available. As such, both women kept a very close eye and ear on the reported escapades of the other, while going at great lengths to avoid face-to-face encounters. However, each of these women lived with a secret desire to be widely recognized as the most amorous, erotic and sensual seductress on Guadeloupe. Such a reputation, Roberto explained would provide a substantial boon to the victor's business concerns.

Roberto then provided his listeners a detailed description of each harlot. Ostrich Katie resided at the Open Oyster Café, and ruled the premises with an iron will, a sharp blade and a wicked tongue. This full blossomed floozy had a reputation for being as vicious as a starving shark. Many of her former patrons claimed that Ostrich Katie would rather cut than rut. She had been christened due to her wardrobe's continual inclusion of huge, brightly colored Ostrich feathers. Robert enlightened us that an Ostrich was a humongous flightless bird that was purported to habituate some remote and distant island to our east. Not one to cross, Ostrich Katie was responsible for a plethora of criminal activities that included every conceivable depravity known to man. Her nemesis, Molly Hatpin was a red haired hellion also capable of all manner of nastiness. Molly's residence was the Hopping Gull Pub, a disreputable and dishonest establishment that was situated not very far from her hated adversary's café. Molly Hatpin was reputed to be something of an actress, with the innate ability to adopt any number of roles as situations demanded. Roberto confided that the slut could transform from a meek and mild young lass to a whip wielding torturer at a moment's notice. It was strictly the preference of each of her customers to choose pleasure or pain in equal measure. Known for carrying long sharp needles in her copious tresses, Molly was quick to deliver mortal wounds if properly motivated.

Roberto reported that the animosity and hatred between the two hussies finally reached its pinnacle and culminated in an agreed competition between the two infamous madams. Christened a doxy duel, this competition would decide once and for all which of the women was most proficient at her art. Further, per the rules of engagement, the loser of this challenge would be forced to vacate Guadeloupe and never return. As a result, the winning harlot would inherit the other's establishment enabling the victor to increase her illicit coffers substantially. The doxy duel entailed counting and totaling each trollop's conquests over a full week's time, with the winner recognized as the whore with the highest number of satisfied customers. Roberto reported a string of detailed descriptions of the various carnal assignations accomplished by each harlot to the extreme delight of his enraptured audience. Concluding his lewd depictions, he divulged that over a period of several days and nights that Molly Hatpin had a slight lead over her nemesis.

Unable to face defeat, Ostrich Katie began scheming methods to defeat her despised adversary. That night, drunk as a seaman on liberty, the bold hussy concocted a plan to end the contest and eliminate her hated competitor permanently. As such, she penned a missive to Molly Hatpin that explained that their rivalry was nonsensical. She reasoned that Guadeloupe was blessed with a plethora of visiting seamen, and as such their rivalry was a waste of both of their talents and time. The note called for a secret parley between the two madams to negotiate a truce and end the hostilities between them. Once clandestinely delivered and duly accepted by her rival, the parley was scheduled late the following evening at a deserted and abandoned house of worship in Shantytown christened the Mission of Lost Souls.

As the time for the trollop's parley neared, both strumpets prepared themselves for battle, as each had deduced that the only method of eliminating each other's opposition was cold-blooded murder. As such, both wenches armed themselves with a bevy of concealed weapons and snuck off unobserved into the tropical night to end their longstanding feud once and for all. Each knew that their burgeoning scheme of elimination would only succeed without witnesses so that the loser's corpse could be disposed of secretly to avoid suspicion, detection or incarceration.

At this point in his narrative, Roberto signaled for a refill of rum to lubricate his parched tongue. Once supplied, the new recruit returned to his darkly humorous account. Given the fact that neither madam could be found the following day, a bevy of concerned sailors decided to search and locate their favorite brothel proprietresses to ensure that each carnal house could continue to conduct its customary illicit business. The two groups searched all day and night but were unsuccessful in locating either floozy. As morning of the second day arrived, the mystery of the missing vamps was solved to a certain degree. With my crew hanging on his every word, Roberto related that the local authorities, based on an anonymous tip, discovered what was left of the two prostitutes inside the Mission of Lost Souls. It was dully reported that each of the tarts' corpses had been savagely torn and mangled into minuscule fragments by some mysterious and exceedingly powerful force. He further related that each of the victim's noggins had been savagely mauled and disfigured far beyond recognition. However, both of their identities were eventually confirmed by the plethora of large hatpins and ostrich feathers uncovered amongst the human wreckage that adorned the forsaken mission.

Unable to understand what had caused the massive amount of damage in this human slaughterhouse, the authorities simply decided that the courtesans had somehow run afoul of a band of villainous pirates, who had viciously slaughtered both doxies for unspeakable and odious past crimes. While authorities could not determine the exact cause of the strumpets' destruction, they had little interest in pursuing the matter further, given the nefarious backgrounds and numerous past depredations committed by each madam. Roberto also mentioned that the authorities were quite perplexed upon discovering enormous feline prints encircling the crime scene, coupled by the unusual fact that each of the tarts' noggins had been found pulverized. At Roberto's conclusion, everyone began commiserating over the sad loss of the island's favorite soiled doves. I, however, had an entirely different reaction. At the mention of giant feline footprints and the tart's crushed skulls, I was convinced that Diable was most assuredly responsible. It occurred to me that the black fiend had taken it upon himself to wrought his own form of justice to these two villainous evildoers. Since I was the one who had freed the gigantic black jaguar, I had to silently admit to serving as an unwitting accomplice in the horrific and mortal demise of these nefarious trollops!

As we continued on to Jamaica, I decided it was the proper time to effect some changes aboard our ships. I had been harboring these changes for quite a while and decided the crew desperately required a diversion. Calling both ships to shore on a deserted spit of land, I announced that I was promoting both Tan and Long Tall Willie to serve as our official combat officers effective immediately. In this role, Long Tall Willie would serve on *Rue's Revenge* and Tan on *Neptune's Revenge*. Both would be accorded the crew's prestige and obedience, along with a larger share of the booty from any future conquests. Breaking out the rum and ship's instruments, we celebrated the event with vigor. After a full day and night of music and merriment, we returned to sea and soon reached the familiar waters surrounding Jamaica.

Upon disembarking, I was quite surprised to receive an urgent summons from the Fort Commander, Captain Houndstooth. While anxious to visit my friends, I nevertheless hurried over to the fort to answer his imperative command. As soon as I was ushered into his office, the military man with a look of utter dismay explained that he had disastrous news to convey. Sensing my concern and utter bewilderment, he quickly explained that the Adams household had been callously and ruthlessly attacked the prior week with devastating results. The entire mansion had been burnt to the ground late one evening incinerating every unsuspecting and sleeping family member including my crewmember, Powder Monkey! Only the bones of the victims, my dear friends, had been located scattered amongst the ashes.

While no positive identification was possible from the charred remains, investigators believed that no member of the household survived the disaster. Now in a state of uncomprehending shock, I listened as Captain Houndstooth expressed his sincerest and utmost regret and consolation. I then questioned the soldier on who was responsible for this dastardly deed. He explained that an extensive investigation was currently underway to determine the perpetrators. Continuing, he sorrowfully elucidated that there were a number of prevailing theories on the identity of the culprit, with most believing that it was the work of the Devil himself.

Realizing that the criminal was indeed human, I questioned the Fort Commander on his specific thoughts and beliefs. Qualifying his next statement as pure conjecture, he answered that he believed it was the nasty work of the nefarious Black Tarantula. Going further, he informed me that he believed that Captain Adams' notorious escape from the fiend's clutches had severely damaged his odious and evil reputation. He rationalized the brutal and merciless attack as both a revengeful repayment as well as an effort to vindicate and further advance this depraved reputation. Swimming in a mental fog, I responded that if it had indeed been the work of the Black Tarantula then there would have been a clear indication of his involvement. Nodding his agreement to my sound argument, the fort commander responded that no clues to the villain's identity had yet been uncovered. Thanking the military man for his concern and compassion, I stumbled out of his office in a totally frazzled state.

Incapable of rational thought, I navigated my way to the home of my dear and now departed friends. Upon reaching the site, I was rudely confronted with the horrors of the situation, as I studied the scorched and blackened ruins of the mansion before me. As I wandered aimlessly around the charred remnants of the once beautiful manor, I was approached by a gentleman who had observed my arrival. Introducing himself as a neighbor, he questioned if I had been acquainted with the Adams'. Explaining that I was a close friend, I begged for any further knowledge he might provide to explain the disaster. Shaking his head slowly, he confessed that he had slept through the entire demonic episode. All that he could report was that the attack occurred in the wee hours of the morning more than a week past, and that the entire event was conducted in a brutal and swift manor since very little commotion had been raised. Confidentially, he informed me that he believed it to be the work of the Black Tarantula. In a sudden moment of inspiration, he divulged that a rumor persisted that a single survivor had escaped the catastrophe alive. Questioning further, I learned that a bruised and battered individual had been seen stumbling away from the blazing home as rescuers arrived to fight the flames. However, he reported that this mysterious phantom had not been seen nor heard from since the night of the attack. Thanking the neighbor for both his information and concern, I continued my aimless tour of the blackened and smoldering ruins.

After untold hours of trudging about in a dreamlike state, I finally made my way over to the small root cellar that housed both Gertrude's medical store and my valuable treasures. Discovering the camouflaged entrance untouched, I lifted the secreted door and entered the dark, damp space. Locating an oil lamp, I kindled a flame and brought light onto my surroundings. Gratified that the structure was undisturbed, I was quite startled to notice movement deep within its far shadows. Navigating closer to examine, I realized that the movement I had noticed was human in form. Taking a closer look, I discovered a figure lying prone on the earthen floor covered haphazardly with blankets. Rushing over to the individual, I recognized him as one of the brothers I had hired to watch over and protect the Adams household.

After a thorough examination, I was relieved to discover, that while he had suffered a slew of traumatic injuries, he would recover fully with proper medical attention. After several hours of concerted ministrations, I had him resting comfortably on a straw bed covered with fresh blankets. After a careful spoon feeding of weak fish soup supplied by a nearby inn, I had him drink a medicinal draught to ease his pain and allow him undisturbed rest to enable his numerous wounds to heal. Having done all that I could do for him, I left him sleeping fitfully and returned to the ship and the soothing company of my crewmates.

As I reached the dock, I realized that I was still operating in a perpetual fog. While my conscious mind registered the horrific loss, somewhere deep in my being I remained hopeful that a few of my friends might have somehow found a way to escape their murderers. Continuing this fantasy, I conjectured that they were currently in hiding until they felt safe enough to seek assistance. While I knew that this avenue of thought was foolish, I somehow clung to this last hope like a drowning sailor to a floating spar. In any event, I was unsuccessful in attempting to get some rest, as the demons that tormented my mind would not subside making my effort nothing more than a good intention. Whenever I gained consciousness, the incredible pain and consummate loneliness flooded back both unmercifully and relentlessly. Shorebirds, I am sure many of you have experienced this same haunting experience due to catastrophic loss. In the shortened timespan since learning of the disaster, it was virtually impossible to maroon my suffering and painful sensations in an obscure corner of my mind, because these loathsome and repugnant memories continually surfaced and navigated their way back to the forefront in a most painful manner as soon as my guard was down!

My loss was both painful and devastatingly self-consuming. I had lost three charming aunts and a good friend when the Adams sisters and their nephew perished in the conflagration. In addition, I had lost my closest confederate and adopted brother with Powder Monkey's passing. I was very tempted to drink my sorrows into oblivion in an attempt to avoid the mind-numbing fog that had invaded by being. However, I realized that an alcoholic-induced haze would only delay the intolerable pain that now tormented me. I decided that my best defense was to remain as completely engaged and fully occupied as I could contrive in the short term. Constructing a quick mental list, I fixated on the number of necessary chores that required my attention. I had an injured patient to heal, a meeting ordained by the Adams sisters' solicitor, a further consultation with the Fort Commander and a Captain's never-ending duty to ensure that all was right with my ships and their crews. Certainly not daunting in scope, but enough to keep my suffering mind in tight check and fully occupied.

Chapter 8: Future Plans Unfold

With plans formulated, I returned to the scorched mansion the next morning to check on my patient. Entering the root cellar, I found my charge alert, but still in considerable pain. Quickly concocting a pain-relieving tonic, I dosed the poor wretch and sat waiting on a nearby stool while my healing draught had a chance to work its magic. After a few hours, he awoke and gave me a brief sad smile. Moving to his side, I questioned him on his current condition, which seemed satisfactory. Even so, he seemed racked with pain along with deep-seated remorse. I began my queries attempting to uncover exactly what had occurred, and the party responsible for wreaking the senseless catastrophe on the Adams household. Before he had a chance to respond, I realized that I had never really took the opportunity to learn he or his brother's name. Deciding to rectify this omission, I sheepishly quizzed him on their names. He informed me that his name was Rufus Pennington, and his brother had been christened Jamie. Upon casting his thoughts on his brother, I observed the instant pain and devastation that flooded his facial features. Providing the poor suffering soul a small sip of rum, I continued probing him on the specifics of the Adams debacle. Settling into a somewhat comfortable position, he began his tale.

He divulged that the attack took place the preceding week during the early morning hours. As it just so happened, it was Rufus' night off, and he was in the midst of an unplanned celebration with a few of his chums at a nearby alehouse. He had left his brother a few hours earlier near the mansion to conduct standard inspection rounds that would routinely continue throughout the evening. Upon imbibing more than he intended, Rufus, nonetheless, decided to return in order to check on his brother. As he stumbled and weaved his path back to the Adams manor, he thought he recognized a bright light emanating in the same direction he was navigating. The brightness continued to increase the closer he staggered. Upon reaching his destination, he was alarmed to ascertain the Adams mansion ablaze in a fiery conflagration. Shocked completely sober, Rufus immediately set out towards the flames in search of his brother. Wandering the grounds aimlessly, Rufus discovered his brother on the far edge of the property in a state close to death. From a quick inspection, Rufus ascertained the extent of the grievous injuries and the horrific abuse that his brother had suffered. Jamie was still breathing, but even that simple task was arduous given his serious injuries. Cradling his brother in his arms, Rufus began to slowly and carefully question him on the events that had transpired in his absence. Jamie related that sometime after midnight a slew of malicious marauders had made their presence known. Several of the scurvy scum initially raced to the mansion to secure the doors trapping its occupants. Meanwhile, the remaining force gathered a variety combustible materials and proceeded to drag it to various locations outside the manor and set these piles on fire to ensure that the resulting blaze would destroy all.

As the marauders went about their evil work, Jamie neared the mansion on his assigned security round and was immediately attacked. Once subdued by the cowardly criminal swarm, he was strung up between two nearby trees and questioned endlessly on the location of my ship and crew. Choosing to endure the brutish torture rather than reveal any information, Jamie bravely answered their queries with false and misleading information, which his tormentors seemed to believe. He divulged that my ship and crew were on a long mission back to England as a favor to the sisters.

Barely conscious at that point, Jamie informed his brother that nobody inside the home had stood any sort of chance of survival. Jamie confided that his tormentors continued to administer further punishment even though they had exhausted their questions. Having completed their fun and believing the poor victim in mortal danger, they simply cut him down and left him to perish in utter agony. Before losing consciousness once again, he informed his brother that the fiends continually referred to their leader as the French bastard, without divulging his actual name. However, since the flames consuming the mansion were so bright, Jamie was able to identify the saboteur's leader as he continued to direct the savage onslaught, Captain LeMerde! After his confession, Rufus informed me that his brother simply expired quietly in his arms.

Once his brother was gone, Rufus found a spot away from the blazing manor and hastily covered his brother with brush so he could perform a proper burial at a later time. He then began wandering the grounds in the hope that he might encounter the rogues responsible for the insidious attack. Hearing muffled voices and horse whinnies, Rufus headed in that direction. Upon reaching the source of the sounds, Rufus was able to spot a horse-drawn wagon being boarded by a number of black-garbed hooligans. As he neared his quarry, the marauding swine detected his presence and the driver of the wagon spurred the horses forward directly into Rufus' path.

Unable to recognize the immediate danger, Rufus pressed forward and was trampled by both horse hooves and the wagon wheels. Presumed dead by the wagon's passengers, the vehicle continued its hurried retreat from the burning mansion. Rufus confessed that he was in and out of consciousness from that moment until I happened upon him in his hiding place, which had been revealed to him by Aunt Gertrude long ago. In a moment of regretful sorrow, Rufus apologized for he and his brother's failure to protect the mansion as I had previously arranged. Informing him that the tragedy could not have been scuttled by the efforts of any two men, I ordered him to lie back and get some rest so that his wounds could mend. At these words, Rufus collapsed into a sorrowful heap and was soon fast asleep. Sure that my patient would fully recover, I exited the root-cellar and made my way into town for a meeting with the Adams' solicitor, who had sent word earlier that my presence was required immediately.

I made my way to the solicitor's office still in a state of utter shock and depression. Once inside the building, I was told that the lawyer was in conference and would be free shortly. Taking a seat, I reminisced on Rufus' account of the night of the murders and felt the burning fires of revenge kindling in my soul. As witnessed, the perpetrator of this heinous crime was my old enemy, LeMerde. Cursing his name, I made a solemn pledge to chase the scoundrel to the ends of the earth if necessary and obliterate him once and for all. As I made this sacred oath, I was informed that the man I had come to visit was free and would now see me.

As I entered the office of Simon Beardsly, I could not help but notice the absolute clutter and discord that ruled his place of business. While the small man behind the desk was neat and prim, it was difficult to understand exactly how he was able to conduct business in the utter chaos that surrounded him. Peering up at me behind his oversized spectacles, he invited me to take a seat directly across from him. My initial impression was that I was face-to-face with a creature that had lived underground his entire life. His skin tone was the ashen-grey color of a corpse. While I could sense that this human mole held nothing but disdain for me, I nevertheless was quite curious to uncover the reason behind his summons.

Once I was settled, Simon Beardsly unctuously informed me that he had been retained as the legal guardian of the Adams' fortune for the last twenty-five years. Given the unforeseen and horrific deaths of all three sisters along with their last surviving relative, Captain Adams, the attorney confessed that it was his sworn duty to ensure the sisters' last requests were handled promptly and properly in accordance with English law. With this pronouncement, he held up a legal document and whispered that it was the last will and testament of the three sisters. Still completely dazed and confused, I questioned the legal expert why that mattered along with the motive behind my summons. Realizing my total ignorance, the attorney removed his eyewear and gave me a measuring glance. Once performed, he smiled in a most ghastly manner and divulged that I was the sole beneficiary of the enormous Adams' fortune. Shocked and utterly confused by this pronouncement, I shrilly questioned the man's sanity for making such a ridiculous statement. Holding up his hands in order to quiet my outburst, Simon Beardsly questioned if I was indeed formally known as Echo Eden. Nodding my assent, he continued by informing me that all three sisters considered me a close friend, worthy of their unbridled love and absolute respect. He explained that all three Adams sisters had recently demanded a special meeting in order to fashion a substantial revision to this last will and testament.

In doing so, they had informed him that I had saved not only their lives but that of their nephew, and as such had decided to amend their will. This emended last testament expressed their desire to grant me a portion of their property known as Gertrude's Root Cellar in the event of their untimely passing. In addition, they had named Captain Adams as the recipient of their vast fortune upon their deaths. Further, Simon

Beardsly divulged that I was named sole beneficiary of this fortune should Captain Adams precede them in death. Providing a self-evident shrug, the lawyer announced that since all three sisters as well as Captain Adams had perished in the recent tragic blaze, I was entitled to everything the sisters owned. Continuing without a trace of humor, he reported that the will he was holding had been personally witnessed by the Governor, so nobody could question its legal veracity. Since the bequeathed estate represented a truly prodigious sum, Simon Beardsly meekly volunteered to continue his role of managing this fortune until I no longer required his services. Agreeing immediately to his proposal, I informed him that I needed some time to sort out the entire affair. Nodding, he advised me to take as much time as needed and to alert him of any specific intentions or decisions I reached. While I was now wealthier than my wildest dreams, I still ached terribly over the devastating loss that had accounted for this windfall. The sad truth was that I would have gladly traded all of this new found wealth for the return of my dear comrades and friends. With that last thought raging in my mind, I bid the odd looking attorney a good day and exited his office to contemplate my future.

Stunned by this latest news and my heartbreaking losses, I wandered aimlessly around town. I was quite unsure how I would continue to manage my life without Powder Monkey's invaluable assistance and loyal friendship. Aware that I was meandering around in circles and starting to attract unwanted attention, I decided to seek a quiet place to rest and reevaluate my situation in order to develop an operating plan. As I had opted in the past on Saint Domingue, I returned to Shantytown's quiet and secluded graveyard where I was certain I would not be disturbed. Locating a small bench under a large shade tree, I sat and began to collect my thoughts.

As I scanned my dismal surroundings, I focused on the large number of mausoleums that dotted the landscape. These burial dwellings certainly seemed quite solitary and deserted, given that any living being would hardly relish the task of making regular visits to these moldering vestiges of mortality. As I made this survey, a thought suddenly occurred to me. A mausoleum was a perfect hiding place for the invaluable contents of Gertrude's root-cellar. I realized that I could not only construct an impregnable fortress to secure my precious belongings, but also provide an everlasting resting place for my dear departed friends. Continuing this line of thought, I had another inspiration. Since the Adams sisters had bequeathed their entire estate to my keeping, it was only right that I dedicate a portion of these funds to create a beautiful setting for their final resting places. Because all three sisters were quite appreciative of nature, I decided that the entire Adams property would be converted into a lush tropical garden, which would be open to the public to utilize and enjoy. Thinking a bit more, I rationalized that I could easily secret the Adams' mausoleum in a far corner of this public garden placing it directly over the current root cellar's location. This structure would be protected from any outside intrusion by iron entranceways and a stout and formidable fence. It would be like hiding a priceless treasure in plain sight! I also theorized that Rufus could act as groundskeeper and custodian of the memorial to further insure the safety of my invaluable cache. Finally, I decided that Simon Beardsly should function as executor of this project, insuring proper design and construction as well as appropriate maintenance and upkeep.

As I was outlining the various steps required to see my scheme come to fruition, I detected footsteps nearing my position. Instantly alert, I glanced around to identify the source of the disturbance. Striding towards me was a familiar face, Fat Dog! Reaching me, Fat Dog nodded his greeting and took a seat next to me. He opened the conversation by informing me that he was heartedly sorry for my loss. He confessed that he had also experienced this same sort of overwhelming grief over the murder of our good friend, Handy. He confessed that this loss had brought on titanic waves of self-pity and depression that assaulted the very walls of his soul. He divulged that the passage of time was the only solution to such situations. We sat together under the shade tree for a while without saying another word, both lost in our own personal grief!

As evening closed around us, Fat Dog informed me that the villain who had initiated this bloodcurdling act would be apprehended and punished severely. Glancing over at my old friend and pretending ignorance, I questioned him on the scuttlebutt surrounding the tragedy. Fat Dog informed me that he had heard from numerous sources that the attack was the insidious work of the Black Tarantula. Shaking my head slowly, I confessed that an eyewitness had identified the actual perpetrator as

Captain LeMerde. Seemingly surprised by this new information, the pub owner mentioned that he had also been privy to further scuttlebutt on this notorious villain.

His sources had confirmed that Captain LeMerde and his accomplices had fled to the island's interior following his desperate escape from justice. Rumor was, that Captain LeMerde had fallen in with a vicious band of cutthroats, also on the run from the law. Taking command of this group of lawless scum, LeMerde had led a number of successful raids on outlying plantations and small farms. Realizing that his evil reputation and dastardly actions would eventually draw the authorities down upon him, the unconscionable Frenchman decided to take to the sea once again. Fat Dog confirmed that a recent patron had confided that Captain LeMerde and his rogue band had attacked and defeated a crew of visiting pirates, who were preoccupied with careening their vessel. Executing the pirate captain and the majority of his crew, Captain LeMerde had commandeered the ship and set sail for safer waters. At this point in his narrative, Fat Dog drew a flask from his coat pocket and partook of a quick swallow of rum before continuing his report. He had also been told that this band of renegades had made their way to the Cayman Islands, a group of small islands located to the northwest of our position. From this lair, scuttlebutt had it that the insidious devil had led a series of daring raids on unsuspecting merchantmen leading to their ultimate devastation and destruction.

My mind was a raging bonfire given the information I had just received. All I could envision was journeying to this location and obliterating the nefarious dog and his evil horde as soon as I possibly could. As I was musing over these thoughts, Fat Dog interrupted my reverie by announcing that he had a close friend on the island named Big Paul Brown, and would be more than willing to provide me with a letter of introduction. He promised to write the letter as soon as he returned to his pub, so that I could pick it up later that evening. Having concluded our conversation, my friend rose and informed me that he had to return to his pub to make sure that his pet chimpanzees were tended and fed. Shaking hands, I expressed my deepest thanks for both his assistance and his friendship. Waving off my statement nonchalantly, he smiled and bid me a good day.

Realizing that I had to return to my ships to prepare them for immediate voyage, I rose to my feet and exited the cemetery. On the way back to the docks, I made a quick visit to Gertrude's root cellar to check on my patient. Entering, I found Rufus alert and healing quite nicely. I informed him of the will and the sisters' last requests, and, like me, this news stunned him greatly. I then divulged my plan to turn the grounds into a memorial garden. I also disclosed that I required a caretaker for this memorial, and questioned whether he was willing to take on this responsibility. With tears of gratitude, he blubbered that he would be most appreciative of such an opportunity. I informed him that I would draw up the rudimentary plans that he and Simon Beardsly could follow to create a beautiful and lasting tribute to my friend's memories.

With that, I bid him a good day and returned to *Rue's Revenge* to commence sailing preparations. Once aboard, I issued a string of orders to both Lion and Sharkface to prepare both ships for potential conflict. Both officers informed me that nearly all was in readiness, and that we could sail in two days. Satisfied by their response, I returned to my cabin.

The next few days were spent in furious preparation for our journey. I spent several hours the first day drawing up the plans for the Adams' Memorial Gardens and Mausoleum. When I was finished, I made my way into town to meet with Simon Beardsly. Reaching his office, I was immediately shown in, where I found the strange little man pouring over various legal contracts. For the next several minutes, I outlined my plan for the gardens and the final resting place for my friends. Once I had detailed my intentions, I unrolled the parchment with specific diagrams for the design I had just mentioned. I then requested his assistance to continue his work as guardian of the Adams' fortune in my absence. I inquired if he would also take on the role of supervisor and managing director of the planned memorial. Blinking now in utter surprise, he whispered that such a task would be both an honor and a privilege. I also disclosed that I had retained the services of a very trusted comrade, who would act as caretaker for the grounds and report directly to him. Simon confessed that he was not personally acquainted with Rufus, but was sure that I had selected the most qualified individual for the role. I then informed Simon that I needed to complete a vital mission, but would return soon to inspect the work. Wishing me success, Simon promised to initiate the project immediately, and thanked me sincerely for the opportunity to continue to serve the Adams' legacy.

Upon departing the attorney's office, I made my way back to the charred ruins of my friends' home and found Rufus alert and responsive. I discussed my meeting with Simon Beardsly and the detailed plans that would soon be set in motion. I ordered Rufus to report to Simon Beardsly as soon as he was able. Finally, I cautioned Rufus to keep the cellar a secret between us, and explained my devious method of disguising the storehouse so that only the two of us would know of its existence. Finally, I disclosed that I had also made plans for a small cottage on the edge of the grounds for his personal use. Gratified by my show of generosity and concern for his welfare, Rufus promised to guard the grounds with his very life!

Chapter 9: Adventure in the Caymans

The following morning, we set sail for the Cayman Islands. The desire to attain revenge burned brightly within me and threatened to consume my entire being, making me quite anxious and eager to attain total retribution. Prior to sailing, I had a long meeting with my officers to inform them of the reasons behind our sudden departure. Upon learning that we were bound on a mission of revenge, each and every officer voiced positive support. I explained that I was led to believe that LeMerde had been very busy in his new piratical career, and as such had taken numerous valuable prizes. My desire was to seek out and destroy this lowlife renegade and his dastardly crew. Gratified by the news of a potentially substantial reward for our efforts, my officers promised to communicate the particulars to the crew. They were sure everyone would be anxious to defeat the notorious villain, thereby claiming his treasures as our own. With a sharp salute, they were off to prepare for war!

Since I had previously stopped by Fat Dog's Pub to obtain his letter of introduction, I charted a course for the largest of the three Cayman Islands, Grand Cayman. Fat Dog had advised me to generously lubricate the recipient of the letter, Big Paul Brown, in the same manner that all island authorities expected. Fat Dog promised that his friend would assist our effort with both information and any supplies that we might require.

Our voyage to the Cayman Islands was routine without *dirty weather* or other obstacles slowing our journey. I decided to learn a little more about our target, so I sent word for Blind Pig Jeffers to report to my cabin. This nervous little scoundrel had actually spent a great deal of time in the Cayman waters servicing on a variety of different pirate ships. Blind Pig had rightfully been anointed with his unusual moniker due to his extremely poor eyesight. His small and narrow slit-like orbs gave the impression that his eyes were permanently closed at all times. Since this condition severely limited his ocular abilities, he navigated by utilizing his hands to poke and prod his way along any chosen route. This habit gave bystanders the impression that he was certainly blind. He appeared at my cabin door and eventually made his entrance after much fumbling and bumbling.

He reported that the English possession consisted of three distinct islands, Grand Cayman, Little Cayman and Cayman Brac. The largest and most populated of the three was Grand Cayman. The other two islands provided perfect pirate hideouts given their extreme isolation. The area was well known for its ample supply of sea turtles, which provided an excellent source of fresh meat for any passing ship. Pirates, privateers and merchantmen had all traveled these waters for quite some time to replenish food stocks, obtain fresh drinking water and to careen their weed-laden hulls. Given the small population, these islands had long been dubbed "*the islands that time forgot*". Blind Pig reported that these low-lying islands went unprotected during fierce tropical hurricanes, which habitually swept across them resulting in continual death and destruction. Blind Pig was also somewhat familiar with our destination, Bodden Town, home of the first English settlement and provided some scant details.

Not long after, our topman sang out that our objective had been sighted, and we anchored a considerable distance from the southern side of Grand Cayman to avoid the treacherous coral reef that ringed it. As a purely precautionary measure, I instructed Lion to anchor *Neptune's Revenge* an even further distance away in case we met with resistance. Without further consideration, I led a small company to shore in one of our longboats. On the beach, we were met by a small group of islanders, who welcomed us with warm hospitality and well-wishes. Wasting little time, I announced that I wished to meet with their leader, Big Paul Brown, as soon as possible.

As I was led to our destination, I surveyed Bodden Town for the first time. I found it extremely primitive compared to many of the ports we had previously visited. Since I wished to confer with Big Paul Brown alone, I had sent my crewmates on a mission to explore the town, knowing full well that they would not wander far from the first pub they happened upon in their reconnoitering efforts. Meanwhile, I was led to a sizable home that was constructed with island mud and lumber and slightly raised off the ground by stout wooden poles as a protection against flooding. While the home was hardly elegant, I could discern that it was the largest of its kind, and therefore spoke of power and authority in this shoddy community.

My guides stopped in front of the structure and their leader raced up the steps to announce my presence. In no time at all, he returned followed by a powerful individual, who I surmised was Big Paul Brown. Offering me his hand in friendship and welcome, Big Paul smiled a dreadful looking grin that betrayed the fact that his choppers were in atrocious condition. I counted only five teeth remaining in his cavernous maw. Putting that aside, I estimated that Big Paul was the physical equal of Lion, a man certainly not to be underestimated. After a short time trading introductions and pleasantries, Big Paul ushered me into his home to uncover the reason for our visit. Following the brute inside, I checked my pockets to ensure that Fat Dog's letter of introduction was still in my possession. In addition, I had selected a walnut sized emerald from my private stash to lubricate the proceedings.

Prior to launching into particulars, I decided to first establish my credentials. Pulling Fat Dog's letter from my pocket, I handed it to Big Paul and allowed him the time to fully peruse the contents. Finishing his reading, the hulking leader looked up at me and questioned how he might assist me. Taking my time, I provided a concise report on the brutal attack and murders of my closest friends. I informed him that an eyewitness had identified the beast that had led the assault as Captain LeMerde. I divulged that scuttlebutt had spread that the scoundrel was operating out of these waters, but as to a specific location I had no details. Therefore, the reason for my visit was to discover the location of his pirate's lair. Once done, I informed Big Paul that I intended to hunt this unfeeling monster down and punish him severely for his heinous crimes.

Big Paul seemed rather uninterested in both my account and subsequent intentions. Realizing that I needed to provide additional encouragement, I reached into my pocket and extracted the priceless gem that sparkled like green fire as I held it up for his inspection. The avarice and greed written across Big Paul's face told me that I had chosen the proper enticement. Handing the priceless treasure over to the salivating giant, I again approached the subject of LeMerde's current location. This time my query brought a very different reaction from my host. Big Paul sat back in his throne-like chair and seemed to go through an intricate thought process. After some time, he scratched his scraggly beard and informed me that he had been privy to reports on the infamous pirate, and had a good idea where I could locate him. In a most confidential manner, Big Paul whispered that his sources had claimed that the rascal had constructed a series of temporary structures on Little Cayman's western end. Given this island's sparseness, the rogue had been forced to trade with Big Paul's associates for both fresh water and turtle meat on a regular basis. While useful, I could not put aside the growing concern that my host was not being totally honest in providing this intelligence. However, my burning desire for revenge blunted my caution, so that I accepted without question all that I had been told.

Breaking for a moment, Big Paul offered me an island drink named *swankie*, which was nothing more than lemonade! Once our dry throats were wetted, Big Paul's face suddenly lit up as he informed me that he had one additional piece of intelligence. Smiling broadly, Big Paul confided that word had it that Captain LeMerde was currently in the process of careening his ship, naturally accompanied by a *grand carouse*, a pirate's gala of sorts. Continuing, he divulged that the essentials for the *grand carouse* were scheduled to be delivered the following evening. Big Paul then slyly suggested that perhaps this might prove to be a fortuitous opportunity to launch a surprise attack on the French rascal and his dastardly crew. Having come to this same conclusion, I quizzed him on who was in charge of supplying the pirates with food, drink and entertainment. Big Paul responded that his comrade, Jack Bitteroot held this honor, and provided specific instructions on where I could locate him. Smiling now, I thanked Big Paul for his invaluable assistance, and made a hasty exit in order to locate Jack Bitteroot. As I exited, Big Paul wished me luck with my mission and promised that we would celebrate my certain victory upon my return.

I followed Big Paul's directions and located Jack Bitteroot. A brief conversation confirmed Big Paul's intelligence, and after a quick round of pricey negotiations, it would now be my crew delivering the *grand carouse* essentials the following evening. Having completed this arrangement, I rushed back to my ship to initiate all necessary preparations. My scheme was rather simple in nature. In order to gain entrance to the *grand carouse*, our crew would pose as suppliers of the debauchery's essentials. To accomplish this, we needed to purchase various disguises in order to deceive our treacherous enemies. Once accomplished, my disguised deliverymen would be joined by the remainder of our company, who would attack from the island's interior after successfully flanking the villains.

I was certain that my ships and crews could have easily bombarded our quarry from the water as they participated in their *grand carouse*. However, the lust for revenge prevented me from pursuing this easy course. You see, I desperately needed to face my sworn enemy so that I could experience first-hand his rightful demise. My scheme did not stop at substituting my crew for the islanders charged with delivering the party essentials. I plotted that several of my men would be disguised as trollops including attire, make-up and wigs to utterly deceive our targets and allow us an eager welcome to the festivities. Further, I planned to lead the frontal assault, so that I could locate and dispatch LeMerde personally.

In order to effect the proper disguising of selected crew members as doxies, I was forced to choose a number of smaller members. My choices included Tan and Long Tall Willie along with several other smaller men. Once selected, I personally directed the dress and proper accoutrements for each man, or should I say woman! So that we were properly armed and prepared for combat, I secreted a vast arsenal of weapons in the bottom of each small boat that would act as our transportation into the midst of the reprobates' party. Late the following day, we were prepared for attack, and I ordered our ships and the small convoy to proceed to the designated location. My orders were rather simple regarding battle conduct, no quarter and no mercy!

Since the boats that transported the frontal attack force were exceedingly slower than my two ships, I was certain that our flanking force would be situated in their designated spots long before we made our appearance. Directing our advance, I took the opportunity to inspect my men's disguises one final time. While the harsh sunlight revealed flaws here and there amongst my actors, I knew that our planned arrival under the cover of darkness would certainly mask all. Nearing our rendezvous point, I called for the musicians in our group to strike up a lively tune to announce our celebratory arrival. As expected, the entire beach used for careening was aglow, and we could make out vague figures cavorting around the huge bonfires dotting the shore. However, there was no ship in sight! Our boisterous music and voices carried to our foe's position, which brought a resounding and approving roar from the renegades. Anxious for a taste of rum and lusting for the approaching wenches, the murdering swine ran to the water's edge emphatically urging us to hasten our arrival. While I was fairly certain that my flanking force was in position, I cautioned the helmsmen in each boat to delay our arrival to the best of their abilities to allow our men the opportunity to move even closer to their targets. As planned, I instructed our grenado specialists to prepare their weapons and to launch a barrage as soon as we came into range. When unleashed, these lethal bombs would dispatch a number of enemies and signal our flanking troops to attack.

When we were nearly ashore, I issued the order to release our granados. The effects were devastating as the battle commenced. Once on the beach, my men grabbed their sabers, muskets and dirks and rushed into the fray issuing bloodcurdling screams and yells. With one particular target in mind, I joined the fray hacking and severing anything in my path. I continued to navigate the battle arena in search of LeMerde.

Given their rigorous training, my crew made fast work of the pirate brutes, who were falling dead all around us. Unable to locate LeMerde, I continued hacking and cutting my way through the pirate scum. Realizing that very few were still alive, I called a halt to the slaughter and ordered my men to secure anyone living so that interrogations could commence. As the survivors were herded into a group, I was startled by serious cannon fire coming from the west. Momentarily confused, I hazard a guess that the commotion had been initiated by Lion, but could not fathom an explanation. I then surveyed the field of corpses searching for LeMerde, but there was no sign of the poisonous serpent. Since only four survivors remained, I ordered a *sand bath* prepared for their enjoyment. Once the first three unfortunates were buried up to their necks in wet sand, the fourth member was very willing to disclose all that he knew!

As his companions wailed over their predicament, I began my interrogation. Without introduction, I quizzed the unburied pirate on the whereabouts of his leader. Blinking in extreme fear, the reprobate divulged that Captain LeMerde had received an urgent summons from Big Paul to return immediately to Grand Cayman. Accompanied by more than half of their company, the pirate leader had made his departure earlier that day. When questioned on the reason for the urgent summons, he laughed and informed me that he had absolutely no idea at all!

However, the fool did disclose that Captain LeMerde was quite friendly with the good people of Bodden Town. He also divulged that the entire crew were treated like entitled lords whenever they spent time amongst these uncommonly friendly villagers. He summed up the relationship by informing me that Grand Cayman was most certainly a home away from home. Realizing that the wretched fool was spouting the truth, I switched subjects and probed him on the cannon fire we had all heard during our short but brutal battle. Laughing now, the delirious pirate answered that he had no idea about the source of the commotion. Pleading for his life, the sorry scum stated that he had divulged all he knew. Realizing he had been truthful, I ordered him consigned to his place on the beach and strolled away to his trailing child-like screeches. You see, a *sand bath* consigned an unlucky participant to be buried at a beach's shoreline during low tide. As the tide slowly rose, the condemned would experience a slow drowning death as water coursed slowly over his noggin sending the accursed blackguard to meet his new master, Satan!

With the exception of a few injuries, my men were in excellent condition having bested the celebrating pirates rather easily. I was still confused and extremely curious on the mysterious cannon fire as one of my crew spotted *Rue's Revenge* sailing into view. Once anchored, Sharkface came ashore to report. With a look of sad regret, Sharkface related that all had gone according to plan. However, he divulged that the same could not be said of our sister ship, *Neptune's Revenge*. Once the cannon fire was detected, Sharkface had sailed past our position to check on the clamor. With a saddened look, he informed me that *Neptune's Revenge* had been assaulted by an unknown aggressor, who had dealt significant destruction and death to our unsuspecting ship. Once this dastardly deed was accomplished, the vessel had simply turned tail and vanished. Sharkface reported that besides the loss of masts, spars and sails, *Neptune's Revenge* had incurred significant structural damage requiring immediate refitting and repair.

As far as the crew, Sharkface reported that Doc and Lion were seriously injured. Additionally, several of her crew had died in the hailstorm of enemy shot. Included in the list of casualties were several close friends such as Monkey Faced Bill and Jumping Jimmy. Sharkface also reported that no warning had been given by the phantom attacker. The sneaky renegade had simply approached our ship and opened fire. With Doc injured, there was nobody to treat Lion, who I was told resembled a human hedgehog given the number of wooden splinters adorning his entire body. Having heard this distressing news, I ordered my entire company back to *Rue's Revenge* so that we could rendezvous with our disabled sister ship and assist with the injuries and devastation incurred by the insidious surprise attack.

Once aboard and our longboats secured, we set sail. Upon approaching *Neptune's Revenge*, we could easily glimpse the extensive damage previously reported. I was the first aboard, and I raced to the Captain's cabin to check on Lion's condition. I found my friend in his bunk in tremendous pain and in a feverish state. Without preamble, I immediately went to work by providing Lion with a mild potion to ease his pain. Once done, I began removing the nasty wooden splinters that dominated his entire frame. After several hours of concentrated work, I had succeeded in removing the worst of these wooden spikes, and provided my commander with a special draught that induced sleep so his body could begin to heal. While I was ministering to my patient, my crew attached several sturdy cables to our stricken ship so that it could be towed to a safe harbor for repairs. I gave orders to sail towards Grand Cayman where I had an unannounced appointment with the sneaky rogue responsible for the deadly ambush. When we were near our target, I chose a small boarding party that was comprised of my finest warriors. They would accompany me to Grand Cayman while the remainder of the crew and ships would sail back to Jamaica so that work could initiate on our damaged vessel. As I watched my two vessels slowly disappear, I began to formulate the tough questions I harbored for Big Paul Brown!

Chapter 10: Grand Cayman, A Viper's Nest

On our short journey back to Grand Cayman, I fought to regain my composure given the deceptions that had crossed my wake. I realized that I had acted far too hastily upon the false intelligence that I had received from the good citizens of Grand Cayman. Due to my extreme bloodlust, I had ignorantly placed my vessels and men in harm's way, and had paid a very dear price for this unforgivable oversight. I was also aware that Big Paul represented the highest authority on these islands, and I would need to proceed with extreme caution in dealing with this traitorous scum.

As we had neared our destination, I made sure that our longboat was launched far enough away from the island to prevent any possible shore observations. In addition, I had utilized extensive theatrical make-up along with dirt and blood encrusted bandages to disguise my arriving party as severely wounded and defenseless survivors. Adding slings, splints, crutches and litters to the mix, our wounded and ragged appearance would guarantee that we posed no threat to anyone onshore. This deceit would allow us an opportunity to discover the extent of the conspiracy against us. Since I required the combative services of both Tan and Long Tall Willie, I installed Tiger Eyes as second in command to Sharkface. I had also provided Sharkface with ample coin to ensure quick and proper restorative work on Jamaica, as well as funds to allow the crew a joyful and pleasant liberty. At the same time, I liberated further coin from my private stock to assist in my retribution efforts on Grand Cayman.

On the way to shore, I secured the coins and a generous supply of herbal ingredients with Long Tall Willie for safekeeping. Since I was unsure who was friend or foe, I provided my landing crew with instructions to maintain their ploy of acting as helpless and wounded convalescents, while keeping a constant surveillance on everything occurring around them. Their seemingly woeful and damaged conditions would provide me the perfect opportunity to visit each of them daily to tend to their injuries, thereby avoiding any conjecture of conspiracy on the part of the deceitful islanders. Once beached, I ordered them to remain in the longboat until temporary domiciles amongst the traitorous scum were secured. I then separated and using a wooden crutch limped my way alone to Big Paul's residence.

As anticipated, my reception at Big Paul's manor was both warm and friendly, mixed with ample measure of pure feigned confusion. The sneaky scoundrel whisked me off to his private study to question our exploits against the insidious pirates. Playing along with his deceptive game, I provided a detailed account of our costly battle with the thieving villains, along with an accounting our significant injuries and the complete destruction of our vessel, never mentioning our second ship. Informing the conniving rascal that only I and a few fortunate crewmen survived the devastating encounter, I petitioned him for short-term residences until my wounded had an opportunity to heal. To seal the bargain, I delivered a magnificent ruby pendant to cover any expenses occurred during our stay. Big Paul fairly snatched the beautiful bauble from my hands, while informing me that I could count on the islander's hospitality during our recovery. He also disclosed his sincerest sympathies for our losses, although I knew these words were totally spurious. Providing me with a hearty meal, he showed me to a spare bedroom that would be placed at my disposal for as long as I remained on the island. Big Paul then excused himself and informed me that he would see to all of my injured crewmen's accommodations before nightfall. Making myself comfortable, I awaited the arrival of darkness.

Once evening descended, I scurried over to the window and eased my way out of the house. It was a moonless night that sported a continuous riffling breeze that was sure to keep the flying bloodsuckers at bay. I cautiously made my way to meet with my two combat officers. Upon reaching our prearranged spot, I ordered Long Tall Willie and Tan to select a target from amongst the obvious pirates roaming the settlement. Once this individual was waylaid and subdued, I instructed them to interrogate him to ascertain more intelligence. With plans set, we dispersed silently to maintain vigilant watches on our nefarious hosts.

I returned to Big Paul's residence and was about to make my way to my bedroom window, when I noticed strong light emanating from his study. Creeping silently along the outside of the house, I positioned myself directly below the lighted window, and peeked in to receive an eye-opening surprise. Big Paul was in conference with two swarthy-appearing rogues, who just happened to be the former junior officers of LeMerde! While I could not make out their hushed words, I could attest to the friendly nature displayed among the two villains and my illustrious host. I was now quite convinced of Big Paul's guilt in the matter of the *grand carouse*, but I continued my surveillance nonetheless. Eventually, the two pirates concluded their business and took their leave.

Big Paul then strode towards my eavesdropping spot and shuttered the window completely closed. Upon checking, I realized that one louver was misshapen and allowed a peephole into the room. As I peered in, I witnessed my host sneaking over to an ancient bookshelf and removing several large and ponderous tomes from its bottom row. Setting these aside, he reached into the newly created space and extracted a miniature strongbox that he carried over to his desk. Once seated, he opened the box to reveal a significant treasure trove and promptly deposited my recently provided bribes into the mix. Staring at his horde with sheer greed lighting his features, he finally closed the box and returned it to its concealed niche. As he was accomplishing this task, I quickly made my way back to my room and crawled back through the window. Hearing stealthy footsteps approaching from down the hall, I kicked off the boots and jumped directly into bed pulling the thin blanket over my clothes. Feigning deep sleep, I heard the bedroom door squeal lightly as it was opened. I then heard Big Paul's labored breathing as he glanced around the room to make certain that I was in bed and asleep. Vowing to take even greater caution in the days ahead, I finally fell deeply asleep.

The next morning, Big Paul invited me to breakfast. Feigning continual sympathy for our plight, Big Paul reported that he had found temporary homes for all of my injured crewmen. He then provided writing paper and ink so that I could commit our entire saga to paper for presentation to the proper authority. I realized immediately that this effort would keep me quite busy for the next several days, which I was sure was the devious devil's intent all along. Bidding me a good day, Big Paul strode from the house. I retreated to a shady spot in the adjoining garden to begin my report as well as to devise a scheme to topple the criminal element that infested this community.

When the brute returned for dinner, he stopped by my room to check on my report's progress. Given that I was nimble with a pen, I had several pages to show for the day's passage. Nodding his approval, he announced that dinner would be served shortly as he made a fast retreat. Our dinner conversation was careful and contrived by all in attendance. As the meal progressed, I informed Big Paul that as soon as my report was complete, I would provide an account to the entire settlement so that everyone could be made aware of our failure and defeat. Going further, I advised that such vital information could prove useful to him and his neighbors, since the lawless brigands that attacked us might decide to turn their attention on them at any time. I realized that this deceptive criminal would be forced to comply with my recommendation, given that it was his notion to have me document our exploits. Grimacing, he reluctantly agreed and informed me that he would host the affair in two night's time. With an evil smirk, he laughed and told me he hoped that I had enough time to finish my account. Wincing in a prescribed manner, I stammered that I would do my very best!

Since nothing more needed to be accomplished, I begged for my retirement due to my injuries. Convincing in my effort, I was dismissed and forgotten as I hobbled back to my room. As planned, I awoke in the middle of the night and scurried into Big Paul's study to liberate a number of the smaller but extremely valuable baubles from his secret cache. Safe and secure back in my bedroom, I sewed these baubles into my inner pant leg and planned to deliver them to my mates the following day.

The next day passed uneventfully as I hobbled around the town observing all that was occurring. In making these rounds, I met with each of my invalid men to fill them in on my newest scheme. Long Tall Willie announced that they had chosen and detained a despicable pirate drunkard for interrogation the previous night. Upon rigorous questioning, the sea sot had divulged that the entire settlement was involved in trading by stealth, a seaman's description of black market smuggling. The townsfolk were in league with a multitude of pirate crews and regularly purchased their booty in exchange for coin. These black-market goods were then traded to other island's merchants at prices well below market value. The captured pirate informed my interrogators that for the most part the citizens of this community consisted of former pirates, who had decided to move their plundering habits to shore.

In addition to trading by stealth, the townsfolk were also known to waylay unsuspecting merchant ships, who had the misfortune of anchoring in port for fresh food and water. These innocent traders were unwittingly captured by the locals and their goods purloined, their crews murdered and their ships either sold to cooperating pirate bands or sunk offshore. My men informed me that the villainous townsfolk had a unique method of disposing of unwanted outsiders. The scoundrels utilized a small cove on the opposite side of the island that was the natural habitat for an army of man-eating sharks. The unscrupulous miscreants would ferry any captured prisoners to this death hole and dispose of the poor unfortunates in a neat and tidy manner. In addition, my men had learned that Captain LeMerde had an ongoing agreement with the townsfolk to supply stolen booty and trade goods from his piratical attacks. They also uncovered that LeMerde had established a temporary lair in town by converting an abandoned church cellar into his booty trove headquarters. Sadly, there was no further information on the whereabouts of my French nemesis. The pirate that was questioned simply stated that his leader had sailed away on some unspecified business and was unsure when he would return. In his unexplained absence, the reprobate had left behind a captured sloop to enable his remaining skeleton crew a means of transport. As my men finished their informative report, I was not surprised in the least by any of this news. Now that I had the proof I required, I outlined the next step in my plan with my remaining crew.

I assigned roles to each crewman for our upcoming engagement. Each man was given the charge of discretely shadowing a different citizen in order to discover the hidden location of each reprobate's treasure. Since I was positive that there was no trust amongst these criminals, I was sure that their ill-gotten booty would be secreted close and continually checked by each of these hooligans to prevent discovery and theft. Once we were aware of the specific locations, we could proceed to the second phase in my dastardly game.

Chapter 11: Distrust and Anarchy Prevail

The following day the entire residence was alive with preparations for the evening's promised gathering. Food was being cooked, wine and rum kegs were delivered from the cellar and the house was cleaned and prepared for its role as host for the town's elite. During these furious preparations, I found it easy to deliver a mixture of *Datura* and *Wormwood* into both the wine and rum kegs designated to appease the raging thirsts of the invited guests. With all in readiness, I retreated to my room to complete my report, which I would be delivering to the assemblage later that evening.

The town's blackguards began to assemble at dusk and were hard at work eating, drinking and conversing with each other when I made my grand entrance. Accompanied by lukewarm applause and encouragement, I marched to the front of the assemblage and proclaimed my intention of reporting details of our disastrous encounter with the pirates. As I proceeded, I intentionally kept my account dry and extremely tedious which resulted in further alcohol consumption, which was exactly my aim. As I began to become aware of the effects of my ministrations of herbed intoxicants, I decided the time was right to enact my plan.

Gaining the full attention of the now addled crowd, I confessed that our resounding ambush and defeat did serve one very important purpose. Intrigued by this announcement, my drugged listeners became very attentive as I continued to explain my pronouncement. In a calm and nonthreatening voice, I advised all present that I believed these same pirates would eventually turn their thieving ambitions on the poor townsfolk. Given my prognostication, I begged them all to be extremely vigilant against these bloodthirsty monsters, who I was sure would soon attack and wreak devastation and ruin.

Well my dire warning had its desired effect as the fully sedated locals scattered and ran blindly from Big Paul's residence. Screaming, blubbering and swearing could be heard as they pushed and shoved their way towards the safety of their homes. Given the mild mixture of *Wormwood* and *Datura*, I knew that each would suffer only a short time from impaired reasoning. I also was aware that these greedy and deranged criminals would immediately fret about the safety of their private stashes, and would dutifully check on them as soon as they possibly could. As I watched their delirious and panic-stricken retreat, I was certain that my men would secretly trail each to discern the location of their treasure repositories. Turning to my host, I made a quick apology for the fear and trouble I had caused. Waving away my apology, my host continued to imbibe the spiked liquor, and ordered me to return to my room. A short time later, Big Paul sent his servants to bed and locked himself in his library to protect his own personal treasure trove.

The next morning, I made my usual rounds to monitor last evening's exploits of my feigned injured crewmen. To my utter delight, they all reported that they had shadowed their targets and had discovered the hiding places each had chosen for their ill-gotten booty. Informing all that no further action was required, I issued implicit orders on the next stage of my scheme. At the same time, I entrusted Big Paul's stolen valuables to Long Tall Willie for safekeeping.

Returning to Big Paul's home I was treated to the howls and wails of my host as he crashed and banged his way around the house. I met the unhinged fool in the hallway and immediately questioned him on the cause of his concern. Staring at me with the gaze of a total madman, Big Paul announced that he had discovered several of his most priceless possessions had gone missing. Feigning ignorance, I offered to assist in the search for his valuables. Glancing in my direction with his furious bloodshot eyes, he growled that he alone would conduct the search and required no assistance. Going further, he pointed an accusing finger in my direction and announced that I was most likely responsible for the disappearances. Appearing stunned by his words, I responded that I was woefully sorry for any trouble I might have caused, and that I would depart the moment the right opportunity became available. Smiling in a harsh and cruel manner, Big Paul disclosed that perhaps I would be vacating the island sooner than I had anticipated. With that he turned and stormed down the hallway towards his study.

I had the good fortune of not encountering my host the remainder of the day as he roamed from room to room tearing apart anything in his path. Deciding it was a good time to take a long walk, I exited the house and began a meandering stroll around town. As I neared the beach, I discovered that an English merchantman was in the process of anchoring offshore. As I continued to watch, I was joined by several of the town's leaders, who had survived the night without being slaughtered by marauding pirates. Buoyed by the sudden appearance of prey, the men began to laugh and whisper amongst themselves, obviously anxious to increase their wealth at the expense of the newly arrived Englishman. Not long after, a longboat was launched from the anchored ship and the Captain and his officers rowed swiftly to shore. Once safely aground, the contingent was met by the assembled leaders as they welcomed their guests to Grand Cayman.

The English Captain, named Brownstone, explained to his reception committee that he was bound for the Spanish Main to trade with towns and settlements along the coast. He announced that he intended to return to the island on his way to Jamaica before sailing back to England. However, before this could be accomplished, he expressed the dire need to refresh both his water and food supply. The townsfolk informed the Captain that both were plentiful, and promised to take the necessary steps to see that his ship's needs were fulfilled. Breathing a sigh of relief, Captain Brownstone thanked his gracious hosts and questioned who was in charge of the settlement. Speaking up for the first time, I introduced myself and gave a brief description of the plight that had befallen my ship and crew. Noting his sympathetic look, I informed him that I was currently taking refuge at the island leader's home, and would be more than happy to direct him there. With a deep bow, the Captain acknowledged and accepted my offer and we both turned and began our trek to Big Paul's home.

As we made our way, I made several covert references to the strange behavior of the settlement's citizens. Confused by my words, the English Captain questioned my exact meaning. Taking a moment to collect my thoughts, I informed my new associate that the townsfolk seemed exceptionally friendly with all manner of pirate and brigand who regularly visiting this location. Continuing, I confessed that there was also a tremendous amount of wealth concentrated here that certainly did not result from providing visiting ships with fresh food and water. Pressuring me for further explanation, I whispered that I harbored secret suppositions on the real nature of the business conducted here, which I was quite sure was far from legal. Begging me to elaborate, I confessed that I had witnessed known pirate elements consorting openly with the town leaders. In addition, I had witnessed a plethora of trade goods inventoried in secret warehouses meant for commerce with other islands.

Frustrated by my implications and hints, the English Captain demanded that I speak plainly on my vague suspicions. Stopping abruptly and begging for his strictest confidence, I blurted out in a terrified tone that I believed this settlement was in league with the scourge of the sea, pirates! My news had its desired effect as Captain Brownstone made the sign-of-the-cross on his breast at the mere mention of pirates. I continued by informing him that I suspected this settlement was composed of thieving land pirates who preyed on innocent traders just like him. I told him that I was certain that trading vessels were routinely seized and sunk by these insidious islanders. Shocked now, Captain Brownstone had the good sense to question the fate of the crews from the captured ships. Whispering, I replied that they were in all likelihood murdered and their bodies disposed of to prevent detection.

Beginning to exhibit real fear, the English Captain questioned what he should do about the situation. I replied that I was merely conjecturing based on limited observation, but I was fairly certain I was right in my suppositions. I then cautioned Captain Brownstone to keep alert and to limit his stay on the island. Further, I again made him promise to keep our conversation private, since word of my suspicions would lead to considerable harm for me and my surviving crewmembers if our hosts discovered the extent of our knowledge. Agreeing to my requests, Captain Brownstone informed me that all that passed between us would remain confidential. With his agreement, I turned and led the way to Big Paul's home.

Once introductions were made, I was rudely dismissed by Big Paul, who desired a private conversation with the Englishman. As I made my retreat, I heard Big Paul announce that the island would provide a gala welcoming feast for all aboard the English ship the following evening. Since I was moving away from the conversation, I heard no more. Anxious to meet with my men, I left the house and scurried around town. Visiting with Tan, I filled him in on the latest development and provided instructions for the following evening. Understanding my orders implicitly, Tan saluted and promised to bring his crewmates up to speed. Taking my time, I continued to wander aimlessly before eventually returning to my foe's residence.

Dinner that night was relatively subdued as Big Paul seemed quite distracted. Given his behavior, I was certain that he was devising plans to attack and pirate the English ship resting at anchor offshore. Knowing that much preparation was required on my part prior to tomorrow's celebration, I made my excuses and retired early. In my room, I carefully prepared the secret arrangements that I was sure would result in a most memorable celebration.

Part of this groundwork included the manufacture of a special herbal concoction to ensure the festivities were a complete and roaring success. I mixed a generous and potent mixture of *Datura* and *Belladonna*, which was certainly a wicked and serious combination. When imbibed by my treacherous hosts, this herbal elixir was guaranteed to elicit the absolute worst behavior on each of their parts. The next day, I provided Long Tall Willie the mixture along with specific instructions on the exact usage and timing for introducing it as part of the evening's gaiety. Meanwhile, Big Paul continued to roam the house still beside himself with the mysterious disappearance of his treasure items. While he had no idea who had stolen his booty, he continued to harbor suspicions that I and my crew were somehow involved. Because of this belief, he watched me constantly, and had ordered my room, my meager possessions and my person searched several more times. Having no success in this endeavor, Big Paul was completely stymied, but his consummate greed and overall stubbornness would not allow him to cease his desperate recovery efforts.

As yet, I have failed to provide a description of the female counterparts to these insidious land pirates. For the most part, these women were hard and weathered creatures, aged prematurely by a demanding and difficult lifestyle. Cruel, stingy and pure hellions, these landlubbing hags would certainly claw your eyes from their sockets for nothing more than a cross stare issued in their general direction. Their brutal nature was conditioned by their continued harrowing existence in this den of thieves and murderers. To divert their attention from their everyday woes, they adorned themselves with the ill-gotten plunder of unsuspecting merchants in the form of the latest European fashions and elaborate accessories, including pretty baubles borrowed from each of their mate's treasure troves. They reminded me of preening pirates on land adorned in utmost finery and fashion, in all, totally out of place. These women were just as greedy as their husbands, yet twice as mean and vicious. To be sure, they were best avoided at all costs!

To prepare myself for the evening's affair, I attempted to brush and clean my only set of clothes to the best of my ability. As I wandered outside to inspect the food, drink and decorations, I found that all was in readiness. I noticed that the island's elite had begun to assemble as I made this inspection. The guests of honor were not expected to arrive until later that evening, allowing the deceptive thieves an opportunity to begin their celebration early. This opportunity also allowed these cutthroats to drink their needed courage prior to committing the necessary atrocities that were planned for their English guests. I knew that this would be the perfect opportunity to introduce my special elixir to the town's populace without the danger of affecting any of the visiting English crew. What I required was a diversion to hold everyone's attention, so that Long Tall Willie would complete this task.

I had been told by a number of citizens that every important gala always included a lively band performance. I knew with certainty, that if a band was present, that there was only one sure way to utilize it to divert the crowd's attention, my phenomenal singing voice. As I pretended to hobble around the assembling populace, I kept careful notice of the band members as they made preparations to perform. Just before they began, I hobbled up on the stage and announced to all that I intended to serenade my wonderful hosts as partial payment for the many kindnesses they had extended to me and my crew. Having very little choice in the matter, the bandleader questioned my choice of song. After a brief conference, we agreed on several tunes, and the band struck up the first number.

As I joined in with an exceptionally strong tenor's voice, the eyes and ears of everyone in the audience turned in my direction. From that moment on, I had them all in my total control. As I performed, I observed Long Tall Willie secretly doctoring a gigantic bowl full of rum punch, the delectable turtle stew bubbling away in a humongous cauldron, a full keg of beer and a slew of opened rum bottles. With the trap set, I knew it was time to direct my unsuspecting prey to sample the doctored refreshments. Since the crowd was under my spell, I begged for a short break to wet my parched throat so that I could continue to entertain them. Cheers, yells, shouts and whistles answered my request. As I prepared to step off the stage, I urged everyone to take full advantage of the short break by partaking in the sumptuously prepared food and drink. Requiring no further encouragement, they practically mobbed the refreshment tables like a pack of ravenous wolves. In no time at all, they were consuming the medicated fare. I knew that it would not be very long before they began to exhibit some highly unusual reactions.

As I stepped back onto the makeshift stage, I noticed the arrival of the English party. To welcome them properly, I broke into a lively rendition of *Grommet Billy's Lament*, which halted their advance as they listened to my magical voice. Once I finished, there was a huge roar of approval and thanks from all present. Smiling now, I welcomed the English crew and announced my next song, *Hook-nosed John's Voyage*, which I was certain would elicit a pleasurable response from my adoring fans. I continued to perform song after song to the audience's rousing cheers and encouraging hoots. As I did so, I began to notice some very strange antics on the part of my enemies.

As I peered into the crowd, I observed one grown man sobbing uncontrollably off to the side. He was pleading with anyone in earshot to assist him by removing the filthy drooling trolls that were clinging to him. He suddenly stood and ran directly into one of the blazing fires in order to dislodge the insidious invaders. It took six burly men to drag his smoldering body to safety, as he fought and struggled insanely to return to the cleansing pyre. He was finally restrained by stout ropes in order to prevent him from turning himself into a human torch. As my gaze shifted, I spotted one woman standing on the roof of a nearby house, swatting at the invisible fiends that had driven her atop this precarious perch. As she weaved and stumbled along the roofline, she suddenly lost her footing and plunged screaming to her death. Her death dive caused a huge stir, so I ended my performance and joined the multitude investigating this tragedy. As I closed on the inert corpse, Captain Brownstone came to my side as the town physician pronounced the poor harlot dead. Shocked beyond reason, the ship's commander questioned what in blazes was happening. Shrugging, I calmly informed him that it appeared the islanders were suffering from some mysterious form of mental dementia, highly contagious and extremely dangerous. Strictly conjecturing, I stated that it was highly likely that the fresh water source of the island was tainted, which would certainly explain the utter madness we were witnessing. At that moment, a wild-eyed pirate staggered in our direction shouting nonsensical warnings about plague laden harpies that were out hunting for him. Having provided his dire alert, he stumbled, scuttled and crabbed his way away from us, while maintaining a constant watch for his murderous foes.

Just then, Big Paul suddenly came into view chasing one of his neighbor's wives with murderous intent in his crazed eyes. Screaming incoherently, he blamed the dirty strumpet for the theft of his precious treasure. After a long and exhausting chase, he finally captured the poor harpy and proceeded to administer severe punishment. Utilizing his huge fists, he pounded the woman's face again and again while chastising her as both a thief and robber. Captain Brownstone knew that Big Paul represented law and order in the community and his apparent bout of madness meant that absolutely nobody was safe. Glancing fretfully around, he surmised that the madness had indeed permeated the entire settlement. Well, this was the final nail in the coffin for the good English Captain. Making an instant decision, he turned and instructed his officers to round up the crew and gave sharp orders that he intended to sail as soon as everyone was aboard.

Pulling me off to the side, Captain Brownstone invited us to join him on their voyage, given the utter lunacy that was now in progress. I explained that I was still administering to my significantly injured crewmembers. Continuing, I responded that I required at least another few weeks before any of them could hope to face the rigors of sea travel and survive. Realizing that the frightened commander would probably elect not to return for us, I boldly inquired if I could ensure his revisit by providing a significant inducement. I then informed the good Captain that I had amassed the entirety of our wealth my crew possessed prior to landing on the island after our attack by pirates in order to fully control and protect our holdings. I then offered him half of these valuable coins, a rather sizable sum indeed, to persuade him to return for us following his intended trading excursion. Continuing, I promised him the other half upon his revisit and our transport to Jamaica. Yet uncertain and still a mite nervous despite my most generous offer, Captain Brownstone finally agreed to my proposal, promising to return to convey us back home. Shaking hands to finalize the arrangement, he nervously wished us the best of luck in the short term as he turned and hurriedly made his way back towards his landing crafts with his entire crew in tow.

If the crazed islanders were aware of their guest's hurried departure, they gave no indication as they continued to display the gruesome effects of the lethal elixir I had manufactured. They pranced and cavorted while they screamed and wailed unholy epitaphs and threats to anyone crossing their paths. With the departure of the English crew, I signaled my men to enact the next phase of our plan. You see, each had been previously briefed to return to the hidden treasure lairs and abscond with the booty each held. The next order was to amass and secret all of this treasure in a hidden cave we had discovered farther up the coast. I was certain that once the thefts were discovered that our hosts would be quite incensed and frantic over the losses. Prior to secreting this booty, I told Long Tall Willie to pick out several distinctive pieces from each cache. These easily identifiable valuables were then to be brought back to the lunatic's party for proper distribution. Actually this portion of the plan was quite simple; my men needed to plant these selected prizes amongst any pirates found either dead or unconscious.

Finally sated with the islander's insane exploits, I ventured inside Big Paul's home, and commiserated with the serving staff on the utter madness that had erupted outside. Afraid for my own wellbeing, I confessed to the terrified retainers that I decided to seek the safety of the house. Since many had witnessed first-hand the strange and inexplicable behavior of their master and mistress, they understood my concerns completely. I then warned them to avoid their loony master until the mysterious curse passed. As I had expected, these warnings were met with the traditional superstitious gestures! I then snuck into Big Paul's study and liberated his entire treasure horde which I transferred to Long Tall Willie for safekeeping.

Chapter 12: Demented Loggerhead Delirium Strikes

The following morning, I went in search of my host. I was told that Big Paul was resting in bed after his servants had found him attempting to swim on a dry sandy beach. Knowing that he was sleeping off the effects of my powerful concoction, I decided to canvas the remainder of the hamlet in order to pass the time. What I discovered hardly stunned or shocked me given the potency of the herbal concoction I had employed the previous evening. I was gratified at finding a number of inert community members strewn haphazardly around town following the prior evening's lunacy. While most of these individuals were alive, as evidenced by their ragged breathing, there were a few of miscreants who did not fare as well. The deceased were composed of a mixture of both island residents and pirates. The citizens were being removed from the scene by faithful servants, while the pirates were left to lie in their own filth. I knew that it would be several more days before normalcy of any kind would be restored to this den of thieves.

The remainder of my time was utilized in meeting with my men to plot our next move. That evening, Big Paul finally awoke and called me to his bedside for a parley. In a hoarse whisper, he begged me to relate exactly what I had witnessed the previous evening. I responded that truthfully I had seen very little. I explained that I was frightfully apprehensive about my own safety amid the chaos and madness that had erupted all around me. Due to this extreme fear, I shamefully admitted to returning to the safe confines of my room to shutter out all danger. Shaking his head in his own painful remembrances, he questioned if my medical knowledge and experience could provide an answer to explain the utter madness and chaos of the prior night.

Taking my time to ponder his query, I stated that I had witnessed such insanity only once before in my travels. Anxious to be informed about this event, Big Paul demanded that I recount details of this experience. In a slow and thoughtful voice, I answered that it appeared that many of the town's citizens suffered from a rare malady I entitled *Demented Loggerhead Delirium*. Continuing, I divulged that the dreaded sickness was essentially induced by tainted turtle meat. Since Big Paul knew very little about medicine, he was totally taken in by my fictitious illness. Continuing, I described this disease as being rare but quite serious for the infected. Questioning if I believed that the danger had passed, I sadly shook my head to indicate that the sickness was far from over. Stunned into silence by this response, I informed him that recurrences were sure to manifest again, although in my experience these incidents never proved as severe. In a terror-stricken voice, he demanded to know if there was a known cure. Sighing loudly, I responded in a reluctant manner that I had heard from various healing sources that an unusual remedy had been proven to have some success in treating this vile malady. Begging me to divulge this solution, Big Paul gripped my shoulders and practically shook the information out of me. My answer was short and direct, drink copious quantities of lemon flavored rum and avoid turtle meat at all cost!

Questioning my unorthodox antidote, Big Paul asked for further clarification. In a whispered confidential tone, I confessed that I had been advised by several respected healing contemporaries that a special mixture of herbed lemon rum could ward off a portion of the evil effects of this dreaded disease. Cautioning him that it was far from a cure, I warned that even with this special remedy that the disease's insanity-like spells would only be somewhat mitigated and not entirely eliminated. Hopeful and buoyed by my words, Big Paul called for his servants and ordered them to start collecting lemons. I smiled privately at his command since I had previously dosed Big Paul's entire rum inventory with *Wormwood*. I knew that when my delectable medicine was ingested, the *Wormwood* secreted in the rum would produce milder rounds of hallucinations, which would keep Big Paul in a suffering state and far less attentive to my devious undertakings.

Thanking me for my knowledgeable assistance, Big Paul dismissed me and ordered a bath drawn to clean himself from the previous night's affliction. I retired to my room awaiting the real uproar to commence. A while later, I heard a series of shrieks, moans and wails emanating from Big Paul's study. The servants were once again terrified by these screams, and several of them bolted from the house convinced that their employer was suffering a relapse of *Demented Loggerhead Delirium*. As

I approached the study door, Big Paul suddenly burst from the room with utter madness dominating his entire being. Taking one look at me, he shouted that someone had purloined his entire treasure trove. Before I could respond, he commanded his servants to restrain me while he personally conducted a thorough search of my person followed by my room and belongings. Convinced that I was somehow responsible, Big Paul was quite adamant in his dire promises that he would recover his stolen booty while making the perpetrator pay for the serious transgression with his life. Well, this extensive search was made by my wild-eyed host to no avail. Unwilling to admit defeat, he and his legion of servants continued to ransack the entire house and still discovered no trace of his treasure. Inconsolable, Big Paul retired to his study to ponder matters in order to devise a strategy to see his precious horde returned. Given this welcomed respite, I did not have the pleasure of my host's odious company for the remainder of the day as he plotted and schemed in an exasperated and maddened state.

The next morning, Big Paul emerged from his study with eyes bloodshot and in a very ugly mood. Eyeing me in a most suspicious manner over breakfast, he advised that I should make plans to depart his island at my very earliest convenience. He then sulked back to his study for more of his lemon flavored rum curative. Free to conduct business, I hobbled out of the maniac's household and made my way to my crew's locations with the pretense of tending to their fictitious injuries. This opportunity enabled me to provide further instructions to each man. When I returned to Big Paul's lodgings near dusk, I was not at all surprised to discover that several key citizens were present to report on recent discoveries. As they moved as a pack towards Big Paul's study, I was only able to discern their opening statement. Specifically, they told my host the surviving pirates had been arrested and were presently being held in the town's brig. Any further dialog was obscured as they entered Big Paul's sanctum and the door slammed behind them.

Since it was close to dinnertime, I wandering aimlessly around the house. As I smelled the strong scent of lemon coming from the kitchen, I smiled and whistled a merry tune. You see, I had purposely chosen this delectable combination of ingredients to ensure that my host would quite willingly imbibe copious quantities of my counterfeit medicine.

To hasten the hallucinogenic effects of my treatment, I decided to add a minute amount of *Datura* powder in an empty cup set out for Big Paul's use at the dining table. To further appease my devilish sense of humor, I also sprinkled some into the cup designated for Big Paul's spouse.

It was not so long after that we all sat down for our evening meal. Extremely agitated and overanxious to convey the news delivered by his recently departed associates, Big Paul barked to his wife and I that his colleagues had just reported that they had also suffered similar robberies the prior evening. Sweating profusely, he informed us that these associates had discovered items from their missing treasure troves secreted amongst a number of dead pirates found around town. As such, he related that his friends had ordered the town's constable to arrest all pirate survivors from the prior evening's debacle. Not wasting the opportunity, I voiced my significant concern regarding the overall chicanery and treachery of pirates in general. Going further, I stated that I was not at all surprised that thieving sea thieves had a hand in this insidious travesty. As Big Paul seriously pondered my words, I continued by stating that the only way to establish the absolute truth was to question each of the incarcerated pirates to discern guilt or innocence. Jumping up from the table, Big Paul shouted for his butler, who appeared a moment later in a nervous and agitated state given the strength of the summons. Big Paul issued a string of commands which the butler heeded without comment. The gist of these dictums was to alert the island's constable that Big Paul planned on visiting the brig immediately after his dinner to personally interview each of the pirates held in custody. Big Paul waved his humongous paw in dismissal, and the butler flew from the room to execute his orders. Big Paul resumed his seat and quaffed the lemon rum in his cup in three large gulps in an attempt to calm his strained nerves. At the same time, the harpy-like mate also partook of her drink. Conscious that strange and unusual behavior would manifest in short order, I sat back and waited for the show to begin.

Straightaway, Big Paul's face seemed to undergo a significant metamorphosis, going from a self-satisfied smirk to a fully terrorized gape. He jumped up from the table and demanded to be told why the room had suddenly filled with vicious blue gnomes. At the same time, his hulking bride issued a savage scream, and began itching and scratching every part of her exposed anatomy, while complaining about the horde of bloodsucking bogarts that were eating her alive! The two continued to spout absolute nonsense as they staggered and whirled about the room in a vain attempt to dislodge their unwelcomed tormentors. Hiding my mirth, I played the role of horrified observer right along with the serving staff, rooted in place attempting to understand exactly what was happening.

Eventually taking control, I ordered both Big Paul and his wife forcibly restrained and taken to their rooms. I then prescribed a dose of my curative every hour until the madness subsided. Having done so, I slipped out the back door and navigated my way to the prison where the surviving pirates were being held. Sneaking my way around the back, I located the pirate's barred cell easily as they were the only occupants. Whispering in the shadows to gain their attention, I informed the miserable lot that Big Paul and his associates believed that they had pilfered the islanders' secret treasure caches. Suddenly aware of the grave danger they all now faced, the miscreants started blubbering their innocence to this crime. Hushing them before they alerted the guards, I stated that it made little difference since Big Paul and his cronies believed them guilty. Continuing, I cautioned that they needed to make an escape before matters got fully out of hand. To assist in their plight, I supplied them with a number of sharp blades. As I turned to leave, one of the jailed rascals inquired about my identity. In the same whispered tone, I confessed that I was a friend of LeMerde and was merely returning a favor. Understanding my motives, the brigands proceeded to hide their newly received weapons and resumed their original positions to await an opportunity to escape.

In a rush, I returned to Big Paul's home and slipped back inside through my well-used bedroom window. Opening my door, I immediately made my way to my guest's bedroom to ascertain my devious host's condition. Entering Big Paul's room, I discovered the brute tied securely to his bed with a multitude of charges attempting to dose their master with lemon and rum. Sputtering and swearing, Big Paul was making every effort to continually avoid the blue gnomes that surrounded his bed. Taking control, I ordered the servants to secure their master, while I poured the medicine down his gullet. Once this evil mixture had a chance to take effect, Big Paul increased his frantic struggle for freedom from his miniature marauders.

That entire night the household was kept awake by the moans, shrieks, screams and curses issued by both my host and hostess. In the morning, things appeared to reach a calm and stable level as I navigated my way back to Big Paul's room. As expected, I found my patient in an extremely foul mood as he lambasted his charges for continuing to keep him immobilized. Wishing him a good morning, I cheerfully went about the process of checking his various vital signs. Upon completing my bogus inspection, I asked my patient how he felt. Delivering an additional number of vile curses and threats, he informed me that the madness had passed much to his great relief. Agreeing that I concurred totally with his assessment, I ordered the servants to free their master.

Once untied, Big Paul staggered around his bedroom promising death and destruction to all. Facing the heaving brute, I shouted that the servants were merely following my orders. Gazing seriously into his eyes, I promised that when the next bout of the disease began, the entire staff would simply let him die rather than attempt to assist in his recovery. Shaken by my dire pronouncement, he reconsidered his position and then began thanking us for our thoughtful ministrations. In a shaky and weak voice, he begged me to inform him when he could expect the next bout. Feigning total ignorance, I replied that it would happen when it happened. Realizing that he had little choice in the matter, he nodded and continued his pacing. Almost back to his normal self, he ordered the servants to prepare a bath. Sensing my presence was no longer required, I slipped quietly from the room while ordering the servants to release their mistress once they had seen to the needs of their master.

Later that morning, Big Paul stormed back into the house bellowing that somehow the pirate prisoners had made a successful escape sometime during the night. He disclosed that the thieving scoundrels had mysteriously obtained weapons that they utilized to overpower their guards. Intent on their immediate recapture, Big Paul had organized a hunting party to track the rascals down before they had a chance to escape the island with all of the purloined treasure. Acting mystified, I questioned why the pirates would flee if they were indeed innocent. Smiling evilly, Big Paul stated that was exactly his own line of thought!

Well, I can faithfully report that my plan was working to perfection with both sides now pitted against one another. It was now time to incite the pirates into taking action so that both sides would be operating on the offensive. In order to accomplish this, I had instructed Tan and Long Tall Willie to kidnap three pirates including LeMerde's two henchmen. The two French officers were to be taken to the cave where we had stowed the islander's treasure to await their ultimate fate. As for the third pirate, I ordered him securely bound, gagged and blindfolded upon capture. I was not particular in a choice of a target, other than informing my men to choose a candidate with a smidgen of intelligence. Once apprehended and incapacitated, I mandated that our guest be confined to a rather desolate and solitary underground burial crypt in the community's only cemetery. I had scouted this location out and was pleased by its relative isolation and the overall dread the site naturally inspired.

As I alone entered the eerie and sinister sepulcher, I found my victim trussed securely to a chair, gagged, blindfolded and terrified beyond reason. Standing behind the devil in the deep shadows, I slid his blindfold down a smidgen so that he could view his macabre surroundings. Utilizing my *special voice,* I replicated Big Paul's well known intonation to hoodwink my esteemed guest. You see, I had developed this extremely useful talent as a young lad back in Londontown. To master this handy skill, I had toiled long and hard to cultivate and hone this innate talent so that I could replicate all manner of sounds, most importantly human speech. Over time, I had also expanded the overall effectiveness of this valuable weapon by becoming versed in directing sounds or voices to any specific location I chose, normally a fair distance away from their point of origin. To take maximum advantage of this exceptional gift, I had purposely kept this talent secreted from everyone, including my closest friends and relatives. In addition to employing Big Paul's tone and modulation to induce terror, I further lowered his blindfold a wee bit more from behind and ordered him to glance around the moldering enclosure and choose a spot for his bones to rest for all eternity.

Swallowing quite nervously, the rogue whispered that he was totally at my command. Without allowing him to regain his composure, I barked out in Big Paul's voice that he needed to convince his mates to abandon the island immediately. Advising him that the settlement's partnership with LeMerde was finished, I threatened that they had only one day to make their escape. I then screamed that if my orders were not followed, he and his scurvy mates would be soon joining LeMerde's two junior officers. With that warning, I roared for him to take particular notice of the two new coffins that were resting on the floor directly in front of him.

To complete the charade, I had LeMerde's two junior officers stripped of their uniforms, swords, scabbards, boots and various other personal items that were sure to be recognized. These well-known personal effects had been strewn around the two sealed coffins announcing the identities of the occupants. As planned, the whimpering sea dog glanced at both sarcophagi and recognition immediately crossed his face. Well, this ploy certainly convinced the trembling fool that Big Paul meant serious business. I then imitated Big Paul's bellow to question whether the swine understood my warnings and threats. Whimpering and whining, he whispered that he understood completely. With that, I returned the blindfold and severed the ropes binding him. The terrified pirate then stumbled and bumbled his blind retreat from the house of the dead to alert his confederates.

Once accomplished, I returned to Big Paul's dwelling. Upon checking on my patient, I found Big Paul in a most miserable and unstable mood. At that moment, we were rudely interrupted by an island conspirator who had arrived with important news. After a cursory greeting, the messenger blurted out that LeMerde's pirates had been observed making hasty evacuation preparations. The emissary related that he had personally beheld the slippery swine in the process of packing and moving their stored booty from their repository to the beach for stowing on a ship he had witnessed disembarking. Musing but a moment on the news, Big Paul loudly conjectured that the pirate's retreat signaled that they had stolen the bulk of the settlement's wealth and were now in the process of spiriting it away. Spurred into taking action, Big Paul roared that the thieving scoundrels needed to be stopped at all costs.

Issuing a string of orders, Big Paul began preparing his island troops for war with the retreating pirate cravens. He sent out word that all of his associates needed to immediately arm themselves, adding that the islander's wives should do the same. As soon as his terrorized messenger had been dispatched, he rose from is sickbed and began to dress. His troops began to assemble at his residence near dusk. As ordered, the troop had indeed armed themselves with all manner of weaponry. While the men sported traditional armament, the women were forced to improvise as best they could from their own household items. This meant an odd collection of kitchen carving knives, age old swords, hatchets, machetes and all manner of potentially lethal homemade weapons. Upon being told that the pirates would take a few more hours to complete their frantic transfer, Big Paul decided to wait for full darkness before launching a surprise attack. Given this sanctioned delay, Big Paul ordered his servants to fetch food and drink for his makeshift army. Since the rum that was hastily delivered had previously been doctored with *Wormwood*, I was certain that result would certainly make for a very interesting battle!

As Big Paul's army feasted, I slipped out the back door and scurried over to meet with my crewmen. Once together, I began to issue orders. The first was to avoid getting involved in the brewing war at all cost. I then commanded Tan and Long Tall Willie to shadow Big Paul. When the proper opportunity arose, they were instructed to disarm him, bind him, and transport him to our hidden cave for later interrogation. Additionally, I commanded Angry George to lead the remainder of our men against the pirate sloop with the ultimate goal of capturing her for our own use. Specifically, I directed them to wait for the actual battle to commence and then sneak aboard the sloop utilizing our longboat. Once aboard, their directive was to secure the vessel and then sail it to a safe haven. As every one of my men was fully trained and capable warriors, I was sure that they would have a little difficulty against the panic-stricken pirates. With my orders issued, I returned to the battle preparations underway at my host's manor.

I found most of Big Paul's combatants in his courtyard continuing to be spirited up by the barrels of rum supplied from Big Paul's cellar. The *Wormwood* in this rum had begun to take its toll given the cavorting and utter craziness I witnessed. As I stood and watched, Big Paul provided a rousing speech filled with biblical references such as "*an eye for an eye and a tooth for a tooth*". In listening, I had to smile to myself since he had just articulated my very own motivation.

The rum consumption continued, the insanity intensified and finally it was time for action. Rousing his rabble to battle, Big Paul led the way towards the beach to attack the escaping pirates. Intending on monitoring the slaughter, I followed closely behind to enjoy the plot I had set in motion. The belligerent islanders met their pirate counterparts just off the sandy beach as they were completing the transfer of the last of their purloined booty. The battle began with a sloppy and ragged clash by both sides with mortal wounds being delivered and received. As I watched the murder and mayhem continue, I judged that the pirates would actually triumph in the confrontation. As I had earlier surmised, the pirates were slightly more proficient at warfare and hand-to-hand combat than the ill-armed women, servants and soft-living islanders. However, I also realized that regardless of the outcome, very few of the combatants from either side would survive the night!

As I continued my surveillance, I noticed that Big Paul came to this same conclusion as he began to edge away from the center of conflict. Before long, he had made his way to the outer fringes of the battle, and, with a quick turn, he was off in search of a safe hiding place. I was pleased that I had previously planned for this contingency as Tan and Long Tall Willie would shadow the treacherous island leader from a safe distance away to consummate my orders. Satisfied that my foresight proved accurate and knowing that Big Paul would soon be one more of our captives, I continued to enjoy the brutal conflict, so much so that I lost track of my immediate surroundings.

Suddenly, a blood spattered hulk of a woman lunged in my direction. Stunned totally by her gory and savage appearance, I took several brutal blows to my head from the fearsome club she wielded. Forced to defend myself, I blocked her next attack and managed to knock the club from her hands. Undaunted, she continued staggering towards me with her claws extended and managed to rake the side of my face unleashing a fountain of blood. Painfully incensed, I swiveled and grasped both of her wrists which I snapped via a merciless downward jerk. As she emitted a shrill scream of excruciating agony, I finally recognized her as Big Paul's mate. Ignoring her injury, she lunged forward intent on biting me with her fangs since utilizing her claws were no longer an option. As she approached in a shambling gait, a large red circle appeared to take shape in the middle of her forehead. It seemed that an errant musket ball had found a home in the hellion's forehead irrevocably ending her days on earth.

Having long overstayed my welcome, I turned and began my own retreat. As I was backing away from the battle, I noticed that the pirate sloop was now aflame. Initially alarmed for the safety of my men, I noticed our small longboat racing away from the stricken vessel at a furious rate. Not much later, the pirate ship exploded sending a man-eating wave of flames sweeping its way uninterrupted across the beach and directly into the mass of combatants totally obliterating them. This cleansing inferno spelled the end of the current criminal rule for the settlement!

Chapter 13: The Devil Receives New Troops

Stopping by the abandoned church, I found a trove of discarded trade goods that had been abandoned in haste by the panic-stricken buccaneers. Noting that this horde would provide a strong start for whoever survived the night of cleansing, I moved on towards our hidden cave. Upon arriving, I was pleased to discover three special guests, including Big Paul, bound securely on the cold, damp stone floor. My men had persuaded the rogues to reveal several of their well-protected secrets. Their first bit of knowledge was that LeMerde's two officers had confessed to the cowardly attack and destruction of the Adams' mansion. They had whimpered and mewed that Captain LeMerde had ordered the assault solely as a means of revenge against me. They were also quite oblivious as to who was actually inside the house when the attack occurred. In their own words they had confessed that; "*it was impossible to determine the identity of any victim amid the terrified and hysterical shrieks and screams issued from inside the burning structure*".

The second tidbit was that LeMerde was in league with my insidious nemesis, the Black Tarantula. While this relationship was informal and very loose in terms of specific arrangements, it, nevertheless, was predicated on each partner supporting the other in times of need. Unfortunately, my mates were unable to garner the location of either scoundrel due to the dishonored junior officers' claims of ignorance. They had only asserted that they had been ordered to remain behind on this insidious spit of land to ensure that my destruction was total and complete. My interrogators were also sadly unable to uncover any information on my beloved Rue. While the officers were aware of the Black Tarantula's fascination with the lass, they had not heard of any new developments in his manic search for the French songbird.

They did confirm what we already knew about Big Paul and his cronies' partnership with LeMerde. Each thieving islander had profited handsomely from this arrangement. The final piece of intelligence validated that Big Paul and his cohorts routinely utilized the small cove on the other side of the island to dispose of unwanted victims. Dubbed

Beelzebub's Cauldron, this locale made very short work of any victim thrown its way!

Not long after, Angry George and his boarding contingent arrived safe and unharmed. He reported that a clumsy pirate had knocked over an oil lantern in his haste to stow transported booty. My men had noticed the blaze as they silently approached the sloop, and had wisely opted to abandon the plan to board and capture the vessel. As they remained spectators, they realized that the ship's flames were spreading rapidly. Dismayed by the destruction of the pirate's treasure in the explosion, I buoyed their spirits by reminding them that we had previously captured far more valuable treasure from the pirates living on land.

Before dawn, I ordered my crew to march our three guests back to Angry George's hidden longboat for a fun and relaxing jaunt. Since we had three new able-bodied recruits, I ordered them to the oars to transport us to *Beelzebub's Cauldron*. As an additional measure, I had mandated that Big Paul be stripped of his landlubber slops like LeMerde's subordinates, who had previously been relieved of their uniforms. My reasoning was quite simple in intent. The stripped rogues rowing us would certainly enjoy the full fury of the tropical sun coupled with the ever present flying bloodsuckers providing them continual discomfort along the way. The journey took most of the day and night with our esteemed rowing team complaining continuously with moans, wails and shrieks the entire way. We finally arrived just after sunrise at the hellish spot, recognizable by the array of human bones scattered over the sandy bottom of the cove. I ordered the longboat ashore to await the full light of day.

When the sun finally made its grand appearance, I asked Long Tall Willie to supervise a work detail made up of our three prisoners. Their assignment was to fell a sufficient number of palm trees that prospered just off our position on the brilliant white sandy beach. Once this foresting chore was completed, I had the prisoners lash the logs together to form a crude raft tethered with frayed and weathered cordage that we had scavenged along the beach. These bindings had more than likely served as previous restraints for the poor unfortunates fed to the ravenous predators waiting patiently offshore. I knew that this rotted and brittle cable would certainly not last long as secure bindings, but I was also aware that my scheme only required its cooperation for a brief period of time.

When the crude raft was completed, I ordered it towed out to the middle of the cove and anchored to the bottom using our own stout rope along with a large rock from shore. As these preparations were underway, we noticed gliding black demons circling patiently below our longboat as their feast was being prepared. Our prisoners also spied the hungry sharks, who had once served as co-conspirators and now were relegated to the role of mortal enemies. Their eyes were wide with terror as they stared down into the watery graveyard realizing their end was near. In a clear voice, I demanded to know the location and plans of both Captain LeMerde and the Black Tarantula. Continuing, I also demanded any of their knowledge of my dear Rue.

For the most part, my queries were answered with blubbering, sputtering and mumbling. In the end, they all confessed that they had no idea of their confederate's plans or his whereabouts. Satisfied that under extreme coercion, their answers remained unchanged, I ordered their binding severed. Once accomplished and under the aim of our muskets, I commanded the trio to make their way onto the raft they had constructed. The pathetic sight of these three terrified nude rivals beset by painful sunburn and a host of significant insect bites brought a cruel smile to my face. Our guests continued to plead for mercy as I explained their upcoming fate.

I revealed that the survival game that they would be participating in was dubbed *Last Scoundrel Standing*. The rules of this deadly contest were quite simple, every man for himself. Since there were no rules, I explained that they would battle one another on the raft attempting to dislodge their opponents. The lone survivor of this savage game was promised his freedom with a solemn pledge of no interference from any one of us. At this point, the murderers once again began caterwauling separate pleas for mercy. Shoving our longboat away from the crude raft, I proclaimed that the contest had commenced. As my men and I cheered the competitors, the trio circled each other warily sizing each other up as they navigated the small confines of the raft.

As expected, Captain LeMerde's junior officers joined forces against Big Paul in an effort to dislodge him from safety and into the jaws of death. The only problem was that the two French deserters were used to battling foes with either sword or musket. Big Paul, on the other hand, was quite knowledgeable in hand-to-hand confrontations. Even though the odds were stacked against him, Big Paul's huge fists scored blows far more often than those of his competitors. Waiting for the precise opportunity, Big Paul unleashed a tremendous uppercut that sent one of the Frenchman staggering uncontrollably backwards and off the raft. Flailing and screaming for assistance with his head jutting above water, the two remaining combatants stood transfixed by the poor fool's mortal dilemma.

Suddenly the water surrounding the brute began to roil announcing the hungry sharks arriving for dinner. With a shrill shriek that sounded more like a stricken strumpet, the brute was savaged and dragged below the surface. In moments, the entire pool seemed to magically transform into a bright crimson hue as the scoundrel was shredded from stem to stern. Horrified by this sight, the two survivors regained their composure and reinitiated their struggle. Big Paul now held the advantage as he battered and pummeled the remaining French pirate. Scoring a series of wicked blows, Big Paul knocked the scum down and began to viciously kick him in a sloppy attempt to knock him off the platform. Realizing the dangerous hazard now facing him, the deserter got to his knees and attempted to rise once more. Big Paul took this opportunity to deliver a lethal kick to his foe's face which jettisoned him directly into B*eelzebub's Cauldron*. Once again, the ravenous demons arose and snatched their prey from the surface and dragged the screeching pirate down to his everlasting doom!

Victorious now, Big Paul called over to me to release him from his floating prison as previously agreed. Before answering, I questioned how long he and Fat Dog had been conspiring against honest sailors. Pondering my query reluctantly, Big Paul finally mewed that he was nothing more than Fat Dog's distant consort, trading favors from time-to-time without any sort of formal alliance. Continuing, he blubbered that Fat Dog had not requested any sort of skullduggery against us other than reporting on our everyday movements. His words seemed relatively trustworthy in light of the mortal danger he faced, and gave me some hope that my old friend had not directly conspired against me. Once again, Big Paul begged in a cowardly fashion to be rescued from his floating deathtrap before it completely unraveled, reminding me that I had given my word. Smiling cruelly, I retorted that I had never promised to assist his escape. Rather, I proclaimed that I had only promised that we would not interfere with his escape. I then announced, that if he successfully navigated his way clear of the hungry predators, we would torment him no further. With an expression of utter rage, Big Paul cursed me time and again. Correspondingly, he carefully judged the distance he would be required to swim in order to foil the savage man-eaters waiting patiently below him.

As he was making this critical study, one of the weaker ropes snapped and half of the crude raft came undone and began to float away. Big Paul was utterly terrified as he watched half of his temporary sanctuary making its retreat. Standing rigid with fear, he heard yet another rope snap. This time the remaining structure came completely undone as palm logs scattered in all directions. Big Paul, aware that any attempt to swim was sheer suicide, clung like a monkey to the upper portion of one of the larger logs hoping to ride his savior to safety. The problem was that he still had his arms and legs in the water as he clung atop the floating refuge for dear life. The sharks sensing sustenance rose and began to nip and chomp at his exposed extremities severing his hand and a sizable portion of one of his legs. Bleeding profusely now, the sharks converged as a pack and literally pulled him off of the log with their razor-sharp teeth and dragged him screaming below to his savage and appalling end.

At I watched him suffer grievously and die horribly, my thoughts returned to the many friends and mates that had been cruelly taken from me. While his death was both abominable and beastly, I believed it was just revenge for the nefarious deeds he had perpetrated throughout his lifetime. Revenge, sweet revenge! When the show had concluded, I ordered my men to begin our journey back to what remained of Big Paul's settlement. By their silent scowls of horror, I knew that the cruel and inhuman punishment I had decreed affected each deeply. It was Long Tall Willie who finally broke the somber mood by commenting that our little entertainment had robbed him completely of appetite. Laughing maliciously, I replied that I felt certain that his condition would be rectified once we were back in town!

We returned to discover that the few town's survivors were attempting to restore a semblance of order. The battle with the pirates had purged the community of it less desirable element leaving only a handful of elders, slaves, servants and youngsters. Selecting the most obvious leader from among this group, I led him to the basement of the abandoned church. Once there, I pointed to the remaining goods and announced that this booty was the sole property of the island's survivors so that a fresh start could be made without continuing to consort with pirates and thieves!

A week later, the English merchantman returned from its trading mission. Upon disembarking, Captain Brownstone was quite stunned to discover that the community had dramatically altered in his absence. He was bombarded with news from survivors of the devastating battle between the pirates and the settlers, which had resulted in the total annihilation of both sides. Satisfied that proper justice had been served, Captain Brownstone announced that he would anchor only long enough to restock his food and water stores. With specific tasks to complete, the town's survivors scrambled to fulfill his pressing needs.

Once I provided the promised payment to the good Captain, he ordered me to make preparations to depart for Jamaica. I commanded my crew to amass their meager belongings for our journey. While we had very little to transport onboard the English vessel, we did carry six full hogsheads of rum, which I explained had been purchased to provide a celebration once we were reunited with our mates. Without giving my statement much thought, the English Captain ordered my men and our precious rum supply aboard. I was certain that he would have been utterly stunned by the actual contents of these barrels. For between false walls, we had secreted the bulk of the treasure we had liberated from Big Paul and his insidious associates. On friendly soil, I planned to turn the entire trove over to Tan and Long Tall Willie to distribute to the crew based on merit and position. In all honesty, wealth was no longer a force driving any of my decisions so I was more than happy to donate my portion of the booty to my men. Unequivocally, I had more than enough wealth to last for over one thousand lifetimes!

Chapter 14: Jamaican Travails

Captain Brownstone ensured that we were made comfortable as we departed the Caymans. Since no duties were expected aboard the Englishman, it gave me ample time to reflect on my recent choices. My selection of punishment for Big Paul was both swift and decisive. I felt no lingering regret as I had long ago pledged no quarter would be given to confirmed enemies. Exhibiting pity when harsher methods were demanded invariably opened the door to odious future issues. Turning the other cheek with ruthless antagonists was a sure way to incur pain, hardship or death. Therefore, I had promised myself that I would never again allow adversaries a second opportunity to exercise foul play! Brutal and callous you might think, but certainly a wise course to remain among the living.

Upon reaching Jamaica, we were met by a contingent of British troops led by Captain Houndstooth. Before I had the opportunity to greet my old acquaintance, we were surrounded and summarily arrested. Stunned and confused, I questioned the meaning of this harsh treatment. Thoroughly abashed, Captain Houndstooth explained that the new Governor, Bartholomew Burgess II, ordered him to arrest me for the heinous crime of piracy. Noting my confusion at the name he provided, he quickly explained that the former Governor had suddenly taken flight back to England after his beloved wife had contracted a rare tropical disease. He continued by reporting that the frightened and desperate man had deemed his return vital in order to obtain proper medical attention for his spouse. Continuing in a conscience-stricken manner, he divulged that the new Governor had certainly been misinformed or misled about me and my associates. However, with a saddened expression, he related that both my crews had already been taken into custody and were currently housed in the island's brig awaiting trial. Given the crestfallen look on my face, he promptly assured me that this misunderstanding would soon be rectified given my past heroic deeds and incontestable reputation. Expressing his sincerest regrets over the entire ugly situation, he maintained that he was simply following orders.

Following this brief conciliatory explanation, he barked out a series of commands and we were marched towards the center of town. Included in our company was the good Captain Brownstone, who protested his complete innocence the entire way.

As we were herded towards the Governor's office, crowds began to form along our route with fanatic citizens branding us as pirate renegades and calling for a hempen jig. Per the usual custom, we were deluged with all manner of rotted fruits, vegetables and human waste. Reaching our destination, we were shepherded inside and made to wait while the great man was alerted to our capture and subsequent arrival. Taking his sweet time, we waited nervously contemplating our fates. Finally, the newly appointed commander, Governor Burgess, swept into the room and in precise and perfect enunciation demanded a situation review by his troop commander. A brief appraisal on my part found the new superior to be quite skeletal with a skull that appeared much too large for his slight frame. While not quite ugly, he was not handsome to any degree, sporting an oversized nose that jutted out like the beak of a gull. In many ways, he resembled the gargoyles perched atop certain important structures in old Londontown, hungrily scanning the horizon for prey. Twitchy and jumpy in movement and prissy and formal in tone, he barely listened to the report issued by Houndstooth pointing out that tragic mistake had most assuredly been made. At the briefing's end, he stated that he had been advised by a highly credible source that we were conducting business as pirates. Answering his charge, I questioned the source of this fraudulent claim.

Governor Burgess retorted that the esteemed informant was none other than Big Paul Brown, who had sent a missive branding me a thief and pirate! At these words, Captain Brownstone jumped to my defense. He explained that I had been forced to subsist on Grand Cayman amongst a nest of vipers to protect and tend to my wounded companions. Continuing, he responded that Big Paul and his brethren had proven to be criminals trading by stealth with close associations with pirates. Brownstone then testified that I had assisted his escape from the rogues and was due congratulations not condemnation. He also reported that Big Paul had mysteriously disappeared on the night of the battle between pirates and islanders. The few survivors of this horrific struggle had confided in him that they believed the villain had fled and united with his pirate brethren. Captain Brownstone asserted that Big Paul was definitely not an individual who could be trusted to provide proper testimony on anyone. Brownstone added to his defending declaration by informing the new Governor that the survivors had also disclosed that I had generously bestowed all unclaimed pirate valuables to them to allow them a new beginning. The good Captain declared that this selfless act had certainly demonstrated non-pirate-like behavior. He concluded his strong arguments by stating that he would personally vouch for my good heart, noble intentions and honest demeanor!

Well, I can attest that this information cast serious doubts in the mind of the new island leader. While not entirely convinced of my innocence, his dubiousness seemed to have grown considerably. I then produced the Letter of Marque and arrest warrants for Captain LeMerde and the Black Tarantula. Governor Burgess took an inordinate amount of time inspecting all three. He eventually announced that the documents seemed genuine and legal, but would need confirmation of their validity. Knowing this would take time, I suggested summoning my personal attorney for questioning. Agreeing, Governor Burgess sent one of his troopers to escort Simon Beardsly to his office.

The poor terrified wretch took little time answering the command as he attempted to salvage a proper appearance before the King's new representative. His thin wisps of hair were strewn haphazardly across his age-spotted crown, and he was perspiring profusely from all ports. Without preamble Governor Burgess launched into a series of questions to understand the attorney's credentials as well as our relationship. When asked to provide a professional opinion of my character, Mr. Beardsly reported that I was most magnanimous and good-hearted. As an example, he cited my donation of the Adams' land as a beautiful public garden in my friends' memory. Continuing, he confided that I had inherited a vast fortune from the Adams' estate so there was absolutely no reason for me to take up piracy. Finally, the good lawyer produced several letters bound together with a black ribbon. He explained that they were letters of character and personal worth drafted by each of the Adams sisters prior to their demise.

Selecting one of these missives, the Governor began reading the words crafted by my departed friends. After a while, he abruptly stopped and questioned my role aboard the *Amafata*. Explaining my duties, he then asked if I was the remarkable lad as described personally to him by this ship's Captain. Embarrassed, I managed to agree that the good man had referred to me in that manner from time to time. Still somewhat confused, I inquired how the Governor was acquainted with my deceased leader. Smiling with a wolfish grin, the Governor confessed that my Captain had been his closest friend while attending a small private college in England. With a complete shift in demeanor, he informed me that his friend had stayed in touch by post until his unfortunate demise. Clapping me on my back and wrapping his boney arm around my shoulder, he begged my forgiveness for his grievous misunderstanding.

Turning now to Captain Houndstooth, he issued specific orders to release my crewmen from confinement and to see that they were escorted back to our ships. Since we were certainly not pirates, all charges were dropped and a public apology would be issued proclaiming our innocence. Turning, I gave my sincerest thanks to both Captain Brownstone and Simon Beardsly for their unwavering support and defense of my character. Delighted, both scurried from the room to attend to important matters that awaited their attention. I then conferred with Tan and Long Tall Willie and asked them to accompany Captain Houndstooth to see to the release of our men.

At last, I turned to bid my thanks and farewell to Governor Burgess. Sensing my urgency, the Governor asked if I would sit and enjoy a cup of tea. Certain that he had a reason for the invitation; I accepted without question. When we were served, he confessed that he had an important favor to ask. He then explained that his issue centered on his daughter's perplexing and worrisome behavior for the past several weeks. The Governor confided that his daughter had fallen under some sort of spell and was not behaving normally at all. Inundated with official duties since his recent arrival, the Governor confessed that he had little time to spend at home, but had certainly noticed her abrupt change in behavior. He had questioned his spouse, but she claimed to also be mystified concerning this alarming situation. Made aware of my skillful healing reputation as detailed in Gertrude's recently read letter, he pleaded me to examine his daughter to determine the cause of her strange malady. Having no real choice in the matter, I reluctantly agreed to his great relief. Acting quickly, he suggested that I attend dinner with his family and selected guests that very evening.

My first stop was an accomplished tailor to clothe me properly for the upcoming night's affair. Begrudgingly, the nervous and fretful tailor agreed to accept the assignment only after I offered him an exorbitant sum. Promising to complete my new clothes prior to my dinner appointment, I exited the shop and continued to the Adams Memorial Gardens to ascertain the progress that had been made in my absence.

Upon arriving, I found Rufus supervising the work on the elaborate plans I had mandated. Catching his eye, he hurried to my side with a broad smile and welcoming wishes. Aware of my recent difficulties with the Governor, Rufus was genuinely elated that matters had been set straight and both myself and crew had been exonerated. Commending him on the marvelous progress made since my last visit, Rufus shyly grinned and turned a bright shade of crimson.

Returning back to his old self, Rufus practically dragged me to the completed mausoleum, well-hidden and discreetly disguised by a series of intricate mazes and locked gates. Once he unlocked the final massive iron entryway, he lit a torch and led me down a series of steps to a common vaulted area with securely gated alcoves containing stone vaults holding the charred bones of my deceased friends. Knowing I wished time alone, he lit a second torch and turned to make his exit, informing me that he would be topside seeing to matters.

Taking the torch and the keys Rufus had provided, I made my way around the room reminiscing on fond memories as I passed the final resting places of each of my friends. Making a detailed examination, I reached a small undistinguished alcove in one of the far shadowy corners and discovered a non-gated minuscule vault with a marker memorializing my friend, Powder Monkey. Since his remains were never discovered, the vault was empty. Moving to its back wall, I slid open a stone panel which blended into the surroundings to prevent discovery. Placing it aside, I crawled into the small depression and down a set of narrow stone steps. At the bottom was a small room complete with desk, cabinet, small table and chair for conducting my shore-bound affairs in seclusion.

Ducking down and crawling through the desk opening, I removed the back panel and found another crawlspace leading further down to the old root cellar. I was delighted beyond measure to discover the space untouched. My first stop was my concealed treasure cache, where I withdrew significant coin and smaller jewels that could easily be converted to coin. I then made my way over to Gertrude's workbench and spent some time again familiarizing myself once again with her incredible medicinal trove. Unbuckling my specially designed leather wallet, I refilled its contents. I then proceeded to create a very nasty black sticky substance that I applied on the blades of the ten wicked throwing knives that were housed in yet another specially designed leather girding. I was certain that this new substance would prove handy in dealing with unseen obstacles sure to cross my wake. Once the blades dried, I placed them back in their sheaths and donned the portable arsenal once more. Making sure everything was properly stowed; I exited the root cellar and made my way topside ensuring that all the security measures were reset. Outside, I found Rufus deeply engaged in work so I waved a friendly and understanding goodbye, shouting out a promise to return in the near future before I shipped out.

Making my way back to the ship, I decided to stop at Fat Dog's to pay a visit and initiate a newly conceived scheme. You see, even though Big Paul had not directly implicated my old chum in a conspiracy against me, I still harbored a modicum of doubt. Fat Dog noticed my entrance and came rushing over to greet me. As he navigated his way towards me, I was surprised to observe two large apes trailing in his wake. Noting my stunned expression, Fat Dog introduced his two pets as Stem and Stern. Aware that the simian brutes were now monitoring me closely, Fat Dog explained that his companions served as bodyguards, keeping him out of harm's way. Ignoring the dull-witted stares from the hairy pair, I clasped my old acquaintance in a warm and friendly greeting to reassure his confidence in our friendship and to secret my lingering doubts concerning his loyalty.

Anxious for news of our voyage, he practically dragged me to his private table in a far corner. Once our drinks were served, Fat Dog pressed me on the details of my exploits in the Caymans. True to my burgeoning plan, I informed him that Big Paul had been invaluable and had pointed the way to LeMerde. Continuing, I divulged that our raid had been somewhat successful. However, I confessed that during our initial attack, we had been ambushed by another rogue pirate band resulting in significant death and destruction. I explained that this unprovoked ambush had also allowed the villainous Captain LeMerde to escape. Continuing with my bogus report, I explained that while tending to my severely wounded mates, I lodged with Big Paul. During this time, I recounted that Big Paul and his associates were attacked without provocation by this same crew of savage pirates. Concluding, I informed Fat Dog that both sides were obliterated when the pirate ship's powder magazine accidentally detonated during the battle. When I had finished this entire fabrication, I could sense that Fat Dog was not totally convinced of the veracity of my report. However, he had absolutely no contradicting evidence to refute what I had related to him. I judged him suspicious, and I knew I would have to be guarded in his presence.

To diffuse the situation, I decided to lead the tavern in a series of hearty and bawdy sea chanties and ballads. My opening number was *Pot Bellied Suzie*. Well, you can imagine the response, just short of riotous! The entire house was now in my command and I was not willing to release them. As I began the next work chanty, *Scurvy Dogs Workin'*, I glanced over at Fat Dog who seemed to have temporarily put aside any immediate suspicions towards me.

On my exit, I was stopped by a gorgeous strumpet dressed strangely in traditional gypsy attire. Her hair was long and jet-black trailing down past her waist. Her eyes were dark brown, almost appearing black in the poor light of the pub. She was slight of frame and moved with the grace and agility of a dancer. Grabbing my arm, she smiled and introduced herself as Madame Mystique. Upon chancing on this unusual creature, I stopped and stared for a moment before inquiring why she had arrested my departure. With a self-assured smile, she responded that she was a renowned fortune-teller and offered this service to me. Still a bit stunned by her unusual appearance and beauty, I responded that I had urgent business awaiting me. Not the least perplexed, she retorted that her services were always available. Continuing, she provided the exact location of her sanctum, and boldly informed me that she would expect my presence the following evening at eight. Without a further word, she pivoted and glided gracefully out of the pub.

Chapter 15: Quite a Deluded Lass

My entire journey back to our ship was spent contemplating the hidden intentions behind the actions of the mystical fortune-teller. While beautiful and self-assured, I sensed an underlying nervousness that seemed a bit alien to her overall haughty and confident comportment. Given my brief observation, my internal warning system was on full alert, signaling that Madame Mystique seemed to be serious trouble in the making. There appeared to be something sinister behind those hauntingly beautiful eyes that shouted proceed with extreme caution. I was certain that I needed to be circumspect and vigilant in any dealing with this enchantress. However, I knew that I would keep the appointment she offered!

When I reached the harbor, I was pleased at the progress that Lion's appointed man, Bottom Dog, had been able to achieve while our crew had been unjustly incarcerated. Our temporary overseer had been deprived of his both of his legs due to cannon chainshot that had cruelly severed his lower appendages. However, he managed to navigate adeptly on a small wheeled cart since experiencing this tragic loss. While a cripple in most men's eyes, this seasoned tar was reputed to be an excellent sailmaker and loyal sailor. Under his watchful eye, work had already been completed on *Rue's Revenge*, while more serious repairs were still underway on *Neptune's Revenge*. A detailed appraisal dictated that another two weeks would be required to complete the refurbishment and restore our sister ship to combat shape. Locating Lion and Bottom Dog directing the numerous workers, I joined them and congratulated them on their excellent efforts. Lion was quick to point out that all my accolades should be given to Bottom Dog, since it was his diligent overseeing that enabled the repairs to continue while our men were detained. Turning to the curious specimen, I questioned what role he would like to assume when we eventually made sail. With a sly smirk, the rogue answered that the title of Captain would suffice. Laughing now, I countered that this role was currently filled, which prompted Bottom Dog to opt for an alternative role as sailmaker. Promptly agreeing to his request, I handed him several gold coins as reward for his diligent service. Turning to Lion, I offered him a leather pouch filled with similar coins to enable the hiring of additional laborers to shorten the restoration time.

Once aboard, the first detail I handled for my upcoming meeting with Madame Mystique was unpacking the black hooded robe which had been pressed into successful service several times in the past. To complete the ensemble, I selected dark colored slops, gloves and boots. My objective was to appear veiled in the darkness that any proper séance normally required. In order to disguise my face, I selected black face paint from my theatrical store. While I could not arrive painted black, it would be an easy matter to apply the black coloring once the séance began. The end result would make me virtually invisible and, thereby, in full control in the ritual's required darkness. Knowing that sporting any visible weaponry would be viewed as a threat, I decided to rely on the specially-doctored miniature throwing knives tucked securely around my waist and hidden under my shirt.

As I mentioned, when I visited my underground sanctuary, I mixed up a special concoction following one of Gertrude's formulas. The base ingredient for this deadly elixir was a dark syrup she had obtained from an Indian jungle shaman. The tribe had dubbed the substance *Woorari*, translated roughly as creeping death because of its deadly effect. As Gertrude explained, the Indian shaman brewed the syrup from a special vine that grew high overhead in his homeland's vast rainy jungles. The special property of this substance was its ability to paralyze any living object when introduced into the victim's bloodstream. This mixture spread rapidly throughout a creature's anatomy and arrested all normal bodily functions, including breathing! Thus, this slow and creeping enemy shut down one bodily function after another, and eventually starved the poor unfortunate of air ending its life. What made this death so gruesome was that the victim was fully conscious of the invading calamity, but was helpless to do anything to prevent eventual suffocation, therefore aptly christened *creeping death*!

Gertrude had augmented this potent substance with precious secretions from a rainforest denizen also known to produce similar lethal results. This animal was brightly colored amphibian called a poison dart frog. The secretions from this innocuous creature were used to coat the sharp tips of small thorns which Indians fired from long hollow tubes at prey high in the forest treetops. I had questioned the duplicative nature of the substances, and Gertrude had responded that her experimentation had proven that the addition of the two had made the end result much more potent. But I did not stop there. I had also added several amounts of more dangerous and lethal poisons such as spider and snake venoms and other assorted goodies. While I knew my final product was quite deadly and lethal, I had no way to judge the strength of this new compound. However, I was quite sure that the right opportunity to test my creation would soon be at hand!

That evening, I arrived at the Governor's domicile before the designated time and was immediately ushered into his private study. Upon entering, I discovered my host in a despondent and worrisome state. Without preamble, he confessed that he feared his daughter's condition was worsening. Her recent odd and erratic behavior had become increasingly magnified, and he now feared for the girl's life. Placating him, I promised to apply my entire healing skills to this dastardly problem which earned a brief display of relief on his part. While temporarily reassured, I presented him with a special gift, a magnificent bejeweled dagger, as a token of our new friendship. While the small blade was strictly ornamental, it was quite valuable and exceedingly beautiful. Stunned by my generosity, the Governor had difficulty thanking me as he stammered and stuttered attempting to form the proper appreciative words.

With our business concluded, we made our way to the dining room to join the rest of the evening's dinner party. Upon entering, I was delighted to spot Captain Brownstone amongst the attendees. Rushing to my side, he wished me a hearty and genuine welcome. Clapping me on my back, he inquired how I felt given my narrow escape from the gallows. Smiling broadly, I responded that I was quite relieved to be both alive and well. Turning, he introduced me to a Dutch trader, apologizing that the merchant spoke very little English. The Dutchman shook my hand and made a concerted effort to communicate, but his English was rather atrocious. Somewhat embarrassed by his language deficiency, the man dissolved into a series of muttered thoughts and concerns.

From these whispered snatches and my ability to speak and understand his native tongue, I deduced that he was in a serious predicament with stored perishable goods and no transport back to Holland. It seemed that his planned conveyance had been destroyed in a recent hurricane. I can tell you that the very mention of this natural calamity bestowed an icy feeling of dread.

These vicious storms arose seemingly without warning and certainly possessed no conscience to grant victims pity. Rather, these raging tempests offered only ferocity and wonton destruction across their meandering paths. Shuddering, I happened to harken back to an incident earlier that day involving our newest recruit, Bottom Dog. Lion had pronounced that his friend could provide us with serious assistance regarding weather. Lion had disclosed that Bottom Dog possessed the rare talent of accurately foretelling the approach of *dirty weather*. This ability was solely due to the sensitivity he felt at positions adjacent to his severed leg joints. He had informed me of this amazing talent by claiming that; "*the nastier the storm, the more vicious my ache*". While the promise seemed too good to be true, I reasoned that only time would confirm or deny his boastful claim that "*he could feel the advance of nasty weather in his bones*"!

The next individual to be introduced was the Governor's wife, who proved to be a nervous little bird. Her manner, tone and movements confirmed her high-strung temperament and weak constitution. She seemed intimidated and cowed by the Governor, while at the same time quite oblivious to anything occurring around her. I remembered that recently obtained island gossip had proclaimed her to be a laudanum addict. While I had employed this narcotic to dull excruciating pain during medical surgery, I certainly did not utilize it to treat minor aches and complaints. While beneficial at times, this substance was quite dangerous if foolishly abused, many times leading a poor unfortunate user to die by simply wasting away!

Observing a young woman from afar, who I reasoned to be the Governor's daughter, I could tell that she had once been quite beautiful. Making this curt survey, I concluded that her beauty had long fled leaving in its wake a wild-eyed, unkempt and raving harpy-like creature. As she wandered around the room, she spouted utter nonsense as her eyes danced and flitted in every direction. Monitoring her strange behavior, it seemed she was searching for someone or something. Upon introduction, I realized that any communication between us would prove impossible due to her inability to clearly focus.

The remaining member of this small gathering was the fiancé of the stricken girl. He seemed a soft spoiled brat, who treated all with derogatory contempt and arrogance. He was prissy and self-centered and when introduced issued me a sneer and refused to shake my hand. Obviously, he viewed me as distinct inferior. I also sensed that he seemed totally detached and quite unaware of his lover's serious condition. His behavior was akin to an old nefarious nemesis, Catstalker Gene! While his intentional rebuff was underway, the butler announced that dinner was served and all were asked to take a seat in the nearby dining room. The food was rich, lavish and excessive, and the meal was conducted in quite a madhouse atmosphere. Total chaos reigned with everyone attempting to converse while nobody seemed concerned about listening.

During the chaos, the Governor's daughter suddenly issued an insane cackle and then began to recite quite an odd verse of poetry. Her highly unusual and nonsensical ditty caught me by surprise. Her exact words were:

"A savage pirate roams the briny
In search of riches and plunder
Forever unsated...forever searching
For fabulous booty to appease his hunger"

Stopping for a moment to collect her addled thoughts, she then concluded her rhyme with these balmy final lines:

"Death awaits on sea or shore
Never forget to bolt your door!"

Well, I can attest that this last pronouncement brought the dinner to an absolute standstill, as all eyes in the room turned in her direction. Shrugging off my confusion and utter bewilderment, I questioned her on the source of the rhyme. Instead of providing an answer, she jumped up from the table and ran from the room. As she departed she recited the verse over and over again trailing her progress through the mansion, interrupted by fits of mad giggles all the way! As soon as she disappeared, her mother excused herself professing a need to tend to her daughter. The look of grateful relief on her face gave me reason to believe that her daughter's well-being was the last thing on her mind.

After his wife's departure, the Governor gave me a strained gaze. Consequently, I became aware of the serving maids whispering to each other in their own language. From the time I had spent with Tiger Eyes, I had learned the basics of this language so that I was able to decipher the gist of their communication. As such, I was able to grasp that they were whispering about the poor girl's need to ingest more medicine. Continuing my eavesdropping, I discovered that this medicine had been provided the lass by a fortune-telling she-devil. Little more was uttered as the women attended to the needs of the guests. Promising myself to investigate these whisperings further, I returned my attention to my fellow dinner guests.

As if things were not disruptive enough, the precocious fiancé expressed the claim that he concurred with his intended that pirates, and for that matter, most seamen were ignorant savages, horrific drunks and vicious animals. Glaring directly at me, he professed these strong sentiments as I sat stunned along with my tablemates. Captain Brownstone and I simultaneously disagreed vehemently to his frivolous statement, but the self-centered numbskull refused to recant his words. Since the self-absorbed snob seemed to have specifically singled me out with his incriminating declaration, I felt compelled to defend myself as well as the entirety of my sailing brethren. With righteousness burning bright, I turned my full attention to my accuser and began my defense.

In order to have the offending upstart recount his antagonistic words, I turned to face the Dutchman. Utilizing his native tongue, I informed him that I was quite fluent in his language. Amazed and deliriously pleased, we opened our discussion on the imminent problem he faced. Having reached a strong grasp of his dire situation, I questioned the premium he would be willing to pay to ensure his perishable goods did not simply rot in the brutal tropical climate. He answered that he would be amenable to compensate a bonus of twenty-five percent above the normal transport rate to anyone who could solve his plight. With this knowledge, I now turned to Captain Brownstone to uncover his sailing plans. He confessed he was returning to England quite soon with less than a full load of goods due to disappointing business dealings on Grand Cayman. Suspecting this to be the case, I questioned if he would be willing to incur a small detour on his voyage if it meant more than fair profit. Grinning now, he responded that he would be very inclined depending on the detour I had in mind. Turning back to the Dutchman, I explained the arrangement I had proposed to Captain Brownstone. In no time at all, I had both parties in full agreement to the arranged terms. With much to organize, both men excused themselves so that a loading schedule could be finalized that very night. Before they left, they turned and paid me tribute and thanks for my valued assistance in the matter. They then both offered me a substantial reward for my brokerage service, which I politely declined. With a smile and a warm embrace from each, they took their leave.

Once they departed, I turned to the spoiled young man and retorted that an ignorant sailor could certainly not accomplish the deed I had just engineered. Continuing, I pointed out that the vast majority of the island's nobility could not converse in vernacular beyond their native tongues, while I was quite fluent in well over ten different languages. Pressing my defense, I informed my accuser that an ignorant seaman could certainly not conduct and conclude the type of business arrangement to the mutual satisfaction of both parties with the ease that I had just demonstrated. Therefore, I insisted that he retract his claim that all sailors were nothing more than ignorant savages.

Before allowing him a chance to respond, I continued my defense by concentrating on his second insult concerning the drinking habits of tars. While I had to concede that many of my sailing associates favored *hot spirits*, I affirmed that I had never developed this same habit. I confessed that lemonade was my drink of choice while at sea or on shore. Given this choice, I pled innocent to his charge of drunkenness.

Moving on to the charge of vicious animal, I agreed that I could not refute the fact that I was an animal, since man by his very nature was included in this broad category. As to the charge of vicious, I also confessed that under certain circumstances I could be judged guilty of this descriptor. Explaining myself, I divulged that my personal nature could be induced to become vicious if pushed to the extreme. My contemptuous scowl upon delivery of these words seemed to give the narcissistic twit serious pause.

Concerning the final charge of being a savage, I hoped to dispute his slur by challenging him to a renowned gentleman's game, chess! For the first time since my defense opened, the Governor spoke up and informed me that I might have overstepped my bounds, since this young scamp was the finest chess player on the island. He explained that nobody was willing to play chess with him given his immense skill. Totally undaunted, I confirmed my challenge which was met by my adversary's cruel grinning sneer. The match began with the braggart expecting a quick defeat on my part. As the game proceeded, I methodically captured man-after-man erasing his self-confident veneer into one of total bewilderment. As a pronounced expert, he realized that he was now being schooled on the finer points of the game and his anger quickly rose to the surface. With only his king and a few pawns remaining, he jumped to his feet and dumped the board and its remaining pieces into my lap and stormed out. As he departed, I informed the Governor that the charge of bloody poor loser could be added to his many other deficiencies!

Now that we were alone, the concerned father begged me for my thoughts on his suffering daughter. I responded that I had pieced together a rough diagnosis but required further intelligence to confirm its validity. Confused and utterly baffled, the Governor broke down into desperate sobs as he pleaded for a quick solution. Nodding, I informed him that I wanted to interview his daughter's maid and that I needed him to remain absolutely silent during this process. Dutifully agreeing, he ordered his valet to fetch the maid at once. Almost immediately, a terrified young woman was ushered into our presence. As agreed, the Governor sat off to the side in silence with his head buried in his hands. This unusual sight added immensely to the poor girl's distress and discomfort as she twitched and shook with extreme fright.

Addressing the girl in her own tongue, I introduced myself and asked for her name. The use of the familiar tongue put her instantly at ease as she informed me that her name was Queenie. Quite astounded by my fluency in her language, Queenie questioned how I had learned the dialect of the slaves. Grinning, I explained that I had been taught the language by one of my crew named Tiger Eyes. Nodding, she informed me that his name was well known amongst the slaves for the freedom he had gained as well as the exalted position he held as a member of a sailing crew. She then told me that it was an honor to make my acquaintance. Continuing, she added that my reputation was also noble, and I was rumored to be a fair and honest man and a very good leader. Thanking her sincerely, I confessed that I required her help in a matter regarding her charge.

Blinking in abject confusion, Queenie questioned how she might be of assistance. I informed her that I had been trained in the art of healing. I also divulged that the Governor had become aware of my medical abilities and had enlisted my assistance with his daughter's condition. Queenie now understood my mission, but still harbored doubts about how she could assist in the matter. I informed her that I had heard her fellow maids whisper about the special medicine the lass was taking and wished to learn more about it. Fearing that the direction of this inquiry would cause the terrified woman to lapse into a protective silence, I informed her that should her mistress continue to digress that there was a strong possibility that she would die. Should this unfortunate possibility occur, I quickly explained that Queenie would suddenly find herself out of work and potentially sent back to the cane fields. If that happened, I promised that the harsh toil and brutal sun would age her in no time at all. Well, this statement had its intended effect as Queenie began to sing like an island songbird.

She confirmed that her mistress had been taking a special medicine, which she seemed to rely on more and more each day. She affirmed that this special medicine had been kept a close secret and that the girl's parents and fiancé were totally unaware of it. In order to investigate this mysterious curative, I asked Queenie to fetch some of it for my inspection. In an instant she disappeared and returned with a small brown corked bottle which she placed in my hand. Meanwhile, the Governor, rooted in his chair and still bewildered beyond reason, furiously questioned the contents and the source of the miniature vial that Queenie had just produced. Stifling him by reminding him of his pledge to remain silent, I opened the bottle and sniffed the brownish liquid identifying the contents immediately as rum along with another slight but familiar scent, *Wormwood*! It seemed that somebody was also aware of the disastrous effects of mixing the two substances.

Turning my attention back to Queenie I questioned where this medicine had originated. She divulged that the girl was in the habit of visiting a Gypsy fortune-teller, who provided an ample supply of the healing draught. She also confessed that the girl's strange behavior had begun soon after her first visit and had deteriorated ever since. However, the lass continued to visit the fortune-telling witch on a weekly basis, always supplied with a copious quantity of the curative after each visit. When I inquired about the name of the sorceress, Queenie whispered that her name was Madame Mystique. Things were now becoming clearer by the moment.

Taking the deadly medicine into the kitchen, I dumped its contents out the window to the sheer horror of Queenie. Calming the girl's fears, I asked her to fetch a bottle of rum from the Governor's study. Once delivered, I mixed the proffered rum with more than an equal portion of fresh water and added several calming and healing herbs which created a soothing and curative final product. I then poured this mixture back into the empty bottle and instructed Queenie to replace the medicine in the same place she had found it. I promised that her mistress would soon show signs of recovery, and I charged the maid to keep a close watch on the girl and to report anything unusual to me at once. Nodding her understanding, Queenie practically skipped out of the room to perform the duties I had assigned.

Returning to the Governor's study, I was confronted immediately by the worried bureaucrat. He confessed that he was totally unaware of his daughter's strange medicine. Further, he wailed plaintively that he was also ignorant concerning the girl's daily routines and activities on their new island home as he had been totally immersed in the affairs of state since their arrival. Taking immediate steps to calm the apprehensive and distraught man, I informed him that I had now provided the proper medication for his daughter, I explained that it would take several more days for this curative to take effect. Relieved by my words, the Governor questioned what role he might play in the recovery efforts. I confessed that there was little any of us could do other than keeping a close watch on the stricken girl. With no more to be done, I bid the Governor a good evening and made my way back to my ship.

Chapter 16: A Seance is in Session

The next morning, I made a detailed inspection of both vessels. Where required, I made mental notes of minor modifications required which I later provided Lion. Gratified that Tan and Long Tall Willie had initiated combat school for new recruits, I joined in these classes to become acquainted with the new crewmen as well as to judge their overall battle skills. While I estimated their abilities as mediocre, I was certain that it would not be long before my experts turned them combat proficient. Providing encouragement and commendations, I continued what I considered the necessary task of getting to know each intimately.

The rest of the day passed uneventfully and the time for my appointment with the Gypsy mystic neared. Exiting the ship, I made my way to the location provided by the enchantress the previous evening. The building was nondescript marked only with a miniature sign displaying a crystal fortune-telling ball with rays of light emanating off its surface. Knocking firmly, I was greeted by Madame Mystique dressed in the same vibrant, multi-colored and flowing Gypsy gown. Issuing a warm welcome, she ushered me into a heavily curtained adjoining room that housed nothing more than a wooden table and chairs with a crystal fortune-telling ball sitting atop.

The two chairs were opposite each other at the table, and the room was dimly lit by two tapers also sitting atop the table. Madame Mystique, already seated, smiled and pointed to a seat opposite her, indicating that the séance was about to begin. Once I was comfortable, she announced that she would attempt to make contact with the spirit world in order to obtain answers to any question I might harbor. With a leering wink, she invited me to relax and begin concentrating on the exact queries I desired to be answered. With that she blew out the candles and plunged us into total darkness. As soon as the tapers were extinguished, she began a fallacious soliloquy with the spirit world which I paid very little attention to as I hurriedly applied the black theatrical paint I had toted along with me. Once completed, I donned the pair of black gloves and slipped the black hood of my robe over my head, rendering me virtually invisible in the utter darkness surrounding us. All the while, I kept adjusting my night-sight. In very little time, I began to make out the outline of Madame Mystique as she continued her showman's prattle to raise departed specters. As she had previously cautioned, the wraiths would not speak directly to me, but rather only through her, which I found very convenient indeed! As she continued to invoke supernatural shades, I soundlessly arose and began to scout the room making a hurried yet thorough inspection. This diligence paid off handsomely, as I discovered the heavy breathing of two rogues secreted within the surrounding curtained maze waiting, I was certain, for their chance to do me harm. The reason for this strong supposition was the distinct and robust aroma of gunpowder that wafted conspicuously in the air alongside their pungent and ghastly body odors.

As I completed my exploration, Madame Mystique suddenly voiced that she had indeed made contact with an old associate who wished to converse with me, Handy! In a theatrical-like change-of-tone and inflection, Madame Mystique began speaking for my old comrade and informed me that he was overjoyed to be able to communicate with me once again. Utilizing the same spurious voice, she trilled that he was heartily sorry for the tragic deaths of my friends at the hands of the conniving French scoundrel. Continuing, my friend asked what specific questions I wished answered. From across the room shrouded in black, I used my *special voice* to project my own recognizable vocalization towards my original seated position to fool both Madame Mystique and her lethal accomplices. In a normal modulation, I informed the bogus spirit-raiser that I had several questions that required answers. The first was where could I locate my enemy, Captain LeMerde. Knowing that any reply by the mystic would be nothing but sheer prevarication, I switched my attention to have some sport at the expense of her concealed cohorts.

Again employing my *special voice*, I issued a mournful and bloodcurdling wail that sounded as if it had emanated from the opposite corner of the room. Upon hearing this baleful cry, Madame Mystique emitted a sharp squeal and her hidden compatriots flinched noticeably causing the curtains surrounding them to significantly riffle and alerting me to their exact positions. Given these pronounced reactions, I had a hard time stifling the hilarity that was building inside of me. Gaining a measure of composure, I again projected my own voice back to my original position posturing my second query. "*Whom could I trust on my quest*"? As my hostess returned to her devious, tranquil self, she again utilized the same counterfeit intonation and responded that I could surely trust my old friend, Fat Dog! This admission provided a bit of enlightenment on exactly who had commissioned this counterfeit clairvoyant.

Deciding it was time to test my newest weapon, I maneuvered close to both of the hidden accomplices and again issued a reiteration of the previous ghastly wail. This horrific shriek captured my adversaries' complete attention, allowing me to slice both mid-torso through their curtained shields with two of my miniature knifes laced with *creeping death*. These wounds were quite minor in nature and, in all probability, not mentally registered by the highly preoccupied scoundrels given their complete captivation by the room's wailing specter. To provide time for proper observation of the effects of my lethal formula, I projected my voice once again to my assigned spot and posed my third question. "*Where could I locate the infamous Black Tarantula*"?

Pondering this query, Madame Mystique took a long moment before responding. Before she eventually answered, I was surprised to detect that both curs I had just barely scratched had simultaneously slumped to the floor issuing no further movement. Checking their breathing, I was stunned to discover that no evidence of life could be found on either brute. I did uncover a slew of lethal weapons on each of them that I was now sure were dedicated to my destruction. However, the covert assassins were now quite dead and quite unable to do me harm. Realizing the extreme lethalness of my new weapon, I was still highly astonished by the exceedingly brief time it took to have my fabricated poison work its charms. I also instantly discerned that very little of my deadly substance was required to render nearly instantaneous death.

As I was made these observations, Madame Mystique, continuing in her disguised tone, informed me that the Black Tarantula had decided to ply his trade further north amongst the fledgling British colonies. Aware of utter duplicity behind this retort, I made my way silently back to my seat. As Madame Mystique called for my final inquiry, I posed my last question. "*Where could I locate by beloved Rue*"? In answer to my query, Madame Mystique voiced a fictitious reply that my lover could be found safe and unharmed on her own home island. Paying little attention once again to this false intelligence, I heartily thanked Madame Mystique for her invaluable assistance in summoning my trusted friend and companion. Continuing, I boldly questioned who had hired her to conduct this séance. Perplexed by this query and the failure of her assistants to permanently silence me, she sputtered that she had no idea what I meant by this last statement. Standing, I provided a response by grasping the crystal ball from the table and slamming it violently into her face knocking her unconscious. I then collected the false fortune-teller and hoisted her over my shoulder for transport back to my ship for further interrogation by No Nose and his hideous pets!

Once aboard, I deposited the aspiring murderess with No Nose and provided specific instructions on his required interrogation. Nodding, he took the limp form and disappeared to conduct his own séance. Returning to my cabin, I sent word to Long Tall Willie to join me. Upon arrival, I asked him to return to the site of the séance. Once there, I told him to remove the two dead henchmen along with any personal effects found and dump the entire load deep in the nearby swamps where they would never be discovered. My belief was that the trio would not be missed by anyone. After all, they had pretended to be Gypsies and the breed disappeared all the time, in most cases with a purloined precious bauble or two!

About an hour later, No Nose appeared at my door. My adept interrogator informed me that his gull had willingly squawked that Fat Dog was at the heart of the conspiracy. He had hired Madame Mystique to lure me to a murderous end through her fortune-telling sham. Once her henchmen had succeeded in butchering me, they were tasked with discreetly burying my corpse so that my crew could never locate it. In answer to an additional enigma that had badgered me since my visit to the Governor's home, the bogus gypsy clairvoyant confessed that she had been tasked by Fat Dog to provide the newly-appointed Governor's daughter with the loathsome elixir designed to transform the lass into a demented and delirious madwoman. The fraudulent medium revealed it was Fat Dog's intention to eventually provide a cure for the poor damsel's affliction, thereby gaining enormous favor with the new island's leader.

In doing so, Fat Dog hoped to become a trusted colleague of the man, which would enable him to gain all manner of confidential military and governmental intelligence. With my questions and many suspicions confirmed, I ordered a ponderous chain secured around Madame Mystique and commanded Scuttle to row her out to sea so that she could enjoy a refreshing saltwater bath! Before she was hauled from my sight, I spied the baleful and malevolent leer she cast in my direction. Without further provocation, she suddenly erupted in a series of lewd and abhorrent curses wishing untold pain and suffering upon me. Laughing at her weak revengeful effort, I ordered her to be silent and to save her rants for her new clientele, who she would be joining momentarily. I then shouted to my entire crew that the traitorous trollop would soon be plying her fortune-telling talents for the poor unfortunate denizens of Davy Jones Locker. While my men roared in total agreement, I gave Scuttle a curt intended to send the treacherous Gypsy to her deserved doom. Before he could comply, I had a sudden inspiration that called for a more deserved punishment for our duplicitous guest. Forestalling Scuttle's compliance, I revealed my new scheme to my audience which was met by an even louder boisterous and comical reception. With the conniving murderess bound and gagged and hauled off to the bilge, I called Tan and Long Tall Willie to meet in my cabin to plot the next step in my plan to deal with my traitorous friend, Fat Dog! With my intentions vocalized, both expressed grave concern for my safety given the savage capabilities of Fat Dog's simian bodyguards. Attempting to calm their fears, I informed them that there would be a little danger if all went according to plan!

Chapter 17: Fat Dog's Just Desserts

Upon imparting my specific requirements on the plans for Madame Mistique, I departed the ship and made my way directly to *Fat Dog's Pub*. Once inside, I spotted my adversary who appeared summarily stunned that I remained amongst the living. Hustling across the room, Fat Dog questioned how he could be of service. In a hushed tone, I informed him that I had learned some important information in a recently conducted séance which required his wise consultation. Smiling furtively, he suggested that we rendezvous at our previously utilized location in the Shantytown cemetery so that we would enjoy complete privacy. Agreeing completely, I turned and exited his establishment. Guessing that my crafty foe would not come alone, I hurried to the location to prepare a welcoming party for my nefarious guests.

From the start, I had harbored a firm belief that a few of my forthcoming visitors would be quite hairy and utterly ferocious in nature. To mitigate this colossal disadvantage, I had taken a number of precautions. The first of which was to increase the amount of the *creeping death* on each of my small throwing blades. While I was aware that this new amount would end a man's life instantaneously, I was totally at a loss as to its effectiveness against the feral beasts I expected to encounter. The second precaution involved my Gypsy prisoner who had been properly prepared and delivered by my men in advance of the evening's festivities. As I had commanded, she had been outfitted in a set of my old slops and then gagged and securely trussed. Once I arrived at the preordained location, I reunited with my mates who delivered the bound temptress in a less than gentlemanly fashion. I then made a careful scan of this desolate site for an optimal hiding place, which I found atop a mausoleum conveniently adjacent to the rendezvous point. I then made a hurried assessment to pinpoint a spot to situate Madame Mystique. Deciding on an ancient and crumbling stone cross that served as a nearby gravestone, I instructed my assistants to bind the disguised trollop to this masonry marker. Once she was secured, I commanded my assistants to find concealment nearby, but to not interfere unless I signaled them for help. Climbing up on the adjacent mausoleum, I readied two of my lethal shanks and pulled the black hooded robe around me to disguise my presence as I waited for the party to begin. Not long after, I distinctly heard the approaching racket made by my approaching assassins. Grunting and growling, two black shades and their double-crossing keeper burst into view a fair distance away from my lofty position.

For a moment I was stunned with primal fear as I monitored the progress of Fat Dog's powerful brutes, Stem and Stern. Regaining my composure, I firmly gripped two of my blades and prepared for action. I was fully aware that these incredibly savage beasts were capable of my abject destruction, if given the opportunity. Remaining in total seclusion, I utilized my ability to redirect my *special voice* and issued a warm welcoming shout to Fat Dog that would seem to emanate from the vicinity of the bound and gagged fortune-teller. Fat Dog recognized my voice and with a series of quick and furtive scans began attempting to locate my exact position. Not wasting any more time on game playing, I loudly questioned Fat Dog on why he had betrayed both my friendship as well as those of his old mate, Handy. Watching closely, I detected quite a stricken expression cross my opponent's face as he seemed to be internally struggling with the controversial choices he had made. However, this regretful visage did not last very long, as it was replaced with a menacing and vengeful sneer. Once this occurred, he shouted that the answer to my question was money. Continuing, he boasted that his employer, The Black Tarantula, was very generous as he demanded only minuscule bits of island scuttlebutt in return for more than bountiful payment. He then confessed that his demonic overseer was especially interested in my specific activities. Confounded by this revelation, I asked my traitorous associate why the pirate scourge was so interested in me. Shrugging at my query, Fat Dog responded that he had no inkling as to why his employer was so obsessed with such a near-do-well sailor. All the while, my nemesis continued his visual search for my exact location following my voice as guidance. Peering intently toward the area he had discerned as the rightful one, he finally spotted the lone figure standing in the shadows against the cross. Sure now that he had discovered my hiding place, he pointed toward the site and blew three screeching toots on his ape whistle which sent his two charges into motion. Given the order to attack, his simian assassins raced toward their designated target and attacked with beastly ferocity. Helpless to protect herself from the unmerciful onslaught, the would-be murderess was literally torn asunder as the chimps utilized savage claws and fangs to dismember, disembowel and eventually decapitate their pinned and helpless victim. Their brutal actions were spurred on by the shouted encouragements of their nefarious master. While both fiends performed this unspeakable and unholy devastation, I realized that I now had an opportunity to best them. I was also cognizant that any mistake on my part would allow Fat Dog's merciless pets to reach my position and also tear me asunder piece-by-piece.

Taking very careful aim, I released both blades in the direction of the hairy backsides that faced me as the monsters continued their bloody onslaught. To my everlasting relief, both dirks found their mark and entered the unprotected backsides of both chimps with dull thuds. Alerted by these mild pricks, the trained killers pivoted toward the source of these intrusions and in no time at all located me. With a mutual roar, the two hairy scoundrels bounded over to the mausoleum supporting me and began a furious assault on the roof. Fearful now that the lethality of my concoction was insufficient, I glanced around for an avenue of escape, which proved quite fruitless. Extracting two more of my blades, I calmly awaited the arrival of my hairy assassins, resigned to die in one last brutal battle. Even attempts at mimicking Fat Dog's command whistle with my *special voice* had no effect on the two monsters' forward progress as they quickly clambered onto the mausoleum's roof. Baring their fangs and snarling ferociously, Stem and Stern cautiously inched their way toward me.

As they crept closer, I noticed that they both began experiencing slight difficulties with their balance. They both appeared to slip slightly and falter to a degree as they continued their stealthy approach. Before they completely closed, I sheathed my two blades and leapt down from my perch, landing in a rolling maneuver that brought me quickly to my feet. Turning, I watched in dread as the two black shapes also followed my lead. Their landings were certainly not as graceful, as they collapsed into balls of fur, fangs and claws struggling to regain their balance. Realizing that my deadly mixture was wreaking havoc on their bodily functions, I now took a seat on a nearby gravestone to enjoy the show. Before long, both apes collapsed upon the ground and despite their continued frantic and frenzied efforts were unable to rise from these prone positions.

Wandering closer, I observed the spasmodic motions of each ape coming less frequently as they finally lapsed into utter stillness. As I stood watching, Fat Dog raced over and took a moment to assess the situation. Realizing that his beloved pets were dying, he dropped to his knees and began sobbing like an infant denied his mother's breast! Wailing piteously, Fat Dog turned in my direction with a look of absolute malevolence in his eyes, demanding to know what I had done to his beloved companions. Rather than answer, I took four steps forward and delivered a massive blow to the very center of his face. Given the vicious nature of my punch, Fat Dog flopped to the ground like an unchained anchor!

At the prearranged signal, both Tan and Long Tall Willie materialized from their hiding places. Stunned momentarily by the scene of destruction, they eventually questioned what I wanted done with Fat Dog. Without a moment's thought, I ordered them to transfer the traitor to his apehouse for questioning. As far as the chimps, I told them to dump them into the nearby swamp along with the sundered remains of the Gypsy mystic. As I watched my mates collect rendered pieces of the fortune-teller, I experienced a momentary feeling of remorse for the poor wench. Never in my wildest dreams could I have anticipated the amount of human destruction that Stem and Stern could wrought. The results of their feral attack was far beyond belief. However, as I harkened back on the mystic's cold-blooded attempt on my life, the compassion that had begun to swell in my mind quickly evaporated. I reasoned that she was no less a murderess and therefore got exactly what she deserved. Once the beasts and the majority of the dismembered doxy were dispatched, Fat Dog was hefted onto my mates' shoulders, and we swiftly made our way undiscovered to Fat Dog's apehouse. Upon our arrival, Fat Dog was secured to a decrepit oaken chair, while the surrounding caged chimps flew into noisy delirium at our foreign presence.

Deciding that their clamorous din might alert unwanted visitors, I extracted some *Belladonna* powder from my waist wallet and doctored multiple bananas. These special treats were then distributed to the anxious beasts, who greedily consumed the adulterated fruit. In no time at all, the chimpanzees went deadly silent as each sat in their enclosures dazed and befuddled. With preparations complete, it was time to initiate my interrogation of my counterfeit chum.

Emptying a bucket of cold water on the slumped form caused the traitor to sputter awake and groggily take in his surroundings. I informed Fat Dog that I had several questions that required answers. Sneering at me, he spat that he had no intention of providing any sort of information no matter what form of torture I could instigate. With a smiling nod, I crossed the room and stood in front of one of the enclosures holding a dazed ape. Extracting my cutlass, I skewered the beast ending its life to the surprise and horror of my guest. I informed the villain that a repeat performance would occur each time he refused to answer or offered untruthful responses. With eyes blazing absolute loathing, Fat Dog reluctantly nodded that he now understood the rules to the game we were playing.

With that, I began my interrogation with Fat Dog answering in a voice dripping with rancor and malice. My interrogation yielded a plethora of valuable information. In the first place, he confessed to have been operating as a spy for the villainous Black Tarantula for quite some time, providing vital information as it became available. Secondly, he claimed that he was also in discreet contact with LeMerde, who had indeed joined forces with the nefarious pirate scourge. When I questioned him on his involvement with Big Paul in the Caymans, he snorted that his specific instructions to the arrogant dolt were simply to ensure that I did not cause any harm nor interfere with LeMerde's piratical enterprises in that region. Lastly, Fat Dog disclosed that my beloved Rue had been located and captured by the Black Tarantula. To force her complete cooperation, the devilish scoundrel had made her a prisoner aboard his vessel, where she could perform her comforting lyrical serenades at his will. Fat Dog continued his forced confession by divulging that rumors alluded to a mutual alliance that had formed between Rue and the dastardly sea thief.

Not believing this last tidbit, I pressed Fat Dog on the current location of both of my enemies. With a wicked smile, he spat out that both were bound for Marie-Galant intent on wrecking death and destruction on my close friends. Stunned, I pressed Fat Dog for further details of their specific intentions, but received nothing in return as the traitor claimed total ignorance on any further details. His memory did not improve even when I once again threatened the life of one of his precious pets. Resigned to the information provided, I began preparations for the proper punishment of the man I had implicitly trusted. My plan called for a wicked and horrific penance, which I reasoned would somewhat appease the blazing fires within me calling vehemently for revenge.

The first step in my reprisal was to administer a slight slice to Fat Dog's forearm with one of my specially treated knives. I was careful only to administer a small dose of *creeping death* to the rogue, intending merely to cripple and not kill my victim. Before long, Fat Dog's features became frozen along with every muscle in his body. His only movement was the fluttering of his eyelids, which beat out a constant message of intense loathing coupled with unbridled fear. Thoroughly enjoying his predicament, I ordered Tan and Long Tall Willie to sever his bindings and tote his lifeless form to his pub's sporting pit. Not quite finished, I sent them off to procure some rancid cooking lard which I slathered liberally over Fat Dog's entire upper torso and noggin. I then situated my victim face-down in the center of his death arena, and commanded my assistants to arrange for a very special visitor. You see, I intended to conduct my own version of the infamous *Gator Gobble Game*, utilizing Fat Dog as its sole victim.

The ravenous reptile, star of the noxious contest, was dragged hissing and snarling into place inside his protective cage. Cantankerous and frightfully hungry, the beast was finally released to locate any available prey and commence feeding. As the ponderous reptile closed on the truly delectable smell emanating from the only food source in the arena, I thoroughly enjoyed the frantic dance being performed by my enemy's eyelids. Standing transfixed, we all watched as the gator slowly slithered its way over to Fat Dog's inert form. Huffing and sniffing directly in its victim's face, the reptile seemed a might confused since this meal was quite foreign but certainly carried an irresistible aroma. Given its ravenous appetite, the beast took a tentative nip at Fat Dog's lard-smeared noggin, neatly extracting an ear for its effort. Meanwhile, Fat Dog's eyelids fluttering increased in intensity, opening and closing in rapid movements that now resembled a flickering flame! Pleased with the savory taste of its meager nip, the gator began feeding in earnest chomping and ripping sizable chunks of lard-smeared flesh from my enemy. The show ended abruptly when the gator decapitated Fat Dog, swallowing his head in one mighty gulp. Appeased by my traitor's dreadful demise, I signaled Tan and Long Tall Willie that it was time to return to our ship. Leaving the reptilian monster to fully sate its appetite, I began to make a mental list of final preparations required to make both ships ready to sail to Marie-Galant.

Once aboard, I issued a series of concise orders and informed all that we would sail in a day's time. Around mid-morning, word reached us that Fat Dog had suffered a most horrific tragedy. It was reported that he has somehow fallen victim to the reptilian star of the grisly *Gator Gobble Game*. His half-devoured corpse had been discovered inside the sporting arena along with his well-fed luminary. The entire island had been devastated by the ill news. I had a difficult time discerning if the public sadness was in response to the tragic accident that had accounted for the loss of the beloved pubmaster or the real concern that the very popular Gator Gobble Game would in all likelihood be outlawed permanently. In any case, I experienced neither regret nor remorse at the traitorous scoundrel's demise!

Chapter 18: Captain LeMerde's Defeat

Anxious to weigh anchor, I personally supervised the final refitting and restocking of our vessels. Aware that my close friends were in mortal danger, I urged my crew to hasten their efforts at every opportunity. I was well acquainted with the numerous inhumane and dastardly actions perpetuated by Captain LeMerde, who was convinced that he had ample provocation to mount a revenge-motivated attack on my close friends.

As I pondered my plan of attack, I came to the realization that any attempt at a frontal assault would guarantee an instant death sentence for Rene and his family. Therefore, I came to the logical conclusion that utilizing the hidden cove on the far side of the island was the ideal point to allow a clandestine infiltration. I was also certain that Rene's hidden access route would enable us to transport men and equipment safely, expediently and covertly to my friend's plantation.

With a steely voice, I urged my crew to double their efforts until at last we were ready to depart. Issuing orders to weigh anchor, we sailed out of friendly Jamaican waters on our critical rescue mission. The voyage itself seemed interminably long, but we eventually arrived at our intended destination without incident. Gratified that we met no resistance upon entering the well-disguised cove, I issued orders to Tiger Eyes and a few of his men to hasten to the plantation manor to scout enemy numbers, positions and movements as well to ascertain the exact location and condition of the Turbout clan. Once accomplished, he was to immediately return to report his findings.

My decision to utilize Tiger Eyes and his men was rather simple. Because of their skin color, they could easily infiltrate the enemy's lair disguised as plantation slaves. While time was of the essence, Tiger Eyes and his team still required the cover of darkness to avoid accidental discovery or detection. Ensuring that this group was garbed in a close replica of plantation slave-wear, I bid them good fortune and launched their undertaking as soon as the sun set.

With the initial stage of my plan in motion, I made sure that the remaining fighting force was suitably equipped for action. To my great relief, Tiger Eyes and his band returned early the following morning unscathed. Hustling to my side, he reported that the Turbouts were currently being held captive inside their mansion by six or more heavily armed pirates, as well as a dozen additional brutes surrounding the perimeter to prevent any sort of rescue or escape attempt.

Tiger Eyes further revealed that all of the pirates were reported to be drinking heavily at the expense of Rene's fine wine and spirits cellar. Tiger Eyes divulged that he and his team had detected no sign of either Captain LeMerde or the Black Tarantula. Surprised by this intelligence, Tiger Eyes had made contact with several of Rene's slaves to attempt to ascertain more detailed information. However, these frightened retainers were unaware of any further scuttlebutt regarding my two enemies. Tiger Eyes did learn that an additional squad of nearly two dozen heavily armed pirates had been stationed on the cove's beach to ensure that any attack from the sea would be thoroughly thwarted. The slaves also divulged that Captain LeMerde's vessel had been anchored in the very center of the cove to also assist in warding off any rescue attempt. This ship's seaward guns had been loaded and primed for action. In addition, a significant armory of muskets and small cannons had been rowed ashore to bolster the onshore defensive position. He completed his report by revealing that while the Turbout family was still alive, they had been promised a most hideous and painful ending the moment any rescue attempt was made.

Taking a moment to plot our next move, I suddenly remembered the night of the Voodou rite on Saint Domingue which sparked a cunning notion in my mind. Requiring some very special necessities, I sent Tiger Eyes and his men back to the slave quarters to procure a portion of these essentials. Informing him that completion was necessary before the sun set; he saluted and turned to execute my orders informing me that all would be accomplished under the very noses of the drunken heathens.

Once departed, I sent Lion back to our ships to procure the remaining requirements. I then summoned Long Tall Willie to prepare a slew of silent weapons for our use in the upcoming planned assault. Choosing a small team of our most proficient knife hurlers, Long Tall Willie armed each of them with several braces of throwing knives. Lion returned with the goods I had requested, and I went immediately to work disguising my silent death squad. Remembering Grommet Jemme's and my use of the tar, charcoal and ash to replicate the skin tone of island slaves, I proceed to mix up a generous portion of this darkening agent and began applying it liberally on my assault team. Tiger Eyes returned from his foray, loaded with a variety of borrowed slave-wear which my darkened force donned to complete our ruse. Disguised as plantation slaves, our mission was to infiltrate the area surrounding the manor house and silently eliminate all of the drunken thugs. Once the manor was secured, I instructed Lion that I would send word so that a larger force of our men could join us there to initiate the next stage in the plan.

Moving unnoticed to within eyesight of the manor, I dispersed my team to stifle all outside resistance, while Long Tall Willie and I would infiltrate the house and exterminate the vermin inside. Long Tall Willie and I made our entrance through the kitchen toting armfuls of firewood for the cooking stove. Upon entry, we discovered Rene's butler slumped at a small table weeping and moaning with his head buried in his hands. Moving to his side, he glanced up quite confused by our foreign presence. Before he had a chance to react, I revealed myself which brought a huge sigh of relief from the miserable wretch. Sensing his dark mood, I questioned its source. He blubbered that the insidious pirate vermin were currently sequestered in Rene's study burning precious books for sport. He also divulged that the entire squad was utterly inebriated and plotting very ugly mischief. Continuing, he whimpered that he had overheard the fiends plotting to defile both Aimee and Lille, currently hiding in their rooms upstairs. Interrogating him on Rene's location, he explained that Captain LeMerde had taken him with him to pay a formal visit to the Governor. Both were expected to return in no less than two days.

Resuming my hasty interrogation, I questioned him on the presence of the nefarious Black Tarantula. The butler answered that only Captain LeMerde and his nasty cutthroats had made their presence known, and there had been no sightings of the other infamous rake. Commanding him to remain in the kitchen, Long Tall Willie and I crept towards the noisy celebration coming from the den. As we neared, we heard several of the devils beginning to make their way noisily and unsteadily up the main staircase snickering and giddy with lust as they prepared to attend to the captured noblewomen's needs. Pausing to allow them to ascend, I motioned Long Tall Willie to deal with the brutes remaining in the study, while I began my climb to halt the lecherous rapists.

At the top of the landing, I heard quite a ruckus emanating from Aimee's room. They were disturbing sounds of both a loud and vicious struggle coupled with the poor girl's cries and wails. At the door, I was met by Lille who came at me with a dainty dagger intent on causing grievous injury. Disarming my distressed friend, she continued to flail and struggle like a mad woman. Dragging her to her own room, I revealed myself to her which unleashed great sobs of relief on her part. Ordering her to remain behind, I crept towards Aimee's room to deal with the disgusting houseguests. Silently cracking the door, I noted that there were three scalawags in the room. All three were hovered over a struggling form on the bed as I made my silent entrance.

Too intent on their fun to notice my approach, I reached the nearest thug and neatly sliced his throat from ear-to-ear before he was even aware of what was happening. The blood spray from his lethal wound was spectacular, completely drenching his two cohorts as well as Aimee. Confused and surprised, the two remaining brutes turned, and I jammed a sharp blade into the second defiler which entered his gaping maw and continued directly into his brain. The nasty criminal was dead long before his twitching body slammed to the floor.

The remaining pirate reached for his pistol that was lying on a small table beside the bed. Before he had a chance to employ it, I surged into him in a mindless fury and knocked the gun from his grip. Reaching for my brace of knives, I unsheathed one and drove it directly into his bared privates. With a shrill cry of utmost agony, he groped his injured organs with both hands. Completely at my mercy, I drew my razor sharp cutlass and with a vicious sweeping blow decapitated the villain. Like his degenerate partners, his head and torso tumbled separately to the ground twitching frantically with his eyes continuing to blink in a most furious fashion.

Glancing over, I observed that Aimee was utterly horror stricken by the entire grisly affair. As she attempted to scream, I clamped my hand firmly over her mouth and whispered that everything would be fine now. Still quite addled, I realized that she could not recognize me under my slave disguise. In a calming tone, I revealed my identity and informed her that her suffering was over. Eventually recognizing me, she collapsed sniffling, sobbing and whimpering hysterically in my arms. Calling for Lille, I handed the poor girl over to her care and ministration. Before they departed, I questioned Lille if she was aware of Captain LeMerde's plans on Guadeloupe. She hastily informed me that she had no idea whatsoever, other than the pompous ass's pronouncement that he had a very important date to keep with the Governor. Sniffling back her tears, Lille thanked me profusely for my timely appearance and assistance. I informed her that there was much yet to accomplish to rid the island of its evil pestilence, and instructed her to remain in her room with Aimee until I returned. I could sense that she was still frightened to the core, so I promised to send several of my most competent men to protect them both until our work was completed.

Returning downstairs, I found Long Tall Willie who had also made a bloody mess of Rene's beautiful study. I could tell by the evil smile on his face that he had thoroughly enjoyed his heinous redecoration efforts. Summoning Rene's butler, I explained that all of the rogues inside the house had been permanently dispatched.

I then questioned the quaking man on the pirates guarding the cove. He reported that the rascals had been extremely busy constructing makeshift shelters. He had overheard that they had been commanded to lie in wait in these crude lairs to surprise and overwhelm any unwanted intruders. Questioning their numbers, the butler responded that there were at least two dozen savages on the beach and a slew more stationed on their ship.

I sent Long Tall Willie to fetch several kegs of rum along with numerous bottles of wine from Rene's well-stocked cellar. I then ordered the nervous cook to boil a large cauldron of water to which I added some very special ingredients. When the spirit inventory was delivered topside, I dosed each with a generous amount of the cook's newly brewed concoction, knowing that only a small sip of this lethal alcohol was quite enough to fell any living being. Moving outside, I was joined by Tiger Eyes and his squad, who had made very short work of the external sentries. Issuing a series of orders, I directed my men to collect the dead pirates and cart them deep into the nearby mangrove swamp for immediate disposal. I then collected the dosed spirits for the party I planned on the beach.

Upon reaching the waterfront, my men dispersed and began the process of sweeping the area clean of its human filth. Caught by surprise and senselessly inebriated, my team made short work of their assignment. The slaughtered fools were then quickly stripped of their slops and summarily dumped in the nearby marsh. Several of my team then donned the villain's garments and took up sentry duty so as to avoid alerting the anchored vessel of our presence. I then sent Tiger Eyes and a few of his warriors back to guard the women, while Long Tall Willie retrieved the transport wagon loaded with my doctored brew. You see, I had previously mixed a fair quantity of *Devil's Trumpet* seeds and *Belladonna* into the liquor supply, transforming the hot spirits into lethal and devastating poison!

Loading our party supplies into a nearby longboat, Long Tall Willie and I began our journey to the anchored ship. Once alongside LeMerde's vessel, I imitated the slave's dialect shouting out to the curious crew aboard that we had been sent by their mates at the manor to deliver a goodly supply of rum and wine discovered in the owner's cellar. Wasting no time to appropriate this treasure, the spiked spirits were hauled onboard and the devil's own party began across the entire vessel. We were hastily dismissed and rowed dutifully back to the beach to await the outcome of our virulent delivery. Observing the wild celebration onboard, we did not have to wait very long before the festivities came to an abrupt end. Sensing little movement from the enemy's vessel, we boarded the longboat for a return visit. Unnoticed upon arrival, we made our way onto the silent ship and discovered a truly grisly scene. The villains lay strewn dead from bow to stern. Long Tall Willie then rowed back to the beach to fetch Lion and a small company of our crew. I began a careful search of the vessel with dead vacant eyes monitoring my every step. Discovering only a modest amount of plundered booty, I set it aside for Lion to distribute in a fair and appropriate manner to the crew.

After a long and interminable wait on the floating graveyard, Long Tall Willie and Lion arrived with two dozen crewmen. In stunned silence, they began the gruesome task of clearing the ship of its dead. They jettisoned the vast majority, but I ordered a few pirate bodies lashed securely in visible positions all around the vessel of death. I then ordered several of my men to stand guard including two capable cannon teams, since I fully expected the appearance of the Black Tarantula at any moment. I was certain that I had concocted a perfectly baited trap and all that was missing was the infamous sea spider.

Having completed the rescue mission, I borrowed one of Rene's swift transports for a jaunt to Guadeloupe to discover and foil whatever LeMerde's had planned. After cleansing ourselves of our slave disguises and donning appropriate attire, I took only enough crew to effectively handle the transport, including Tan and Long Tall Willie. I informed Lion that I would return as soon as matters were rectified. We arrived at Pointe-a-Pitre's sheltered harbor under the cover of darkness. Alighting on the serene dock, we went unnoticed and unmolested by either the perpetual harbor rats or governmental watchdogs. With orders to scour the dockside dens of iniquity in search of vital information, my men dispersed like silent cockroaches scurrying into the night. Needing time to think, I remained behind to await their discoveries. After an hour, Tan and Long Tall Willie materialized out of the foggy gloom to make their report. In all, the news was quite scant. It seemed that LeMerde and his contingent had landed a day earlier, and had made their way directly to the Governor's mansion. Curious now, I gave orders to separate in order to scout the governor's residence to illicit further information. Daylight was upon us as we neared our target, which was abuzz with activity with servants running every which way around the majestic structure. From initial observations, it appeared as if preparations were being made in advance of some gala celebration planned for that very evening.

Interviewing a few of the workers by providing a modest enticement of coin, I discovered that LeMerde had indeed arrived. With the invaluable aid of Rene's forced testimony and providing a generous bribe to the greedy island leader, the scheming maniac had cleared himself of all past charges. As such, a grand celebration had been hastily announced to welcome the guiltless French officer back into the good graces of the monarchy. The few loyal men who had arrived with my foe were scattered outside the Governor's residence partaking of strong spirits generously liberated from the mansion's stores. I realized that I had to breech this reinstatement affair in order to foil LeMerde's scheme. My first step was to locate the musicians hired as the night's entertainment. With the aid of a few coins, this step was quickly achieved. Upon making my way to bandleader's side, I utilized a hefty sum of gold to convince him to allow me to join their company for the evening's entertainment. Dubious as to my intentions and even more concerned about my musical abilities, I performed a quick audition demonstrating my strong singing voice which easily satisfied the man.

Since the affair was still many hours away, I utilized the time to procure both appropriate costuming along with a near-perfect disguise. Besides tailored clothing to match that of my new troop of musicians, I procured a wondrous mask that would totally obscure my identity. Before joining my fellow entertainers, I gave orders to my men to quietly confront, neutralize and dispose of Captain LeMerde's pirate contingent once the official festivities were underway. I then spent time with my fellow musicians preparing a series of musical numbers that were sure to delight and enthrall all in attendance. As night finally arrived, so did the invited guests who flocked to the gala in droves intent on merriment and debauchery at the Governor's expense.

Time finally arrived for our performance and my small troop of entertainers made our way to an elevated and decorated stage that had been erected on the candlelit verandah. The Governor made his grand appearance to a roaring welcome from his guests. Striding proudly onto the center of the stage, the Governor called the throng to order welcoming and thanking all for their valued attendance. Proceeding pompously, he announced in his booming and cultured voice that the evening's festivities were being held in Captain LeMerde's honor. The Governor explained that all past charges against the illustrious officer had been proved false and as such he was being reinstated to his former rank and post, as island protector!

The crowd erupted with roars of approval at the news, as LeMerde strutted his way vainly and arrogantly in full military regalia to the Governor's side. Hushing the crowd, my devious enemy thanked his loyal supporter and the island's gentry for their unswerving faith in him. Promising to expend his full energy to the protection of all assembled, the crowd erupted in a clamorous round of applause amid individual shouts of thanks and praise. The Governor regained control by wishing all a delightful evening before introducing the evening's entertainers. As all of this official nonsense was underway, I took the time to scan the attending horde for a sign of Rene. I finally spotted him sitting off to the side sweating profusely and wearing a despondent scowl. He seemed totally oblivious to everyone and everything happening around him, most likely due to the intense fear that any blunder on his part would doom his beloved wife and dear sister to a most horrific death.

With our formal introduction concluded, my fellow band members struck up our initial tune. Stepping now to the front of the stage and calling on my *special voice*, I replicated the exact tonality of the French tailor who had produced the outfit I now proudly wore. I introduced myself as Pierre Duval, an itinerant troubadour recently arrived on this lovely tropical paradise. Noting that neither the Governor, Captain LeMerde nor the assembled horde recognized me, I announced our first lyrical melody, a well-known and well-loved French ballad entitled *The Wonders of Paris.* Launching into the performance, I was gratified to discern that my euphoric voice still had a mesmerizing effect, as the crowd quieted and stared up at the stage totally transfixed. This was my exact intention, since I would require their undivided attention when I deemed the moment right. After performing several more hauntingly beautiful melodies, I was sure that I had the entire assemblage under my total control.

Just before we were scheduled to take a brief rest, I addressed my adoring fans and pointed to the guest of honor, Captain LeMerde. In a calm and sure voice, I informed the audience that I had recently spent some time on Jamaica. Noticing the nervous expression that stole across my nemesis' face, I continued by questioning the scoundrel if he was not in fact the same individual who had been tried, convicted and sentenced to hang for several serious crimes. Shocked to the extreme, LeMerde glanced quickly over to the Governor for support. Before either could utter a defending retort, I informed my rapt listeners that the French military man that I spoke of had been convicted of both kidnapping and counterfeiting. Plowing ahead, I also divulged that this nefarious criminal had made a daring escape from English authority. During this escape, this reprobate had murdered several innocent guards so that the title murderer could be added to his list of heinous misgivings.

With a reprehensible and bloodthirsty expression, Captain LeMerde advanced on my position with drawn saber intending to silence the impudent balladeer, who had the utter gall to relate these foul prevarications. When he reached the front of the stage, he began jabbing his sword viciously in my direction. Now facing his barred blade, I fearlessly continued by announcing that I had also recently visited the isle's beautiful sister, Marie-Galant, where I had discovered the entire Turbout family being held hostage by this same nefarious brute. Well, this latest bit of news caused the entire audience to turn their attention on the incensed officer loudly demanding clarification and explanation. At the same time, Captain LeMerde was far beyond furious, as he advanced on me with murderous intentions etched on his features. As he neared, I singled out Rene and quizzed him on the reason why his dear wife and sister were being held hostage against their wills. Shocked completely by this query, Rene attempted to locate his tongue, but was yet unable to muster the ability to speak, as he was yet under LeMerde's implicit orders to remain silent and to not interfere in any way with the evening's festivities.

All the while, Captain LeMerde had closed the small gap between us, naming me a scoundrel and liar in hate-laced screams. Ignoring his words, I glanced over to Rene and informed him that I had good tidings, and reported that both his wife and sister had been rescued. These words produced three simultaneous responses. Rene regained a hint of his old self and demanded an immediate explanation of how his loved ones had been saved. Correspondingly, the crowd began to believe that my words had a ring of truth and shouted question after question to both LeMerde and the Governor. As both occurred, Captain LeMerde, having finally reached my side, swept his saber in my direction intent on murder, while screaming violently that I was nothing more than a prevaricating rascal. Jumping back to avoid his vicious swing, I pulled off my mask and flung it aside, revealing my true identity. With a thunderous voice, I shouted that my name was Captain William Bilge and that I had been officially sanctioned by the Governor of Jamaica to track down and arrest Captain LeMerde for the hanging offenses of kidnapping, counterfeiting, murder and piracy. At that moment, total chaos erupted as all in attendance began screaming and shouting wildly.

Captain LeMerde, shocked to the core at discovering me standing before him, shouted for his men posted around the mansion to converge on his position. Utilizing this momentary lull, I unsheathed my own blade, and the two of us proceeded to trade blows to the absolute horror and bewilderment of the startled bystanders, who promptly turned in a mob-like fashion and fled for safer quarters. Rene, now seemingly convinced that his loved ones were safe, shouted out repeatedly to anyone who would listen that he had been coerced into providing false testimony by the scoundrel, LeMerde.

As our battle ensued, I was in total control and thoroughly enjoying myself. Delivering far more punishment that that of my opponent, I relished taunting the proud peacock as I danced nimbly away from his maniacal feints and thrusts. As we circled one another, I promised him a slow and painful death at the end of an English noose.

As our battle ensued, Captain LeMerde came to the slow and highly irritating realization that he was no longer the superior swordsman. Shouting once again for assistance from his men, he went on a wild and desperate offensive that proved quite ineffectual. Laughing in his face, I divulged that his men would not be attending the festivities this evening since pirates certainly had not been invited! As my enemy finally realized his serious predicament, I went on the attack. In a series of blindingly swift and skilled advances, I hammered unmercifully at his weakened defenses scoring various nicks and slashes on numerous portions of his exposed anatomy. Now bloodied and terrified, the cowardly fiend glanced around for an avenue of escape, which was exactly what I had been plotting since the initiation of this battle. You see, I could have easily cut him down long ago. Instead, I chose a different course since this manner of death would have been far too swift and merciful. My crew's specific orders were to allow the scurvy rascal a chance to escape, and then capture him in an isolated location free from any island witnesses. In this way, I could enact the very special plan I had in mind for the ultimate demise of this vicious swine.

Cut and bleeding profusely from my deadly onslaughts, LeMerde broke off our duel and turned to flee. Before doing so, he reached out and slashed the Governor's arm leaving behind a vicious wound that immediately began to gush a copious amount of blood. He then purposely knocked over a huge blazing candelabra directly onto the Governor's daughter, whose flowing and frilly gown immediately caught fire upon contact. As the poor creature issued shrill screams of pain and terror, the craven criminal bolted from the verandah. I had certainly not envisioned an innocent being harmed in my efforts to destroy my enemy. Forgetting the fleeing coward, I dropped my blade and ran to the girl and lifted her into my arms. I then proceeded to scurry over to the humongous fountain in the very center of the verandah and dove into it. With an angry hiss, the water thankfully extinguished the lethal flames as the stunned lass surfaced sputtering and spitting water. Assisting her gently from the fountain, she was whisked into the manor house to be immediately attended and consoled. As she was conveyed to the mansion, I distinctly heard her grousing about the ruin and devastation of her beautiful gown. In that moment, I realized that she was indeed the Governor's offspring!

Since I was quite sure that my men would obey my order and capture the fleeing French rabbit, I stopped to assist the wounded Governor. As he sputtered my praises, Rene joined us, anxious for news of his family members. Turning in his direction, I calmly reassured him that both Lille and Aimee were safe in the hands of my most trusted crewmen. Breathing a monstrous sigh of relief, he joined the Governor in feeble attempts at thanking me. When normalcy eventually returned, the Governor issued a series of orders to search and apprehend the nefarious villain, who would be promptly hanged for his heinous crimes. Turning to the Governor, I requested permission to exit the island and return Rene to his loved ones. Coming to his full senses, the Governor agreed and begged me to do so at my earliest convenience. Saluting him, I gathered Rene and we made our hasty exit.

Returning to Rene's transport, I filled him in on the daring plan we had utilized to free Lille and Aimee. When we arrived at his small vessel, my men were assembled beside it. I was not at all surprised to notice a large bundle of sailcloth lashed to the boat's bottom, indicating that my men had followed my orders implicitly.

The subsequent reuniting of the Turbout family was moving and stirring indeed. As the numerous kisses and hugs proceeded, I explained that I was yet on the hunt for the other vile pirate who had rumored to be somewhere close in proximity. As such, I sadly divulged that his nefarious presence necessitated my immediate departure. Rene embraced me with tears streaming down his face, while Lille kissed me on both cheeks as was the traditional French custom. Finally, Aimee delivered yet another wondrously amorous kiss, while once again declaring her intense love for me. Exceedingly infatuated and with a head full of angry bees, I informed all that I would soon return. I then explained to Rene that Captain LeMerde's pirate ship was now his to command. Noting his look of utter puzzlement, I continued by stating that this powerful weapon would prove a valuable deterrent against any future unwelcome pests given its ponderous and militant armament.

Assured at last that all had returned to normal, I made my final farewells and promptly returned to my two vessels. Upon my orders, Captain LeMerde, who had been previously captured and lashed in sailcloth, had now been secured in my cabin and was now being properly introduced to No Nose's hideous playmates. Given the unknown whereabouts of the Black Tarantula, I sensed that time was certainly of the essence. Praying that No Nose would secede in liberating vital information to determine this wily pirate's plans, I hurried below to hear the results. Discovering No Nose outside my cabin clearly in a dazed and confused state, I moved to his side and questioned the results of his interrogation. Flashing me a dejected shrug, he confessed that his hairy pets seemed to have very little effect on the bound reprobate. In fact, it appeared that Captain LeMerde seemed to honestly enjoy the hideous trespassers, and, as such, no vital intelligence had been gained. Unhappy with this news, I entered the cabin to face the demonic fiend who had slaughtered some of my closest and dearest friends. Striding over to the subdued villain's side, I was subjected to his leering grin as he greeted me with less than gentlemanly words. Nabbing a nearby chair, I answered his nasty slurs with a beaming smile. Confounded, the rogue proceeded to spout his unwillingness to divulge information no matter the punishment or torture I attempted to institute. Laughing now at his brash boast, I informed him of the hideous demise of his two loyal associates, who had also chosen this very course. Unfazed by these gory and gruesome details, he boldly restated his intention to remain mute. As I studied his proud and haughty features, an extremely black notion entered my mind. Calling Sharkface into the room, I whispered a specific set of commands. My First Mate listened intently and then sprouted a wicked grin of his own as he exited to fulfill my orders.

Chapter 19: The French Captain Sings

Turning my full attention to my nemesis, I sneered that he needed to prepare himself for the next round of queries. Totally undaunted, my black-hearted foe simply glared at me with hate and rage flooding his features. Taking a needed break, I went topside for a breath of fresh air. Utilizing my telescope, I scanned the horizon for any sign of the Black Tarantula, but none was forthcoming. Stowing the instrument, I issued orders to the topman to maintain a sharp lookout for the *Spider's Web* as we continued sailing northward. Sharkface soon appeared at my side with news that all was in readiness.

Returning, I found the defrocked officer spread and secured on a small table unable to move any portion of his body except his mouth and eyes. Bending over the beast, I whispered the ghastly saga of an old associate nicknamed Lipless Billy. I related that the monster responsible for the lad's torture utilized a swarm of leeches to remove the helpless lad's lips. Due to this unholy desecration, Billy had been forced to spend the remainder of his days isolated from his fellowmen to avoid their horrified reactions to his insidious disfigurement.

Continuing, I explained that my plan called for a slightly different tack. I promised my foe that my wee beasties would immensely enjoy their uninterrupted feast on his unprotected privates! My words resonated strongly given the look of dread that now crossed LeMerde's face. You see, I had a strong inkling that this prideful and self-centered pirate would fear the destruction of his manliness more than any other gruesome torture I could hope to invent. In fact, as I pinched and lifted one of the squirming black devils for his viewing pleasure, Captain LeMerde screamed and begged me to cease my nonsense, promising to answer my inquiries rather than being ravaged. Smiling now, I returned the hellish creature to its squirming mates and began information gathering.

My initial examinations were those that I was already well aware of but would serve to test the veracity of my devious opponent. Answering these with his typical sneer, the brute acknowledged his assistance in the long ago attack on Captain Adams, as well as his savage destruction of the entire Adams' household. Since these responses were truthful, I questioned him on the fate of the *French songbird*. Smiling evilly, he divulged that my darling Rue was currently in good hands, performing on a routine basis for the crew of the *Spider's Web*. Noticing my pained reaction, he chuckled menacingly and boasted that the lass had proved a very willing performer, while secretly masking her true intention of plotting to murder her benefactor when the opportunity arose. Continuing, the subdued swine bragged that he voiced this very serious concern to his senior partner, who had concurred totally with his assessment. Consequently, her movements were being closely monitored so that any foolish attempt to launch any sort of conspiratorial attack would be dealt in a swift and harsh manner. With a sly smirk, he spat out that her only interest to his vile partner was the fact that she was closely tied to me. Confused entirely by this admission, I demanded further clarification as I reached once again for a squirming leach.

Noting my serious intent, LeMerde fearfully wailed that the Black Tarantula was quite obsessed with my outright destruction. Aware that my theft of his fortune and slaughter of his First Mate was enough motivation to induce his obsession for my obliteration, I baffingly questioned why his partner would harbor such strong personal hatred, especially since we had never even met. Shrugging, my prisoner confessed that the reason remained one of his partner's many secrets. He did affirm that a multitude of his crew had conjectured that some past transgression on my part had spawned their leader's black hatred. Whatever the motivation, LeMerde concluded that the Black Tarantula despised me and would utilize any weapon at his disposal to insure my ultimate doom.

Bothered by the intensity of these words, I changed the subject by pressing him on the current location of his nefarious partner. Issuing a savage laugh, he informed me that he had not been supplied that information, and that even the assistance of my filthy wriggling friends could not entice answers that were unknown to him. However, he did add that his partner had provided a message for me that had been left behind at the Turbout plantation. With a cruel smile, he informed me that it was a frightful shame that I would not be able to review its contents. Realizing that there was little more to be gained from further prodding; I ordered the vile villain trussed and secured in the hold until a decision on his ultimate fate was made.

Intrigued by his last morsel of information, I signaled Lion to come aboard in order to confer on our course of action. Lion appeared at my cabin door carrying a miniature chest, routinely utilized to secure small valuables. He explained that Rene's butler had rushed the chest into his hands prior to his departure from Marie-Galant. While the butler had no concept of the actual contents, he had overheard the brutes stationed inside of the house arguing about whether to deliver it to Captain Bilge or ransack the container for themselves. With their subsequent demise, the loyal servant had hustled across the island to deliver the container to Lion believing it held something of importance. The small casket easily fit in both of my hands, as I turned it every which way in close inspection. It was made of stretched leather and adorned with multiple metal fittings that were more decorative than functional. Having no key to fit within the miniature lock, I utilized my dirk and carefully probed the tiny catch until I heard an audible click. Prying up the lid, I discovered a single sheet of parchment inside. Unrolling the paper, I found that it was a handwritten missive addressed to me by the son of Satan himself, the Black Tarantula. The demon's dispatch read as follows:

Captain Bilge,

By your inexcusable and unwarranted attack on my Tortuga stronghold, you have declared war between us. This cowardly deed was perpetrated without cause. You have murdered my innocent crewmen, blatantly sacked and plundered my private treasure trove, savagely attacked and damaged my ship and are personally responsible for the death of my most trusted aide, Hurricane Jeffers. For all of these heinous personal affronts, I have decided to seek equal justice for the enormity of my losses.

To start, I commissioned Captain LeMerde to attack and obliterate the Turbout family as the first step in my rightful vengeance. Secondly, I have hunted down and abducted your beloved Rue, who I now hold hostage aboard my ship. While the lass is currently among the living, I am unable to guarantee

that this condition will continue indefinitely.

If you ever hope to reunite with your lover, you must follow these instructions precisely or suffer my vengeful wrath. You must collect all of my pilfered belongings and journey to Saint Domingue. At the site of your lover's former punchhouse, you will deliver my lost treasure to my two agents, who I have instructed to remain in place awaiting your arrival. You will do so alone and without assistance during the last week of the following month and not a day sooner!

Should you fail to follow these orders implicitly, I will be forced to take my vengeance out on your beloved causing her unimaginable pain, suffering and eventual death. I trust that I need not provide specifics given my bloodthirsty reputation of which I am sure you are well versed.

Your enemy for life,
The Black Tarantula

Since we were less than halfway through the current month, I realized that there was still time in which to comply with the specific demands of this raving lunatic. Dismissing his specific instructions, my first inclination was to set sail for Tortuga, viciously attack the demon in his fortress and rescue Rue. However, after my blood cooled and I regained cognitive thought, I realized that my heated impulse was rather foolhardy, since I had no reason to believe that the demon and his captive were even at this location. Taking a measured breath, I concluded that I was woefully short on information vital to battle my insane adversary and rescue my beloved. I also recognized that any foolhardy failure on my part would certainly result in Rue's death. Therefore, I reasoned that further intelligence was vitally required to generate a battle plan that would lead to success. Calling Sharkface and Lion to my cabin, I outlined the gist of the message and ordered them to chart a course for Saint Domingue. Both my commanders hurried away to comply with my command while I sat and examined the delivery chest. The item was indeed elaborate and ornate, probably a specially designed treasure vault for some wealthy Lord. As I studied it, a sudden thought came to me and I called for an immediate audience with Guzzlin' Gooch. Given his proven proficiency with wood, I explained my scheme in detail to the soon grinning tar. Eager to please, he snatched the chest and raced out of my cabin to begin the work I had commissioned.

Needing time to ponder my prisoner's fate and with a grumbling emanating from my belly, I made my way to the galley to appease my sudden hunger. As I made my entrance, I found a group of my men in a rapt stupor listening to yet another sea tale from our renowned storyteller, Angry George. Our shipboard yarn spinner was dutifully outlining the basics of his narrative. In truth, I simply enjoyed listening to these manufactured yarns just as much today as I did in the past as a wee lad. Today's agenda covered a favorite crew pastime, christened a pirate's court.

The premise of a pirate's court was quite simple with individual crewmembers acting the parts of court officials, the offending party, defending and prosecuting counsels, the jury and finally court spectators. Each crewmember played a specific role and was free to extemporize at will as long as parliamentary procedure was followed in an assuredly rough and tumble manner. Basically, this shipboard pastime allowed bored tars an opportunity to dress in crudely manufactured costumes as they ridiculed the landlubber's judiciary system. In the case of pirates, whose lives literally hung in the balance, it was a chance to spit in the face of the devil and survive to celebrate with their fellow mates at the trial's conclusion. Another necessity for success of any pirate's court was the addition of *hot spirits*, which usually provided for novel and hilarious fun on everyone's part. Should any court member get out of hand during these mock proceedings, they were usually pounced on by their offended mates and silenced in any feasible manner short of death. Since it was a unique method of relaxing crew tensions, most Captains simply tolerated the practice if in fact they were even given this option.

Angry George was running through brief descriptions of the main characters in tonight's narrative. The focus of this evening's yarn was a scurvy rascal named Sudsy Scupper, an idiot by birth and a general nuisance by trade. Sudsy's tongue had been previously severed, a condition he attributed to a former pirate's torture session. His crewmates had conjectured that in reality the fool had most likely bit the tip off himself in one of his usual drunken stupors. In any event, the loss had left him incapable of enunciating words clearly or distinctly, mostly issuing nothing but mumbled nonsense. In their shipboard pirate's court proceedings, this bilge-mouthed simpleton had been assigned the role of the infamous pirate, the Black Tarantula! As such, he was being tried for numerous and unforgivable crimes against mankind.

The judge in this drunken courtroom drama was the ship's bully, Skinner Shaw who detested the little maggot in the box with his entire being. Skinner planned to issue extreme pain and hardship upon his victim as a result of the trial's outcome. Since their ship's laws precluded crew fighting, punished by unusually harsh castigation, Skinner had been unable to unleash his physical wrath on his inferior nemesis, while his raging desire to inflict grievous harm dominated his every waking moment. The prosecuting attorney, a close confident and sworn confederate of Skinner's, was named Black Cat Bill. Both miscreants had engineered the entire proceeding in order to finally attain their pent-up vengeance upon Sudsy.

The court session opened with Black Cat's descriptions of the multitude of heinous crimes Sudsy, operating as the Black Tarantula, had perpetrated. These included rape, torture, murder, kidnapping and a slew more. In each instance, Black Cat personified each of these dreadful crimes as having been personally inflicted upon a different inebriated juror. For example, he convinced Pumpkin Rodgers, that Sudsy acting as the Black Tarantula had raped and slaughtered his two precious daughters in a most unspeakable manner. Drunk to the point of insensibility, Pumpkin had to be forcibly restrained as he lunged at the cowering defendant with a wickedly sharp dagger attempting to gut him for the fabricated crimes he had committed against his daughters. The fact that Pumpkin had never sired children to the best of anyone's knowledge meant absolutely nothing to this alcohol-addled lunatic!

And so the trial continued with Black Cat successfully convincing juror after juror that the accused standing in the docket had engineered horrific injustices to their phantom families or friends. With the entire crew agitated to extreme madness, Skinner promptly called for a vote of guilt on the part of the accused idiot. The fact that Sudsy was stumbling drunk and hardly aware of the proceedings that transpired against him meant little to the mean spirited bully. In a unanimous vote, the jurors declared the accused pirate guilty beyond any reasonable doubt.

Acting as judge, Skinner announced a quick and harsh sentence against his enemy. The guilty man was to be immediately hung for the awful and heinous crimes he had never even committed. Energized by this harsh pronouncement, Sudsy was dragged topside by the inebriated mob and summarily hung from a convenient yard ending his miserable life to the sheer delight of Skinner and Black Cat. After this ugly deed was transacted, the entire crew returned to their bottles of rum and drank themselves into further oblivion. Convinced that they had acted with righteous intentions given the ugly crimes committed by the guilty pirate, most of the crew forgot the hanging incident until they awoke the following morning in bleary and dazed states. At this point, they were confronted by the dead corpse of Sudsy swinging listlessly from a topside yard. Ashamed and still quite confused, they eventually cut Sudsy down from his lethal perch and flung his dead corpse into the sea. Once done, they resumed their normal shipboard duties as if nothing at all had ever transpired.

A combination of guilty consciences and snatches of recalled memory haunted each of the crew's daytime thoughts and nighttime dreams, but ever so slowly the insidious deed was expunged from their minds. Skinner and Black Cat suffered no such recriminations and merrily went about their normal shipboard duties, pleased with their successful efforts to eliminate the hated maggot. After a few weeks had passed, the ship returned to normal and the ugly incident was completely forgotten by all.

At this time, a very strange occurrence took place aboard their ship. After yet another evening of hard drinking, the entire crew was rudely awakened from alcohol-induced slumbers by a series of inhuman screams issued from the lower decks. Upon careful inspection, the source of these frightening wails was Black Cat Bill, who had been savagely attacked and mutilated during the night. Frothing blood and screaming unintelligible words, Black Cat was inspected by the ship's doctor, who discovered that the unfortunate was missing half of his tongue. Incensed into a hysterical state, the crew incessantly questioned each other attempting to discover the criminal responsible for the mindless mutilation. These crude inquiries proved absolutely useless, as no wrongdoer could be held accountable for the horrific attack. Once his wounds were tended, Black Cat instituted his own personal investigation by simply collaring individual crew members and attempting to crudely beat the truth from them. This harsh action earned him a knife in his throat from one of his abused mates. Dying in a quick and painful manner, Black Cat and his murderer were sewn neatly in a sailcloth shroud and tossed overboard per the agreed nautical regulations of their vessel.

Over the next several days the crew slowly settled down and resumed normal duties, attempting to forget the entire affair. Skinner, quite shaken by the sudden loss of his close friend, remained quite aloof and distant from the rest of the crew. Continuing to imbibe to extreme, he prowled the ship both night and day for any clue that might help explain the mysterious transgression against Black Cat. He also began grousing to anyone willing to listen that something was stalking his every movement aboard ship. Sure that their mate was slowly losing his mind, most of the crew began avoiding contact with the delirious tar and certainly ignored his paranoid rants and wild suspicions.

Since the entire ship had become quite unsettled by the strange behavior of Skinner, they decided in mass to confine the lunatic to the bilge until they could offload their burden at their next port-of-call. Once accomplished, the crew gathered on the topdeck and proceeded to once again drink themselves into insensibility. Copious quantities of *hot spirits* were summarily consumed and the entire lot descended from drunken stupors into fitful sleep. In the morning, the bleary men were rudely awakened by one of their own, who stood sputtering and shaking on the topdeck pointing upwards and shouting nonsensically. Straining their blood-reddened eyes skyward, the confused tars were greeted by an extremely grizzly sight. Hanging well above them and dangling freely in the wind was their bilge-incarcerated mate, Skinner Shaw.

Confused and bewildered by this unexpected tragedy, several men clambered aloft and cut the poor unfortunate down, returning his corpse to the maindeck. Once again the ship's doctor was called upon to make an examination, and he quickly announced that the poor fool was indeed dead. The doctor ruled the death suicide, but upon close examination could not account for the fact that Skinner's tongue had been crudely severed in the same manner as Black Cat Bill's. Making a hasty sign-of-the-cross, the doctor ordered the dead man thrown overboard to stop the utter panic that had begun to surface on every mate's part. Once accomplished, the men gathered on deck were shocked that Skinner's corpse did not sink into the briny depths, given the weighty length of iron chain that had been securely wrapped around the corpse. Instead, the dead body continued to float in the clear blue sea as if attempting to follow their vessel.

Consummately panicked, the tars armed themselves with muskets and spent the entire day taking target practice at the ghostly corpse which continued to shadow in their wake no matter the course corrections applied by the ship's navigator. When darkness finally descended, the terrified crew was summarily treated to unholy wails and cries coming from the inky-black sea surrounding them. Several crewmembers spoke up and informed their mates that the unintelligible wails sounded very much like those of their long lost mate, Sudsy Scupper! Crazed far beyond reason now, the entire crew surrendered to mass panic and hysteria. In their haste to escape the pursuing devil, they ran aground on a hidden reef and mortally gutted their ship. This dire situation forced them to abandon their dear vessel to either swim or drown. Since most of the fools had never mastered the art of swimming, there was only one survivor to this sailing nightmare. Upon rescue, this lone survivor was virtually impossible to understand. He had been cursed with a speech affliction that caused him to mumble incoherently due to the unexplained result of missing the majority of his tongue!

When Angry George ended his frightening tale, several of my men unconsciously made the perfunctory signs-of-the-cross as they retreated from the galley to perform assigned tasks. For my part, the tale had sparked a diabolical notion, and, smiling devilishly, I thanked Angry George for his enlightening narrative. The next morning, I called all hands on deck and formally announced that I had made a decision on the treatment of our nefarious prisoner. To the absolute delight of all, I announced that a pirate's court would be convened to try our villainous guest, which was met with a rousing chorus of hurrahs from my men.

Chapter 20: Court is in Session

The initial order of business was appointing appropriate roles for our court. Since my judgment was definitely swayed, I excluded naming myself as judge. Instead, I appointed Lion, as Lord Judge and Magistrate. Not to be omitted, I appointed myself Court Prosecutor, since I was fully cognizant of the scoundrel's sordid past. For Chief Defender, I thought the matter over for just a short while before settling on Booby Bird as the optimal candidate. His erratic short term bewilderment would only serve to further frustrate and anger his sworn charge. For Court Sergeants, I chose my two incredibly powerful crewmembers, Sharkface and Tiny Junior. To ensure that order was maintained, these behemoths were each armed with a deadly wooden billet, which could easily crush any man's skull should the need arise. After that, I allowed a jury panel to be selected by the crew in whatever manner they deemed appropriate. Given a need for legitimacy and a flair for proper stage production, I provided each key member of the court with appropriate garb and accruements such as powdered wigs and robes so they could properly emulate their portrayed roles. In all, it was to be a magnificent reprisal of any English landlubber's court. The script had been written, the actors versed and garbed and the curtain was about to be raised!

As Chief Magistrate, Lion opened the proceedings laying out the basic rules for the trial. Once accomplished, he turned to me as prosecuting attorney and demanded that the list of charges against the accused be cited. I stood and began by identifying the defendant as a former French naval officer, disgraced and stripped of his rank. The specific charges I advanced were kidnapping, counterfeiting and murder. In answer to these crimes, LeMerde merely sneered and shouted his complete innocence which earned him a sharp rap on his prideful noggin from Sergeant Sharkface for obvious court disruption. With this painful tap came a blunt reminder that any further outbursts would be treated with a much harsher manner from both of the huge grinning court peacekeepers.

Opening with the first charge of kidnapping, I announced that the victim of this crime was not present to bear testimony. Continuing, I explained that almost every crewman in the courtroom could serve as substitute witnesses to this cowardly deed, since it had been their initiative that had liberated the victim from the defendant's clutches. I also stated that the Jamaican high court had tried this miserable wretch for this identical crime and had summarily found him guilty. Rather than regurgitate any of these prior formal proceedings, I thought it might be amusing for the court attendees to hear a detailed account of the successful deception Aimee and I had engineered that had provided the motivation for her subsequent abduction. As I narrated these events, I glanced over and received continuous murderous glares from the defendant. As I finished my lurid rendition to the heckles and hoots of the entire court, Captain LeMerde shouted out that I had utilized the cover of darkness to complete my ruse, since he was positive that daylight would have spoiled my little game. With a self-assured smirk, I countered that the time of day had little bearing on the issue since the imbecile involved in the charade would have been consummately hoodwinked regardless of the circumstances surrounding this successful ruse.

Moving on to the next charge, I advised the court that once again the defendant had also been judged guilty as a counterfeiter by the same English court. I then questioned the audience if they would be interested in the salient details surrounding his conviction? With a resounding assent, I launched into the tale which I was quite sure the defendant was totally unaware. Producing one of the bogus coins from my picket. I explained the true source of the counterfeit coins. Captain LeMerde surprised and confused by this newly exposed information sat stunned and befuddled. Continuing my revelation, I laid out the detailed plot I had utilized to frame the arrogant brute. As the pertinent details emerged, LeMerde leapt to his feet naming me a prevaricator and pirate, which earned him a harsher thump on his head from Sergeant Tiny Junior. Slumping back down from this wicked blow, I glanced over to LeMerde and was treated to a most ghastly and utterly menacing scowl, a testament to the pure contempt, enmity and utter malevolence he held for me. Long ago in London, I had the misfortune of experiencing a very similar demonic glower at the hands of a yet another detestable and despicable bully. Consequently, my brief recollection of this grisly flashback sent an ice-cold shiver down my spine. While this fearful reaction was receding, the entire court had been enraptured by my account of the consummate dupe played upon LeMerde. As such, my mates erupted into even greater hilarity as various individuals issued animal hoots and cries while Lion banged his gavel attempting half-heartedly to restore a semblance of order.

Simultaneously, Booby Bird leapt to his feet shouting a stringent objection that his client was in fact innocent of the counterfeiting charges, since a conspiracy had been launched to garner a wrongful verdict. He motioned that these specific charges be dropped from the proceedings against his client. At a momentary loss, he bent down and asked the defendant's name once again since it had slipped his mind, which produced further hilarity amongst all. His furious client merely sputtered that he was in the care of an imbecile, and as such requested an immediate change of counsel. Lion banged his makeshift gavel for silence, while Sergeant Sharkface banged the defendant's skull once again to the extreme delight of all. Taking the initiative, I spoke up and agreed wholeheartedly with my drooling counterpart, since it was absolutely true that the defendant was certainly not a counterfeiter but rather a poor deluded simpleton.

Booby Bird, elated by my pronouncement, jumped up and announced that he was the finest defender that ever sailed. This ridiculous statement was again met by a roar of laughter from all, and once again the courtroom was thrown into utter chaos. Lion, banging his gavel with extreme malice, eventually brought the proceedings back to order. He roared that having weighed the matter in all seriousness, he could only declare that the defendant was indeed innocent of the charge of counterfeiting. Continuing, he smiled broadly as he announced that the defendant could certainly be judged a pathetic dimwit!

Chaos ensued and when order was finally restored, I moved on to the serious charge of murder. To this charge, I informed the court that the defendant was responsible for a number of crimes under this broad heading. I outlined the defendant's successful escape from Jamaican authority which had cost the lives of several of his warders. Since this ugly and brutal deed had been witnessed by numerous islanders, I concluded that this crime was factual and substantiated. Stopping for a moment, I petitioned the court to see if there was any interest in hearing the fate of the defendant's co-conspirators in this escape, which was quickly answered with a unanimous and resounding affirmative from my men. Booby Bird leapt up to lodge an objection but was shoved back into his seat by Sergeant Junior Tiny before he could utter a sound.

With that, I launched into a detailed account of our encounters on Grand Cayman, ending with a detailed narrative of the horrific and tragic end of the two villains as sustenance for the pack of ravenous sharks. My frightful tale was met by furious shouts of joy from my men, who absolutely delighted at the grisly end suffered by the two murdering swine. Captain LeMerde leapt once more to his feet screaming that it was I, not him, who should be placed on trial for the crime of murder. Shouted down by all, he received yet another wicked head thump from Sergeant Sharkface for his continued insolence and disruption.

Moving on, I informed the court that our insidious defendant had also ordered and personally led the vicious attack on the innocent Adams sisters, their illustrious nephew and most importantly our former crewmember, Powder Monkey. Continuing, I outlined the atrocious actions of the defendant, who had directed the torching of the Adams' mansion and then remained close-at-hand to gleefully observe the horrific plight of the innocents as they were consumed in the subsequent inferno. I pointed out that two trustworthy witnesses had sworn the guilt of the defendant. Surprised by this bit of information, the defendant convicted himself of this unforgivable crime by shouting out that he had certainly left no witnesses in his wake. Continuing in an unconvincing tone, he attempted exoneration by whimpering that the Adams mansion had most likely burned of its own accord, and therefore was a simple yet unfortunate accident. His outburst earned him yet another savage pounding from Sergeant Sharkface, who in his exuberance nearly crushed the poor villain's skull.

Countering the defendant's claim, I again took control and informed the court that another reliable witness had supplied testimony on the scoundrel's involvement. Citing the well-known name of Fat Dog, I explained to the court that the hospitable pub owner had also sworn to the defendant's guilt prior to his untimely death at the voracious jaws of his star reptilian performer! Numbed by the news of his fallen conspirator, LeMerde screamed that the Adams sisters were witches and surely deserved the flames that devoured them and reunited them with their master. Before either sergeant could react to this latest outburst, I shouted out that the defendant had just professed his own guilt and petitioned the jury members for a guilty verdict.

Before anyone on the jury had the chance to respond, I bellowed that I had one final charge to level against this disgraced officer and confirmed pirate. In a loud and strident voice, I informed all that the fiend had also defrauded and subverted one of their favorite shore games, the *Gator Gobble Game*. This final bit of information sealed the fate of my enemy, as all present called for the rogue's immediate demise. Smiling now, I resumed my seat as my duty as prosecutor had come to an end.

Before the jury announced their verdict, Captain LeMerde spouted that the scurvy scum making up the jury were nothing more than a band of pirates and as such were totally incapable of passing sentence on a gentleman and Officer of the King. Continuing, he sputtered that each and every one of them certainly deserved hanging. Knowing his words only incensed my mates, Lion called upon the esteemed judgment of the jurors to decide the guilt or innocence of the insidious serpent seated in the dock.

The jury took little time in declaring Captain LeMerde guilty of kidnapping, murder and overall vile evilness. Going further, they decreed that the scum be hung from the nearest yardarm that very moment. Standing once more, I addressed the court and suggested that consideration be given to an unusual and unprecedented punishment I had concocted for the convicted, who was now sputtering and spitting curses at all of us. The courtroom dissolved into utter pandemonium, and it took an eternity for Lion to bring the proceedings back to order. In the meantime, Sergeants Sharkface and Tiny Junior continued their vicious assault on the defendant for no good reason except pure enjoyment. Once order was restored, Chief Magistrate Lion questioned what punishment I had in mind. In a menacing voice, I shouted that the villain deserved *sea marooning*, which was met by a series of totally confused and befuddled expressions. However, once I detailed my suggested punishment, Lion banged his gavel one last time declaring the trial ended and the punishment wholly appropriate. LeMerde was dragged bleeding and screaming topside to face his doom!

To execute this punishment, I commanded a small team to assemble a crude raft. This death platform was provisioned with leg and wrist shackles secured to each corner. Stripped entirely of his uniform, the murderer was fastened spread-eagled to these restraints in a most uncomfortable manner. True to the sentence, the raft was lowered over the side of our vessel and secured to our stern by a sizable length of strong cable. Knowing that we had more than a week at sea prior to reaching our destination, I had ordained that this floating brig would be dutifully dragged in our wake the entire time. Given its crude design, I knew that my hated foe would surely endure a briny voyage straight from hell!

As the prisoner's raft followed us that day, Captain LeMerde was exposed to the full brutality of the merciless sun and gusting wind with no shelter to protect his fair complexion. At night, the cold and salty spindrift continually drenched his sunburned hide, delivering additional pain and agony to his scorched frame. Upon orders, each evening at dusk the raft was towed back to our ship so that I could personally check on the knave's condition, prior to returning him to his proper place. After a full week of this insidious torture, Captain LeMerde's pitiful condition had reached fatal stage. His burned torso was completely blistered exhibiting huge patches of molting flesh. His lips were unrecognizable and resembled rancid beef liver rather than anything remotely human. His eyes were also quite useless as they had been seared by the sun's harsh rays. In all, he resembled a pathetic lump of suffering flesh! Upon careful study the absolute destruction wrought by my brutal and beastly punishment, a portion of my consciousness seemed to soften and I began to question if my treatment of my old enemy was too severe. In the next instant, I had a vision of my close and dear friends, the Adams sisters and Powder Monkey awash in flesh-eating flames screaming and wailing in abject misery as they slowly burned to death. This nightmarish reminder hardened my heart and suspended all thoughts of discontinuing my enemy's deserved punishment.

On the seventh night I performed my daily check. Staring intently at the gory mess, the beast's ravaged milky-white orbs suddenly flashed open. I was certain that he could distinguish little since the intense tropical sun's rays had blinded him several days past. Upon hearing my voice, he croaked out that he would soon see me in hell. Staring down without pity, I responded that I was quite sure that he would not require my company since he was sure to have a bevy of vile and despicable comrades to provide eternal companionship. Wishing him a speedy journey to meet Old Scratch, I ordered him returned to the sea. As I had conjectured, his actual death occurred sometime that night. When he was drawn toward us on the eighth night, I pronounced the villain dead and at home with his master, Lucifer. Grabbing a nearby axe, I severed the umbilical cord between his hellish raft and our vessel and watched as it slowly slipped off into the night!

Chapter 21: Saint Domingue, War Preparations

Once the roguish French officer had been dispatched to his watery consignment, I gave orders to proceed at all haste to Saint Domingue to rendezvous with Black Tarantula's agents. My thoughts centered on the approach I would need to adopt to garner the necessary assistance I required from Saint Domingue's Governor. Scant scuttlebutt obtained on this functionary led me to believe that he might be operating as my foe's agent either through intimidation, outright fear or bribery. In any case, I was certain that the situation called for devising a clandestine ruse to garner his assistance while avoiding any of his suspected treachery. To this end, I began cogitating an approach to circumvent any chicanery on his part.

At last, we arrived at our destination. As my vessels were securing berths, Bottom Dog asked for an audience, which I readily granted. Scooting into my office, he announced that every joint in his body detected the approach of *dirty weather*, which he was convinced would occur within the week. While he believed that a brewing hurricane was imminent, he further confessed that the storm's might would surely produce a significant blow. He urged me to find shelter for both ships to avoid potential damage due to his ominous apprehensive forecast. Heeding his inclinations, I called for Sharkface and Lion to join us in my cabin. Once assembled, I summarized Bottom Dog's concerns and ordered my leaders to locate and anchor our vessels in a deserted and protected haven close to our present position. I instructed them to commence their search for this location as soon as I was safely ashore. Once they reached this spot, I commanded that both ships be careened and refitted as soon as the storm passed. Saluting, the two were off to initiate their search. I thanked Bottom Dog for his vital warning and sent him smiling to the galley for a reward of a strong tote of rum.

With my officers' exit, Guzzlin' Gooch was at my door to report on his undertaking. Unveiling the small treasure casket that I had provided, he explained that he had transformed it into the deadly device I had commanded. He explained that he had added a series of tiny hidden needles that would release when the chest was opened. Since this container was small and easily handheld, he pointed out that the projecting sharp points would most definitely wound any unsuspecting villain attempting to open the chest. I intended to coat each of these stinging lancets with *creeping death*. Since I planned to return the treasure box to its owner, through his emissaries, I hoped that my deadly surprise would serve to end his miserable life. Aware that my ruse had only a small chance of success, I continued to plot and design a full offensive against my nemesis. Congratulating Gooch on his excellent work, I filled the container with a goodly amount of counterfeit coins, slathered on the deadly mixture on the protruding needles and finally locked the container tight.

Having one more detail to accomplish, I called Long Tall Willie to my side and explained my need. Surprised by me request, he nodded and hurried off to comply. After only a few hours, he returned with the exact item I had described, and I thanked him elatedly for his fine effort. I added this article to a coin pouch that was partially filled with silver and gold coins. Cinching the sack closed, I descended to an awaiting longboat for my trip to shore.

Upon arriving at the Governor's office I was met by his assistant, the Vice Governor. This little man was a squint-eyed weakling, who sported large round spectacles that seemed to enlarge his eyes to enormous proportions. Since he had the overall appearance of a familiar nocturnal avian predator, I mentally christened him Owl Eyes. The nervous little fool seemed very aware of my name when it was offered and also acted as if he had anticipated my visit. He introduced himself in faultless French as Claude Anton Gustaves, and formally announced that I was under arrest. A trio of guards suddenly appeared and stripped me of my weapons and hustled me off for a private conference with the Governor. It sure seemed like this rude welcoming was becoming a commonplace occurrence on every new isle I visited. Hustled away, I was roughly dragged before the Governor. The great man was seated behind his desk as I was shoved into his office. He was a rather short, rail-thin individual who spent an inordinate amount of time twitching and squirming like a fish out of water. He sported a rather angry looking scar that ran from his balding pate down to his jaw. His eyes were light gray in color and seem to reflect a rather cold and distant nature. A half empty decanter of wine and a half-filled goblet sat squarely in front of him, and his behavior suggested that he had been seriously imbibing prior to my visit.

Owl Eyes opened the conversation in French explaining that I had been identified as a pirate by several reliable sources. Deciding to secret the fact that I was fluent in French, I replied in English that I could not understand a word he had just uttered. Exasperated by my bewilderment and ignorance, Owl Eyes repeated his statement in less than perfect English. I denied his serious charge by explaining that I carried proper documentation on my ship that certainly mandated otherwise. Neither of my accusers offered me the chance to produce these documents, as Owl Eyes sniggered to his leader that my papers were most likely forged. Taking the initiative, I informed them both that my reason for visiting their fair isle was to supply and refit my ships in preparation for a battle with the Black Tarantula. This blatant statement perked their interest, but, as words that flew between them, they expressed their doubts on my veracity along with the shared opinion that the demonic pirate was invincible.

The Governor, sensing my utter confusion, explained that the Black Tarantula had recently invaded their island and caused all manner of horrific crime. Besides being maimed for life as his facial scar testified, he sputtered that he had been held captive by the scoundrel along his wife and child. He had been promised harsh and painful deaths for his precious brood if he interfered or opposed the villain in any way. In addition, the demon pirate guaranteed his return to cause even greater pain and suffering island-wide if he discovered that he had been betrayed in any manner. I responded that the only sure method of ending this curse was to soundly defeat and destroy the beast. Owl Eyes broke out in a series of hysterical giggles at the conclusion of my statement, confiding in French that he was quite sure that I was both an idiot and a madman.

Attempting to change the subject, I announced that I had brought gifts for the Governor, which garnered a look of greed on the faces of both men. Drawing the pouch from my pocket, Owl Eyes quickly snatched it and tossed it onto the center of the Governor's desk. With trembling hands, the petrified coward picked up the pouch and dumped the contents onto his desk causing the coins inside to scatter in every direction. However, it was the strange item that tumbled out with the coins that drew both men's total attention. You see, I had sent Long Tall Willie to procure an island Voodou doll, much like the version delivered to Rue long ago. Aware that the majority of islanders were quite fearful of the dark side of their slave's religion, I had specifically included the grotesque item to capture their full attention and to send a wave of terror across their bows. Shocked by this discovery, both men jumped back from the desk as they made signs-of-the-cross to ward off evil spirits. Speaking in unison, they demanded to know the reason for the abomination's presence. Explaining that the doll was nothing more than an insurance policy to guarantee that I was not harmed on my visit to their isle, I picked up the crude image and gave it my full attention. Owl Eyes blurted out that I was not only a pirate, but also a witch who required immediate incineration to end my evil ways.

Laughing at his ridiculous statement, I informed both fear-stricken cowards that I had previously liberated a group of slaves from a sinking *blackbirder*, slave trader to you landlubbers. Subsequently, several of these men had joined my ranks. Among them was a Voodou priest, who had personally crafted this despicable icon to ensure my safety. Owl Eyes immediately ordered the guards to free their pistols and aim them in my direction to preclude me from attempting any further foolish maneuvers. He then turned to his boss and spat out that I should be hung immediately with my dead body thrown on a roaring blaze to end my witching days! Again snickering at their palatable fear, I announced that any dramatic action taken against me would force my priest to visit unspeakable horrors upon them both. Owl Eyes responded first by snatching up the doll and passing it to his soldiers ordered that it be burned immediately. In response to his drastic solution, I explained that the ugly little doll was merely a replica and that my priest held the actual Voodou charm in his possession.

Regaining his voice, the Governor demanded to be told what silly nonsense I was spouting, since the slave's beliefs and religion were strictly relegated to the ignorant and uninformed. With a steely gaze, I responded that my Voodou priest had promised to channel his black magic upon anyone who lodged threats or injuries against me. With a hysterical laugh, Owl Eyes explained that my priest could absolutely have no way of knowing what had transpired behind these closed doors and ordered his men to drag me off to the military prison until a final determination of my fate could be made. Before the guards were able to move in my direction, I utilized my *special voice* to produce a hideously loud wail which imitated a hell-crazed banshee in eternal search of human souls. As all eyes in the room moved in the direction of the demonic scream, I leaned over and slipped a generous portion of *Datura* tonic into the Governor's half-filled wine goblet.

As calm returned, the visibly shaken Governor grasped his wine and drained it in hopes of calming his shattered nerves. Meanwhile, Owl Eyes kept questioning over and over what had caused the terrible commotion we had all heard. Ordering the guards to check the outer office for intruders, he staggered over to the governor's side for moral support. As the guards exited, I stated in a calm and sure voice that the wail had been caused by a demon sent by my priest, since he had obviously divined the Governor's harmful intentions towards me. Continuing, I promised that this malignant demon would surely continue to haunt them day and night!

The Governor shakily poured himself another draught of courage, as the guards returned with terror stricken expressions dominating their features. They reported that they had found nothing amiss outside. Taking the opportunity, I issued yet another terrifying wail that seemed to come from the large window directly behind the island's leader. As all eyes moved to the window, I dosed the wine decanter with a further quantity of *Datura*. Meanwhile, the thoroughly shaken Governor demanded to be told what black magic I was employing. In a sincere and hushed voice, I informed the Governor and his cringing assistant of the impending catastrophe they had unwittingly unleashed.

Continuing with my prediction, I hissed that my Voodou priest would now be forced to wreak havoc with the island's weather. Both the Governor and Owl Eyes gazed at the tropical sunshine outside the office window and laughed nervously at my prophecy. Ignoring their mirthful reactions, I further promised that a ghastly demon would haunt the Governor personally causing him nightmarish visions, pain and hardship. Acting the role of a brave soul, the Governor responded that he was far more fearful of the Black Tarantula than my silly little doll which he ordered burned. With that, Owl Eyes called for my immediate imprisonment and I was dragged forcibly by the guards toward the office door. Turning in the Governor's direction, I promised the fool that I would see him very soon and, with a knowing grin, predicted that hell itself would now be unleashed because of his ignorant actions.

From the Governor's office, I was roughly escorted by armed guards directly to the nearby military prison. The brig was situated in a cellar below the Fort Commander's headquarters. The prison itself was a dark and damp underground hell, where an unbelievable number of convicts were shackled to every wall within the vast warren of rooms that filled this massive space. As we entered, the noxious vapors of human filth and depravity assaulted my nostrils. As my eyes adjusted to the sudden darkness, I witnessed the outlines of the half-starved, suffering and pathetic prisoners seemingly waiting for death to deliver them from their torment. Peering intently, I beheld that these creatures were beset by huge weeping sores as lice and vermin crawled freely across their frames. As I was roughly dragged deeper into this earthbound Hades, I noticed the audible crunch of all manner of insects and pests under my boots, while voracious rats roamed the brig's perimeter. In all, it reminded me of my childhood spent in the hellish basement of Saint Agnes and a comforting smile lit up my face.

Eventually, an empty shackle was found and I was cruelly shoved against the adjoining wall as the ankle bracelet was roughly secured to my leg. The Master Jailer made his appearance as the guards hastily departed. His wicked expression promised nothing but continual pain and torment. With a hearty laugh and an angry sneer, he proceeded to administer several vicious lashes from his filthy whip as he officially welcomed me to hell. With his formal introduction complete, he turned and stalked away leaving me bleeding and stinging in utmost pain. As soon as the beast departed, the convict on my left began to mock my cultured and fine appearance. Glancing over, I saw that the voice originated from an enormous brute, who had a variety of serious scars adorning every portion of his monstrous carcass. With a loud and commanding voice, he informed me that he was now my new master and as such would take any liberty he pleased.

Peering down at my boots, he boomed that the first order of business was my repayment for the excellent lodgings he had provided. To recompense his hospitality, he demanded my fine boots to cover initial expenses that I had incurred at his wondrous establishment. Laughing at the oversized buffoon, I informed him that his lodging price was far too high, and, subsequently, I would be forced to take my business elsewhere. Snarling viciously at my impertinence, he inched menacingly closer to restate his demands and to deliver deserved corporal punishment to cower and bend me to his will. Enraged at facing yet another bully, a savage countenance overtook me, and I reacted with utter rage and ruthlessness. As he progressed closer, I delivered a swift and brutal punch to his ponderous gut followed by a lightening quick elbow to his nose which completely shattered upon impact. Enraged by my defiance, he unleashed a killing round-house punch which I easily evaded while delivering my straight flexed fingers unerringly and expeditiously into his bulging windpipe which was savagely crushed. Gagging and sputtering in an attempt to draw a breath, he collapsed back against the filth-laden wall whimpering and vomiting profusely. He then slowly slumped to the filthy floor and lost consciousness as he expired without uttering another sound.

I then cautioned every prisoner surrounding me that a similar fate awaited anyone who dared to irritate me in any way. With time to kill, I squatted and leaned back against the moldy dripping wall listening to my fellow prisoner's muffled moans and wails as I calmly awaited my next appointment with the Governor. As I relaxed, I heard the small man on my other side muttering about the consummate injustice done to him. Since I knew that innocence was a very cheap commodity in any brig, I chose to ignore his protests and wait for my expected summons.

A few hours later, the prison guards returned to serve a weak slop of unidentified origin for the day's fare. Upon examining the bowl of gruel thrust into my hands, I could see that it was worse than any meal I had ever the displeasure of consuming on water. The liquid glop was littered with dead maggots and unidentified bits of gore and gristle. Declining to consume the substance, I dumped it on the floor for the roaming vermin to feast upon. When the guards reached the deceased giant slumped on the floor, they kicked him viciously to gain his attention, but received no response to their brutal summons. Realizing the brute was dead; the guards immediately roused the Master Jailer who demanded to know what had occurred to cause the creature's death. Since the entire prison population was too terrified to answer, I responded that the thug had been in the process of eating the vermin that roamed the floor when he suddenly began to viciously choke and gag. Panicked by his adverse reaction to this hellish meal, he seemed to lose all control and plowed directly into the prison's wall. I then explained that the giant collapsed to the floor from this blow and had not been heard from since. I added that he had probably ingested some poisonous breed of vermin and that mistake had led to his ultimate demise.

My reasoning did not sit well with the Master Jailer as he regarded me with utmost contempt and suspicion, attempting to determine if I was being humorous at his expense. In reality, I knew that he was looking for any excuse to administer corporal punishment for the unexplained death. The rest of my companions remained mute, except for the small Spaniard adjacent to me. In halting and stuttering English, he confessed that I had professed the truth and the brute had expired just as I had reported. Unsatisfied with both our responses, the Master Jailer provided us both several sharp lashes before his anger finally dissipated. Ordering the deceased reprobate removed and disposed of, he stalked away muttering curses at us all.

When peace returned, I thanked the little man in his own tongue, which completely delighted him. Asking for his name, he introduced himself as Pablo the Pigeonman. Amused mightily by his moniker, I questioned him on how he had come to be imprisoned. In a hushed whisper, he divulged that he had arrived recently on the island accompanied by his son and precious pigeons. He confessed that he had been in pursuit of his wife, who had deserted him on Spanish Cuba for a French degenerate. Having landed and discovering no evidence of their presence, he had rented a minuscule hovel in Shantytown while he planned his next move. Concerning his unusual name, he revealed that since birth he had been taught the breeding and training of a very specific type of bird, one he termed a messenger pigeon. Unaware of this specific breed, I urged him to tell me more.

Pablo explained that these birds possessed the remarkable ability to navigate their way back to their homes after being released from distances very far away. Sounding quite absurd, I questioned his sanity.

Professing his statement to be true, he related that the Spanish military had employed these birds to deliver missives during times of war. Since Spain was constantly at war with one nation or another, his services were quite valued. In fact, it was a royal decree that sent he and his family to Cuba in order to train birds for military use in the New World.

Once he arrived, he was ridiculed greatly by Cuban military leaders, while his bride found her existence on the isle intolerable and longed to return home. Chancing upon the French lover, she had taken matters into her own hands and had deserted him and his son in the process. His inquiries about their whereabouts upon arrival had raised suspicions amongst the locals, who had branded him a Spanish spy. Without a fair trial or a chance to relate his story, he had been thrown in this hellhole to await death while his young son had been left to fend for himself. Pablo was also very concerned about his darling pets which would certainly perish if not properly cared for. In truth, I could not discern who the poor suffering unfortunate worried more about, his only child or his pet pigeons. Continuing in Spanish to keep our words between us, I questioned whether his birds could really perform the unbelievable feats he had boldly asserted. Without hesitation, he announced that he would prove his claim if he was ever released from our present predicament. However, his saddened eyes disclosed that he was quite aware that his freedom was a vain aspiration that eventually would follow him to his grave.

As he finished, the Master Jailer hurried back to our position, accompanied by a full military detail. Without a word, he quickly unlocked the fetters securing my ankle. The soldiers roughly knocked the brute out of their way when this deed was accomplished. Grabbing both of my arms, they forcibly dragged me topside to discover the tropical calm of yesterday had altered considerably. The wind now howled and hurled any unsecured object along a meandering path. Dark storm clouds dotted the horizon, as I was inwardly thrilled that Bottom Dog's prediction had proved true.

Hustling me back to the Governor's office, I was shoved into a seat facing the stricken creature, with Owl Eyes teetering nervously by his side. Glancing up at me with a crazed and terrified expression, he inquired if my Voodou priest was responsible for the storm that now threatened his island. Laughing heartily, I reconfirmed my predictions which included the arrival of *dirty weather* brought on by their foolhardy disregard of my dire warnings. Continuing, I questioned the terrified idiot if he had been visited by the spiteful spirits I had predicted. In a horse whisper, he confessed that huge yellow and black snakes had made their dreadful appearance not very long after I had been imprisoned. Chuckling at his torment, I replied that I could guarantee that his decent into evil had just begun. Nodding his acceptance of my dire pronouncement, he questioned what I required of him to ensure that the Voodou curse was broken.

While Owl Eyes was not in total agreement with his leader's sentiments, I realized that the Governor was entirely convinced and willing to comply with any demand I might lodge. I began by requesting the short term use of two of his many island schooners to act as transport vessels for necessary supplies and materials for my ships. Due to the fact that I held no real trust for either functionary, I had decided to mask my real intent behind this request. Continuing, I promised to return these borrowed vessels as soon as our refitting and restocking efforts were completed. Since this demand was relatively benign, I promised that this loan would not place either of them in harm's way with their feared and hated adversary. I even offered to make a substantial payment for the loan of these vessels, which earned grins of avarice and greed from both of these disgusting creatures. My second petition was that both individuals would promptly inform me of any communication they might receive from my enemy, the Black Tarantula, regardless of its nature. Owl Eyes seemed to bristle in a pronounced manner at this demand. Reiterating, I stated that failure in this mandate would result in my priest unleashing further havoc. With a nervous gulp, the Governor nodded his reluctant agreement.

Lastly, I demanded the immediate release of the prisoner called Pablo the Pigeonman as well as the services of the Master Jailer for a brief time, with the solemn promise to return the latter safe and free from harm. Completely stymied by these last requests, the two administrators found them quite trivial and readily agreed. I vowed that as soon as I was reunited with my crew, I would order my priest to lift his powerful spell. However, I added that my savage cleric was powerless to end the hurricane that was now raging across the island. With that warning, I cautioned the two leaders to take normal precautions to survive the nasty storm. Totally agreeing to my demands and with great relief flooding their features, the pair issued the appropriate orders to set my petitions in motion. Wishing them both a good day, I exited the office with a satisfied smirk adorning my face.

Chapter 22: The Black Tarantula Reigns

Once free of the conniving pair, I made my way to the harbor to reunite with my crew, who I had previously warned that my absence might prove lengthy depending on the vagaries associated with my meeting with the island's head-of-state. Upon making contact with Angry George, he was delighted to see me safe and sound. He reported that the crew had been made aware of my arrest and subsequent imprisonment through local scuttlebutt. As such, all had been exceedingly apprehensive concerning my safety and wellbeing. With pleasantries and a short briefing exchanged, I ordered him to send word to Lion and Sharkface to join me immediately. Understanding that we had very little time before the full fury of the hurricane descended, I commanded my two leaders to secure the loaned French schooners and convey them to the safety of our protected anchorage, where the entirety of our rework and refitting could proceed in secrecy. Not long after, a frightened squad of soldiers delivered my new Spanish friend along with our trembling prison tormentor. I assigned the grateful pigeon trainer to our ships, and directed Angry George to convey his flock of birds along with his son to our secret location. Pulling Pablo aside, I confessed my plans for his marvelous pets, and understanding my intended stratagem, he beamed with unabated pride. He promised that I would be extremely delighted with my decision to liberate him and place my trust in his winged messengers.

Turning to the business of the nasty prison master, I called Tiny Junior to my side and ordered that the louse be provided ample hard labor and the reward of the *cat-o-nine-tails* for any dereliction of duty. Whispering in the Master Jailer's ear, I promised equal or better punishment for his intentional mistreatment of prisoners over his tenure as self-appointed torturer and inquisitor. With a solid thump on his head, Tiny Junior sent him scurrying to the launch that was headed out to our two newest vessels.

Turning to Long Tall Willie and Tan, I plotted the delivery of the Black Tarantula's treasure to his awaiting agents. I was gratified that the pair had brought along Gooch's reworked casket for this planned rendezvous. The winds continued to intensify resembling an insane howling demon as the storm beat its steady approach. Gazing out on the harbor, I was delighted to see both of our newly borrowed vessels weighing anchor and pressing a hasty escape, bound for our sheltered sanctuary.

Since we had little time to waste, I shared my plan for my foe's designated delivery with my waiting men. I would personally make the actual delivery, while Tan and Long Tall Willie remained hidden nearby. They were then ordered to shadow the recipients to determine their ultimate destination. Pocketing the small but deadly treasure box, I made my way to the former site of the Rue's tavern. The remains of this once grand pleasure house was now a massive pile of rubble and utter devastation, a sorry sight indeed given my fond memories of the venue. As I stood and surveyed the scene, I was approached by a pair of swarthy miscreants, who demanded to be told my intentions against the howling backdrop of the storm's approaching fury. Informing them that I had business to conduct with certain agents expected to be stationed at this exact location, I identified myself to the visible relief of the duo. Without providing their names, the pirates advised that they had been commissioned by the Black Tarantula to accept my offering, which they would promptly return to their master.

Removing the miniature box from my pocket, I simply handed it over to them without further pomp or ceremony. Providing a mock salute, they pivoted to make their escape as they nervously glanced about to ensure that I was indeed alone. Prior to leaving, one rascal turned and shoved a folded piece of parchment my way explaining that it was a missive from his master. With their duty accomplished, the scurvy pair scuttled away aware that the hurricane was now on our doorstep. Realizing that I needed to locate some sort of shelter from the imminent tempest, I wandered in aimless circles searching for a place of safety to survive the tropical gale. My erratic wandering brought me to the old Shantytown cemetery, where Rue and I had consummated our love. Locating a solid and sturdy mausoleum that had its entrance on the leeward side of the approaching storm, I used my pistol to eliminate the ancient lock and chain guarding its gateway. Prying apart the rusted grating, I stepped inside to discover that my chosen hiding place was indeed safe and secure from the dangers of the hurricane. Stumbling upon an antiquated oil lantern, I lit the device and settled down on one of the numerous vaults that dotted my new domain. Since I had nothing but time on my hands, I extracted the crumpled note that I had been given and began to read. The dispatch read as follows:

Captain Bilge,
Since you are now reading this billet, I trust that you have fulfilled your end of the bargain. Although I had sworn to return your dear lover upon receipt of my precious possessions, I remain doubtful as to your honesty and integrity in this manner.

Given that you have proven by your past actions to operate with duplicity and chicanery, I have no choice but to assume that you may have not faithfully fulfilled the bargain offered to you. Therefore, I have had a change of heart concerning the exchange that was promised in my last missive. Whether you have acted in good faith or not, I no longer trust your deceitful nature.

Your new instructions are to proceed directly to my fortress on Tortuga to conclude the bargain originally proffered. Once I am assured that my stolen booty has been dutifully restored, I will comply with my earlier promise and return the French songbird to your safekeeping. However, should you in any way act with skullduggery and deceit that you have demonstrated routinely in the past, I will be forced to reward this treachery by destroying your lover in the most reprehensible manner you could ever imagine.

The onus is now thrust upon you, and your French trollop's life is totally in your hands. Do not fail her as you have others in times past by your arrogance, insolence and conceitedness. Failure to comply with my specific demands will result in hardship and eternal pain which will surely follow you to your grave!

Your enemy for life,
Black Tarantula

Reviewing the dispatch several more times, I concluded that my prior estimate of the fiend's dishonesty had been rightfully postulated. Regardless of my actions in the matter of his treasure, the beast never intended to honor the bargain he had originally proposed. While this revelation came as no real surprise, I nevertheless ached for the opportunity to face and destroy the demon forever. I was confident that the calculated scheme that I was in the midst of engineering was the only sure method of concluding this conflict successfully. While I anguished over the precarious position facing Rue, I had been certain and correct in my belief that the deceitful beast would not have simply released her once his missing treasure was restored. Remembering the confession of LeMerde, I was also positive that for whatever reason the hypocritical villain relished my untold sufferings and sought my utter destruction in a manner that entirely suited his obscene machinations.

Further, the perplexing and baffling reference to failing others confounded me utterly. Perhaps the rancorous snake was referring to the Adams's disaster or possibly his devilish plan to eliminate the Turbouts. I thought more about the specific words in the missive and came to a startling conclusion. Surely the reference was to my tragic loss of Powder Monkey, who I had treated as a younger brother throughout our brief time together. In any case, the triggered remembrance of Rue's plight awakened a renewed sense of loss and despair that now dominated my entire being. At the same time, the ever increasing gale-force winds that assailed the island seemed to reflect the wails, moans and cries of my lost comrades, as they screamed out for retribution and revenge. A sudden powerful gust of fury seemed to shake the entire structure as it awakened me from my sorrowful recriminations. Moving over to the entrance, I gazed out at the full ferocity of the chaos that surrounded me. The air was filled with all manner of life-threatening debris uprooted and made to dance haphazardly at the whim of Mother Nature. Roofs, trees and other assorted detritus were being rearranged across my field of vision like some sort of apocalyptic nightmare. Retreating back to the safety of the enclosure, I laid my head back against a crypt and fell into a restless slumber, dreaming of happier days with dear departed friends!

Upon awaking, I realized that peace and quiet had returned to the tropical isle. Gaining my feet, I ventured outside to survey the damage wrought by the violent tempest. As suspected, many of the structures of Shantytown had simply disappeared in the hurricane's wake. This observation came as no surprise since most of the buildings in this section of the city were casually thrown together with no thought of longevity due to their rude construction. The isle's lush trees and shrubbery had also been dealt a telling blow as the storm had simply stripped this flora away completely. The driving rain coupled with the powerful winds had amassed huge piles of assorted objects including human corpses, which appeared to peek out of these monstrous dams with unblinking eyes. As I meandered toward the harbor, I encountered traumatically shocked and slack-eyed survivors, wandering aimlessly in pursuit of acquaintances and loved ones. Their continuous and sonorous hailing to their loved ones were both haunting and surreal. Reaching the harbor, I was not at all surprised to find it virtually emptied of ships, since many wise Captains had elected to attempt a desperate race for survival rather than face being blown onto the shore. Hopeful that our crafts had fared well, I located Angry George who had engaged a small punt for the short journey to our concealed cove.

Upon entering this secluded inlet, I was gratified to observe that all four vessels appeared relatively unaffected by the recent hurricane. Greeted warmly by Lion, he reported minimal damage to our fleet and that alterations and specifications that I had ordered were currently underway. Pleased by his report, I traipsed from ship to ship encouraging my men who were all hard at work. Our borrowed schooners were anchored securely in the cove as crewmen toiled on every portion of their structures. My specific designs for each of these ships was to turn them into exacting replicas of *Rue's Revenge* and *Neptune's Revenge*, down to their colors, gunports, deck constructions, figureheads and every other miniscule detail including the installment of our haunting company flag. These two vessels would play a vital role in the upcoming battle with the forces of evil and their exacting resemblance was a crucial factor in my plan. Additionally, I had elected to increase the cannon power of each of these schooners. To accomplish this feat, additional gunports were cleverly crafted and painted to be invisible amidst their surrounding hulls, until such time as they would be unveiled in the heat of battle to surprise and confound our enemy.

Additionally, I ordered all of our sails made battle ready which meant the use of heavier sailcloth soaked in alum to prevent fires. I had also decreed doubled running riggings to ensure continuous steerage, canvas affixed to all rails to reduce flying wooden splinters, blankets and water tubs topside to arrest any fire threats, oaken plugs handy to attain quick repairs for potential cannon damage to any vessel's structure, filled sand buckets on the decks to provide sure footing and absorb any bloodspill and the sides of every ship greased to complicate enemy boarding efforts. I had also sent Angry George and a company of men back to the city's harbor with ample coin to secure additional powder, shot along with two extra longboats for each new ship. Lastly, I ordered every vessel careened and weed-free to allow maximum speed and maneuverability. Since war was on our agenda, I was fixated on providing every small advantage I could muster.

As I continued my inspection, I noticed that the corpulent Master Jailer had been assigned the filthy and backbreaking job of careening two of our beached ships. Ambling over to the noxious brute, I was pleased to witness new lash marks adorning his backside for dereliction of duty. As previously ordered, Tiny Junior stood very close to the self-imposed torturer to administer any required encouragement with his whip should the brute's effort lag in any regard. Hopefully, this hard lesson of humility and pain would serve to amend his evil inclinations, but if not a wondrous *sand bath* would serve the villain well! I also found Guzzlin' Gooch and his hard working assistants dutifully engaged on the beach adding updated grenade launchers to our musket and grenado ketches. In all, the work was furious, backbreaking, sweat-inducing and totally necessary for our upcoming confrontation.

Turning towards the jungle that surrounded and protected our location, I noticed Pablo the Pigeonman and a small boy emerge from the dense thickets hefting armloads of sapling branches. Upon spying me, he hurried over to my side and introduced the young bright-eyed lad as his son, Bunkey. Questioning him on his progress, he reported that he was currently manufacturing comfortable coops to house his special birds on each of our ships. He explained that he had enlisted the aid of two young crewmembers and was training them to handle his pigeons. He divulged that once the suitable pigeon accommodations were installed and when his special birds became accustomed to their new homes, he would initiate the intricate training regimen to acclimate and ready his pigeons for active duty. Satisfied with his report, I congratulated him on his hard work and urged him to hastily continue his vital charge. With a gleeful wink and a snappy salute, he was off to complete his ordained tasks.

Just before darkness overtook our frenetic efforts, Tan and Long Tall Willie made their appearance with only one of the Black Tarantula's agents in tow. Securing the rascal in the hold of one of our new vessels, they reported back to me. Launching into their account, they detailed that they had followed the pair to a nearby pub where the two had taken shelter to avoid the nasty weather. Upon settling, the duo proceeded to drink themselves into oblivion, and in the process became less guarded and progressively louder in their conversations. My men had secured an adjacent table to allow them to eavesdrop on almost every word the pair spoke. As it turned out, their ultimate destination was Tortuga, specifically to the impregnable fortress of their master. However, as they continued their spirits' marathon, a significant rift developed between the two blackguards. The greedier of these varlets, emboldened with liquid courage, argued for prying open the small container in order to liberate a small sample of the booty prior to returning the cache to the Black Tarantula. His argument was that his master would have no way of knowing the exact contents of the container, and would in all likelihood not miss any small extraction. The timid one of the pair argued against this plan, insisting that their wily Captain would somehow sense the discrepancy and punish them severely for their crime.

This argument raged back and forth until the defender advocating no action passed out from copious spirit intake. At that point, my men witnessed the aggressor drunkenly fiddling with the chest's locking mechanism, spelling his doom. As soon as the thief broke into the treasure box, he suddenly slumped forward and expired without uttering a sound. Tan and Long Tall Willie then collected both pirates and dragged them to a rented room they had procured in order to wait out the storm's fury. Once the hurricane ended, they promptly abandoned the deceased scoundrel, and carted his unwilling partner back to our location for interrogation. Upon completing their report, I thanked them both for their wise and quick thinking and sent them off for a hearty meal and some much needed rest.

While I was a bit disappointed that my poisoned contraption did not end up directly in the hands of my enemy, I reasoned that it would be far more satisfying to destroy the demon pirate in a face-to-face confrontation. As such, I ordered the surviving pirate to be brought before me for questioning. Once he arrived, I asked him for his name, and he responded that his mates called him Swamp Frog. Sure that this miscreant would require the proper motivation to loosen his tongue, I began plotting a way to ensure his total cooperation. When the rogue was fully secured, I decided to attempt a direct approach before resorting to extreme measures. As I guessed, the survivor was indeed terrified of his master's harsh and demonic nature, and refused to answer any of my initial inquiries. In a halting and awestruck voice, he proceeded to inform me of the insidious punishment the Black Tarantula had commanded as a result of our successful raid on his fortified lair.

He began his tale of woe by informing me that a total of fifty pirates had survived our foray on Tortuga. These unlucky survivors had then been forced to each draw a single bean from a large pot that contained only six black beans and the vast remainder white. Anytime an unlucky black bean was chosen, the unfortunate crewman was separated from his fellow tars. The exercise continued until all six black beans had been selected. These terrified star-crossed creatures were then securely lashed to the riggings of the recaptured *Spider's Web*. Their fiendish Captain then commanded that fishing tackle be delivered topside. Unaware of the hideous fate awaiting them, the Black Tarantula fashioned sharpened hooks to both ends of six individual fishing lines. One hook from each of these lines was then secured to a different sensitive part of the bound prisoner's anatomy such as his privates, his eyelids, his lips and other nasty locations. The Black Tarantula then proceeded to flay a slice of flesh from the thighs of each captive and utilized this bloody meat to bait the hooks at the other end of each line. These baited hooks were tossed overboard to await the eventual strikes from the hungry fish that constantly prowled the waters around their ship in hopes of being rewarded with routinely dumped refuse.

Eventually each of these baited hooks were taken by a ravenous sea denizen, and the taut lines yanked and tore at each prisoner's hooked sensitive flesh until the attached fish eventually strained hard enough to tear the opposing hooks loose from their points of origin, maiming and brutalizing each suffering individual in the process. Once this destruction had occurred, the Black Tarantula called for a new set of hooks and line and the sick game was reenacted all over again with a different body part nominated for disfigurement. While this demonic punishment was being administered, the entire crew had been ordered to remain topside to witness the torment and pain of their fellow mates. Any fool who diverted his eyes from the ghastly presentation was assured a spot hanging in the riggings as punishment for his abject cowardice. Choking now in terrified gulps with tears streaming down his face, Swamp Frog divulged that the last of these poor devils did not expire from his grievously inflicted wounds until the end of three monstrously long days. Concluding his repellant account, the poor fool lapsed into uncontrollable sobs as he pleaded with me to question him no further.

Leaving the petrified tar to regain some semblance of order, I promised that I would return soon to continue our discussion. Once outside, I called Long Tall Willie and had him produce the lethal treasure chest that had been recovered and returned with his captive. Instructing him on what I had planned for the closed-mouthed villain, I left our prisoner to be properly prepared for my next interrogation session. Returning to the cabin after having been informed that all was in readiness, I found the shivering thug bound securely to a chair with the lethally miniature chest strapped into his trembling paws. As ordered, the fool was also gagged tight to prevent him from uttering a sound as I laid out his options. Upon his continued refusal to answer my queries, the first option was opening the deadly apparatus affixed to his hands, which I explained would result in the identical painful death that felled his thieving compatriot. The second and more humane option was his cooperation and agreement to answer some very basic queries after which he would be freed and permitted to make his escape from us. Questioning if he fully understood his options, the petrified rake nodded his head. Undoing the filthy gag, I quizzed him on which option he preferred. In a high-pitched and faltering squeal, he demanded to know whether I was totally honest in my offer to allow him to escape unharmed if he complied with my wishes. Nodding firmly, I promised on my departed mother's grave to adhere to the bargain I had struck if he indeed provided the truth. Taking but a moment's time, he spat out that he would divulge all he knew for a chance to survive!

My first question was what role he played as part of the Black Tarantula's horde. Gulping in nervousness, he explained that he served as a Master Gunner responsible for several gun crews aboard the infamous *Spider's Web.* When the opportunity arose to partake in the special mission, he leapt at this chance in the slim hope of discovering an avenue to escape the vile clutches of his insane leader. Confessing that he was an expert with cannons, he had hoped to find suitable employment that would spirit him far away from the demon's dominion.

Satisfied that Swamp Frog was being truthful, I moved to the next subject quizzing him on the condition of my beloved Rue. Blinking with mild surprise, he stated that the Black Tarantula had captured the lass, who had been eventually located after a long and furious search. As to her condition, he confessed that his Captain had specifically constructed a devilish torture chamber in his cabin which he utilized to keep prisoners like the poor lass in permanent bondage. Demanding further details, he stuttered that the fiend had been slowly starving the cursed woman to death, thoroughly enjoying her prolonged pain and suffering. Stiffening at this vile news, I questioned the brute's ultimate plan for my beloved. Nodding understanding, Swamp Frog warned that he believed that his vicious boss had no intentions of ever freeing the girl, and seemed rather content to continue his horrid torture until the poor creature eventually expired.

Shaken to my core, I begrudgingly moved to the next subject by inquiring about my nemesis' location and any short term plans he might have revealed. Choking back a sob, my prisoner moaned belatedly that the sadist kept the majority of his plans to himself, never trusting any of his crew with particulars concerning the future. All that he was privy to was that he had been ordered to Saint Domingue to await my arrival, and subsequently transport any items I delivered back to his degenerate commander on Tortuga. Weeping uncontrollably at this point, he whimpered that he had been honest and forthright in his responses and could reveal no further information on his leader's plots nor course of action. Removing the dreaded casket carefully from his sweating palms, I stated that I had faith that he had been truthful in answering my questions. Informing him that I was a man of my word, I ordered him to be released from his bindings and free to leave!

Noting the utter relief caused by my words, I probed where he intended to flee given that his insidious leader seemed to have spies and confederates virtually everywhere. Slowly nodding agreement, he shrugged and confessed that he really had no viable plan of action, and as such would probably suffer a piteous ending at the devil's hand sooner or later. Agreeing with his wise assessment, I suggested that he consider joining our ranks in our effort to end the wicked reign of his degenerate commander. Continuing, I informed him that when we had succeeded in this task that he would be freed of the lethal threat haunting his very existence. Intrigued by my offer, he questioned my motives for placing my trust in a former crewman of my enemy. Responding, I confessed that I was critically short of men possessing his unique cannon talents. I also informed him that his service to the brute had unconsciously conditioned him to gage the Black Tarantula's inclinations and proclivities that might prove quite useful in our upcoming confrontation. Besides, I affirmed that the fiend was a mortal enemy to both of us now which naturally made us compatible allies.

Stunned into silence by my logic, the confused tar slowly gained his senses and began to smile, realizing that I had provided him a viable course that might finally free him from the clutches of his villainous Captain. Grinning, he shook my hand and swore his total allegiance to our cause and command. Signaling Lion, I ordered our newest recruit be assigned to one of our new vessels where he would operate as Cannon Master and loyal aide. As he turned to follow Lion, he stopped and swiveled back in my direction informing me that he had just recalled a vital bit of knowledge. He blurted out that he and his deceased partner were also ordered to keep the Vice Governor apprised of their activities while sequestered on the island. In this regard, he was quite certain that this local functionary was somehow in league with the Black Tarantula. As such, he cautioned that the Vice Governor should not be trusted. Ecstatic by this new intelligence, I thanked Swamp Frog heartily before sending him away on his new assignment.

Chapter 23: Owl Eyes Reveals Secrets

With Swamp Frog's revelation, I called for Tan and Angry George to report to me. As soon as they appeared, I filled them in on the critical knowledge received on the island's Vice Governor. Intent on questioning the deceitful emissary, I commanded my two wily veterans to return unseen to town and covertly snatch the suspected spy and spirit him back to our location for interrogation. Winking, I informed them that No Nose's pets had been idle for far too long and were in dire need of an unwilling playmate. Understanding my meaning, they provided beaming smiles and mock salutes and were off in a flash.

Returning to my inspection rounds, I was pleased to observe that our new vessels were being transformed into mirror images of our dear ships. Calling Lion and Sharkface to my side, I explained the ruse I had utilized with the Governor concerning the intended usage of these ships. Since we remained sorely in need of further armament and supplies, I suggested that these new vessels be employed on regular trips to town to transport the detailed list of necessities I had assembled. Aware that we were also critically short of men, I dictated that these regular forays include enlistment efforts. Given the significant damage caused by the recent storm, I assured them that I was convinced that the town was rife for attracting viable candidates, as long as enough coin was offered in the bargain. Lastly, I cautioned them to conduct all of their affairs in total secrecy and under the cover of darkness, since our mortal enemy might have additional agents reporting on our actions. Warning them to fly English colors and to cover the new figureheads with sailcloth, I directed them to respond to questions posed by authorities or inquisitive locals with nebulous and inane responses to further shadow our intentions. With total understanding, they returned to their supervisory roles with knowing smirks on their faces.

The next morning, I was rudely awakened by a commotion occurring outside my door. Stepping over to investigate its source, I found the unhappy and threatening face of the isle's Vice Governor glaring at me. Upon recognizing me, he launched into a series of threats and slanders in his typically arrogant French tongue. Snapping a response back in French, I ordered him to calm himself or face severe penalties. Upon hearing my words, Owl Eyes went immediately silent. In a hushed voice, he inquired if I truly spoke French or had merely mastered a smattering of phrases in my nautical wanderings. Smiling coldly, I retorted that I spoke excellent French as but one of the many languages I had mastered in childhood. Gulping back his concern, he hastily apologized if any of his prior statements had caused me pain or hardship. With an evil leer, I promised that the slate would be more than counterbalanced once I had finished with him.

I directed his abductors to secure him to a sturdy chair in my cabin, while he continued to lodge threats and extreme displeasure over his rough and unwarranted treatment. Calling No Nose, I filled him in on his assignment and made my way to the galley to enjoy the first meal of the day. Surprisingly, I was able to detect the shrill cries and wails that emanated from our new guest as far away as the galley. Providing my chief interrogator ample opportunity to ingratiate his subject to his horrid pets, I sat and listened to the ship's latest *scuttlebutt*. It was reported that the Master Jailer's work effort continued to be woeful at best, prompting continuous punishment from Tiny Junior. Smiling at this piece of news, I arose and wandered back to my cabin to begin my own questioning of the Vice Governor.

Upon entering the cabin, I detected a horrid stench coming from our guest's direction as the coward had voided himself due to extreme terror. Several of No Nose's spiders roamed freely over the poor fool's torso, as he eyed each with his oversized orbs nearly bulging out of their sockets. Pleading and promising to divulge anything we desired to know, I signaled No Nose to collect his meandering atrocities, and took a seat in front of the wretch to initiate my queries. My first question was quite straightforward. I asked him how long he had been acting as an agent for the Black Tarantula. Feigning ignorance and innocence, he shouted that he had no idea what I was talking about as he played the role of spy for nobody. Turning back to No Nose, I ordered him to once more unleash his killing demons, which brought a renewed mask of terror to Owl Eye's guise. Hastily amending his retort, he spouted that he had been passing innocuous information to the demon pirate for little over a year's time. Nodding acceptance, I then demanded to be told exactly what information he had conveyed to my enemy concerning our intentions to engage him in battle. The scum thought about my words, but failed to produce an immediate response as he brooded over an appropriate answer. Sensing this hesitation meant further duplicity, I nodded to No Nose indicating his assistance was again necessary. After a brief reintroduction to his hairy abominations, Owl Eyes regained both his honesty and memory and begged for the session to proceed without further visits from No Nose's horrid pets.

Repeating my prior query, the trembling coward informed me that he had reported that I intended to assault the pirate's stronghold on Tortuga with both of my ships within a month's time. Thanking him for the truth, I then probed him on the reasons his confederate abhorred me to such a great extent. Expressing nervous ignorance, he spat out that he was unaware of the specific reasons, but was absolutely certain that his boss thirsted after my painful and gruesome demise. Suddenly laughing hysterically, the slobbering functionary informed me that my plan to defeat the Black Tarantula would surely end in failure since the Tortuga fortress was impregnable and impervious to attack. Pressing for further details, he wailed that he was totally ignorant on any other particulars. Sensing his continued dishonesty, I motioned to No Nose once more which seemed to cause Owl Eyes a startling recovery of memory. With his eyes trained on No Nose, he divulged that the Black Tarantula had several more deceptions that as yet remained unveiled. Intrigued, I demanded exacting details. His continual wailing, sobbing and pleading persisted throughout the remainder of our discussion, but several salient details eventually emerged. It seemed that my nemesis also employed duplicate ships, two *Spider's Webs* in fact! The utilization of these two vessels coupled with his bloodthirsty reputation enabled him to double his prizes, while thwarting all efforts by proper authorities to end his evil reign. When threatened, he routinely anchored one of his ships in the protective cove below his formidable cannons to entice any foe to attack. In the heat of battle, he would then swoop down on these unsuspecting tormentors with his second vessel catching them in a deadly crossfire and obliterating them in the process. This carefully laid trap had been utilized by the villain numerous times in the past.

Additionally, I was stunned when Owl Eyes revealed that he had also been privy to rumors that the Black Tarantula had enlisted the aid of an extremely formidable partner, who was also committed to my utter destruction. No amount of added threats could produce further intelligence on this rumored ally. All that I was able to dredge up was that my opponent was a master tactician, who was always two steps ahead of any opponent. The Vice Governor prognosticated that this mysterious co-conspirator would team with the duplicate *Spider's Webs* to guarantee an end to my existence. With this pronouncement, he lapsed into hysterical laughter promising that if the Black Tarantula did not destroy me then he would certainly employ his position of power on the island to ensure my rightful obliteration.

Realizing both the truth and subsequent danger behind his last statement, I formulated a quick scheme in my mind. Keeping the cowardly knave trussed, I concocted a mixture of *Datura* and rum that was sure to cause the undercover agent some serious behavior modifications along with hellish hallucinations. With several of my men holding the squirming cur down, I managed to pour a goodly amount of the deadly mixture down his gullet. Gagging him afterwards to prevent him from spewing out my special brew, I waited for the fun to commence. After less than an hour, I noticed the whelp beginning to twitch and cavort in his restraints, as if attempting to dislodge some sort of imaginary tormentor. Loosening his gag, he began wailing about the monstrous hairy spiders that continued to crawl all over his frame. Gratified that my mixture was having its desire effect, I instructed my team on the next step of my planned deception.

My scheme called for me to pay an unscheduled visit to the Governor. Concurrently, Owl Eyes would be covertly transported to the unguarded rear of the Governor's office. Once in place, my men were instructed to liberally dose the fool once again with the potent rum and *Datura* mixture. I ordered them to then muffle him and hold him quiet until the drug induced its deadly result. At that point, my instructions were to release the madman inside the back entrance of the building where his disruptive presence would soon be detected. I was sure that once released and discovered, he would be brought before the Governor to determine what should be done with the delirious madman.

All proceeded according to plan. As I was comfortably seated in front of the Governor negotiating the payment terms for the borrowed ships, a loud commotion erupted within the edifice. As we both glanced toward the entry door, it suddenly burst open and several guards dragged the raving Vice Governor into the office. The Governor shouted his annoyance for the rude interruption, but was immediately quelled by the mad antics being enacted by his second-in-command. Owl Eyes was clawing at his torso, as he screamed for aid to help rid himself of the grotesque creatures that were viciously attacking him. Still under tight restraint, the squirming and twitching imbecile fought for his freedom in order to turn his full attention to the imaginary pestering pestilence plaguing him.

Upon witnessing this insane demonstration, the Governor, frozen in confused alarm, turned to me silently professing abject bewilderment. Seizing the initiative, I blurted out that as a trained medical practitioner I had witnessed similar symptoms by patients in the past. Begging me to continue, I announced that the vivid hallucinations along with the pronounced delirium were indications of a rare tropical fever. In a hushed whisper, I confided that in such a desperate state the infected was quite dangerous to himself and anyone nearby. Now terrified beyond description, the Governor shouted for more guards to ensure the proper restraint of his deranged assistant, while screeching for his personal physician to be summoned immediately.

When the good doctor finally made his grand appearance, there were a total of eight struggling guards fighting to contain Owl Eyes. After a cursory examination of the balmy bespectacled human worm, the doctor confessed that he was stymied by the highly unusual symptoms and rather at a loss at recommending a curative. Stepping forward, I advanced my theory that it appeared to be a form of rare tropical fever. Unable to deny my pronouncement, the doctor questioned what I would recommend in the way of treatment. I responded that some success had been evidenced in the past by utilizing a strong purgative tea made from various natural elements to help combat this deadly ailment. Noting the good medic's dubiousness, I questioned the hesitant medical practitioner if he personally had any success utilizing leeches to regularly bleed his patients afflicted with fevers. Sparked by a curative which the pompous dolt was totally familiar, he brightened and issued a knowing smile.

As I fairly shouted my query on leeches, the stricken patient's eyes flew wide-open in horrified appall. Summoning every ounce of manic strength, the slippery eel broke free from his guards and ran directly towards the large window located behind the Governor. Desperately seeking an opportunity to escape a squadron of twitching and slimy bloodsuckers, Owl Eyes burst through the window as the Governor cowered and vehemently whimpered for assistance. Since the office was on the third floor, the deluded escapee fell screaming and wailing a long time before a stone patio ended his pain-wracked serenade. Rushing over to the destroyed window, I gazed down at Owl Eyes' body, which was sprawled face down on the stones below with his neck twisted at a highly unnatural angle. Turning back to the doctor, I announced that the good doctor could save his leeches for other cases, since the Vice Governor no longer required their ministrations. Marching out of the office, I was both happy and relieved that the cowardly spy had sent his last missive to his nefarious boss!

Upon returning to our hidden location, I was quite pleased to discover that all four ships had now been successfully careened. Since this brutal backbreaking labor had ended, I inquired on the status of the Master Jailer. Lion reported that the odious lout had been kept busy with additional manual labor, but this meant keeping a watch on him at all times. Weary and disgusted with his skedaddling antics along with his surly demeanor, Lion suggested that it was high time to return him to his former life. Agreeing wholeheartedly, I summoned the revolting creature to my cabin for a farewell discussion. Upon arriving, I informed him that he had performed his service to us in an admirable fashion and it was now time to return him home. Sensing imminent freedom, the fool sneered that he would repay my kindness some day in the very near future. Filled with a sense of false security, he threatened to alert authorities about the transformation of the Governor's two vessels. Grinning and nodding like an addled child, he taunted that our secret would not remain concealed much longer. Aware of the danger in his ominous threat, my mind went to work on inventing a method to eliminate this danger without our implication.

Realizing that I could not simply make him disappear without becoming personally involved, I began to strategize a method to negate any testimony he might direct against us. Snickering at his vile threat, I mentioned that the hard labor to which he had been assigned had physically served him well. I further complimented him on his loss of unhealthy weight, along with the wholesome color and muscle he had added in the process. To compensate his valued service, I proclaimed that I intended to reward him with a magnificent ornate dagger along with a half dozen bottles of our finest rum, which would accompany him home. To seal the bargain, I arose and procured a bottle of rum from my private stock, which had previously been treated with a strong dose of *Wormwood*. Uncorking the bottle, I offered it to him to quench his raging thirst. Slurping a mighty gulp, he thanked me for my generous rewards, and recorking the bottle made ready to return.

Ordering six more bottles of rum to be delivered to my cabin, I expertly doctored each in the same manner. As for the dagger, I coated its extremely keen blade with *creeping death*. I was fully cognizant of the fact that any new blade was invariably tested for sharpness by its new owner. This was normally accomplished by dragging the new weapon's blade over the possessor's fingers, thumbs or palms to judge the sharpness of its edge. Coupled with the doctored rum, I had faith that the tormenting villain would significantly slice himself testing the gift as soon as he was in a safe and secure location so as to not broadcast the fact that he owned such a fine and valuable possession. Once done, the *creeping death* would seal his lips permanently.

To ensure that he did not elect to validate the blade's keenness any earlier than planned, I informed him that many of my men remained dubious as to his character. I explained further that brandishing such a weapon in their midst would prove to be a life-threatening act on his part. To mitigate this danger, I divulged that Lion would hold his treasure safe and return it to him once their vessel reached town. Distrustful as ever, the brigand began to lodge an argument for immediate possession. However, after a moment's thought about my words of warning, he reluctantly agreed to the proposed arrangement. With a spiteful wave, he bid me goodbye and followed Lion's pointed finger to the waiting transport.

Handing over the medicated rum and prized blade to Lion, I ordered that he return our repulsive guest back home safe and sound. Nodding his reluctant acceptance, Lion turned to collect his ill-favored cargo. Before he was away, I also cautioned him to avoid inspecting the dirk's blade as I had treated it with a very nasty surprise for our most unwelcome guest. Flashing a quick grin, he saluted and took his leave.

As the vessel departed, I could still hear the drunken threats issued by the revolting landlubber, but was certain that my special brew and treated dagger would severely complicate his happy homecoming more than he would ever know. When Lion returned early the next morning, he reported that he had followed my orders implicitly. However, he chuckled that the corpulent rogue had begun to descend into stranger and stranger behavior the closer they neared their destination. By the time they delivered the lout to his abode along with his liquid reward and valuable dirk, he was raving, jabbering and making absolutely no sense at all. Believing him intensively intoxicated, they simply dumped the repellant ogre on his doorstep and made their escape.

Two days later Scuttle returned to our company with his initial inventory of replacement grenados. As he made his report, he informed me that he had heard a story concerning our temporary laborer, the Master Jailer. It seemed that the scoundrel had been discovered mysteriously dead in his house the same day of his return. Because the investigating medical man could deduce no foul play in the matter, the cause of death was judged natural but unknown. When I questioned Scuttle on the disposition of the valuable dagger I had awarded our indentured servant, he answered that no mention of the blade had been made in any of the island's scuttlebutt. At this news I laughed heartily knowing that some thieving knave was in for the surprise of his life when he also tested the blade's edge. Thanking Scuttle for his report, I sent him off for some rest and nourishment.

As our work continued at a frantic pace, our newest recruit, Swamp Frog, was busy training our new cannon teams on the proper loading, aiming and firing of the massive guns. Due to our need to properly defend our two new vessels, his work continued night and day as Lion and Sharkface constantly supplied additional fresh recruits for training. While the guns remained silent to protect our location and intentions, the crews dry-practiced continuously and many were becoming quite proficient in their skills under their new mentor's crafty and tireless tutelage. When we reached open waters, these new cannon crews would certainly have the opportunity to display their newfound proficiency.

Pablo the Pigeonman and his son had also been very engaged during this time acclimating and training their small birds to return to their nests aboard our ships. Since the pigeons required daylight to navigate, the pair rowed out to distant locations each morning where they would release their pigeons, which for whatever miraculous reason always seemed to navigate their way back to their shipboard homes. Additionally, they stocked each off our two new transport ships with the small birds. The unerring navigational ability of these tiny creatures never ceased to amaze me as well as my officers.

As last-minute preparations were now underway, I began to finalize my battle plan. As the Vice Governor had warned, the Black Tarantula was a clever strategist, who carefully planned each of his moves with utmost care and thinking. I knew that we were involved in a real-life game of chess where losing spelled ultimate destruction and death. Since I was also a master of this game, I was determined to come out on the winning side. Like my nemesis, I had a few new tricks to unveil, which I was sure would confound and confuse our enemy and tip the balance of power in our favor!

Chapter 24: Spider Hunt

In order to give us every opportunity to claim victory, I made the decision to thoroughly scout our enemy's fortifications and deduce his militaristic intentions. Since I had been fortuitously forewarned of my foe's unidentified collaborator, I ordered Tiger Eyes and a small cadre of seasoned sailors to locate a suitable craft for this vital but dangerous reconnaissance mission. A short time later, he returned with an ancient and decrepit fishing ketch complete with moldering nets and timeworn equipment that was sure not to raise enemy concerns if spotted. His specific assignment was to scout the Tortuga stronghold, and then attempt to uncover any unpleasant surprises our opposition might have concocted. In order to communicate his findings in a timely fashion, I commissioned him to tote along several of Pablo's pigeons. Realizing that these marvelous creatures were quite useless without a seasoned handler who could communicate the team's discoveries, I summoned Pablo and requested his son, Bunkey, volunteer for this dangerous mission. While not very pleased with my request, the stalwart Spaniard agreed reluctantly to my petition.

Prior to launching, I met with Tiger Eyes to impart some last minute instructions. I dictated that all of his daytime reconnaissance should be accomplished while posing as local fishermen. This specifically meant deploying his tattered nets as he trolled the waters anywhere close to his ultimate target. During the hours of darkness, I commanded that his ragged and worn sails be replaced with newly fabricated tar coated sheets to add speed and maneuverability while allowing little chance of detection. Lastly, I divulged a special bit of knowledge that I hoped would allow him to ascertain the enemy's secondary position and intentions as well as his mysterious ally. Nodding understanding, he hopped aboard the derelict vessel and sailed away.

Since I still had more than a week left in my enemy's deadline, I ordered our small fleet to raise anchors and head south. Settling on a distance far enough away to avoid alerting nearby settlements of our warlike intentions, I commanded that full combat practice be initiated in order to sharpen our militaristic skills to a precise and dangerous level. Given these firm orders, cannon practice was inaugurated in earnest. While our seasoned veterans accomplished the majority of the initial target damage over the first several days, Swamp Frog's personal direction of each of the newly created cannon teams proved invaluable as these hastily thrown together newcomers also proved their worth as considerably proficient gunners. Eventually, they matched the efforts of even some of our finest seasoned cannon teams.

Close at hand, our grenado boats were summarily engaged in practicing their deadly arts to the constant beat of ship's drums coordinating their efforts to hunt prey like a pack of wolves. Utilizing their vicious grenados and lethal muskets, competition was held amongst each team as they strove to execute drummed orders swiftly and accurately. In a short time, a certain rhythm and exactness developed on each team increasing their ferocity, their fleetness, and their overall maneuverability to the drummed commands. They were virtually unstoppable, too small and fast to be destroyed by enemy fire and too devastating and destructive as they functioned as coordinated units. Consequently, they proved their worthwhile potential as a deadly and vicious weapons ready to be unleashed in our upcoming conflict! In addition, our highly precise and efficient grenado catapults were also installed on the upper decks of both *Revenges.*

Guzzlin' Gootch and Chips finalized their marvelous transformation of our two borrowed ships, turning them into exacting replicas of our original vessels. Once completed, I ordered the portside hold of each new vessel crammed with the remainder of undistributed gunpowder purchased through our Governor's kind assistance. Each vessel then conducted a series of specific drills and exercises. Each mate aboard these ships had specific assigned responsibilities with Tan and Long Tall Willie acting as demanding overseers.

Pablo continued to labor with his pet messengers along with the continued training of his chosen charges personally selected for handling his marvelous birds. I was certain that the critical role of these diminutive creatures would soon be put to test as we gravely awaited the initial report from Tiger Eyes' scouting foray. Finally, after four long days of waiting, the first pigeon arrived with its initial espionage missive. Pablo translated his son's communiqué. Having successfully run reconnaissance on our enemy's Tortuga fortress, Tiger Eyes reported that the *Spider Web* was peacefully anchored in the cove with its seaport guns primed and ready for action as our villainous foes awaited our anticipated arrival. Tiger Eyes also reported that the fort's cannons were also fully manned and armed for imminent attack. Lastly, he disclosed that he planned to head south to scout for the Black Tarantula's second vessel and his anonymous conspirator. I thanked Pablo for this news and continued battle preparations.

My crew's warfare practicing pressed on unabated through the remainder of the week as their battle proficiency escalated with each passing hour. Their overall mood was positive, but I sensed an underlying nervousness gripping each as they conducted these necessary exercises. Nevertheless, they hungered for the opportunity to face our enemies in full combat and seemed confident of attaining victory given the increased mastery of their battle skills. However, I was aware that as time was running short, the necessity for further intelligence from our scouts was indispensably critical.

That evening, I joined my crew in the galley for a welcomed warm meal after our long week of practice and preparation. With most of the crew present, Angry George seized on the opportunity to launch yet another of his mesmerizing sea tales. This evening's fanciful yarn centered on a saga that had been imparted by a grizzled old pirate and aptly centered on a bird, an appropriate subject since every crewmember had observed Pablo's pigeons training vigorously over the last several weeks. His narrative initiated with a fearsome pirate crew that happened upon a derelict vessel in their continual prowl for booty. This hapless ship appeared to be drifting aimlessly on the currents. Fearing an insidious trap, the pirates fired a series of warning rounds from their batteries. Receiving no response from this clamorous gesture, the rascals edged closer and closer to their victim. Having received absolutely no sign of resistance from the seemingly abandoned ship, the pirates came alongside and utilized grappling hooks to close the final distance. Once side-by-side, the raucous animals stormed aboard the helpless merchantman. What they discovered confused and befuddled them entirely. While their prey was fully loaded with valuable cargo and prodigious supply of *hot spirits*, there was nobody left onboard. The merchantman was utterly deserted!

Somewhat unnerved by their discovery, the scoundrels hurriedly went about their work of stripping the valuable find of any item deemed worthwhile. As they scurried about this happy chore, the Pirate Captain and First Mate made a careful search of the officers' quarters hoping to uncover valuable coins or gems. They tore each cabin asunder and located a small bounty of prized booty in the form of gold coins. While they performed this pillage, a pirate tar reported that a single living creature had been discovered in the galley, a bright and colorfully feathered parrot. This sole survivor of the ghostly merchant ship seemed well trained, as it perched peacefully on the reporting pirate's shoulder as he confronted his Captain. The docile creature proved quite fluent and rattled off a slew of meaningless words and phrases that delighted all within listening range. Dubbing the fowl, Lone Survivor Sam, the Captain took immediate ownership as the tropical bird hopped compliantly onto his shoulder and began issued numerous friendly welcoming remarks. As soon as the merchantman had been successfully gutted of all valuables, the Captain ordered it fired and scuttled.

Life aboard the pirate ship resumed normalcy as the crew partook in uncontrolled drunkenness with their purloined spirits and eventually lapsed into ungoverned soused beasts as they continued their hunt for prey. The pirate leader mesmerized by his new pet roamed the ship delighting in the words and phrases spouted by his new avian companion. However, he was somewhat confounded by some of the words uttered by Lone Survivor Sam, especially those that infrequently dealt with death and murder. One such phrase especially drew his complete attention and chilled him to his core was the ominous parrot's declaration; "*Beware of the sea hag*"! Since the majority of this popular creature's words were utterly harmless, the Captain dismissed this strange phrase outright and continued in his absolute enchantment with his new pet's antics and vocalizations.

With an ample alcohol supply now onboard, the crew continued their liquid orgy, refusing any semblance of sobriety as they meandered across the calm tropical seas. The spirit binge proceeded unabated for a full week, and with the liquid inventory still in good stead the contented drunks saw no real end in sight. On the eighth night, the drunk and delirious pirate crew were sleeping rough, aimlessly scattered across all decks, when they were rudely aroused by a frightful din originating from the lower decks. Unsure of the racket's source and yet quite inebriated, the pirates discounted the loud screams and wails as nothing more than fanciful imaginings as a direct result of their liquid diets.

Waking groggily the next morning, the pirates began questioning each other on the ruckus they had all overheard the previous evening. To a man, they confessed that the disturbance indicated acute human suffering and pain, but were unable to pinpoint or identify its source. Mildly shaken and a mite nervous over this occurrence, they took their concerns to the Captain to see if he could shed some light on the mystery. Their leader, fully cognizant of normal shipboard clamor, explained their concerns away by reminding them that all ships sounded like insane asylums during sleeping hours. He verified that loud obnoxious noises were certainly the norm during long nights at sea. You see, men crammed into tight spaces, exhausted by daytime duties and plied with strong spirits provided the perfect opportunity for all manner of loud commotion. Some tars talked incessantly in their drunken stupors, others shouted or screamed while a few even issued vile and obnoxious involuntary bodily outcries. Convinced now that nothing was truly amiss other than normal chaotic nighttime cacophony, the crew dragged themselves to the galley for sustenance for their grumbling bellies.

Still slightly spooked, they settled down at their morning repast as they laughed and joked in unison at their own foolishness. As the meal progressed, one mate suddenly jerked alert searching for his close confederate, who was not amongst them. Separating himself from his munching mates, he initiated a search of the vessel for his friend. Sure that the rascal was in hiding, the tar wandered the entire ship intent on locating his missing chum. As his search progressed, other pirates joined his quest but to no avail. The missing fool had simply disappeared! With his absence confirmed, panic renewed and the crew again confronted the Captain, who appeared mildly perturbed by this news. At the same time, Lone Survivor Sam began chanting mechanically, "*Beware of the sea hag*", which deepened the dread and consternation of all. Taking firm control, the Captain provided a plausible explanation for the missing man by explaining that he most likely stumbled overboard while drunk as he attempted to relieve himself of excess drink. Continuing, he theorized that the screams heard the previous night were nothing more than the poor fool's cries for assistance as he floundered in the nighttime sea. Mollified by this sound reasoning, the pirates returned to their bottles continuously saluting their fallen comrade.

The result of their actions was that by nightfall every tar aboard was pleasantly inebriated and totally numbed to the loss of their missing mate. Sometime later that evening, the ship was once again rudely wakened by inhuman screams and piercing wails from an unknown location aboard the vessel. Dazed and bleary, the men wandered around bumping rudely into one another as they searched for an explanation for the unholy clamor. Unable to deduce the source of the cries, the pirates huddled and shivered in small groups as they awaited the upcoming light of day. When the sun finally made its brilliant appearance, the scoundrels took a quick inventory of their numbers to discover to their absolute horror that two more crewmen were missing. Once again, a resulting ship-wide search proved fruitless and the rascals were now on the edge of utter panic. The aftermath of their extreme terror led to a dramatic tapering of the consumption of strong spirits, with the universal belief that clear heads were required in order to avoid further disaster.

Postulating that Lone Survivor Sam's declarations prophesying that an evil entity, a sea hag, was responsible for their troubles, they conspired to plot a course of action to defeat this demonic creature. As night arrived, the now sober crew grouped into clusters across the vessel armed to the teeth to keep a close watch so as to avoid any further disappearances. As the night progressed without further incident, the men became increasingly drowsy and the majority slipped into fitful sleep. As daybreak approached, a series of frightful howls and screeches awoke all. A number of the pirates swore that they had observed several crewmen being dragged off the ship by a pair of long bluish arms ending in long and wicked black claws. They proclaimed that the unfortunates were summarily dragged below the waves by the hideous-appearing clawed appendages as they issued panicked shrieks before being silenced forever.

Several crewmembers on the topdeck had hurried to the spot where their mates had entered the water to search for signs of them. They were rewarded with an eerie sight as they peered into the brightening sea, which caused each of them unimaginable dread and foreboding. To a man, they described witnessing the horrible blue-blotched face of a wizened and grotesque old woman complete with long tangled silvery hair just below the water's surface. Further, the witnesses avowed that the facial expressions of this sea demon were utterly repulsive, malicious and sinister in nature. Adding to their hideous description, they divulged that the creature's face sported sharpened rows of rotting teeth, horrid moles and warts along with dangerous and savage red eyes. Upon close observation, the witch seemed to smile in a most unpleasant manner, as if sizing each up as its next victim. Horrified and hysterical, the entire crew went into a state of absolute panic upon hearing these lurid details, convinced that they were all doomed to suffer the same dreadful fate as their lost companions.

Frantically informing the Captain of these sightings, the terror-stricken men described in detail the appalling horror they had been beheld. They postulated that their ship was certainly under attack by an age-old nautical superstition, a sea hag. The pirates proceeded to plead with their commander to vacate their surroundings before any more of their mates were treated to the same gruesome fate. They also argued that Lone Survivor Sam was surely a familiar of the malicious sea hag and as such needed to be dispatched immediately. Perplexed and confused, the Captain agreed with their boisterous demands of taking flight, but implicitly refused to slaughter the innocent parrot, to which he had made a strong attachment. Ordering all sails unfurled and a new course set, the Captain grabbed the helm and guided the vessel on this new path.

Seemingly at once, the bountiful breezes that had filled their sails died away completely, leaving the vessel bobbing motionless on the glassy water's surface. Terrified by the wind's sudden disappearance, several pirates scurried below in a vain attempt to seek safety from the pitiless monster that hungered for their deaths and destruction. As the Captain stood rooted on the quarterdeck in abject confusion, a sudden and ghostly fog bank descended upon the vessel enveloping it entirely. With his crew in frightful disarray, the ship's leader decided on a repellant and labor intensive maneuver to extricate them from their cursed location. He ordered two longboats launched in order to manually row the vessel from their dangerous surroundings. Selecting a totally unwilling crew for each boat, the Captain commanded his forced volunteers to manually tow their ship forward until a suitable breeze arose.

The wary and nervous volunteers clambered down into the tiny dinghies, affixed tow cables to their ship and began to slowly row out ahead of their vessel. As they disappeared into the cloying fog, each turned a baleful eye to their comrades on deck, who offered up meager well-wishes and encouragements. Not long after their disappearance in the fog, the pirates aboard were subjected to grim and horrid howls and shrieks coming directly out of the fog bank. Fearing for the welfare and safety of their comrades, a number of them grabbed the tow cables and hauled the small rowboats back towards the ship.

As the dinghies came into sight, the crew were astonished and summarily stunned to discover that both were completely empty, save a mass of bloody gore that now decorated the insides of each tiny rowboat. Terrified and well past the verge of sheer panic, the remaining pirates abandoned the upperdeck, seeking safety on the vessel's lower confines. But as fate would decree, they discovered the folly of their flight in no time at all. As the day progressed, crewmen after crewmen were roughly dragged from their temporary hiding spots by the horrid blackened claws of their tormentor through hatches, portholes and even through the ship's hull leaving large gaping holes in their wake. As their numbers continued to dramatically dwindle, the Captain ordained that their vessel was indeed cursed and ordered survivors to launch longboats in a determined effort to vacate the jinxed ship. Before deserting his vessel, the Captain set various fires aboard the tormented ship in a hysterical attempt to end the reign of the tormenting witch by destroying the supposed source of the insidious curse. Abandoning Lone Survivor Sam in his cabin, the Captain slowly lowered himself into one of the tiny boats, as flames quickly consumed his vessel transforming it to a fiery inferno. Hopeful that they had left their troubles behind, the survivors pulled long and hard on their oars to distance themselves from the evil machinations of the murderous sea hag.

Unable to free themselves from the curtain of fog that continued to envelop them, both longboats remained quite close as the pirates inside continued to labor furiously at the oars. Not long after, a helpless victim in the lead boat was dragged screaming to his watery grave to the shocked astonishment of his terrified mates. Given this hideous development, fear intensified as did the pirates rowing efforts. However, as time slowly passed, their mates were systematically torn off each rowboat by the witch's sharp talons. Pushed beyond the point of total exhaustion and petrified by fright, the remaining mates flopped into the belly of each vessel consigning themselves to their ultimate fate. Nevertheless, the ghastly abductions continued at irregular intervals until all but one lone crewman remained trembling and shaking in the bottom of his ketch.

This poor devil was eventually rescued by a passing trader and delivered at their next port-of-call to a medical man for treatment. On the way to port, the ship's doctor coaxed the frightful tale from the stricken rascal and word of the mysterious disaster spread throughout the rescue ship. Once in port, the poor devil was lodged at a local punchhouse and the town's physician was summoned to tend to his physical ailments. However, his psychological afflictions went far beyond the doctor's meager expertise, so the scoundrel self-treated his manic condition with copious quantities of rum. On his deliberate voyage to inebriation, the terrified pirate confessed the entire abhorrent encounter with the ghoulish sea hag which had accounted for the ghastly annihilation of his mates to a captivated pub audience. Reaching the point of complete drunkenness, he was assisted upstairs to an empty room by the accommodating innkeeper.

Several hours later, the pub denizens were aroused from their alcoholic stupors by a series of inhuman screeches and wails emanating from the tavern's upper floor. Several of the more courageous patrons reluctantly climbed the stairs to investigate the source of the commotion. As soon as they arrived outside the cursed survivor's room, the caterwauling ceased entirely. Hesitantly pushing the door open, the terrified landlubbers gingerly entered with lamps held aloft to illuminate the tiny room's interior. Surprised and confounded, they ascertained that the lodgings were completely empty, as the surviving pirate was nowhere to be found. The sole window in the small enclosure was wide open and the floor was sloppy wet with numerous puddles dotting the floorboards, but the stricken pirate had somehow disappeared.

As they continued their fruitless search, a bird suddenly flew in through the open window and perched on the bed's headboard. Stepping closer to investigate, the fainthearted patrons realized that the intruder was a tropical parrot. The brightly plumed creature responded to the attention paid him by calling out a single declaration; "*Beware of the sea hag*"! With this fateful pronouncement, the horrified pub rats panicked completely and retreated back down the tavern's stairway shoving, elbowing and colliding with one another in their haste to vacate the cursed establishment. Gaining access to the ground floor, they abandoned their half-empty tankards and fled like a maddened horde from the alehouse. Authorities were summoned and a comprehensive search ensued, but no evidence of the haunted pirate was ever found. Word quickly spread that he had simply vanished into the night at the beastly claws of the demonic atrocity that had also claimed every one of his fellow mates.

Well, I can report that Angry George's tale of terror caused widespread fear and consternation, as many of our more superstitious tars initiated a hasty sign-of-the-cross on their persons to drive off any lurking demon, ghost or witch. Chuckling to myself at their irrational fear, I returned to my cabin to continue finalizing plans to defeat my crafty and nefarious opponent. Later that evening, Pablo reported that a second pigeon had returned with a missive from Bunkey. The message was simple and straightforward in content. The precise translation was, "*South of Tortuga. No sign of enemy. Devilfish spotted and following its course*". I was not at all surprised by this strange account. You see, I had specifically instructed my men to keep a sharp eye out for this demonic creature, that was known to keep company with the Black Tarantula's vessel, in order to lead them to our foe's hiding place. Thanking Pablo, I returned to my plotting and scheming.

Early the next morning, a third pigeon arrived with further news from our scouts. Once again, Pablo arrived at my cabin clutching the small scrap of paper that had just been delivered. Clearing his throat nervously he translated his son's curt message. The exact words were, "*Devilfish led to small cove south of fortress. Two ships at anchor. Will proceed to investigate*." Immediately recognizing the insidious plot of my adversary, I summoned my commanders for a war council. Lion, Sharkface, Tan and Long Tall Willie appeared in no time at all, anxious to be versed on the latest news from the avian messenger. I had previously promoted both Tan and Long Tall Willie to positions of Captain and assigned them the responsibility for each of the two cleverly disguised imitation vessels. With all my leaders present, I laid out a carefully drawn map I had devised from my nautical charts to illustrate our specific plan of attack.

I had already briefed each of them on a general battle strategy based on the vital intelligence provided by Swamp Frog and Owl Eyes on our foe's characteristic combat tactics as well as the crucial knowledge of his unknown confederate. Now that I had the latest report confirming the villains' hiding place along with his fleet's strength, it was time to initiate our own response and retaliation. I slowly laid out the carefully planned trap that I had engineered to defeat the miscreants and rescue Rue. Each commander was issued a specific set of orders that included location, timing, target and an alternative course of action should all not proceed as I had envisioned.

Lion's objective was to circumnavigate *Neptune's Revenge* around Saint Domingue in order to approach the upcoming conflict from the east. Additionally, he was charged with blocking any and all enemy retreats. Tan and Long Tall Willie were commanded to approach the Tortuga fortress from the west. Once arrived and cleverly acting as our decoys, their mission was to engage and destroy the harbored vessel and the fortress's stairway access. In the meantime, Sharkface and I in *Rue's Revenge*, would trail behind to the west of the fortress and make our attack only when the time was judged right. To ensure that this complicated battle plan was executed to perfection, we reviewed and verbally rehearsed each step in the elaborate undertaking time and time again until each knew their role by complete chapter and verse as my deceased uncle, the Old Ghost, was fond of spouting!

Given that Lion required the most time to proceed to his assigned location, I dismissed him and wished him well. With a serious salute, he promised that *Neptune's Revenge* would execute orders to perfection and bid us all well wishes as he made his exit. Since we had a few days yet at our disposal, I urged my Captains to utilize this precious time to further drill their crews on the specific duties that soon would be required of them. With plans set and in motion, I awaited further intelligence from

Tiger Eyes through our winged messengers. Since I expected this word to arrive no sooner than the following day, I went up to the maindeck, assembled our shipboard band and proceeded to accompany them in a series of battle anthems aimed at bolstering the crew's morale and resolve.

The following morning, the last pigeon arrived and the news was swiftly brought to my attention. Tiger Eyes and team had successfully completed their reconnaissance mission and were now headed back to our position. This last missive read, "*Spanish Man-O-War commanded by old enemy, Captain Viola. Armed with thirty guns. Returning at once!*" The news on my long lost nemesis, Captain Viola surprised and astounded me greatly, as I had believed that I had seen the last of him on the snake-infested cove to our far south. He had somehow resurrected himself from the dead, taken command of yet another lethal combat vessel, joined forces with my arch-enemy and plotted to fully participate in our ultimate destruction and death! Had I not been forewarned by Owl Eyes, my fleet would have sailed unwittingly into an insidious trap and appeased my enemies' unabashed appetites for bloodshed, death and destruction! However, I still had a few devious tricks of my own.

Chapter 25: War Preparations Continue

The very next morning, Tiger Eyes and his scout team returned in their decrepit craft and were welcomed back with rousing shouts and calls from all aboard our ships. Alerting Sharkface, Tan and Long Tall Willie to prepare to sail the following day, I awaited my trusty scout to make his full report. Once onboard, I questioned him endlessly on any and all details I conceived, including any word on my beloved Rue. While his information was indeed detailed on our enemy's armament and crew size, he sadly divulged that he had no intelligence whatsoever on my captured lover. Deflated by this ill news, I nevertheless digested all of his keen observations before ordering he and his brave band of scouts to the galley for a warm meal and deserved rest. The remainder of that day was spent in making numerous trips to each of my ships to inspect for the last time the crucial preparations I had ordained.

That evening, I signaled Tan and Long Tall Willie to weigh anchor and proceed to their designated positions, which needed to be accomplished prior to the sun's appearance the following morning. Next, I issued orders to Sharkface to proceed at a leisurely pace northward, so that *Rue's Revenge* would also be in the proper position for combat engagement. I had previously conferred with Bottom Dog on the upcoming weather forecast and was gratified to learn that clear sky and calm weather were predicted by his joints which eased my dread that *dirty weather* would spoil our plans. Informing all to gird for battle, I returned to my cabin to nervously await the initiation of war.

Just prior to dawn on the day of Rue's promised deliverance, my vessel was anchored to the west of the southern tip of Tortuga awaiting a call to action. All sails were reefed with crewmembers standing by to unfurl and deploy them to initiate our advance at my given command. My positioning was purposeful as an isle's natural outcropping helped to mask our presence, while still providing an excellent view of the area surrounding the pirate's lair. Utilizing my scope at our protruding bow, I spotted our two French look-a-likes anchored offshore of the demon's fortress awaiting the arrival of full-light, which would serve as the agreed upon signal for the initiation of conflict. As I had decreed, their assignment was to anchor far enough offshore to avoid the deadly guns on the bluff, but close enough to allow catastrophic damage to both the anchored *Spider's Web* and the summit's stairway access. Their orders were simple; destroy the moored enemy and stone stairway. Once accomplished, they were commanded to remain anchored and wait for the anticipated arrival of the Black Tarantula and his Spanish confederate, sure to be alerted by the distinctive sounds of thunderous cannon roars that would travel fast and sure over water. It was my fervent hope that our two decoys would completely deceive the enemy reinforcements into believing that both *Revenges* were vulnerable to a surprise attack utilizing their superior firepower. In reality, my two replicas were merely acting as *staked goats* tempting the enemy forces to attack.

As daylight finally intensified, the battle commenced with our guns barking their ominous discharges. As I trained my scope on the scene, I was delighted to see that our comprehensive and diligent training proved invaluable as both of our ships scored direct hit after hit on the anchored enemy vessel, destroying its masts, yards and arms, relegating it powerless to maneuver. Once accomplished, the canon teams then concentrated on the vessel's lower decks and in unison sent wave after wave of leaded death into our now helpless enemy destroying and disabling a majority of their guns and unlucky crewmembers stationed aboard.

Once completed, our deadly grenado boats were ordered into action by a series of crisp drumbeat signals. These small messengers of death approached the stricken enemy and began their own furious assault on any pirate foolish enough to forsake cover. The devastation that ensued was both brutal and utterly extensive as the enemy vessel's return fire was summarily curtailed. As this all occurred, the fortress' battlement opened fire in an attempt to destroy my two pesky invaders. Per my stringent order, our two angels of death remained outside of their gun's range. While these stronghold cannons belched fire and smoke at our ships, their cannonballs fell harmlessly into the sea far short of their intended targets. Now finished with the counterfeit *Spider's Web*, our two vessels trained their cannons shoreward concentrating on the stone staircase supporting the only access up or down. With a series of well-aimed strikes, the guns pounded the stairway into oblivion, trapping the pirates stationed above and rendering them helpless and isolated.

Watching intently with my scope for the presence of enemy reinforcements, I observed the grenado boats returning to their ships, having dispatched the vast majority of piratical forces aboard the anchored ship. As I continued a close watch, I ordered our anchor raised in preparation of joining the party, which would begin as soon as the demon pirate and his Spanish toady made their appearance. Time passed excruciatingly slow during this wait and I began to fret that my adversaries had devised alternative plans. My apprehension was finally allayed when our topman sang out that sails approached. Breathing a huge sigh of relief, I continued my surveillance as I ordered our sails unfurled and felt our slow headway towards the approaching adversaries.

As we began to close the sizable gap before us, the Spanish *Man-O-War* raced forward to engage our two ships who had dared to initiate combat. This was the exact maneuver that I had anticipated, fully aware of the aggressive nature of Captain Viola coupled with the cowardly tendencies of the Black Tarantula. I continued to monitor the action as the Spaniard's numerous gunports slammed open and premature firings commenced. Since the Spanish behemoth was still out of effective firing range, I assumed that their strategy was to terrify their smaller and less powerful foes into submission, a true pirate tactic! As planned, our two ships prepared for the deadly assault by having armed all seaward guns while purposely keeping their gunport's shuttered in the face of the Spaniard's swift approach. I had also given emphatic orders that all crewmen on both vessels were to station themselves below deck at the first sighting of the enemy's approach to avoid needless injury or death. As the massive Spanish floating fortress continued to bear directly down on our smaller ships, their deadly shot inched closer and closer.

Both of our vessels remained quiet and almost oblivious to the approaching aggressor. Eventually, the Spaniard's barrage began to wreak serious damage on everything exposed on our ships. Our masts were shattered and destroyed raining sailcloth and splintered wood on the vacated lower decks. As I scrutinized this awesome display of sheer power, I noticed two things. The first was that the cowardly Black Tarantula remained a spectator to the action, as his dastardly crew on the maindeck continued their *vaporing*, cavorting and skylarking, to induce utmost terror and offer moral support to their more powerful ally. While the fiend could very well have spied our sails approaching which might have stalled his advance, my guess was he was merely playing the role of a consummate craven. The second occurred at the point when the Spaniard closed the gap to deliver final death blows to our helpless ships. Just then, I witnessed our gunports on both counterfeit vessels suddenly fly open. As the Spanish colossus wrecked continuing mortal damage, the numerous guns on both of our ships blazed a mighty salvo that sent a legion of chainshot into the upper regions of their harasser, ripping and rending their way through wood and canvas. A goodly portion of Spanish sails were virtually shredded into flapping rags in this initial volley along with the elimination of a bevy of wooden masts, yards and arms. This destruction resulted in a murderous rain of wooden death that descended down upon the unsuspecting Spanish pirates stationed topside, maiming or eliminating a prodigious score of them in the process. Per my strident orders another furious volley of mixed shot was then unleashed that further ripped, tore, splintered and destroyed additional Spanish sails, cables and wooden supports. Once completed, all of our offending gunports slammed shut on both vessels to avoid any direct shot from easily penetrating their gundecks. However, both of my decoy ships were now doomed as the infuriated Spanish giant continued its vicious cannon assault. Unable to maneuver easily due to the considerable loss of sail and riggings, the superior enemy continued to close on our helpless ships intent on boarding and massacring each and every one of its pesky adversaries. This was exactly the outcome I had planned for as a devious smile played across my face.

Continuing our advance, I was thankful to observe numerous grenado boats pulling away from each of our doomed ships, as the Spaniard launched wave after wave of grappling hooks. The Spaniard was quickly drawn alongside both of our vessels and an army of pirates descended down upon each deck. At this point, the plan I had concocted was quite simple. Remaining sheltered on the shoreward side of each ship, the musket teams fired shot after shot at the maddened Spanish boarders. Their work was efficient and deadly, as Spanish pirates were torn apart by both leaded shot and the multitude of lethal grenados landing in furious succession amongst them. As I had earlier predicted, the Black

Tarantula's *Spider's Web* remained rooted in place and far away from this bloody action, while its topside crew ceased their *vaporing* as they watched their allies now being torn apart.

Enraged by the wanton obliteration of his men, Captain Viola sent another horde of screaming marauders onto our two ships with orders, I was sure, to give no quarter or mercy. As this occurred, our grenado boats began a steady retreat from the fight, as they headed for the deeper safety of the enemy's cove despite the furious volleys of the fortress' cannons directly above them. I knew that our small launches made for extremely elusive and difficult targets so that the resulting bombardment provided only an unwelcomed bath for my tars as the enemy's shot splashed harmlessly in the surrounding sea. Far enough removed from the Spanish musketeers, too tiny to provide any real target for the fortress' guns and having destroyed the access stairwell, these small dinghies made their way further and further into the shelter of the pirate cove to await the next step in my insidious plan.

As I peered through my scope, I noted the sight of a multitude of bloodthirsty Spaniard's cavorting and dancing on the topdecks of our two stricken ships, as they celebrated their easy victory sending vicious jeers and taunts at our retreating longboats. Watching intently, I was delighted by the thunderous explosion that emanated from the bowels of both of our doomed vessels. These devastating blasts literally blew both of my decoy ships into minute splinters, as smoke and raging fires dominated the scene. When the bilious clouds of smoke began to clear, I was elated to discern that the Spanish *Man-O-War* had been critically wounded by this apocalyptical explosion. No longer tethered to its prey that had disintegrated in the cataclysmic detonation, the Spanish warship immediately began to list toward its severely damaged side as she took on gallons upon gallons of tropical seawater. Her fate was now sealed and her crew doomed. Several foolhardy souls abandoned their sinking ship intent on swimming to the safety of the nearby beach. However, this dream was rudely interrupted by our waiting grenado boats, as these craven deserters were riddled by savage volleys from our boat's muskets. The majority of the pirates, unable or unwilling to swim, crowded the upper deck racing from stem to stern like maddened curs in a burning kennel desperately seeking an avenue of escape.

Let me take a moment to explain the devious stratagem that I had employed. You see, I had ordered several special modifications made to both counterfeit ships to affect this deadly concussive result. Firstly, I had added secure locking mechanisms to every hatch and entranceway on both of my *tethered goats* to prevent enemy incursion below decks. As soon as any pirate reinforcements were sighted, my firm orders called for my crews to retreat to the lower decks to avoid being slaughtered by cannon or musket fire that was sure to follow. As they raced below, I entrusted several tars to effect temporary security for the lower decks by buttoning down all entranceways with the stout sliding iron bolts to defy our foe's immediate breeching. The false gunports on both ships were actually exit ports for my men sequestered below when the time was judged right. Rope ladders allowed my crews to climb safely down to the waiting grenado boats and make their escape. The last modification I had ordained was the addition of false wooden hulls on each vessel's lower larboardside decks. Between these additional oaken hulls, I had my crews cram them full of kegs of gunpowder that would transform each of my decoy ships into lethal fireships. Primed with a series of slow matches that could be easily reached through purposely drilled access holes, these man-made powder repositories provided the violent explosion that had crippled and doomed Spanish battleship.

Observing the stricken and mortally wounded Spanish vessel drift slowly in the prevailing currents as it continued its measured death plunge, I was extremely satisfied with the results I had so carefully plotted. Ordering all sails employed, we now flew at full speed at both the sinking Spaniard and the Black Tarantula's *Spider's Web*. As I continued my telescopic surveillance, I viewed a lone longboat launched from the Spanish *Man-O-War*. This small craft scuttled rapidly over to the Black Tarantula's craft, and its occupants were quickly hauled aboard. Even with the considerable distance still between us, I was able to determine the identity one of these fortunate Spaniards, Captain Ricardo Inez Viola. Not long after my enemy's retreat to safety, the topman on the *Spider's Web* spied our onrushing presence. At that point, any pretense of assisting further Spanish comrades was summarily abandoned, as the Black Tarantula's vessel took immediate flight heading due east as I had anticipated.

As soon as it was evident that the Spanish warship was doomed, every one of our grenado boats raced further out from the cove's shelter to continue their systematic elimination of desperate survivors either in the water or still clinging to its listing deck. Continuing my monitoring, I witnessed the grisly result of their ongoing attack as every Spanish pirate was eventually eliminated in a brutal and merciless manner. There would be no survivors of this conflict, and Satan would surely claim numerous new candidates for his legions of hell when the day had come to a close. Meanwhile, the stranded scum on the fortress' battlements had ceased their own dancing and skylarking as they stood transfixed keeping a close watch on their Spanish ally slipping slowly below the waves. Additionally, they fretfully witnessed their cowardly leader, the Black Tarantula, initiating his frantic retreat which left them abandoned to face their own doom.

Realizing at that instant that I had foolishly forgotten my deadly brace of throwing knives in my cabin, I hurried below to retrieve them. As I bustled into my cabin, I felt a presence materialize from behind the opened door before my world descended into utter darkness. When I slowly returned to consciousness, I discovered that each of my limbs seemed frozen and my vision remained terribly blurred. Any attempt to call for assistance proved utterly useless, as my mouth was crammed full of some unidentifiable fabric. As my vision began to slowly allow better definition of my immediate surroundings, I glimpsed some sort of dark shape prancing and dancing before me. Completely dazed and utterly confused, I had the impression that I was actually in a sitting position rather than laid out prone from my accidental tumble. As my mind and wits slowly cleared, I perceived a series of insane mumblings like those of a deranged lunatic voicing absolute nonsense. My vision finally returned and a quick assessment told me that I was secured tightly in one of my own cabin's chairs, completely immobilized. Standing before me was an odd figure dressed entirely in black dancing a sailor's jig around my cabin while mumbling nonsensical phrases that I found impossible to comprehend. As the creature became aware of my return to consciousness, the deranged jester leaned in close repeating my name over and over.

Shaking the remaining cobwebs from my mind, I took a closer look at my tormentor. As I had previously perceived, he was garbed entirely in filthy black rags that were coated with all imaginable manner of crud and corruption. While he was a somewhat sizable specimen, he cavorted in a strange hunched manner that disguised his true stature. His face was contorted in a mask of insane fury with red glaring eyes that bespoke utter madness. He sported an angry and wicked looking scar that adorned the entire left side of his face, running somewhat horizontally from his mangy hairline across to his jutted chin. Realizing that I had gained my full senses, he whispered that I had reached the end of my miserable existence. Unable to respond to this mad threat because of the foul rag that had been stuffed down my gullet, I shifted left and right to avoid the noxious aroma that emanated from his grinning drool-filled lips. Understanding my inability to respond, he issued a series of low grunts and groans that I found to be impossible to discern. Leaning in yet closer, he hoarsely murmured that his name was Dizzy Jeffers, brother of my departed enemy, Hurricane Jeffers, the Black Tarantula's deceased First Mate. Salivating like a hound about to savor a meat-laden bone, he explained that his sole mission in life was to extract revenge for my ill treatment and subsequent death of his dear departed sibling. Instantly aware that I was in extreme mortal danger, I made a brief scan of my cabin for any sort of weapon I could employ to save myself. Sensing my purpose, the demented knave gave another maniacal leer before extracting one of my poisoned throwing knives from my brace that was now strapped around his ponderous gut. Providing a truly rabid grin, he snarled that he had located my fancy little weapons and now planned to employ them to dice me into fish-bait. His threat was entirely believable, since I knew that only a minute nick from one of these dirks would spell my everlasting doom.

Nodding my reluctant understanding, I raised my brows silently questioning how he had successfully managed to sneak into my cabin. His unhinged mind seemed to grasp my query and he launched into a rambling explanation. Continually gibbering and drooling, he confessed that he had stolen aboard while our vessel had been anchored off Saint Domingue. Since that time, he had patiently concealed himself inside the dark and damp depths of our ship's bilge, avoiding all contact with my crew. Realizing that the entire ship was quite preoccupied with numerous chores, battle preparations and combat drills, I was not in the least surprised that a stealthy stowaway could manage to avoid detection under these frantic circumstances. He continued his confession by informing me that our hulking cook had nearly discovered his loathsome hiding place inadvertently on more than one occasion, but *Lady Luck* had smiled on him as nobody had detected his most unwelcome presence. Continuing in a daft manner, he divulged that he had been forced to wait patiently until the order for battle had been announced. In the chaotic confusion that ensued, the fiend had snuck his way like a poisonous serpent into my cabin to await my eventual return. Grinning maniacally and issuing a huge slobbering drool, the villain announced that it was now time for me to die!

Prior to initiating further action, Dizzy stopped abruptly and stared dully in my direction. He then acknowledged that his illustrious leader lusted at the opportunity to end my life. He divulged that he was totally unaware of his leader's motives or the reasons behind the primal hate and anger he held for me. Nevertheless, he confessed that the action of taking my life would draw the extreme rancor of his pirate Captain. He spouted that he was totally aware that he would face a most unpleasant punishment for his unsanctioned attack, and that he expected his castigation to be quite harsh and atrocious in nature. Regardless, he was steadfast in his plan to eliminate me. Seemingly pleased and immensely enjoying my palpable terror, the insane cur suddenly revealed that his dead brother had confided in him that their skipper had once bragged about murdering a helpless relative of mine. Confused mightily by this bewildering admission, I raised both my brows signaling abject befuddlement in the hope of eliciting further scuttlebutt from my tormentor.

Somehow understanding this silent signal, Dizzy retorted that he had no idea what his Captain meant by the disclosure. Continuing, he did admit that I had been ordered consummately off-limits under the threat of horrendous reprisal and resulting mortal pain and suffering for deliberate disobedience of his maniacal Captain's mandate. Then, the crazy fool lapsed into uncontrollable shrieks of laughter citing that his disregard and defiant insubordination was absolutely necessary in order to avenge his brother's murder. He then boldly announced that the Black

Tarantula would only savor a lone murder within my family, since he was committed to ending my miserable life on his own volition.

The grinning madman then switched subjects and began to ramble about the plight of my lover, Rue, as he continued to frolic about my cabin. He suddenly ceased this manic activity and blurted out that he was certain that I would never again see my beloved alive, since his demonic Captain had no intention of ever returning her to me despite any of his deceitful promises. Like previous informants, Dizzy explained that the Black Tarantula had no real or special interest in Rue, and had taken her prisoner in order to torment and torture her in the hope of drawing me into his filthy clutches. Dizzy confessed that he and the entire crew were quite awed by the wench's strength of will, as she quietly and heroically withstood the horrendous treatment and the vicious torture to which she had routinely been subjected. Promising me with a gleeful squeal that the doxy was in all probability dead, he seriously advised me to forget her and concentrate on my upcoming demise.

As the unhinged tar slowly raised my knife up to my blinking eyes, a sudden pounding began at my cabin door. Since Dizzy had judiciously wedged a spare chair under the entryway, access had been intentionally denied. The unidentified crewman pounding on the door and shouting my name seemed quite confused by his inability to enter and continued to hammer at the door while roaring for me to respond. Dizzy's insanity cleared momentarily and he recognized his present danger. Pressing the sharp dirk against my throat, he cautioned me to remain still and not ruin his plans. Whispering in my ear, he demanded that I send away the nuisance banging mechanically at the door or suffer my throat being slit.

Aware that the dagger at my throat was laced with instant incurable death, I compliantly nodded my acceptance of his stringent demand. Holding the blade firmly against my throat, he yanked the filthy rag out of my mouth. Gasping and clearing my throat, I shouted to my concerned mate, who I recognized as Sharkface, that I would return topside momentarily. Continuing, I commanded that all haste be made to close the distance between us and the enemy's vessel. Whooping his excited agreement, I heard Sharkface stomp away to fulfill my order. Aware that even the slightest pinprick from the knife at my throat would prove lethal, I let my eyes drift over to the wedged door, while monitoring my wily opponent out of the corner of my eye. Curious as to the reason behind my purposeful shift in gaze, Dizzy altered his scrutiny and took a few steps in that same direction. Given this brief opportunity, I utilized my *special voice* to project a vocalization that sounded like it had originated from the opposite darkened corner of my cabin. In Hurricane's distinctive voice, I proclaimed Dizzy's name over and over.

Recognizing his dead brother's familiar tone, the deranged pirate eased the blade from my throat and moved in the direction of his brother's voice. Continuing, I curtly questioned the lunatic on his intentions. In a quaking croak, the dimwit responded that he was about to revenge my untimely death at the hands of the cringing coward seated before him. Aware that I had little room for error, I shouted out to Dizzy that as a departed brother I was extremely gratified by his demonstrated loyalty. I urged the slobbering imbecile to proceed with his work with utmost patience so as to inflict the most grievous and agonizing injuries possible before relegating his victim to *Davy Jones Locker*. Salivating freely again at the opportunity to initiate his fun, Dizzy dutifully nodded to the empty darkened corner where he believed his brother's ghostly spirit was communicating with him.

Continuing in Hurricane's clear commanding voice, I questioned the simpleton on the sharpness of the blade he was sporting. To complete the task right, I announced that the dagger must be honed to razor sharpness in order to neatly slice away thin layers of his victim's flesh. Confused to the extreme, the dimwitted dolt just stared vacantly into the empty dark corner, unsure of his next move. Taking this opportunity and using his brother's harsh gravely tone, I shouted that he needed to test the weapon for keenness prior to initiating his vicious fun. Confounded again, Dizzy remained rooted in place awaiting further clarification. In an unrestrained roar, I ordered the dunce to run the blade over his own palm to determine if the weapon was suitable for the task at hand. Dutifully obedient to his brutish brother, Dizzy ran the blade across his palm instantly drawing a thin red line of blood. Gibbering with delight at discovering the knife's keenness, the idiot turned back in my direction to initiate his unholy butchering.

As he turned back to me, Dizzy suddenly stumbled and seemed to temporarily lose his balance. I was quite heartened by the potent effects of my virulent herbal concoction. In no time at all, the villain was experiencing significant difficulty with any sort of movement. Confused and concerned at the numbness spreading over this frame, he attempted to lift the sharp blade towards my neck, only to discover that his arms no longer responded. Additionally, he experienced disconcerting difficulties breathing as he gasped and gulped in a terrifying battle to inhale fresh air. With his entire being now frozen and unwilling to respond, his eyes registered complete panic and confusion. Staring fixedly at me, I responded by ordering the fool to die in his brother's own voice. With a mask of furious recognition emerging on his face, he slumped down and then completely collapsed to the cabin's deck as his life slowly ebbed away. In no time at all, he was dead and now free to join his malicious brother in hell.

With this odious moron dispatched, I began to vociferously call for immediate assistance. Sharkface and several burly crewmen forced their way into my cabin to discover my predicament. Confused by my trussed plight and the dead filthy pirate lying at my feet, they quickly untied me. I shouted that I would explain the complete tale some other time, as I hurried over and stripped Dizzy of my precious blades. With no time to spare, I bounded through the door and raced to the upperdeck to survey our situation. My mind, however, was still fixated on Dizzy's statement concerning the Black Tarantula's confessed murder of a relative of mine. This was the second reference to a death of someone quite dear to me at the hands of this monster. Assuming the admission was once again in reference to Powder Monkey, I realized that the only true answer to the dilemma would need to come from the beast himself. As I raced upward, I heard the distinctive sound of cannon fire signaling that Lion had entered the fray! With the scope trained on the horizon, I spied a pair of sails some distance away. Since we were already at full sail, all we could do was continue our breakneck course as we edged closer and closer to our target.

As I glanced around our ship, I noticed Tiger Eyes making a sheepish approach. He wore a strange and guilt-laden expression on his face, and appeared nervous and agitated as he skittered from side-to-side waiting to open a discussion with me. Since we were about to enter full battle mode, I realized that whatever was on his mind had to be important and deadly serious in nature. Turning in his direction, I questioned what was on his mind. Hesitating, he explained that he had not been completely forthright on all of the details concerning his recent scouting mission. Urging him to hurriedly continue, Tiger Eyes apologized continually for his omissions which he now needed to detail. Realizing that our time was short, I pressed my loyal crewman to divulge his deep dark secret.

Before initiating his confession, I stole a quick glance at our situation. Lion and my enemy's vessels were furiously spitting cannonballs at one another in frenetic fashion. Lion had launched his grenado boats, and I could discern that they were harassing the infamous pirate ship in the midst of the lead barrage. Since the wind was optimal, our full sails continued to push us rapidly in the direction of the conflict. Additionally, the enemy's crew was completely enmeshed in battle and had either opted to ignore our expeditious approach or had yet to spy our advance. Turning my full attention back to Tiger Eyes, I urged him to articulate his pressing concern.

Providing another baleful stare, my loyal tar divulged that he had been less than truthful on the details he had reported concerning Rue. Urging him to explain, he heaved a protracted sigh and launched into the particulars of his dilemma. He confessed that during a nighttime encounter with the enemy, his entire scouting party had been subjected to a series of inhuman cries denoting extreme suffering and pain coming from the Black Tarantula's schooner. Pressing on, he explained that the source of the mournful howls was certainly recognizable as female in origin. Since the entire party was aware of Rue's predicament, they had decided in unison to omit this awful detail from their report in order to spare me further grief and consternation. Fighting off a rising wave of anger and disgust, I promptly thanked him for the kind consideration he and his mates had shown. I then promised that the evil tormentor of my innocent lover would soon be punished severely for his crimes. Relieved at my nonchalant acceptance of his dreadful intelligence, I calmly ordered him to his battle station as we sped closer and closer to the heart of the hostility. Vowing in my heart to end this conflict once and for all, I steeled myself for war.

Utilizing my telescope, I was dismayed to discover that an unlucky shot had struck Lion's mainmast, severing this vital component in two. With his navigation sharply hampered, Lion continued the fight although the outcome now appeared quite foreboding. Following my specific orders, he patiently waited for our arrival while his vessel was being fragmentized. Shouting terse commands to ready our guns with chainshot, to prepare all grenado boats for action and to load our deck grenado catapults, we bore directly down on the scurvy scum bent on death and destruction. No quarter! No mercy!

Chapter 26: A Demon Pirate's Demise

Hefting my scope once again as we flew expeditiously onward, I witnessed my adversary continue his heated exchange with *Neptune's Revenge*. As I had previously deduced, the opposition's guns had placed Lion's vessel in an extremely precarious predicament. From our considerable distance, I confirmed that my sister ships' navigation abilities had indeed been seriously reduced as the demon's guns continued to pulverize it.

Calling Pablo's son, Bunkey to my side, I gave him an order to send a message to his father stationed on *Neptune's Revenge*. The missive was intended for Lion with strict orders to counterattack with all guns to hold his foe's complete attention and allow us to continue our stealthy approach. Once we sailed into view, he was commanded to then turn tail and beat a hasty retreat. Bunkey jotted the missive and released the pigeon which dutifully flew swiftly ahead of us to convey my message. As soon as word reached Lion, he obliged by issuing intense renewed aggression, as a furious cannon and grenado barrage suddenly erupted from his vessel surprising and confounding his aggressor. Not to be outdone, the devilish pirate retaliated with his own mindless onslaught which was exactly the reaction I had hoped for! As this hostility was occurring, we continued to bear down relentlessly like an avenging angel prepared to indiscriminately deliver fire and brimstone to all quarters. Grateful to Lion for keeping our nemesis occupied, we arrived at last. At that moment, the pirates finally detected our surprising presence, but by then it was far too late. Adroitly positioning our vessel, we unleashed hell's fury upon our despicable foe. Our guns roared in unison as we neatly broadsided the *Spider's Web* with a furious barrage of deadly grapeshot and chainshot that wreaked extensive havoc to our foe's topside, obliterating a slew of sails, masts and riggings. Like *Neptune Revenge*, the Black Tarantula's navigational abilities had now been severely curbed.

As we passed unhampered, the enemy's gunports facing us sprung open as the fiend's guncrews shifted positions in order to countermand our surprise attack. Meanwhile, I spied Lion moving away from the conflict as swiftly as his damaged vessel would allow. Simultaneously, my crew topside launched a cluster of deadly grenadoes to cause further death and destruction to our now crippled nemesis. While the grenado launchers thrummed a welcomed cadence, our musketeers harassed any foolhardy adversary who dared to make a topside appearance.

As we cleared our enemy's vessel, I ordered the launching of our lethal grenado boats to assist in our savage engagement with the pirate spawn. Utilizing terse drum commands, I coordinated both launched longboats along with Lion's previously dispatched crafts to perform a series of well-coordinated strikes on the now severely impaired *Spider's Web*. Operating like an angry horde of bloodsucking insects, these wee ketches stung and retreated again and again, successfully eliminating a slew of pirate adversaries. These miniature death merchants were too small and agile for any sort of effective enemy counterattack, as they merrily danced on the water easily avoiding the errant cannonshot delivered against them by our frustrated foe. Meanwhile, the grenado launchers on these boats were kept fully employed as they delivered their highly explosive charges onto the ship's topdeck as well as into any opened gunports. Once delivered, these iron fragmented clouds of destruction flew in all directions mutilating, rending and destroying all targets in their path. Our opposition's war chants and cries soon reverted into wails of pain and agony as our attack intensified. Due to the copious blood-spill, their topdeck seemed to transform into a crimson pool that shifted from side-to-side following the motions of the current and waves. A few foolish, but brave souls, attempted to scale the tattered riggings to attempt hasty repairs on their damaged sails. These cretins became live targets for our sharpshooting musketeers, who systematically dispatched these vermin and forced them to perform comical yet fatal dives onto their decks or into the surrounding sea. Concurrently, I witnessed Lion nursing *Neptune's Revenge* into greater motion in his attempt to escape further damage. While his ship's movement was ponderous and halting, I knew that in a short while he would be entirely free from the deadly predicament he had faced moments ago.

During our meticulous attack, I also beheld a monstrous black shape racing toward one of our nearby grenado boats. Unaware of the creature's advance, the beast rose swiftly to the surface and launched itself out of the water landing directly onto the much smaller ketch. As the demon crashed down onto the sea's surface, it smothered the grenado boat and began to drag both the boat and its unlucky crew down to their deaths. A moment later, the sea surrounding the doomed longboat erupted in a furious flume, spraying seawater along with huge chunks of the demon's flesh far and wide. Given the absolute power of the blast, the filthy monster's internals began raining down indiscriminately upon us. The scattering of this bloody viscera drew an immediate audience of hungry predators anxious for a delectable meal. Hazarding a guess, I surmised that one or more of our grenadoes had been lit prior to the fiendish devilfish's attack. These grenadoes had in all likelihood ignited disemboweling and obliterating the leviathan and consigning it to a watery grave, certainly without the traditional thirteen stitches! Disheartened by the loss of our grenado boat's crew, I turned back to the battle at hand intent on gaining revenge for these poor lost souls.

Continuing the onslaught, we made several more passes on our floundering foe and continued to pour copious cannonshot into viable targets aboard their craft. At last, it seemed as if they had run out of pirate crewmen, as a ghostly silence descended over our battered and pummeled nemesis. Realizing the opportunity that now presented itself, I made preparations to board our opposition and rescue Rue. As I prepared my boarding party, I issued specific orders to proceed cautiously given our foe's disreputable nature. Summoning a nearby grenado boat, my incursion contingent climbed aboard for a short journey over to our enemy. As we made our way onboard the infamous *Spider's Web*, we met little resistance as the vessel was deathly still, a floating graveyard for sure! There continued to be little signs of life as we cautiously crept along her topdeck. I proceeded toward the ship's stern and targeted entry at the quarterdeck's hatchway. As my men advanced, they encountered horribly maimed and critically wounded enemy survivors, who were swiftly dispatched and sent to Satan as fresh troops.

Dodging any of the scum's remains along my path, I reached the quarterdeck's hatchway which would provide access to my enemy's lair. As I neared, I was met by a giant masquerading as a pirate who had appeared out of nowhere. He was more than three times my size with bulging musculature on all ports. The villain was bald, save a long braided queue that hung down to below his waist. His terrifying leer displayed an absence of the majority of his teeth with the distinct exception of two golden upper fangs that only added to his overall menacing appearance. The upper region of his mammoth frame was adorned with a series of pagan tattoos that seemed to wriggle and slither as he flexed his ponderous muscles. With a malicious grin, the scoundrel informed me that my journey had come to an end and my right to proceed below had been revoked. Smiling cruelly, I advanced on the brute in a mindless rage, aware that this menacing obstacle needed dispatching so that I could finally reach and rescue Rue. With a roar resembling a savage beast, the giant rushed to meet my advance as our cutlasses collided midair ringing out the news that a serious engagement was underway.

With my sword hand practically paralyzed from this initial violent clash, I stepped back to reassess my foe. Perceiving my movement to be one of retreat, the creature unleashed another mighty bellow and rushed forward on the attack. Out of sheer self-preservation, I ducked under his whistling blade, that surely would have decapitated me. I then dove neatly through his spread legs and somersaulted to my feet to face the behemoth once more. By now our battle had drawn the attention of my boarding party, who began hooting and hollering their encouragements. While my loyal mates could have easily entered the fray at any time, they chose to remain neutral and enjoy the show, trusting in my combat abilities which I had routinely demonstrated during our onboard battle practices. Realizing now that my slim advantage of speed and agility would soon succumb to his inhuman strength, I gazed around for an alternative means of defeating this colossal barricade. Spying a dangling cable that hung limply from an above spar, I began formulating a plan of action. All the while, I was forced to dodge and evade his numerous murderous advances. I sensed that my energy was waning due to this strenuous effort, while my men continued to delight watching the deadly dance I was performing. I briefly considered calling on their assistance but my stubborn pride seemed to stand in the way of doing so. However, given the size and strength of my opponent, I reasoned that loss of pride was a far better alternative than loss of life.

Deciding to forestall a call for aid and realizing that strong measures were essential to my survival, I reached down into my herbal wallet around my waist and extracted a powdery substance. As the crazed brute executed his next lunge, I blew this powder directly into his face while executing another proficient dive through the beast's opened legs. The powdered lime I had utilized served its purpose as the villain screamed that he had been blinded and clawed savagely at his two stricken orbs. Taking advantage of this respite, I wrapped several revolutions of the dangling rope around the blind giant's neck and managed to dart away before his flailing cutlass could cleave me in two. Struggling to free himself from the offending cable and raging about his blindness, the leviathan was quite preoccupied as he performed a comical jig of absolute frustration. Utilizing this lull, I managed to score several vicious slashes to his immense torso before he began to recover his senses.

Wounded, irate and blinded, the monster forgot about the cord around his neck and made a frenzied rush in the direction of my taunting voice. Retreating away from this charging bull, I backed into the gunwale and clambered atop continuing to taunt the beast all the way. As my opponent closed, I executed a perfect dive over his head and somersaulted safely onto the deck. My foe's furious momentum could not be checked, and he slammed into the deckrail and flipped over the vessel's side. The rough noose I had secured around his ponderous throat remained in place as the miscreant plunged seaward unimpeded. When the cable line eventually tautened, the behemoth's downward progress was immediately halted in a clamorous snap as he frantically dangled and fidgeted for freedom while slowly suffocating. His struggles seemed to take forever but finally his frantic efforts to free himself ceased, and he joined his deceased comrades in hell to the absolute delight of my supporting spectators. With nothing now impeding my forward progress, I raced to the hatchway and entered the sanctuary of my archenemy.

Once below, I raced down the darkened passageway intent on destroying the sinister beast and liberating Rue. As I made my way along the inky-black and filth-strewn corridor, I was assailed by an awful odor. In truth, it was worse than any Londontown cesspool! Actually, this noxious reek had a distinct resemblance to that of the scorched flesh of a suckling pig and permeated the entirety of the lower decks. Breathing through my gullet to circumnavigate these putrid fumes, I adjusted my night sight in the enveloping darkness as I crept toward the Captain's cabin. As I continued my stealthy approach, I finally reached the door of the demon's lair and barged into the room.

Chapter 27: Secrets Revealed

Like the corridor I has just traversed, the cabin was quite dark and shadowy with only a few miniature candles illuminating its sparse interior. Glancing around, I noticed that the rear galley windows of this stygian chamber had been purposely boarded shut by seemingly damaged and rotted boards, that allowed only scattering snatches of natural light to penetrate the inky cabin's gloom. It seemed odd to me that the Black Tarantula would prefer continual darkness in his private abode, but then nothing concerning this villain seemed to resemble normalcy. As my night vision began to adjust, the entry door was slammed shut behind me and I heard a privacy bolt being noisily thrown. Turning in that direction, I found myself facing a trio of scurvy rascals, who were openly grinning at the predicament into which I had stumbled. Blinking in surprise that anyone had survived our vicious attack, I immediately recognized the leader of this motley crew as he stepped forward into the weak candlelight, Captain Ricardo Viola. Leering at me like a glutton prepared to devour a sumptuous meal, my Spanish foe barked out a cruel laugh, and with a sweeping bow welcomed me aboard the infamous pirate ship.

Aware that Viola or his two toadies might attack at any moment, I drew two of my deadly throwing knives sheathing my cutlass in the process. Snickering like a condemned madman, the Spanish villain confessed that he and his men had been ordered not to engage but instead guard against any interruptions from my fellow boarders. Pointing at the far side of the Black Tarantula's cabin, Captain Viola informed me that his leader would soon be available for our reckoning. At the same time, he expressed grave misgivings at not being allowed to slaughter me outright for the vile deception I had engineered that had placed he and his crew on the snake and bug infested atoll so long ago. He divulged that my nefarious deception had eventually been responsible for the horrible deaths of the majority of his loyal crewmates including his beloved uncle. As such, he hungered for the opportunity to repay me for all of the pain and suffering I had caused.

As he persisted with his mindless palaver relating the horrific details of his ordeal and eventual escape from the isle's clutches, he continually glanced over to the darkest side of this abominable dungeon that I had imprudently invaded. Following his crazed gaze, I noticed with my acute night vision that this area was comprised of a series of diminutive stalls like that of a miniature livery stable. There were a total of seven of these stalls in all. Each of these enclosures was equipped with a pair of dangling manacles attached to upper beams along with a matching pair of leg irons secured to the floorboards. Six of these wooden chambers appeared quite empty while the furthest unit was blocked from scrutiny by a filthy hanging sailcloth screen that was stretched across its mouth. As I continued to stare, I noticed that the wooden floors and bulkheads of these mysterious structures were stained a dark hue which I guessed was the result of serious blood loss from previous occupants. Suddenly realizing I was witnessing the private torture chamber of the Black Tarantula, I shuddered at the possibility of being shackled and secured in one of these miniature prisons at the total mercy of the bloodthirsty beast who claimed this floating dungeon as his own hell on earth. As I continued my hasty surveillance, I thought I detected the muffled groans and whimpers of a suffering unfortunate in extreme agony and distress. Since these horrific cries and moans seemed to emanate from behind the curtained cell, I was unable to determine their exact source. However, I judged that this screened torture chamber doubtlessly held my beloved, and I began cogitating a means of rescuing her from her dreadful plight.

Still rooted maniacally in place, Captain Viola continued his rant by bellowing that only three members of his original contingent escaped the horrors of his island prison. Rescued by a passing Spanish trader, he had since slaved unceasingly to regain the power and wealth he had once enjoyed. Summoned eventually by the Black Tarantula with promises of fortune and renewed privileges, the maniacal Spaniard boasted that he had joined forces with the Scourge of Caribbean to plunder and savage any innocents who unwittingly blundered into their hands. Together, they had liberated the *Man-O-War* that I had ingeniously destroyed by the use of my duplicitous *fireships*. Grinning evilly like an aroused serpent, the brigand confessed that he owed a great debt of gratitude to his new leader, who had virtually resurrected him from the ranks of the dead.

As I continued to survey my bleak surroundings and contemplated an avenue to reach Rue, both of Captain Viola's deranged animals decided to take matters into their own hands and made an unprovoked rush intent on cleaving me into bits of flesh and bone with their flashing sabers. Sensing this unsanctioned charge, I unleashed my poison dirks, skewering both renegades hilt-deep in their chests. Stumbling from my vicious blows, the scoundrels vainly attempted to dislodge my blades. Before they could manage even this, the *creeping death* lathered on the intruding blades took effect as the brigands dropped to their knees and began to jerk and writhe before expeditiously collapsing face down on the filthy floorboards, inert and unmoving. Captain Viola turned each over to investigate their injuries and roared that the simpleminded fools were dead. Stunned into terrified inertness by their prompt parting, Captain Viola remained frozen in terror and confusion, unable to perpetuate further aggression or retaliation. Eventually leering diabolically after gaining a measure of false courage, my Spanish foe promised that I would soon earn my just rewards for the slaughter of his mates by outright witchcraft.

As he concluded this idle threat, the curtain covering the end stall parted slightly and a true specter of death emerged. While I had been informed through numerous eyewitnesses of the Black Tarantula's unequivocal abhorrent and disgusting appearance, nothing could have prepared me for the gruesome nightmare that now materialized before my eyes. Frocked entirely in black from head-to-toe, this living demon closed the curtain and scuttled his way towards me in a series of odd lurching motions. Once he entered the dim candlelight, I could discern that his entire ebony ensemble was exceedingly filth-covered. The fiend was caked with bits of gore and grisly debris, which presumably accounted for the appalling odor that accompanied his every movement. Bowing as low as his deformed anatomy would allow, the demon formally welcomed me to his humble hellish abode. Since he sported the famous ghastly black mask that I had been forewarned about, it was impossible to judge the true meaning behind his beguiling offer of hospitality, but I nevertheless had a distinct impression that it spelled nothing but doom.

At that very moment, a thunderous pounding came from the bolted entryway announcing the arrival of members of my boarding party. Untroubled by this inconvenient interruption, my hideous host pointed in the direction of the opposite darkened corner of his wretched abyss and demanded that I take careful stock of the surprise he had devised for any uninvited intruders. Leveling my gaze in the direction indicated, I caught sight of a slew of stacked powder kegs with loose black powder sprinkled liberally over this entire deadly stockpile. Shocked by my discovery of this dangerous accumulation, I returned my full attention to my loathsome host. In a growling voice straight from the lower environs of Hades, the Black Tarantula croaked, that should we be disturbed in any manner, his loyal partner had been instructed to ignite the powder and blow the vessel and everyone aboard into infinitesimal fragments of blood, flesh and bone!

Realizing the legitimacy of his claim, I responded to the frenzied shouts and poundings of my men by emphatically commanding them to abandon ship, pursue our retreating sister ship and assist in tending their wounded and injured. Initially reluctant to obey, my rescuers shouted questions challenging my decree. With a feigned carefree voice, I confided that all was in order and that Lion required their vital assistance immediately. Continuing, I announced that my work aboard would conclude shortly and that I would soon reunite with them. Grumbling their many concerns through the locked doorway, I heard my intended saviors eventually retreat back to the vessel's upperdeck to fulfill my strident commands.

Cackling in an obscene manner after their retreat, the Black Tarantula sternly ordered Captain Viola to remain stationary and not interfere further with the business between us. With a truly saddened expression, the degenerate Spaniard unsheathed his saber and moved over in front of the curtained enclosure effectively cutting off any rescue attempt on my part. Turning back to me, the black-cladded fiend formally welcomed me aboard his ship addressing me as Echo Eden and not Captain William Bilge, which shocked me to my very core. The odious rogue opened by complimenting me on my battle strategy in utilizing the two French decoys to lure he and his Spanish partner into attacking these cleverly disguised *fireships*. Still a mite stunned that he was aware of my ancient landlubbing moniker, I impatiently questioned him on Rue's whereabouts, as I glanced in the direction of the curtained chamber. Chuckling evilly, he confided that the courageous lass was indeed nearby and our joyful reunion was close at hand. Unsatisfied by this snide response, I inquired about his motives for harming the helpless young lass. With an insane outburst of glee, he taunted that I should know full well the answer to my own question. Deciphering the ultimate confusion written across my face, the Black Tarantula adopted an entirely new tack by demanding why I had failed to recognize him as an old comrade. Since I had no idea what he was referring to, I confessed to a serious lapse of memory. Reaching under his repugnant cloak, he extracted a foul and revolting red rag which he proceeded to hold out for my closer examination. Still stymied by his games, I responded that I had no clue as to his identity, while demanding that my beloved be released immediately. Shaking with sinister merriment, the madman raised the filthy red scrap of cloth to his face. A moment passed before the dreadful recollection dawned on me, Scarf Rockingham!

Upon this insane revelation, my mind underwent a series of jumbled thoughts. *No, No, No, Impossible, Unbelievable, Inconceivable, Unthinkable, No, No, No*! These were the raging sentiments that echoed again and again in my mind. This was surely a nightmare of the worst sort, and I prayed that I would awaken soon from this bedeviling dream. I knew in my heart that there could be no way that my old nemesis had escaped death after our monumental battle eons ago. Consequently, my mind clouded over and my breathing seemed to still attempting to process this startling discovery. Everything around me seemed to go deathly quiet and exceedingly still as I pondered the Black Tarantula's astonishing revelation, or should I say Scarf Rockingham's confession. While my old nemesis was surely capable of the numerous atrocities attributed to this demon pirate, the concept that Scarf and the Black Tarantula were one-in-the-same was certainly incredulous and seemingly beyond the bounds of possibility, a tale worthy of a child's wildest fantasy. Yet, the devil dressed entirely in black standing before me proffering my archenemy's moldering red scarf had declared this fairy tale to be true.

Sensing my extreme consternation, the devil began rattling off a series of facts that only my boyhood nemesis would have known. He trilled that he had used leeches to punish little Billy Wilder. He also informed me that my closest kin were a brother named Toby and an ancient half-blind Uncle, who served as some sort of ecclesiastic at Saint Agnes' Basilica. Not done yet, he giggled as he taunted that the aged clergyman had met his end by a series of malicious stabbings performed with a small penknife that bore my name. Stopping for a brief moment, he inquired if I needed further proof of his outrageous claim.

Without waiting for my answer, he reached into his despicable robe and extracted a small item which he tossed in my direction. Snagging this offering mid-air, I held it up to the weak light for examination. What I discovered upon scrutiny sent me further into a dazzled state as I effortlessly recognized the tiny penknife gifted to my brother, Toby, by our mutual friend, Handy. This knife I held before me bore the crude etching of my brother's name and for the moment I was again caught in the same waking nightmare.

No, No, No, Impossible, Unbelievable, Inconceivable, Unthinkable, No, No, No! In spite of these strenuous mental denials, the evidence was quite clear. The villainous pirate standing before me was in reality Scarf Rockingham, the Black Tarantula! With his heinous truth revealed and acceptance of this monstrous confession slowly sinking into my frazzled brain, all I could conceive in my delirious state was that this nightmare required a hasty ending in a most permanent fashion.

Still entirely flabbergasted by his ugly revelation, I questioned how he had managed to survive our last hand-to-hand battle at Slugger's Emporium. In a grisly and spiteful tone, he informed me that a guardian angel had rescued him from certain death after being dumped half-dead into the Thames by Slugger's goons. This angel of mercy had tended his numerous injuries and had painstakingly nursed him back to full health. Mentally postulating the baleful fate of this *Good Samaritan*, I once again questioned what he wanted from me since our childhood feud had ended many years in the past. Screaming in utter rage that our hostility had never culminated, he divulged that my timely death would settle the matter once and for all. Reminding him that he had murdered both my uncle and brother in cold-blood, I questioned why he felt so obligated to continue our quarrel with another innocent life hanging in the balance. Sputtering now with abject incomprehension, he confessed, that while had had indeed slaughtered the useless old blind goat, that I alone was responsible for my brother's demise.

Dumbfounded by this statement, I responded that I had found the grave that he had directed me to, but sadly all that it contained were the rotting remains of a stranger and certainly not those of my brother, Toby. Laughing maniacally, he explained that I had unearthed the wrong grave.

Confused and completely stymied, I challenged his exact meaning. Taking a step closer, Scarf challenged me to think back on my discovery in the London graveyard so many years ago. I immediately responded that the grave I had desecrated bore a headstone with the name of Toby and an inscription that read, "*He got what he deserved*". Once unearthed, I related that I had wrongly desecrated this tiny gravesite only to reveal the remains of the unrecognizable rotting corpse. Snickering with delight, Scarf challenged why I had neglected to spot the final piece of the puzzle. Shocked by his revelation, I thought back but could not recall any additional signs or clues that he had just mentioned. Sensing my utter bewilderment, Scarf poured out a few more of the gory details. It seemed that he had indeed buried my brother alive in that very graveyard that I had performed my wrongful defilement. He crowed that he had provided me all of the necessary clues to assist me in saving Toby's life, but I had failed miserably in my assigned task.

As he took careful stock of my addled demeanor, my lifelong enemy spouted that perhaps it was the right time to revisit the demise of Toby Eden. Sensing my outright irritation, he turned to his stationary Spanish partner guarding my only avenue of escape or rescue and questioned if he might be interested in listening to a story of a young scamp who got exactly what he deserved. Upon hearing these timeworn words uttered in such a disingenuous and duplicitous manner, I moved to unsheathe my cutlass intent on immediate combat. Holding up a hand to signal me to shelve my aggression, he ordered me to relax and enjoy the tale he was about to impart. Scarf then nodded conspiratorially to Viola, who had silently made his way behind me and had swiftly pressed his own blade against my backside. With a roar, Scarf ordered him to relieve me of all weapons and associated trickery. Under Viola's keen blade, I was stripped of my brace of lethal dirks, my medicine wallet, and several more secreted knives, basically my entire arsenal. Announcing that I was now ready to listen to his boss's saga, Captain Viola administered a powerful kidney punch as he retreated back to his guard-dog position. Under his total command now, Scarf scuttled back and forth before me as he mentally prepared to deliver his manufactured version of my brother's tragic eradication.

Scarf opened by explaining to his loyal cohort that my brother was a mean-spirited troublemaker, who delighted in landing poor Scarf in serious and dire trouble. Shrieking maniacally, Scarf launched into a series of imaginary reminisces that painted my dead brother in the very darkest of terms. He insisted that as a wee lad, the vicious child persisted in taunting him on the significant deformities he had suffered as a result of his bout with a dreaded pox. Incensed by these fanciful and fraudulent falsehoods I attempted to interrupt this fictional account, but halted abruptly when I once again felt Viola's sharp blade poke the nape of my neck. Turning and gazing intently at my tormentor, I surveyed the revengeful madness that dominated the Spaniard's entire being. Drooling like a maddened hound, Captain Viola literally ached to skewer me with his sharpened saber. With another harsh command, Scarf ordered him to lower the blade and return to his position as watchdog.

Facing me in his hellish mask, Scarf informed me that if I persisted in offering any further commentary during his narrative that he would delight in stuffing his filthy and moldering red scarf down my gullet. Continuing his fanciful account, Scarf explained that Toby conspired with the aid of another clever associate to implicate him in a serious crime, the theft of his boss's prized pocket-watch. Because of this treachery, Scarf whined that he had been viciously beaten and tossed half-dead into the Thames River to expire in a slow and agonizing manner. Shaking his head in amusement, Scarf spat out that he had once again bested the *Grim Reaper*, and had luckily survived this deadly ordeal. However, the madman bemoaned the fact that this conspiracy had cost him the finest job he had ever held, fighting dog trainer and handler. Sadly, recounting this monumental loss, Scarf confessed that besides piracy, training fighting hounds was the profession that suited his innate talents best.

Breaking his unpleasant reverie, Scarf further recounted that Toby's sinister plots renewed the moment the young thug discovered the fact that his victim had miraculously survived. Scarf related that in order to end Toby's villainous reign, he managed to thwart the tot's next nefarious scheme while capturing the young beast in the process. Maintaining utmost control, I calmly stood and faced my nemesis displaying no emotion whatsoever during his latest account steeped in lies and deceit.

Giggling in fond recollection, Scarf questioned if I remembered how much Toby feared savage dogs. As I nodded reluctant acknowledgement, Scarf taunted that he had imprisoned Toby in a fighting dog kennel where the beasts were allowed to savage him repeatedly. On each of these occasions, Scarf avowed nursing my brother back to health so he could enjoy further playtime with the vicious brutes. Scarf revealed that when he had buried Toby alive, the boy was near death and in all probability destined to perish. Chuckling evil and challenging my meager medical expertise at the time, the villain crowed that even if I had discovered his location there was little chance that I would have been able to save him. Scarf confided that Toby had surely secured a well-earned date with Satan and as such had got exactly what he deserved!

Scarf continued his blustering by boasting that he was nothing short of a magnanimous individual at heart. As proof of his extensive generosity, Scarf disclosed that he had certainly provided me infallible clues that provided me a foolproof opportunity to rescue my interned brother. Glancing in my direction, he croaked that I was not quite clever enough to save my brother's life. No, he ascertained, I was certainly not as clever as some believed! At this point, I erupted and spouted that I had desecrated an innocent child's final resting place by following his infernal clues. Barking out a gruesome squawk that I surmised was a laugh, the repugnant bully squealed that I had simply chosen the wrong grave. Smirking demonically, he divulged that I had missed the most important clue, a crudely drawn arrow on the reverse side of the tombstone I had located directing me to the proper location of Toby. Blinking again in righteous and unrestrained fury, I shouted that there was no such arrow nor did my innocent brother deserve such a gruesome and horrific fate.

Snorting contradictorily, Scarf retorted that Toby could hardly be considered innocent. The deranged pirate then went on to reveal that, per the arrow's pointed direction, Toby had purposely been buried in the grave adjacent to the one I had defiled. Gleefully, he crowed that Toby had certainly heard my frantic excavation efforts. Since the spiteful imp had no means of communicating that my efforts were misplaced and inaccurate, Scarf cackled that the boy was forced to resign himself to face a most horrific end. Scarf chided that the fate of being buried alive would force anyone to slowly lose their mind given the limited amount of space to maneuver, the lack of nourishment, a limited air supply and the eventual loss of hope of ever being rescued from a living hell. As the fiend muttered false regrets for Toby's horrific demise, I felt the white hot surge of anger race through my entire being. Stifling this rising fury, I questioned my lifelong rival as to what he planned for me.

Delighting wholeheartedly at my unequivocal antagonized state, Scarf laid out the rules that would govern our upcoming battle. Turning to his associate, Captain Viola, he commanded him to remain strictly impartial throughout our duel and to not interfere with its outcome no matter the result. He then hissed that should I somehow prevail that the maniacal rogue was free to deal with me in any manner he wished. Turning back to me, Scarf emphasized that we would only employ our cutlasses during this confrontation and that any demonstration of my usual tricks or ploys would result in allowing the crazed Spaniard to intercede. He concluded by announcing that should I prevail over both he and his dedicated henchman that I was free to collect Rue and make an unmolested escape. However, he once again cautioned that interference by any of my crewmen would result in the Spaniard igniting of the stockpiled gunpowder which would blow each and every one of us into everlasting eternity. Nodding my reluctant acceptance of his one-sided rules, my cutlass was tossed at my feet by my now jovial and jubilant rival. As I bent to retrieve it, I began to mentally prepare for my bout with evil incarnate!

Chapter 28: The Final Battle

I rationalized that to survive this grisly encounter and provide Rue a chance at freedom, I needed to remain calm and clear-headed. Should I lapse into revengeful fury, I was certain that I would face defeat in a most painful and agonizing manner. To prepare myself mentally, I silently recited a mantra that I prayed would enable me to prevail. Over and over the words of restraint echoed in my mind. They were, *maintain objectivity, maintain focus and maintain control.* Limbering up my taut frame, I raised the blade and signaled that I was fully prepared to begin. In a weak effort to appear civilized, we crossed our blades. Once done, we began to warily circle one another searching for any sort of opening or weakness. As we danced, Scarf maintained a constant dialogue prodding and tormenting me with further details of the demise of my friends and associates.

He confided that he had commissioned the insidious Captain LeMerde to eliminate my confederates on Jamaica. He taunted that the three old hussies and their heroic nephew were incinerated per the standard dictums of punishing the guilty for the practice of witchcraft. His one regret on this dark episode was that he had personally missed the delicious conflagration along with the sheer enjoyment of listening to the hapless screams and wails as the hungry flames consumed each of my close associates. Ignoring my firm resolve to remain level-headed, I pressed my attack with vigor and managed to score several nicks and gashes on my enemy. While they were purely superficial wounds, I nevertheless was somewhat delighted in the discomfort and minor pain they elicited.

Scoffing that my furious effort had produced little damage, the beast went on the offensive and scored some minor wounds of his own. Breaking off this skirmish, we again circled one another like predatory animals. As we continued this combative dance, Scarf jeered about the loss of my dear departed uncle, the Old Ghost. He divulged that he had delighted in plunging my own childish blade into my aged mentor time and time again until his frail life-force slowly slipped away. Delighted now by the remembrance, the villain informed me that my feeble and ancient relative cried for my assistance the entire time the numerous stabbings were inflicted. Tauntingly, he proclaimed that I had once again failed to protect a close and dear member of my family. Proceeding further with his incessant ridicule, he spat that I really only cared about myself to the fateful detriment of anyone close to me. With my anger reaching a fevered pitch, I implemented another series of well executed maneuvers, but once again scored only minor damage. Assessing the situation, I realized that I had miscalculated the fiend's dexterity and agility as he continually scuttled out of harm's way. Rationalizing that our duel would probably last for quite some time, I vowed once again to repress my feral anger as well as conserve vital energy that eventually would be required if I hoped to prevail.

As we continued to circle, Scarf continued his verbal assault by reminding me of my lost comrade, Powder Monkey. Comparing the lad to my deceased brother, Scarf recounted that the slaughter of this innocent lad was also my fault since I had abandoned him to the clutches of the demonic Adams witches. In a sarcastic tone, he informed me that the young man's presence in the Adams household had been providential and a development that he had not planned or taken into consideration while formulating his scheme for demise of the insidious Adams clan. I responded that I was convinced that my friend was still alive, since his remains had not been uncovered in the smoldering ruins. Cackling in an obscene manner, the unprincipled bully answered that no living being could escape the righteous cleansing flames that engulfed the entire mansion. Utilizing this opportunity to return his teasing, I conjectured that perhaps Powder Monkey had not been present during this cowardly attack, and thereby had survived the ordeal. Stunned by my announcement, Scarf questioned where I had come across such a fanciful tale. Continuing the ruse, I explained that a neighbor had claimed to have witnessed a youngster departing from the household long before the deadly combustion ignited. Scarf roared that he had commissioned the French officer to ensure that each and every one of my friends suffered the same horrific fate, which meant that this neighbor was either delusional or simply spinning a tall tale. Given his extreme preoccupation on the matter, I was able to bypass his defenses and score a clean slice to his left leg. Hobbled by this injury, Scarf's evasive abilities were somewhat lessened which provided me brief hope for his eventual defeat.

My somewhat serious wounding of my mortal enemy gave me further confidence as I continued to press my attack on Scarf. Caught off-guard by my latest barrage, Scarf managed to sneer that I was up to my old tricks once again. With much of his former bravado dissipating, I responded that I had spent many long hours practicing for just this type of duel. Sputtering his disgust at my boast, Scarf cursed me repeatedly as a sign of his growing frustration and fear. At that moment, another loud banging came from the bolted cabin's door signifying that my loyal men had not heeded my order to abandon this cursed vessel. Acknowledging their ensuing calls, I calmly shouted that the ship had been rigged to explode at any moment. Given this impending disaster, I once again commanded them to vacate the vessel immediately in favor of the shelter of *Rue's Revenge*. In my strongest tone, I shouted that they needed to guide our vessel as far away as possible from this floating powder-keg. I also added that I would join them shortly once I had finished with my pressing business. Grumbling and mumbling their extreme discontent through the bolted entryway, I eventually heard them making their retreat to the ship's upper deck to escape the serious danger I had just revealed.

Turning my attention back to Scarf, I informed him that our fight could now resume without further interruption. With that pronouncement, I went on the attack scoring severe strikes on various portions of his anatomy. My fervent participation in our combat training had transformed me into a formidable opponent, and I utilized every trick I had been taught to punish my adversary repeatedly, including a vicious wound to his left arm. The conflict's tide had swung in my favor, and I reckoned that Scarf's time amongst the living was slowly drawing to a close. Sensing this same unfavorable outcome and bleeding profusely from both the leg and arm injuries, Scarf opted for an entirely new tactic to distract my attention away from our battle.

Losing precious blood, the scandalous swine began to question me on the object of my quest, Rue. Attempting to ignore his prattling, I continued my one-sided barrage. In a moment of desperation, he revealed in passing that Rue was actually very close at hand. Halting my furious advance, I questioned him on his exact meaning. Pointing at the curtained torture cell, he sneered that my beloved had waited to be rescued for some time and would be ecstatic at my timely arrival. Sensing more of his foul chicanery, I renewed my attack. Realizing that his defeat was immanent, the malevolent varmint continued coaxing me to uncover the secret behind the concealed enclosure. Deciding at last to investigate his vile claim, I shoved past Viola and used my cutlass to part the secreting screen. What I glimpsed upon exposing this space was a nightmare of the highest order!

Bound hand and foot was a skeletal replica of my long lost lover, Rue! At the sight of her dreadful and repugnant condition, my breathing all but ceased, my mind dimmed and blurred and all of my motor functions stalled. I quickly distinguished that she had been deprived of nourishment for quite some time as her skin hung and sagged all over her frame. In fact, she was no more than a helpless and starved bag of bones! Her beauty had been mortally vandalized by this brutal treatment. Her cheeks were sunken to exceedingly great depths and the hollowness of her vision conveyed the loathsome punishment that she had been forced to endure. In many locations, her once smooth and delicate skin had been savagely flayed away to appease the unholy carnal appetite of her persecuting torturer. Other areas of her anatomy had been wickedly charred. My once beautiful lover had been reduced to a gruesome abomination suitable to roam the lower regions of Hades!

Utterly gleeful at observing my pain-wracked and devastated expression, Scarf whispered that his acute ministrations had transpired over the past two months. He then gleefully confessed that he had been astounded by Rue's resiliency and inner strength, since any normal mortal would have long succumbed to his harsh and brutal ministrations. Completely dazed and utterly dumbfounded, I stood transfixed as tears rolled steadily down my face. Scarf then addressed the human monstrosity shackled before me. Softly calling Rue's name, the maniac informed her that her savior had finally arrived. Upon hearing these words, her scabbed eyelids slowly opened and a light of recognition shone in them as she vainly attempted to mouth my name.

Trembling uncontrollably with horror and shame for allowing this vile travesty to occur, I stepped closer and whispered her name. Rue attempted to smile with her raw withered lips, but the end result was nothing short of gruesome. She then attempted to speak, but the sounds she emitted were horse and garbled, quite impossible to comprehend. Witnessing my extreme confusion, she simplified her message and whispered my name and a brief declaration of her eternal love. Returning her love oath, I also whispered that I had come to set her free. With a despondent smile, she croaked out that she was well beyond saving and then struggled to voice her next declaration. Mustering a supreme effort, she stared dully into my eyes and mouthed just two simple words, "*Kill him*"! Having successfully completed this vitally important message, she heaved a great sigh as her eyes rolled back in their sockets and her ragged breathing ceased. In that tragic moment I knew that my love was gone forever!

With tears coursing down my face, I called Rue's name time and again hoping for her miraculous return to the living. Meanwhile, Captain Viola comprehended my outright vulnerability and, against his leader's strict orders, went on the attack. Issuing an animal-like shriek, he rushed at me from behind intent on evening the score for my past transgressions. Alerted to his intentions by his inhuman screech, I moved away from Rue's prison cell toward the stern of the cabin and turned to face his maddened advance. Barely ducking under his wild saber swing, I utilized my own blade to severely slice the villain across his midsection which caused him to instantly double over in abject pain and agony. Moving adroitly behind him, I raised my foot and planted it on his protruding backside. With a mighty kick, I sent the vile fool stumbling unimpeded towards the rotted barricade covering the galley's rear window. Issuing a scream of paramount rage, my opponent blasted into the wooden barricade which thoroughly shattered on impact. His furious forward momentum was barely slowed by the decayed barricade, and he continued through the impaired planks and into the bright sunlight. Issuing a trailing screech, the brute disappeared from view as a mighty splash announced his entry into the surrounding sea.

Scarf, utilizing both distractions to his full advantage, had managed to wrap a crude bandage around both his leg and arm wounds somewhat staunching the flow of blood. While I was distracted by Viola's disappearance, he stealthily charged and drove the blade of his cutlass into the side of my chest hoping to skewer my heart, which given Rue's passing was now shattered into numerous miniature pieces. Fate intervened with my mortal enemy's lethal plan, as his blade somehow skimmed off my ribs and deflected outward sparing my life temporarily. While the wound was not mortal, it was intensely painful and debilitating as I struggled to avoid further punishment from my hated enemy's flashing blade. Eventually righting myself with enormous effort, I staggered into the center of the cabin, bleeding profusely. As I instinctively backed away from his continuous and furious onslaught, I ran directly into the cabin's lone table causing my knees to buckle as my strength deserted me. Collapsing backward onto this scrap-strewn trestle, I felt completely helpless and reasoned that I would soon be reunited permanently with my lover. Bending down to leer at my dire predicament with his cutlass pressed against my throat, Scarf sneeringly promised to be slow and deliberate in dispatching me, since my new boss, Satan, was in no hurry for my esteemed company.

As I stared into Scarf's revenge-maddened eyes, a furious fire of revulsion and rage ignited in my very soul and provided a spark of life that had been momentarily missing. As my weak and fumbling fingers skittered over my chest in an attempt to discern the extent of my latest injury, I happened to come across the wooden cross dutifully strung around my neck. Grasping this talisman which had long ago been supplied by my Voodoo protector, Papa Legba, a sudden thought dawned on me, and I rejoiced mentally at the boldness and deviousness of this novel scheme. You see, Papa Legba had previously shown me that the cross was much more than a protective amulet. Utilizing a simple yet appropriate maneuver, this talisman could be separated to expose a wickedly sharp blade of unbelievable hardiness and efficacy. Scarf, on witnessing a radical change in my facial expression, demanded to know my thoughts. Utilizing this opportunity in order to provide a necessary distraction, I calmly whispered that my spiritual protector would avenge both Rue's and my murder the moment this evil deed was consummated.

Somewhat alarmed by my warning, Scarf rose up and glanced back and forth in a frenzied effort to identify the guardian angel I had just mentioned. Utilizing this minute diversion, I called upon my *special voice* in order to deceive my detestable adversary one last time. Adopting the old crone's voice utilized in conjunction with the moldering statue of Saint Agnes that had long ago completely fooled the rogue, I directed her growling tone in the direction of my departed lover. As if addressing Scarf from the afterlife, the old crone's voice emanating from Rue's position boomed out his name. Continuing, the voice Scarf was well familiar with, demanded to be told why he was so intent on committing another murder. In a timid and child-like squeak, Scarf responded to the dreaded voice, explaining that he planned to end the life of his mortal tormentor to even the score once and for all.

As he was rationalizing his actions to his intensely feared vocal tormentor, I took the opportunity to grasp my wooden cross and appropriately twist it to dislodge the very special blade concealed inside. With this weapon now firmly in my grasp and Scarf's attention targeted on my dead lover corpse, I continued in the crone's highly recognizable voice to inform him that his evil actions would certainly damn him for all eternity. Managing a weak child-like giggle, Scarf replied that this outcome was long foretold and his destiny was eventual damnation whether he murdered me or not. He then turned his full attention back to me and squealed that it was time for me to die. Summoning all of my remaining strength, I rose up and drove the cross's blade directly through the horrific black mask and deep into his left eye. Given the utter sharpness of my concealed dirk, the blade slid unmolested all the way up to its hilt, skewering soft tissue until it entered his brain. Shooting upright and screeching with unbearable misery and torment, the pirate demon instantly dropped to his knees and then crumpled into a fetal ball as he writhed and contorted on the vile cabin's deck.

Wasting no time, I arose painfully from the table and made a cursory examination of the situation. With Captain Viola's rude departure, I only had my seriously wounded advisory with which to contend. While Scarf continued his contortions of agony, I retrieved my medicine wallet and hastily treated my nasty wound. After this quick ministration was hastily completed, I bent over my despicable foe and rudely reclaimed my secret dirk which I swiftly reassembled and rehung around my neck. Turning my attention to Rue, I moved to her side and planted a goodbye kiss on her stilled lips as I wished her a safe journey to heaven, a fate she surely deserved. Having bid her a final farewell, I returned my full attention to the Black Tarantula.

Well aware that this insidious viper had cheated death so many times previously, I began to plot his final and everlasting demise. Rue's dying words also echoed loudly in my mind demanding a final settlement of accounts for this vile and disgusting monster. Visually searching the barren cabin, my eyes alighted on two oil lamps that had been discarded in a far corner. I retrieved both lamps and was gratified to discover that they were nearly full of oil. Holding the lamps over Scarf, I poured both of the lamp's contents on my wailing, moaning and squirming archenemy. Unaware of my specific actions or their intent, Scarf continued to writhe in abject agony on the filthy decking. Grabbing one of the lit candles, I wished the spiteful bully a painful journey to hell before tossing the candle in his direction.

The lamp oil ignited immediately and in no time at all Scarf was washed in flames. As I continued to savor his tormented screams and anguished wails, he suddenly leapt to his feet and began racing crazily around the cabin in an attempt to extinguish the searing flames. His mindless meanderings drew him closer and closer to the store of deadly gunpowder. Given his mindless meanderings, I suddenly realized that my very existence was once again in serious jeopardy. As this reality dawned on me, the human torch stumbled, flopped face-down and then began crawling directly towards the lethal black powder stockpile. Harkening back to the shattered galley window, I made an instant decision. Racing towards the stern of the cabin, I dove cleanly through the opening and into the welcoming daylight. As I flew through the breech abetted by my frenzied flight, a dazzling white light filled the entire world and then seemed to explode in outright fury. Shoved away from the source of the devastating explosion by what felt like a thousand invisible hands, I entered the warm tropical waters with a huge splash after losing consciousness somewhere along the journey.

The warm briny sea eventually brought me back to full awareness, as I found myself floating on my back comforted by its salty embrace. Treading water to remain afloat, I slowly lifted my head to reconnoiter my surroundings. The *Spider's Web* had now been fragmentized and transformed into fiery chunks of floating wooden debris that were scattered everywhere. Latching onto a portion of one of the vessel's masts, I swiveled around and around searching for signs of survivors. As I made this hasty examination, I sighted a few mangled and bloodied pirates clambering atop some of the ship's largest remaining sections in an effort to escape drowning. Amid my furious search, I identified absolutely no sign of my lifelong tormentor nor his nefarious compatriot, and I conjectured that both had surely failed to cheat death a final time.

As I paddled my way towards the largest surviving section of the vessel's hull, I heard a plaintive voice shouting for assistance. Making my way over to the source of the desperate plea, I was shocked to discover that at least one of my enemies had survived the cataclysmic explosion, Captain Viola. As I navigated my way to his position, I felt nothing but vacant emptiness. I knew that a vital portion of my very being had been cruelly severed by Scarf's brutal torture and murder of my lover in his demonic thirst to avenge my imaginary wrongs. With Rue lost there was little that mattered except the possibility of avenging her insidious death. Moving closer to my foe's position, I could clearly hear the fiend begging for mercy and immediate assistance so as to avoid drowning. Nodding my understanding, I questioned him on the extent of his injuries. As I did so, I noticed the appearance of fins slicing the water behind him as they heralded the arrival of dreaded sea scavengers. Latching firmly onto the collar of the severely bleeding reprobate, I again asked about his injuries. In a weakened voice, he confessed that he was gutted by my blade, and as a direct result his life's fluid was draining copiously away. As he made this admission, I realized that the ravenous predators had probably smelled the blood trail in the water and were swiftly closing the gap in search of sustenance. With a bitterly revengeful spirit, I informed the helpless pirate that I would indeed provide him assistance. Eternally grateful for my pronouncement, the brigand made an insincere apology for my rough treatment and Rue's horrific death.

With his words sparking consummate fury in my soul, I pulled the villain along with me towards the floating wooden fragment I had chosen as a temporary sanctuary. While he profusely continued to expressing his utmost gratitude, I suddenly released my hold on the scurvy scum. Treading water, I raised both my legs and gently kicked out sending the severely hemorrhaging package towards our unwelcome visitors as I gleefully wished the Spanish cur bon voyage and safe travels. I then turned and quickly swam to the fragment of surviving wreckage and painfully attempted to claw my way upon it. Swiveling my vision, I was greeted with the gruesome sight of Captain Viola being torn to shreds by the hungry marine monsters. His ongoing screams of pain and torment were pure music to my ears! While my actions had cleansed the world of pure conniving evil, it mattered very little and would certainly not return Rue to me.

Eventually succeeding in navigating my way agonizingly onto my sanctuary, I clung to this slowly sinking portion of the ship as I observed a few scattered wounded and injured survivors also succumbing to hideous deaths at the wicked jaws of the ravaging and rampaging sharks. Meanwhile, my mind reeled with self-doubt and recrimination. I knew for the most part that I had miserably failed all those that I had cared for most in the world. I had failed my only brother and condemned him to perish most horribly in a cramped and confining prison below ground. I had failed my Uncle Arch and allowed him to be butchered like a fattened swine at the hands of my mortal enemy. I had failed the Adams family and my good friend Powder Monkey which resulted in their cruel incineration by the mad French naval officer. Finally, I had failed Rue, who had been brutally starved and tortured by my evil childhood nemesis, Scarf Rockingham. While I had successfully revenged each of these murders, my loved ones were gone and there was nothing I could do to bring any of them back to me.

I agonized back and forth as to whether I should attempt to survive or simply slip under the waves to join their much desired company. I had nothing to live for and no hope for a joyous future. Perhaps this was the moment of my life that Aunt Willamina had foretold in reading my fortune so very long ago. This was a true parting of the ways, a decision to live or die! Then I heard Rue's voice in my befuddled mind asking me how I could be so selfish, so self-important and, most importantly, so infernally stupid! She continued her vicious admonishment by informing me that if I took the coward's course in this decision and simply surrendered to my overwhelming grief and pain that I would be dishonoring each and every one of my lost loved ones. More importantly, I would be rewarding my enemies with a glorious victory by my own death. I found this one dominating and haunting thought to be highly offensive by all accounts and deemed it utterly unacceptable and highly repugnant.

The decision was solely mine to make, live or die. While I reckoned that I had led less than a perfect life, I was cognizant that I had endeavored to respect my fellow man and to treat the weak and helpless with kindness and consideration. While I had not treated all brothers as friends, I had treated all friends as brothers. I finally realized that Rue would be eternally furious and utterly disappointed if I chose the path of a pathetic coward! I also realized in that moment that I did have something very important to live for, that being to honor the memory of everyone I had lost!

As I continued to ponder my fate, I thought of my loyal crew who depended on me for direction and leadership. I also reminisced of the many happy moments I had spent with my close friends, the Turbouts. To my everlasting shame, I also harkened on Aimee and her numerous declarations of love. As I brought all of these thoughts into careful consideration, I suddenly had the strong urge to survive, to finish the remainder of my life's journey no matter its outcome. I was assured that I would never want for fame and fortune since both had been graciously bestowed upon me. I also realized that I had so much more to experience in my life given that I was still a relatively young man. In short, I decided that I wanted to live!

Since my loyal crewmen were very near, all I needed to accomplish was to remain alive until they had the opportunity to return and rescue me from the jaws of the continuously circling predators. After all, I was not yet checkmated! I needed a plan and I needed it fast before the chunk of wood on which I was marooned slipped below to join the rest of its sunken counterparts. While I was aware that I could summon assistance from my Voodou protector, Papa Legba, I judged the situation as less than dire and certainly not completely hopeless in nature. Grasping the wooden cross between my fingers for comfort, I suddenly spotted a bobbing water cask which ignited a sudden inspiration. With a knowing smile, I began preparations to continue to live and experience the eventful future that lay before me.

To be continued...

CHARACTERS AND NAMES

Book Three: Demon Pirate

London, England

William Echo Eden (Captain William Bilge and Bilge Rat)- Orphan, galley slave and narrator
Toby Eden-Echo's younger brother
Arch Deacon Williamson Archibald (Old ghost and Uncle Arch)- Echo's elderly uncle
Scarf Rockingham- Vicious bully
Slugger O'Toole- Owner and operator of Slugger's Sports Emporium

Amafata - English Merchantman

Jedediah Potts (Handy)- Galley master and Echo's friend and mentor
Captain Samuel Conway-Amafata's Captain
Mr Bass- Malevolent first mate
Jemme Buttons (Grommet Jemme and Zombie Jemme) - Suspected Jonah, dullard and Echo's friend
Geovanni Perilli (Doc)- Shipboard physician
Moses Hayes (Chips)- Shipboard carpenter

Saint Domingue

Cap-Francis- St Domingue's major city
Rue La Montaine- Monique's daughter, barmaid and Echo's lover
Babar Kismet (Lion)- Turkish Pirate and valuable crewmember
Black Tarantula- Pirate Scourge of the Caribbean
Angry George- Pirate storyteller and crewmember
Papa Legba- Voodou Loa and self-appointed protector of Echo
Ding-Ding- Island mistreated mutt and Papa Legba's familiar
Adams Sisters:
- Gertrude- Naturalist and Healer
- Wilamina- Palm Reader
- Hortence- Aspiring stage actress

Gene Fabrege (Catstalker Gene) - Miscreant and torturer of small animals
Long Tall Willie- Dwarf seaman and knife expert
Claude Anton Gustaves (Owl Eyes)- Vice Governor of the Island
Pablo the Pigeonman- Carrier pigeon trainer and handler
Bunkey- Pablo's son

Swamp Frog- Pirate mate on Black Tarantula's Spider Web
Lne Survivor Sam- Parrot in sea hag tale

Jamaica

Kingston- Island's main city
Fat Dog's Pub- Renown Island pub
Fat Dog- Owner and operator of Island's popular pub
Stem and Stern- Fat Dog's simian bodyguards
Sir Jonathan William Brisbane III- Island plantation owner, bully and master duelist
Powder Monkey- Sir Jonathan's Slave and cannon expert
Captain Ronald Shuster Adams- Nephew of Adams sisters and commander of Jamaica's Fort Charles
Sergeant Dale Houndstooth- Captain Adams' second-in-command
Rufus and Jamie Pennington- Two strong-armed brothers hired to protect the Adams household
Simon Beardsley- Adams' family attorney
Madame Mystique- Gypsy fortuneteller
Governor Bartholomew Burgess- Newly appointed island leader
Queenie- Governor's daughter's handmaiden

Midnight Crow - Pirate Ship

Rambling Dirk Shivvers- Pirate Captain
Booby Bird Doyle- Addled pirate crewman
Black Monk- Ghost story of cleric who was convicted of demonic worship
Jumping Jimmy- Pirate storyteller
Tiger Eyes- African slave and son of a tribal chieftain
Scuttle the Hunchback- Rescued castaway and accomplished blacksmith
South Seas Tan- Pirate crewmember and hand-to-hand fighting expert
Neptune's Revenge- Privateer vessel and sister ship to Rue's Revenge
Monkey Faced Bill- crewman

Guadeloupe

Pointe-A-Pitre- Island's major city
Governor Louis LaCouturie- Avaricious island leader
Captain Jean Bernard LeMerde- Dishonored French naval officer in command of the island's marine defenses
Francois Rene Turbout- Plantation owner on nearby island of Marie-Galant and Echo's friend
Lille Turbout- Rene's wife
Aimee Turbout- Rene's sister
Lieutenant Alexandre Devereau (Winking Blinking Alex)- Captain LeMerde's second-in-command

Doctor Baptise Broome- Incompetent self-important local physician
Sanglante Noir Diable (Black Demon Pub)- Most notorious drinking establishment on the island
Andre Mimosa (The Corsican)- Known criminal and owner of the Black Demon Pub
Leatherface- Champion bare-knuckle brawler of the Black Demon Pub
Daible- Immense black jaguar utilized in animal fights at the Black Demon Pub
Doxy Duel participants:
Ostrich Katie- Proprietress and madam of the Open Oyster Café
Molly Hatpin- Proprietress and madam of the Hopping Gull Pub
Pierre Duval- Disguise name of iterant troubadour utilized by Echo

ABC ISLANDS—Aruba, Bonaire and Curacao
Captain Ricardo Inez Viola- Spanish Captain of Man-O-War patrolling southern Caribbean

St Lucia
Sharkface Topper- Owner and operator of Island's pub

Tortuga
Hurricane Jeffers- Black-hearted knave and scoundrel who operates as the Black Tarantula's First Mate
Spider's Web- Black Tarantula's vessel
Dizzy Jeffers- Hurricane Jeffer's brother

Cayman Islands - Grand Cayman, Little Cayman and Cayman Brac
Bodden Town- First English settlement on Grand Cayman
Big Paul Brown- Island leader
Blind Pig Jeffers- Rue's Revenge crewmember with knowledge of Cayman Islands
Jack Bitteroot- Island merchant
Captain Brownstone- English merchantman Captain visiting islands
Beelzebub's Cauldron- Shark filled cove on Grand Cayman utilized to dispose of undesirables

Rue's Revenge - Captain William Bilge's Vessel
No Nose Nottingham- Angry George's friend
Guzzlin' Gooch- Extreme drunkard
Rambling Roberto- Mate and vessel storyteller
Bottom Dog- Legless mate and weather forecaster
Tiny Junior- Humongous mate
Sudsy Scupper- Victim in fictional pirate court drama
Skinner Shaw- Sudsy's foe

Black Cat Bill- Sudsy's foe
Pumpkin Rodgers- Mate in Sudsy's tale
Bottom Dog- Legless mate and weather fore

Glossary of Pirate Terms

CANNON ORDINANCE

During the Golden Age of Piracy cannon shapes and sizes varied across the board. Because of this fact, the ordinance utilized to fulfill their deadly mission also varied in size, shape and use.

Bar shot..... A close relative of chain shot except that a bar replaced its cousin's chain. Like chain shot, this ordinance wrought havoc and destruction on ship's riggings, spars, masts and sails.

Bundle shot..... A close relative of grape shot, this ordinance featured packs of short metal bars bundled together with rope or cable. Upon firing, the bindings loosened and sent a wave of murderous destruction down upon enemy vessels and crewmembers.

Canister shot..... Another relative of grape shot, this ordinance utilized a metal canister filled with all manner of destructive materials such as small metal balls or pieces of metal. When they were not readily available, scrap items such as nails, spikes and rocks were employed. Once fired, the canister disintegrated in flight sending a wave of destruction towards the enemy.

Chain shot..... This ordinance was made up of two iron or lead balls that were chained together. Once fired, they whirled their way to their enemy target causing widespread devastation on a foe's riggings, masts and sails to reduce precious maneuverability and speed.

Grape shot..... This ordinance was made up of small iron or lead balls that were bundled together in a canvas sack. When fired at an enemy, the spread out in flight and acted like modern shotgun pellets causing massive destruction. While they caused little damage to vessels, they proved devastating to opponent's crews.

Heated shot..... This ordinance was simply round shot that was heated to a white-hot temperature in order to incinerate wooden and cloth parts of an enemy's vessel.

Round shot..... This ordinance was the traditional cannonball that was normally fashioned out of cast iron material. This shot could be either solid and hollow in construction, with the latter able to travel greater distances due to its lighter weight. This shot could easily pierce a foe's hull and send the ship down to Davy Jones Locker if properly placed.

Split shot..... This ordinance was yet another close relative to bar shot. Instead of utilizing whole spheres as was the case with its cousin, the spheres were split which lessened the weight thereby increasing the distance the shot would travel.

PIRATE COINAGE

During the Golden Age of Piracy, a vast variety of coins circulated across the West Indies. Rather than attempting to relate the entire list of endless possibilities, the following will concentrate solely on the most widely circulated coins.

Doubloon..... This highly prized Spanish gold coin was one of the most frequently utilized monetary units throughout the Caribbean. The name originated from the Latin word dupus meaning double because it was valued at two escudos or dollars. However, gold coins or escudos were minted in denominations of one, two, four and eight escudos. Struck in Spain, Mexico and South America, this coin typically featured images of the Spanish ruling class with the reverse side bearing images of the Crusader's Cross, a lion or a castle.

Pieces of Eight..... This Spanish coin was the silver alternative to a Doubloon. In all probability, this coin was the most widely circulated coin in the Caribbean. It attained its name due to the fact that it could be cut into eight pie-shaped wedges in order to manufacture change when required. In many instances, holes were drilled into these coins so that they could be worn as decorative jewelry or to enable them to be secretly pinned to the inside of an individual's clothing for safekeeping.

Guinea..... This English gold coin derived its name from the British colony of Guinea (Ghana) where its gold was mined. The majority of these coins bore an image of an elephant as a testament of their African heritage. This was one of the first machine-struck coins in existence and carried a value of one sterling pound. It was also the standard coinage of the British East Indian Trading Company. Lastly, the edge of this coin was one of the first to be specifically milled to prevent felonious clipping or filing.

Sovereign..... This gold coin is also English and carried a monetary value of thirty shillings. As such, it was more valuable than the Guinea which was valued at twenty shillings. As its name suggests, the images portrayed on these coins were reigning English sovereigns.

Leeuwendaalder..... This was a prominent Dutch silver coin that bore an image of a lion. Over time, the name of this coin was shortened to Taalder and Taaler to Daalder and Daaler. From this abridgement, the American dollar got its name. Nicknamed the lion dollar, this coin was utilized extensively by the Dutch East Indian Trading Company, who dominated the spice trade from the Far East. Since this organization was a world's trading power by supplying over half of Europe with exotic Far East spices, this coin was widespread in distribution and highly sought after by marauding pirates. In most cases, it was the coin of choice for foreign trading. Although not nearly as common, this coin was also minted in gold.

GENERAL SHIP LOCATIONS

Bow..... The front of a vessel

Stern..... The rear of a vessel

Larboard..... The left side of a vessel facing forward

Starboard..... The right side of a vessel facing forward

Galley..... The kitchen of a vessel

Bilge..... The lowest inner hull of a vessel

GRAND CAROUSE
Basically a wild shore-bound party complete with strumpets, hot spirits, combative contests and games-of-chance. These wild affairs occurred when a ship was in the process of being careened. This was the necessary process of exposing a ship's hull for maintenance and repair below the water line. These repairs included dry rot repair, hull rupture patching due to cannon shot or reef damage and the removal of clinging hitchhikers (barnacles, seaweed and burrowing Teredo worms). This laborious and time-consuming chore was necessary every six months or so in the warm Caribbean waters to ensure a ship's maneuverability and speed maximization.

The process was undertaken in multiple steps. The first was to expose the hull so that work could be conducted. Since the Caribbean had very little tide variation, this meant beaching a ship and hauling it over on one side to expose the hull for repairs. Once accomplished, the next step involved laborious sanding and scraping the exposed hull free of all hitchhikers. The third step was to repair all damaged areas of the hull by adding new planking where necessary or caulking the less damages areas with oakum (separated twine mixed with tar) that was jammed into cracks, seams, crevices and holes. The fourth step was to tar the entire hull for future protection. Once this process was completed, the entire operation was repeated on the opposite side of the hull.

HERBAL ARMAMENTS
Belladonna (Deadly Nightshade).....
This deadly poison has been utilized for centuries as medicine and a cosmetic beyond its lethal intent. The name translates to Beautiful Woman and was used in ancient times by women as eye-drops that dilated their pupils to provide a seductive appearance. While Belladonna is one of the most toxic plants on the planet, it was utilized by early physicians as an anesthetic for surgeries and a painkiller for common ailments such as toothaches, headaches and ulcers. The plant is commonly known under a series of names such as Banewort, Death Cherry, Devil's Herb, Beautiful Death and Deadly Nightshade.

The plant itself contains tropane alkaloids which cause bizarre delirium and severe hallucinations in weaker concentrations. While the entire plant is highly toxic, the roots are generally the most potent.

Quina (Jesuit's Bark)..... This marvelous and miraculous natural curative received its name after being discovered by Jesuit missionaries in Peru between 1620 and 1630. The Andean Indians revealed the healing properties of the fever tree bark to the Jesuits as a specific remedy for the dreaded tropical fever-inducing disease, malaria. The bark of the Cinchona tree is native to the Andean forests of South America. The main active ingredient of this wondrous bark is quinine.

History also contends that the wife of a Spanish Viceroy to Peru (Countess of Chinchon) returned to Spain having been cured of malaria by the miraculous tea made from the bark of this New World tree. As a result, she transported huge quantities of this special bark home with her to introduce it to her homeland.

Devil's Trumpet (Datura)..... This innocent looking plant has a long history of causing hallucinogenic delirium and painful death to its victims. The entire plant is quite dangerous but its seeds are its most potent portion. Loaded with tropane alkaloids, these lethal substances of this deadly plant cause a victim to experience utter delirium, bizarre and violent behavior, pronounced amnesia and eventual death. Over time, this lethal plant has been called multiple names including Thorn Apple, Jimson Weed, Devil's Snare, Moon Flower, Mad Apple and Hell's Bells.

Wormwood..... This is an age-old herb that had both psychoactive and medicinal purposes. The active ingredient in Wormwood is thujone, and its effects are severely heightened by the addition of alcohol. The herb has been utilized over the centuries as a curative to aid digestion since its extremely bitter taste activates gall bladder activity.

Large doses coupled with alcohol can result in headaches, dizziness, tremors, convulsions, loss of intellect, vertigo, giddiness, sleeplessness, foaming at the mouth, permanent mental deterioration, seizures, delirium and severe hallucinations.

Senna..... This natural medicinal aid is derived from the leaves of the Senna plant. This substance, containing the substance Sennosides, works by interacting with the bacteria in an individual's digestive tract. The result is a contraction of the individual's intestines that provides a strong laxative effect. Common side-effects of Senna include severe abdominal cramping, nausea, explosive diarrhea and vomiting.

Senna plants are native throughout tropical regions of Central and South America. Many ancient cultures, including the Aztec Indians, utilized this herbal remedy to relieve constipation for untold centuries.

PIRATE WEAPONS

During the Golden Age of Piracy (1700 to 1725), standardization of weapons had yet occurred. For the most part, pirate weaponry were highly creative and often hand-crafted and one-of-a-kind makeshift designs. The most important attribute of any piratical weapon was trustworthiness and effectiveness in battle situations since an individual's life hung in the balance.

Therefore, a vast majority of pirate weapons were fashioned from ordinary sailor's tools and implements. Additionally, pirates also utilized psychological weapons to cow prey into easy surrender to avoid loss of life and more importantly the potential damage or destruction of plunder. The following is an extensive yet not exclusive list and descriptions of pirate weaponry.

Belaying Pin..... These implements were necessary tools found on any sailing vessel. They served a vital job on any sea voyage. The device was a solid wooden club-like tool utilized to secure running rigging lines. This removable wooden pin fit into holes on a ship's rail to act as secure anchors for the lines responsible for a vessel's rigging. In combat, these pins could easily be removed from their rail holes to be used as vicious clubs in close-quarter fighting.

Blunderbuss..... This weapon was basically a shotgun with the firepower of a small cannon. The design was typified by a flared or fanned-out barrel that dispensed lead pellets over a broad sweeping area. A user normally braced the weapon on his hips or side to absorb the considerable recoil. It was basically a close range equalizer capable of sweeping a deck clean of opponents.

Boarding Ax..... This was a necessary tool also found on any sailing ship. As such, it serviced a number of vital jobs on any voyage. The axe consisted of a two to three foot long handle topped with a sharpened iron hatchet on one side and a blunt hammer on the other. During engagement, it could serve a number of necessary functions such as acting as a human cleaver, a boarding hook releaser, a destroyer of shipboard encumbrances such as doors and hatches as well as a handy clean-up tool to remove downed riggings, masts and sails.

Boarding Pikes..... These were long wooden spears that had a metal end fashioned in a variety of aggressive and dangerous designs. In conflict, they could be used to stave off boarders or simply thrown at opponents. They also served as highly effective defenses against swords and daggers where room allowed.

Buckler..... This was a rather small shield that ranged in size from eight to fifteen inches in diameter. The device was gripped in one hand while the other hand was left free to wield a sword. Because of their diminutive size, they provided little defense against musket or pistol balls. However, they were extremely lightweight and easy to wield in either an offensive or defensive situation. Their best advantage was achieved in close-quarter clashes.

Caltrop..... These insidious devices were also known as Crow's Feet. They were designed as life-sized jacks with four sharpened points. These iron burrs were specifically manufactured to always land with their sinister sharp points sticking straight up in the air. Scattered on the ship's decking, they provided a dreadful defensive weapon against aggressive barefoot invaders. These weapons inflicted crippling injuries, chaotic confusion and positive resistance to invading adversaries. Gripped in a defender's hand these insidious devices could also inflict major damage in close quarter struggles.

Cannons..... These serious guns ranged from six to thirty-two pounds (referring directly to the ability to fire these sized cannonballs). Cannons came in an unbelievable variety of sizes and designs based on their manufacturing origins. While the material utilized for their manufacture varied, iron became the material of choice over time due to its ease of use and economical production cost. Cannons were extremely heavy and difficult to handle aboard ships but provided prodigious firepower in armed conflict.

Dagger (Dirk)..... This was a small multipurpose knife absolutely necessary for routine seafaring chores. The usual design featured a straight blade with a protruding hilt to protect the user's hand from sliding down onto the sharpened blade. This design also avoided very deep penetration which could cause the blade to become stuck and render it useless in battle. The weapon's design called for thrusting rather than slashing during combat.

Cutlass..... These short but thick sabers were manufactured with either a straight or slightly curved blade which was honed to a wickedly keen cutting edge capable of slicing through bone. Their hilts were either cupped or had rounded guards to protect the user's hand. This design also made the sword easier to grip and harder to dislodge in battle.

Cutlasses were specifically designed to be short enough to be effective in confined spaces and close quarter conflicts. Boarding aggression was not like a gentleman's duel, but rather a crazed rush to eliminate any and all opposition. Given this purpose, the cutlass became a prized weapon for its ability to hack and slash rivals. Cutlasses also required virtually no training or practice in order to utilize it and achieve crippling results.

Grappling Hook..... These devices consisted of three to four metal hooks that were equally spaced with a rope attached to an eye on the opposite end. Designed to catch on opponent's vessel outcroppings, they carried enough weight to cover ample distances with accuracy. In closely contested man-on-man fighting, they could also be wielded by aggressors to inflict serious damage.

Grenado..... This device was a round cast-iron ball about the size of a grapefruit or coconut. In fact, the earliest designs were fashioned from hollowed out coconuts, glass bottles or clay pots. This hollowed out device employed an access hole to allow gunpowder, grapeshot or shrapnel to be inserted inside topped by a fuse.

Incendiaries..... These were nothing more than buckets, bottles or small barrels crammed with furious and malevolent materials that were thrown onto enemy vessels to inflict painful injuries, crew panic and utmost confusion. Contents and design of these weapons varied widely depending on the materials available.

A subset of these weapons were stinkpots. These devices were small glass bottles or clay pots that were packed with chemicals such as brimstone or other evil smelling materials like rotted fish, crustaceans or human waste that were ignited and thrown at a foe. They provided battle chaos and panic to any opposition.

Marlin Spike..... This everyday shipboard tool was normally fashioned from wood or metal in an icepick-like design. They were normally six to eighteen inches long. Utilized for various routine tasks, they were extremely tough, unyielding and durable making them quite suitable for inflicting blunt trauma injuries and stab wounds in close quarter combat.

Musket..... This was a longer-ranged gun used primarily for sniping rather than close quarter fighting. It was capable of crippling an opponent's crew without the danger of inflicting serious damage to the prize. After firing, it also suffered a long reloading process and because of its overall length was unwieldly in close quarters.

Pistol..... This firearm was designed to be small in size and light in weight. Pistols were capable of only a single shot before requiring a time-consuming reloading exercise which could take thirty seconds at best. Since this time delay was both lengthy and impractical, multiple pistols were usually carried into battle along with a trusty cutlass and dagger. Pistols usually supplied a lethal boarding volley as well as being utilized as a club once the device was fired.

Psychological Weapons..... Being natural cravens at heart, pirates relied on psychological weapons to cower prey into submission without a fight. Primarily, a bloodthirsty and ruthless reputation went a long way into frightening prey to surrender upon confrontation. Additionally, the red or black decorated pirate flag promising death to all was successful in gaining peaceful capitulation. Other psychological methods included skylarking (prancing, cavorting, shouting and screaming) prior to battle coupled with an invader's band playing loud and militaristic tunes serving the purpose of cowering prey into submission. Lastly, the strategic employment of a cannon warning shot was substantial inducement to force a non-bloody takeover.

Rope Clubs..... These were simply lengths of rope that were stiffened by saltwater or tar and used to inflict blunt trauma injuries in close quarter conflicts.

Swivel Deck Guns..... They were essentially small cannons that rested on a swivel stands and were attached to the upper decking to allow a very wide movement arc. Their short term use was primarily short-range anti-personal sweepers. They fired deadly grapeshot and proved quite effective in repelling boarders or sweeping an entire deck of enemies. Because of their design, they were extremely portable and highly versatile.

POISON DART FROG

These are a group of small amphibians native to tropical Central and South America. Like woorari, local Indians would rub their arrows or blowgun dart tips on the creature to create lethal projectiles. Their poison rendered victims paralyzed and allowed hunters to easily collect helpless prey. While the frogs are small in size, they are quite lethal in design. In fact, there is no known cure for the creature's poison, as it can swiftly cause death in as little as a few minutes.

While most amphibians choose camouflage as a standard defense, the same is not true for this species. These frogs are usually brightly colored with brilliant patterns to warn off aggressors as to their extreme toxicity. A single poison dart frog harbors enough toxin to kill ten grown men. In fact, simple handling of these deadly creatures can prove to be fatal. As such, they are one of the most poisonous creatures on the entire planet.

POX

DA general term used to describe a variety of sexually transmitted diseases during the Golden Age of Piracy. In truth, there was an overall ignorance and clear lack of understanding as to the disease's cause or cure. Because of this widespread ignorance and misunderstanding, the transmission of the illness continued to populate with unsuspecting partners. For the most part, women were wrongly blamed for the spread of the disease.

General opinion deemed that the pox was a direct result of unmitigated passion and vice and as such undeserving of understanding or charity. The disease was viewed as an individual's rightful punishment for lewd and sinful conduct.

In the early 1700's, there was no cure for the pox. As such, the infected were subjected to a vast number of dubious medical treatments. It was also well known that, left untreated, the end result of the malady would produce severe pain, hardship, madness and possible death. Physicians at this time rationalized the non-curability of the pox as proper restitution for the gross failing of the infected.

Barbaric treatments of the time that provided no curative power included the following:

1. The wholesale use of Mercury either ingested, applied directly to body parts or utilized as an inhalant. A victim's copious darkened drooling after the Mercury treatments was viewed as a sign of recovery while in actuality a result of Mercury poisoning.

2. Sores and eruptions on private parts were cauterized with hot branding irons.

3. Leeches were applied directly on the infected sores.

4. Sweat baths were prescribed to induce salvation and perspiration as a method believed necessary to eliminate the bodily poisons. Holywood (Guaiacium) served as a blackened tea was administered to induce sweating in order to drive out the pestilence. This herbal tea came from a flowering West Indies tree and proved to have no medicinal benefit other than being a mild laxative.

5. Slamming or smacking an individual's infected privates with a hard object was also employed to force the infection out of a suffering individual. A harsh example of this felonious treatment was slamming a heavy tome closed on a patient's privates.

6. A variety of purgatives and steam baths were also employed. In fact, sweating cloths were developed by cutting thin strips of cloth and soaking them in a Lead or Mercury solution and applying them directly to a sufferer's body.

7. Various mixtures were provided by medical men whose ingredients included arsenic, sarsaparilla, iodine, Jesuit's bark and Heartsease (wild Pansy) mixed with various amounts of deadly Mercury.

Regardless of the treatment utilized, the primary symptoms of the pox eventually disappeared resulting in the belief that a cure had been achieved. The healed individual invariably returned to his or her old way of life enabling the further spread of the malady.

VOODOU LOA/PAPA LEGBA

Voodou is an ancient religion brought over from Africa as a result of the New World's slave trade. A central belief of this unique religion is that nothing in life happens by chance including accidents or coincidences and that everything serves a purpose. This purpose is determined by a multitude of spirits called Loa. They serve as intermediaries between God and man and guide an individual through the physical journey of life. These Loa are not saints or angels but rather distinct beings with their own likes and dislikes. There is also belief that specific rhythms, songs, dances and symbols exist to honor an address each of them. They are called upon by a Voodou priest (Hougan) or priestess (Mambo) to make earthly appearances to guide their faithful flock. One very important Loa is Papa Legba.

Papa Legba is the spirit or lord of the spiritual crossroads, the gatekeeper in effect. He is the first and last spirit invoked in any Voodou ceremony because he has the power to open or close the doorway between humans and the other Loa. He is the gatekeeper between the world of spirits and that of flesh. No Voodou ceremony can take place without his permission. He is known as a master communicator (can speak all human languages) and quite benevolent in his actions. His sacred symbol is the sun and the cross and his sacred day is Tuesday. He is known for his polite and caring nature and is much loved by all believers. His favorite foods are grilled vegetables and meat and his favorite drink is a spiced peppered rum (Clairin). He also has the ability to ride (take possession) of humans and control their actions and speech.

Papa Legba is believed to take a particular form when he makes his appearance. He is accredited to appear as a crooked (sporting a crutch or cane) lovable old man in a broad brimmed straw hat with a small tobacco pipe in his mouth and a straw bag filled with bits of food at his side. His body is covered with sores and he usually has a familiar (mangy dog or rooster) at his side. His favorite colors are green, rose, red and yellow.

WOORARI

This deadly substance is an alternative name for the material Curare. The substance is a shiny black resin extract prepared by Central and South American Indians from the bark of specific local trees. This toxic material is then used to coat arrow and blowgun dart tips for use in hunting forest animals or to during warfare with neighboring tribesmen. When introduced into the bloodstream, it produces muscle paralysis including significantly affecting lung function leading to asphyxiation and subsequent death. Woorari blocks the junction between nerves and muscles causing this paralytic effect without affecting a victim's consciousness.

Woorari has no effect on an individual when ingested but can prove quite fatal when introduced into the bloodstream. Because of this, this lethal substance can be safely tasted in order to judge its overall strength.

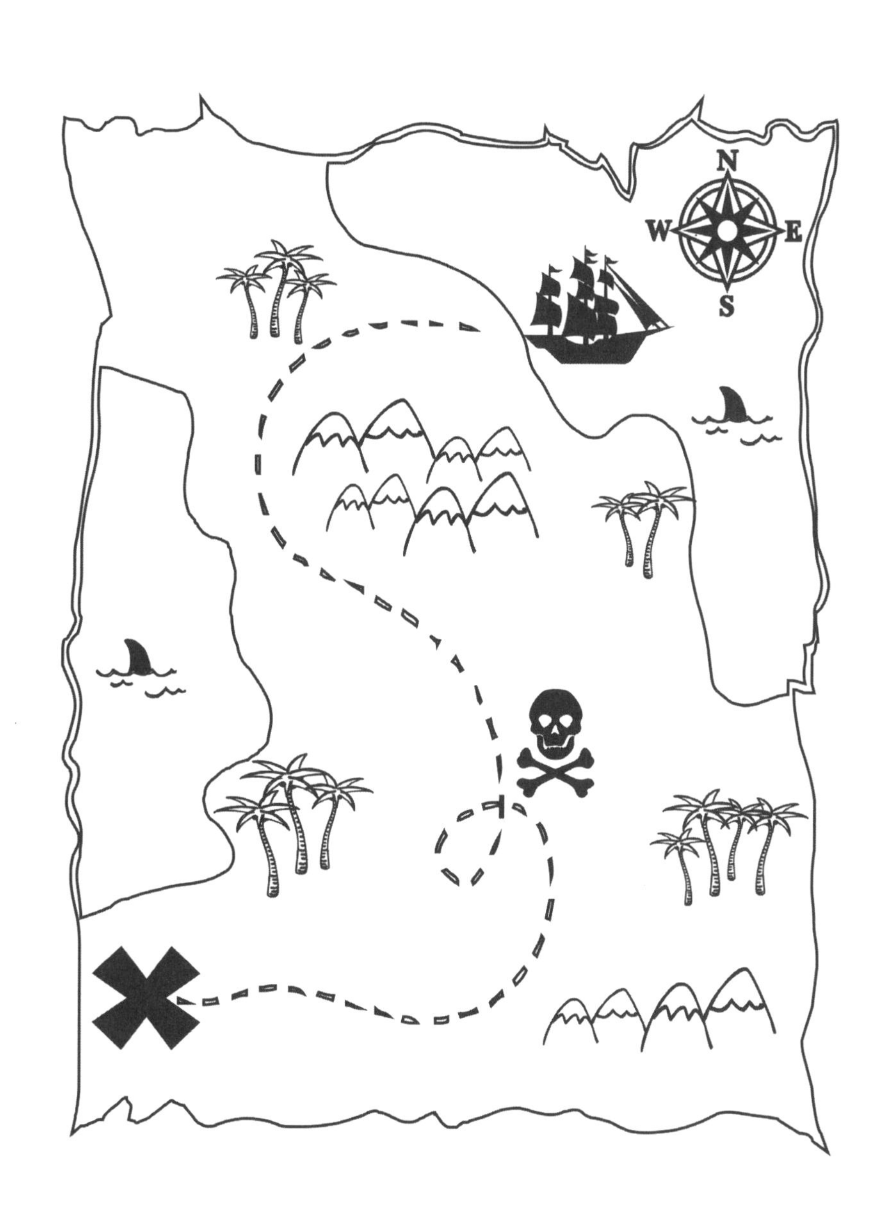
N
W
E
S